STAY HERE

LYNN STEWART

UP WIND SYSTEMS, LLC

For Sweet Petunia

How did it get so late so soon? Its night before its afternoon. December is here before its June. My goodness how the time has flewn. How did it get so late so soon?

— Dr. Seuss

PROLOGUE

Two Years Earlier
September 12, 2002

John Butterfield stood in front of an art gallery on Mercer
Street. He pulled the *Times* article out of his pocket, unfolded
it, and double-checked the address, moving his eyes from the
building to the street sign on the corner, then back to the
building, squinting to see the number above the door. Frustrated, he
folded the article and shoved it back in his pocket. This building
didn't look anything like the art galleries he'd been to before, and
God knows his ex-wife had dragged him to many. Even the unusual
ones in obscure neighborhoods seemed to smell of art — this one
smelled of decay. John didn't want to be anywhere near this building.
It reminded him of the kinds of places criminals squatted in, back
when he was a cop. After four years of not being a cop, he'd lost his
edginess and some of his hawk-like ability to see things and react
quickly. His old leg injury — the ender of his career — painfully

reminded him that entering this building — only to find out the Times had printed the wrong address — would hinder his ability to run the hell away.

John stared at the building, silently begging it to tell him to go home. Instead, the building snickered: *What better place for an art gallery than in a transitional, almost-hip neighborhood like this?* He backed away and crossed the street, regarding the building from a safe distance. He noticed a young couple go in. Then a few more people. A man in a gray suit. A photographer. Another couple. And another. Perhaps the *Times* did, indeed, print the correct address. He couldn't seem to break out of his paralysis — the proverbial deer in headlights. A woman nearly ran into him, turning to yell over her shoulder.

"Get your head out of your ass!" John scooched away from more oncoming foot traffic, feeling like an idiot.

The Starbucks that he'd passed a few blocks back offered safe haven. Any excuse to procrastinate. He retraced his steps away from the art gallery and took refuge inside the coffee shop, safe among crowded chatter and the smell of freshly ground espresso. He ordered a grande, black, and figured he could sip it very slowly while talking himself into going home. Shit. He didn't want to go home, not really. Did he even want to see Annie? After all this time? Maybe he wanted closure. The city seemed to have moved on, but he hadn't. Yesterday, the anniversary commemorations and endless loops on TV yanked the Band-Aid off his broken heart. Until the eleventh day in September stopped showing up on the calendar, he'd never move on. He blew on his coffee and pulled a threadbare sheet of paper from his wallet. He carefully unfolded it and studied Annie's face on the flyer her family had made when they thought she was missing after the attacks. The note she'd written to him on the back of the flyer — faded to almost nothing from a year of his fingers sliding across it like braille — taunted him, as he recited it to himself, the words he'd memorized.

Outside, dusk reached its fingers down from the sky to grasp the city. John had no other choice but to go back to the art gallery. He had to see Annie and told himself he didn't have to talk to her; a glimpse of her would be enough. Then he'd move on — something he should have done when he found the note last year. He had plans. Shorty wanted to sell half of the pub to him — they'd be co-owners and partners. So, yeah, he needed this closure.

He left his untouched coffee on the table and walked into the limbo between light and dark. No longer afraid, he hurried up the sidewalk, not quite running but propelling himself forward as fast as possible, wincing every time his right foot hit the ground. He crossed the street without waiting for the light to turn green. He wasted no time and flung the gallery door open, nearly stumbling as he took the stairs two at a time. A door, propped open on the landing, revealed a massive loft. He stopped, out of breath, and held onto the door jamb for support as he scanned the room, letting his gaze drift over the paintings lining the walls. He knew, from the *Times* article, that Annie's exhibit celebrated and represented the people lost last year, the faces from the missing-person posters that had peppered the city. The photographer he'd seen earlier floated from painting to painting, simultaneously taking photos while trying to cause the least amount of disruption. The usual opening night accouterments — wine, namely — didn't exist. Neither did trays of crudités or prosciutto-wrapped figs.

John didn't know how long he'd been standing in the doorway when he saw her. Her hair, a haphazard mess piled on top of her head, was just as he remembered. Wait a minute. His sweater? The raggedy old sailing sweater he'd found her wrapped up in the day after 9/11 — that first morning when she'd been a refugee on his boat. His old wool sweater! Wrapped around her shoulders tonight like a stole. Quite the contrast to her long, black dress and pearl necklace. He looked all over for that damned sweater last winter. His sweater — a bridge between the day Annie disappeared and now.

He stepped across the landing and slowly made his way around the room, wiping away his tears as he went. He didn't want her to see him like this — a raw jumbled mess. But it was too late. He felt her standing behind him — the same forcefield that he'd felt in her presence before, the one he agonized over for the past year, the one he couldn't quite define. He turned around and touched her cheek, wiping away the first of many tears that evening.

PART I

1

John

His mission seemed simple enough: buy an engagement ring for a woman who didn't want to marry him. Did the fact that he'd spent the last few weeks combing Manhattan in search of a ring make him one of those fools who took the word no to mean maybe or not yet? John stepped out of the jewelry shop, feeling very much like a fool. Who was he kidding? No meant no. He zipped his fleece jacket all the way up to his chin in deference to the wind, clutching a red gift bag by its flimsy handles. Despite an unseasonal warmth in the breeze, John felt chilled and hoped he wasn't coming down with something. Halfway up West 17th Street, the bag caught a gust and expanded like a paper lantern. He lost his grip, and it tumbled to the sidewalk, somersaulting ahead of him, the weight of the small box catapulting the bag as if it were trying to escape. In one swift and graceful motion, John lifted his good leg and slammed his foot down, pinning the bag. He extracted the box and shoved it deep into his front pocket. And the bag, now crumbled and empty, went into the trash bin.

It didn't feel Christmassy. Not by a long shot. The clouds, wind, and fits of rain created a dreary tableau. Not even the festive window displays made up for it. It felt more like early spring — that gray and brown period when nature isn't ready to face the world and hits the snooze button. On TV this morning, Al Roker seemed excited to report the balmy conditions. Sixty-two degrees. Sixty-two! In mid-December! In New York City! This might as well be Florida. And John hated Florida.

He stopped at a consignment shop and regarded the window display: a group of stuffed penguins at a festive table, complete with a rubber chicken on a platter. He laughed, remembering that his new cell phone had a built-in camera. He pulled it out of his back pocket and fumbled with the buttons. Annie would love this. He snapped several photos, then regarded them on the small screen before closing his phone. He patted the front of his pants to make sure the box hadn't somehow fallen out.

Annie had said no three times already, not that John was counting. But this time would be different. Wouldn't it? Sooner or later he'd wear her down, his counter to her point seeming stronger by the day. If her sole reason for not wanting to marry him boiled down to her having incurable cancer, then he needed to assure her that legalizing their relationship had its upside. Hospital visitation rights, for one thing. But more than that, she had already outlived the most optimistic of her doctors' assessments of her time remaining. Just yesterday they took a cab to Central Park and jogged three miles, well, she jogged, and he shuffled. How many people with incurable cancer could jog? His persistence and logic — miracle of miracles — finally wore down Annie's son, Henry, enough to cede to his side of the argument. With an eye-roll perfected and universal among 13-year-olds, Henry's popular refrain was *just marry him already!* Having Henry on his side offered a glimmer of hope. Did Annie have another few years? Maybe. Maybe not. Her latest scan revealed that the tumor at the base of her spine had grown slightly. And she now sports two new, albeit small, tumors on her ribs. Metastatic breast cancer at its finest.

One raindrop, then another, then a few more plopped down on the top of John's head, landing on the spot where his hair had thinned to almost nothing. The window display beckoned, and he opened the door to the shop. He gravitated to the jewelry display case and scanned for rings, the search so automatic that he found himself second-guessing his original choice.

"Are you looking for anything in particular?" The woman behind the counter startled him. Her earlobes drooped under the weight of earrings the size of dinner plates. He ignored her, shaking his head. *Wait a minute. What's this?* He tapped the display case with his finger and pointed at a ring with a diamond in the center of a silver compass. North. South. East. West. Tiny emeralds dotted the band. Green. Annie's favorite color. It looked like her. He realized, with much embarrassment, that his eyes were moist. He cleared his throat and tapped harder on the glass.

"I'll take this."

The woman placed the ring in a velvet lined box, and when she started to lower it into a bag, he said he'd take it just as it is. He shoved the box into the pocket with the other ring and hailed a cab. He had two hours before he had to be at work in Jersey City. He would stop at his house first and hide the two rings. He wasn't sure what he would do with the first ring. He didn't want to return it. Perhaps he'd give it to Annie on their first wedding anniversary. First for first. Yes, that's what he would do. He was so excited that waiting until Christmas morning to propose, like he and Henry planned, would be torture. This would be a real proposal. Not just marriage-talk, but an honest, from the heart, from the gut, from the soul proposal. He no longer felt cold, and the sixty-two-degree, mid-December day, with its wind and fits of rain, as non-Christmassy as any day could be, made him smile.

2

Annie

What is a deadline? Isn't it just an arbitrary point in time, moveable to the right in most cases? A day on the calendar or time on the clock. As long as lives wouldn't be lost, what was the harm in flipping the page or choosing a later time?

Annie Wells stared at the mountain of blank notecards she'd piled on the chairs around her kitchen table — five hundred notecards, to be exact. She'd set an arbitrary deadline during an ambitious period just before Halloween when she'd been feeling pretty good, physically. Four weeks to create the hand-painted holiday cards for the gift shop in the art gallery, her friend Ted owned. Realistic. Doable. Roughly a hundred cards each day. Easy. Her deadline came and went. And now, almost two months later, the notecards still sat — unpainted — on the chairs.

She set another deadline. And another. Ted had been gracious the first time. And accommodating the second. Finally, he told her they'd revisit the notecard project after the holidays, maybe get them into the shop for spring. And that was when Annie decided she would not give in to defeat. She would beat herself at her own game.

She stood and stretched, standing on her toes and reaching her arms up toward the ceiling. Arching her back. Bending at the waist, side to side, then down toward the floor. She rubbed the sore area on her lower back. She ran her hand through her hair and took a deep breath. All five hundred cards today. Easy. She closed her eyes and willed the cards to paint themselves. She opened one eye, then the other. Damn. Still blank.

She hated using cancer as her excuse. She didn't do it often, and when she did, she berated herself. But for the past few weeks, her back hurt in a new way and she tired a little bit more easily. So, it wasn't an excuse, not really. When she mentioned it to Ted, he softened on the deadline and gave her an out. That's when she decided that she would not let cancer have the final say. Nope.

The microwave beeped. Annie didn't remember putting her coffee cup in there. She pulled it out and held it in both hands, blowing on it, grateful for the warmth. She stared at the blank cards, trying to force inspiration. Her original plan — holiday cards — became obsolete the minute the calendar pages turned, leaving Hanukkah in the dust and Christmas a heartbeat away. People only sent cards this late when they'd received one from someone, not on their original list.

She picked up a notecard and tapped on it with her fingers, wondering if she should use acrylics or watercolors. Both dried fast. If she could stay focused, she could have all the cards completed before bed. She would stay up all night if she had to.

A tube of blue acrylic caught her eye. She mixed in a bit of white, making the color that of a cloudless sky, and mindlessly swirled the paint on a piece of scrap paper. The result looked a lot like a snowflake. She sighed and added a few dots of lime green. She stood up and regarded it. Snowflakes. Winter's extended stay meant it could technically snow at any point during the next three months. Snowflakes weren't too Christmassy. And, they'd be perfect for those who did indeed wish to send a last-minute holiday card. Each card a different version of a snowflake. No two exactly alike. A representation of the people who'd died on 9/11. Like all of her exhibits in Ted's gallery, any money made, in donations or sales, went directly to their non-profit, helping to lift the financial burdens of those who'd lost loved ones on that horrible day.

ANNIE PUT the finishing flourish on the last of the cards when the phone rang. She'd painted all day feverishly, stopping only for the absolute necessities, like peeing. Henry could have come home from school and plopped himself at the table next to her, and she wouldn't have noticed. Wait a minute. Henry? Where was he? She answered the phone. Then she remembered. Henry was with his dad tonight.

A bit disoriented when she heard John's voice, she chatted with him for a few minutes, waved him off when he suggested coming over, then said goodbye while she carried the last card to the living room to join the other cards drying on the floor. She carefully set it down, completing the mosaic. From a distance, it looked like a colorful rug. The cards had taken her much less time than she'd anticipated. She hadn't yet eaten dinner, and it was already past seven. She cracked an egg into the pan on the stove and called John back, feeling guilty for wanting to be left alone.

"I'm frying an egg," she said. "I'm too hungry to wait to eat with you, and I'll probably be passed out on the couch when you get here." He said he'd see her soon, and that was the end of that. Hurt feeling crisis averted. Her egg sizzled, begging to be checked. She carefully pierced the yolk with the tip of a steak knife, releasing a tiny bead of liquid gold. Beautiful. She flipped the egg over and let it sit for another few seconds before sliding it out of the pan and onto the waiting plate. She pushed the egg to the side and complemented it with a handful of arugula and a few slices of avocado.

She wished she hadn't called John back. They'd spent the day together yesterday, and the night before that. It was a problematic dichotomy — she wanted to be with him, but she also relished her personal space and the freedom to be independent — a state of being she hadn't experienced in such a long time that the novelty of it still felt new. She and Alec had been together for twelve years before their marriage fell apart like the buildings on 9/11. And Alec still, to this very day, remained convinced that John had caused their marital demise. Alec — shrink and rewriter of history — had to often be reminded that he'd been the one who left. Yet she couldn't stay mad at him. He loved their son, never missed a child support payment, and still told her that he'd take care of her if and when that came to be. She didn't need his help. She had her sister, and she had John. And while she would hang herself before letting John change her diapers (God forbid it should come to that), she loved the idea of him being the one to hold her as she lay dying.

She heard John's key opening the door, startled that forty minutes had gone by. He walked into the kitchen, set a greasy bag on the table, bent down, and hugged her tightly. She melted into his arms, suddenly happy, oh so happy to see him.

"You didn't eat much of your dinner," he said, dumping the contents of the bag — fries from Shorty's — onto her plate.

"I have a better idea," she said, getting up. She retrieved a baking sheet from the cupboard and slid the cold fries from her plate onto the sheet. Into the oven, they went.

"Brilliant," he said. "Hey, close your eyes for a minute and take my hand."

Annie's heart stopped. John had been on a marriage soapbox lately. If things were different, yeah, she'd marry him. But things are as they are — she had cancer and would likely die from it within the next few years. Why bother with marriage and all it entails? She took his hand and let him lead her onto the landing by the door.

"Stand right here," he said. "And no peeking." The door opened and closed, and she could hear John fumbling and banging and rustling. "Okay, you can open your eyes now," came his voice from outside the door.

Annie braced herself. She half expected the door to fly open to reveal a Mariachi band and John on bended knee. But that's not what she saw when the door did, finally, open.

He held the door with his foot while he wrestled with a tangle of green, dragging the Christmas tree through the door, leaving a trail of pine needles in its wake. She was so relieved that she laughed, and laughed, and laughed until the smell of burning French fries broke the spell. She ran to the kitchen and pulled the tray out of the oven. By the time she returned, John had already dragged the tree into the living room and put it in its stand. She hugged him, thankful that the ruckus hadn't disturbed her notecards, and grateful that John's surprise didn't involve a velvet box.

"Let's leave it for tomorrow," she said, taking his jacket and nudging him toward her bedroom.

"Wait, it needs water," he pulled away, smiling, while she tried to hold him tight — no match for his height and weight. He disappeared into the kitchen and came back carrying a pitcher of water.

A half-hour later, wrapped in sheets and around each other, sweaty and groggy from having fallen briefly asleep, he showed her the picture of the penguins from the window display.

THEY STAYED UP LATE, very late, stuffing the cards — all five hundred of them — into boxes. Finished and unable to sleep, they snuggled on the couch and watched TV: *Seinfeld*, *The Golden Girls*, and an infomercial for an automatic hard-boiled egg peeler.

Annie stood in the kitchen, pouring Cheerios into two bowls when she heard the doorbell. She abandoned the task and let Ted in, hugging him, apprehensive of how he might react to the cards, feeling like she was giving him something that she'd thrown together. She opened one of the boxes, muttering all manners of apologies. He pulled out several cards.

"Oh, hey John," Ted said. John shook his hand, hugged Annie, and disappeared into the kitchen.

"Are they okay?" Annie watched as Ted's attention turned back to the cards. She couldn't quite read the look on his face. He put the cards back in the box and pulled out a few more. "I could add more color if you think that would help."

"Stay for breakfast, Ted?" John called out from the kitchen. "I'm trying something new. You don't want to miss this."

"Sounds enticing, but it's my turn to take Elijah to preschool."

Annie pried the cards from Ted's hand and let them fall back into the box.

"Well?" She crossed her arms.

"They're perfect." He kissed her on the forehead.

"I'll help you carry them down," John said, emerging from the kitchen and wiping his hands on his jeans.

"Thanks," Ted said. And then to Annie: "I love them. They'll be sold out before the weekend."

ANNIE TOOK a second bite of the massive waffle tower that John shoved in front of her. "What was wrong with Cheerios?"

"You didn't eat your dinner last night," he said. "I know you have a busy day today. I wanted to make you something hearty."

"You've got to stop fussing over me." She took the stack apart, one layer at a time, and set each piece around her plate. She didn't want John to see her annoyance, but she feared he already knew. It was hard to hide the tone that seeped through her clenched teeth. She focused hard on the plate — her canvas — and examined the components of John's creation before reassembling: waffle, refried beans, egg, bacon, another egg, more bacon, topped with a second waffle. She took a deep breath and reminded herself that his concern sprang from his love. "I think it needs more syrup." She squeezed the Log Cabin bottle and saturated her plate. She took another bite. "Yep. It's amazing."

"Phew," he said, attacking his own stack. "I'll have to try it out on Shorty tonight. I think I may add it to the New Year's Day brunch menu." He smiled.

"The perfect antidote for a post-New Year's Eve hangover," she said, shaking her head. "You could throw in a Bloody Mary, too."

Annie got up from the table and brought her plate to the counter. She'd eaten half the stack — a feat in itself given her absence of hunger. Her back throbbed. *Think happy thoughts.* One happy thought: Ted's reaction to the notecards. Another: John's enthusiasm for the silly waffle thing, and the way he threw pieces of himself into the atmosphere and onto the menu at the pub. Shorty gave him leeway, even more than what would be expected of a co-owner. She only wished the pub were closer. Jersey City wasn't San Francisco, but it was far enough away make things hard sometimes. Most of the time, she liked their life just like this. But her sore back and the new information that the scan revealed, the new parts of her body slowly being invaded by cancer...well, she felt sorry for herself.

She put her plate in the sink and turned on the water. She sniffed and cleared her throat, then wiped away fresh tears with her sleeve. She wanted to call her sister but didn't want Kathy to worry in the middle of her holiday vacation. She missed her. Terribly. Especially now, right in the middle of December. That magical point on the celestial timeline when the days grow as short as they ever will be, but the holiday lights and the sweet longing for hope and together-ness keep things festive and bright. With so much weighing on her body and soul, she needed to let the season be a happy distraction. There. Another happy thought. She forced herself to remember how blessed she was, how lucky to have, at least for now, cheated the odds of a disease that would one day kill her — but not today and not tomorrow. How lucky to be healthy enough to work, paint, and be a mother to Henry. And of course, John. She felt so blessed to have him in her life. She loved him so much that it hurt sometimes.

"Ted told me there's restaurant space for lease on Clermont." She tried to sound nonchalant as she sat back down at the table. She usually swallowed the urge to suggest John leave Shorty's and open his own place in Brooklyn.

"Yeah, well, I can't do that to Shorty, not yet anyway." He looked up from his plate. "But, if you marry me, maybe I'd —"

"Please don't start that again." She covered her ears and got up, angry that she allowed herself to feel vulnerable and needy. A minute ago, she'd even had the fleeting thought to uproot Henry and move to Jersey City. But not anymore. The thought evaporated faster than it had formed. She grabbed her cell phone and her address book from the counter and carried them into the living room. She sat down next to the bare Christmas tree and found the number that her sister had scribbled down. Annie didn't remember if London was five or six hours ahead — dinnertime nonetheless. She didn't want to disturb Kathy and Dee, but she couldn't help herself and started to dial.

"There you are," John sat down and wrapped his arms around her, resting his chin on her shoulder. She closed her phone and set it down. "How about we put some lights on this pathetic tree?"

"I'm out of time." She felt herself soften. She wasn't ready to turn to mush, so she feigned seriousness. The elastic band on the cheap Halloween mask snapped, and her serious face fell to the floor. She touched one of the tree branches, then pointed deep within the tree. John inched his way closer to see.

"Ha, a pine cone." He moved away from the tree and looked hard into her eyes, taking her hands. "I have something I want to give you before you leave."

Annie swallowed. "John, please, don't, not now, not right before I have to meet with a new patient." She choked out a sob, unprepared, and a bit unnerved by his persistence. She needed this right now, like she needed a unicycle. She touched her jaw, suddenly realizing that she'd been clenching her teeth.

"Here." He tossed a small, white box in her direction. She caught the box with one hand and hesitated. "Go on, open it," he said, then winked and grinned.

Reacting to his change in tone, she opened it and pulled out a porcelain penguin, as cute as could be. She hung the new ornament on the branch with the pine cone, feeling shaky and weak with relief.

"What?" He looked at her. "Were you expecting a proposal or something?" And when she didn't respond: "Why on earth would you think that?" He smiled, proud of his hijinks.

She threw the empty box at him. He threw it back. They carried on like this until Annie looked at her watch. John stood up and offered his hand, which she gladly accepted. He pulled her up.

She stared at him, trying to read his eyes. She interlaced her fingers with his, studying them. His fingers were the first thing she noticed the day they met, on 9/11. She'd been so dazed, so confused. His fingers — a beacon of hope that day. Her anti-marriage stance hurt him, she knew this, his eyes confirmed it. He stood silent as if lost in her analysis. She buried her head in his chest and breathed him in. His smell. Part river, part ocean, part pine, part Irish pub. She took in as much of him as her lungs and senses allowed, never wanting to breathe him out.

"I love you." She said it into his chest so softly that she didn't think he'd heard. But he must have. Because he squeezed her in response.

"Can I walk with you to your office?" John spoke into her hair.

She didn't answer right away. Then: "I wouldn't have it any other way."

ANNIE SPOTTED a bench and angled toward it. They still had a long way to go, and the throbbing in her back made it difficult to walk. She sat down. John sat down next to her and raised an eyebrow.

"I'm calling a cab," he said.

"No. Please don't. I need fresh air. I think I overdid it jogging with you the other day."

"Yeah, my leg is pretty sore from that. I'm just happy I can jog again." He put his arm around her. "It's finally Christmas weather." He touched his bald spot. "I should have worn a hat."

They got up and started walking again. In the hullabaloo of John's crazy waffle breakfast, and then his trickery with the ornament, she'd forgotten to take her medication. Five minutes later, she sat down again. She opened her purse and pulled out a bottle of Tylenol, letting two tablets fall into her hand. She flipped them into her mouth and swallowed without water.

"Tylenol?" John looked skeptical.

"I forgot to take my new meds after breakfast."

"I'll run back and get them."

"It's too late now, I've already taken something."

"You'll have them for later."

"Thank you." Desperation had a way of making one humble.

"Now, about that cab."

"No way." She smiled then, got up, and braced herself against the cold, glad for the distraction.

THE PSYCHOLOGY PRACTICE that Annie's ex-husband opened a year after their divorce occupied the ground level of a converted brownstone, a little over a mile from her apartment. Alec, who during their marriage didn't take Annie's art therapy profession seriously — poked fun of it even — had recently read a paper on art therapy and decided to incorporate it into his practice. He hired her as a consultant. The money wasn't great, but it offset some of the expenses of being a single parent. Alec marveled at the difference art therapy made in his patients and frequently apologized for having been such a skeptic.

She walked into Alec's waiting room drenched in sweat. She took her coat off and hung it on the coat rack in the corner, then opened the door and stood on the street, holding her arms out as if welcoming the world, but in reality, merely airing out her pits.

"I don't know where I'll be when you come back with my pills," she said to John as she let the door close behind her. "You can just leave them with Alec." She hugged him, long and hard.

"Eh-hem." Alec stood in the doorway to his office. When Annie saw him, she gently extracted herself from John.

"Hey, Alec." John extended his hand and Alec took it, letting the handshake end a fraction of a second too soon.

"John will be back in a bit with some of my meds," Annie said.

"Sure," Alec looked at John. "Just leave them on the desk through that door." He pointed at the only door in the room, as if John wouldn't have been able to figure it out himself. John hugged Annie again, whispered that he would see her tomorrow, and walked back out into the cold. Alec rolled his eyes to the ceiling, then shook his head.

"I don't know what you see in that guy." Annie ignored him and followed him into his office. "So, I need to brief you on the fellow you're going to see today." Alec sat down at his desk. "Mel is an interesting guy. Early forties. Almost a quadriplegic. He can use his hands a little."

"Was he in an accident?" It fascinated Annie that she and Alec could have such a productive working relationship. He treated her as a respected colleague. Gone were the hundreds of little ways he'd made her feel inferior during their marriage, his snide remark about John aside.

"Sort of," Alec said. "He tried to commit suicide, planned to jump in front of a train. It was a very slow-moving freight train. Decided at the last minute that, no, he didn't want to die. He got away from the train but tripped and rolled down a steep, rocky hillside."

Annie cringed, wondering why, of all the ways a person could commit suicide, they would choose to jump in front of a train. What kind of desperation, at the moment before the train came barreling down the tracks, would empower a person to follow through? The roar, the vibrations. She could understand this man changing his mind. Or at least deciding to change the methodology. Her cancer diagnosis, on the heels of a miscarriage and Alec's cheating, had her fantasizing about doing herself in, and swiftly. But by train? Pills and a good bottle of wine, maybe. But not a train. She feared meeting this man, feared she wouldn't know how to engage with him.

"Is he able to hold a paintbrush?"

"I don't know." Alec shrugged. "I'll leave that for you to assess. I've been working with him for about a year. He seems stuck, and I think you might be able to help him." Then, abruptly changing the subject: "What are these pills John's dropping off?"

She didn't want to talk about this with Alec, but, as Henry's dad, he had the right to know the status of her health. She took a deep breath.

"I had a scan last week." She looked at the floor. "The spot on my spine has grown a little bit." She didn't want to tell him about her ribs but decided to anyway. And before Alec could comment: "But I'm still holding steady. Dr. Chapman says the breast cancer itself hasn't progressed. That's excellent news."

"That doesn't sound like excellent news to me, Brenda," Alec said. "You sound like you're in denial."

"I didn't ask for your opinion. It's not your business. And I go by Annie now, you know that."

"Whatever. Anyway, it is my business, as far as Henry is concerned." He softened a bit. "Henry said something to me last night that makes me think he doesn't quite grasp the gravity of your condition."

"What did he say?" Annie took great care to keep Henry's life as sane as possible. The topic of her being sick rarely came up. She mostly kept him informed of her doctor appointments and mostly told him the truth about significant changes in her condition. She didn't tell him about last week's scan. Her motherly instincts kicked in, wanting to protect him. Because she knew in her gut that her health wasn't as rosy as it had been for the past three years. If living with cancer could ever be rosy. She could pretend, though. At least for now.

"It wasn't any particular thing, exactly," Alec said. "He talked about all the things the three of you plan to do in the future."

"What's wrong with that?"

"You don't have a future." Alec caught his breath. "That's not how I meant it. Let's be realistic. I don't want you leading him to believe that you'll be around forever."

"Nobody will be around forever." Annie stood. She didn't want to have this conversation. The Alec that divorced her was emerging before her eyes. The old Alec, as she sometimes referred to him, particularly in moments like this, stood before her.

"Look, I'm sorry." The new Alec groveled his way back. "I'm really sorry. I guess I'm just worried about you. Worried that you're not taking your health seriously enough. Maybe it's time you think about chemo."

The bells chimed, thank goodness, alerting them to someone entering the waiting room. Annie sat in the office while Alec went out to greet the patient. The weight of Alec's words — bricks on her chest — threatened suffocation. For the first time in months, she acutely felt her horizon getting closer. She longed for the days when her horizon seemed far away — undetectable with the naked eye. Her initial diagnosis three years ago brought her horizon closer, and she'd grown accustomed to its new position in her field of vision. She knew she would die from cancer. That was a given. But she felt well most of the time. She relished the blissful moments when cancer wasn't the first thing that popped into her mind each morning. Lately, though, her horizon felt painfully close. She could see it in all its color, in all its horror, in all its beauty. She would walk toward it very, very slowly.

ANNIE ARRANGED her workspace with paper, watercolors, brushes, acrylics in the primary colors, canvas boards, markers, crayons, pencils, pens, and a shoebox filled with images cut from magazines. As with all new patients, she had no way of knowing how the session with Mel would unfold.

Annie stuck a classical music CD — for focus and clarity — into the stereo system, but planned to ask Mel what kind of music he liked. She had a vast collection, and if she learned anything from working with Alec's patients, it was that music stirred the soul in unexpected ways.

"I suppose he told you why I'm here." Mel entered the art room in his motorized wheelchair, obviously referring to Alec, who trailed a few paces behind.

"Mel, this is my colleague, Ms. Wells," Alec said. It was strange to hear him address her so formally, and with her maiden name. As they say, old habits die hard, and on more than one occasion, he'd had to correct himself mid-sentence.

"Please, call me Annie." She smiled at Mel as Alec left the room. "Dr. Arnstein told me a little bit. That you're a botanist. That you were in an accident about eight years ago. And that you've been having nightmares about terrorist attacks." She paused. "That's about it."

"I wasn't exactly in an accident," he offered. "It was a botched suicide attempt."

"Yes, he told me that too," she said. "But I wouldn't exactly characterize it as botched. I don't think you wanted to die."

"You have no idea," he spat.

"You're right. I don't." She searched for compassion. "But I get it. I wanted to die too, three years ago. I won't go into the gory details, but suffice it to say, I understand."

Mel motored closer to the table and picked up a paintbrush with a shaky hand. "So, are we going to paint, or what?"

"We'll get to that later. Let's chat for a bit." Looking at his hands, she wondered if he could control a cup of coffee or tea. Maybe water. She decided to be direct. "I can see that you're comfortable holding a paintbrush. How about a coffee mug? I'm going to have a cup of tea. Would you like anything?"

"Got any scotch?"

"Not exactly."

"Well, forget it then."

She excused herself and went to her makeshift coffee station by the window — a mini-fridge on top of which sat a Mr. Coffee and an electric tea kettle, along with a can of Maxwell House and a basket filled with different kinds of teas. She selected a packet of Darjeeling and filled her mug with hot water.

"What kind of music do you like? Not everyone is into classical."

"Got any Kajagoogoo?" Mel put the paintbrush down. He looked into her eyes, something he hadn't done since Alec brought him in.

"Of course, the one thing I don't have. *Too Shy*. I loved that song back in the day."

"You don't have that, and you won't give me a scotch."

"How about just a generic 80's mix," she said, ignoring his commentary. "Top 40 type of stuff."

Mel shrugged and slowly wheeled himself down the length of the art table. Annie loaded a CD into her player and turned up the volume a little bit. The Tylenol she'd taken earlier had worn off, and she wondered if John returned with her meds. She excused herself and went looking, leaving Mel alone in the art room. She saw a small brown paper bag sitting on Alec's desk, her name scrawled in John's handwriting. She reached in and pulled out her bottle of pills. *Thank you*, she mumbled into the bag.

She returned to the art room and stood in the doorway, watching Mel dig through the shoebox, *Groovy Kind of Love* the current song. Several pictures were scattered on the table around him. After much digging, he pulled a photo out of the box and stared at it. She couldn't see his face or the subject of the picture, but by his body language alone, she could tell that this picture (and maybe the music) stirred something wistful in him.

Not wanting to break the spell, she slowly walked toward him, keeping a respectable distance. The picture showed fancy porcelain plates of varying colors and patterns. Blue and white — the perfect vessels for little sandwiches to be served at an English high tea. She thought of her sister and grew wistful herself. This would be her first Christmas without Kathy for as long as she could remember.

Annie found it interesting that Mel had gravitated toward the shoebox. She typically started there with new patients, particularly patients who deemed themselves unartistic. Adults and children alike seemed to find it much less intimidating to choose a picture cut from a magazine than to be handed a pencil or paintbrush and told to create something. Often, the selected images came together in profound ways, offering insight that would never otherwise have been gleaned. That alone tended to unblock the patient — leaving them ready to continue on their therapeutic journey with Alec. Mel turned toward her, still holding the dish picture. Annie handed him a piece of white poster board and a couple of glue sticks.

"I know how eager you are to paint something, but I like what you're doing. This is where I like to start." She studied his face. "Without overthinking anything, keep doing what you're doing, but I'd like you to glue the pictures to the poster board."

"I feel like I'm in kindergarten." He pushed the shoebox away, knocking the glue sticks over. Annie caught them as they rolled toward the edge of the table. She wanted to tell him to stop acting like a kindergartener but decided instead to just ask him to trust her. She pushed the box back toward him and placed the glue sticks upright next to the box. He grumbled and shot her a sideways glance.

While Mel worked, Annie made her way to what she referred to as her perch. Just an old leather armchair positioned in such a way that she could observe her patients from a safe distance. Every patient had a different personal space bubble, but in general, her perch kept her close enough to assist, yet far enough away as to not crowd. Nothing killed creativity more than having someone on top of you.

"Why did you want to die?" Mel's question startled her. She realized that she never went back to finish her initial conversation with him. To learn more about him, to find out his goals for the session. To come up with a schedule. She figured the pictures would do the talking but never expected the conversation to turn back to her. She didn't want to discuss her life. Yet something compelled her to open up. A little.

"I had several things converge on me at once. I had a miscarriage, and was diagnosed with cancer a few days later." She left out the part about Alec's affair. Mel nodded and continued selecting, arranging, and gluing.

Annie sat in the pool of blood from the wound Mel had innocently opened. She knew it was an oxymoron, but she felt her life was better now. As if in her imminent death, her life found her. She didn't often dwell on her discovery of Alec's infidelity, but now, with her freshly opened wound still oozing, it was all she could see, all she could feel. She took a deep breath, sopped up the blood, and walked over to Mel. Not a speck of white remained on the poster board.

"I think I'll take water if you have some." Mel seemed parched as if this exercise had sucked him dry. She went to her mini-fridge and returned with a bottle of water. She opened it and set it down next to him.

"The pictures you chose are interesting," she said. Pictures of bananas radiated outward from the middle of the colorful dishes. Six or seven different images of bananas. Why did she even have all those bananas in her box? She stood up and stepped back a few paces. From a distance, the bananas weren't apparent as bananas. The closer she got, the clearer the images became. Surrounding the bananas, he'd glued a woman's face, a fortune cookie, a building with a fire escape, and a pink and yellow polka-dot umbrella.

"Are we done here?" He looked around the room and wheeled himself away from the table. Annie looked at the clock. They still had fifteen minutes or so.

"We have a little bit of time," she said. "I'd really like to chat some about this, and get to know you some. You must like bananas — a lot."

"I hate the damned things." He rolled his chair back to the table and looked at her with sincerity in his eyes. "I'm sorry about your cancer," he said. "And your baby." Annie nodded but didn't respond.

"Tell me about the woman in that picture," she said, pointing.

"She reminds me of someone I knew a long time ago. In college." Mel shrugged. "I spent a semester in London."

"Did she live there, in London?" Annie guessed that the answer was yes. The porcelain plates and the umbrella. Maybe even the fire escape. But the bananas?

"She went to school there, but was from Boston," he said. "Her London flat was in a building with a fire escape."

"What about the bananas?" She couldn't help herself.

"I don't know." Mel grew quiet. Then: "Are we done here?" He backed his chair away from the table, turned around, and started motoring toward the door. "My wife will be here to pick me up. I don't want to make her wait." Annie got up and opened the door for him, but he didn't motor through. "Thank you," he said, still hesitating by the door.

"I'd like to talk more about the pictures you chose," she said. "How about this time next week?" Mel nodded.

She followed him out of the art room, down the hall, and into the waiting area. He rolled out the door without saying goodbye. She stood at the door, watching Mel's wife open the side door of a specially equipped van. Mel motored up the ramp and positioned his chair. His wife climbed in and secured the chair to the floor. She belted him in, lifted the ramp, closed the door, and got into the driver's seat, easing away from the curb into the traffic.

Annie slowly made her way back to the art room, hoping to avoid Alec. She sat down in her chair and regarded Mel's scraps, scattered about the table. Was she in denial, like Alec said? Maybe. She slid her hand behind her back and rubbed. Her new pills took the edge off the pain. The denial came quickly when she felt good. Unmedicated though, the pain might as well be a billboard with the word cancer printed boldly in neon letters. Acute pain somehow made the pages of the calendar slow down — in the midst of it the days dragged on without end. But the pain also reminded her that her life would be cut short — she wouldn't grow old, wouldn't live to see Henry grow into a man. The calendar pages turned in rapid succession like an animation flipbook, bringing her horizon closer and closer.

She would tidy up her workspace tomorrow. She wanted to go home and be there when Henry walked in the door from school. She picked up her phone to call a cab but stopped. She would walk, needing to feel Christmas in the air, needing to feel alive.

3

———————

Pearl

Three nature preserves in one morning — a record for Pearl Butterfield. She dumped the contents of her Home Depot bucket on a patch of hard-packed sand near the water. Using the bucket's bottom as a chair, she sat down and began sorting through her treasures: conch shells, sand dollars, cockle shells, and other odd bits and pieces. She found some sea glass too and planned to add it to the collection that she kept in a jar on her kitchen counter. Her grandson, Luke, would love the sand dollars. At six years old, there would be countless ways to entertain him in the coming days: crafts, cookies, and swimming. Her community had a lovely pool and a small water park for kids. And of course, the beach. And the nature preserves. She'd bring him here, just the two of them, to look for more shells.

She carefully placed the shells into her bucket, then looked at the water, confused. She squinted in the sun, cursing the day she moved to Florida. She bunched up her shirt collar and wiped her sweaty neck. Damn. Where the hell did she park her motorcycle? In the parking lot just up the beach? Shit. She couldn't remember. Could she have parked near the trail where she sometimes photographed fungus? Yes, probably the fungus trail. She walked in that direction.

The more she walked, the more convinced she became that the fungus trail wasn't even at this nature preserve. She stopped walking and looked up at the sky, the sun nicely concealed by a lush, green canopy. She stood still, hoping her bearings would find her. *Be logical, Pearl.* She reminded herself that there were only two possible places at this park. With multiple trails leading from the parking lots to the beach, she was bound to find her motorcycle. She tried not to think about her neighbor — seventy-seven years young, just like her — who'd been recently diagnosed with Alzheimer's.

"Get it together, Pearl," she said to the sky. "When you hear hoof-beats, think horses, not zebras." She used to tell this to her daughter-in-law, Marina, who frequently drove herself into a panicked frenzy over inane things. Pearl's mother used to say it, meaning, if you have a headache, it's probably just a headache, not a brain tumor. Maybe she should call her friend. Sally would roar with laughter and stay on the phone while Pearl tried the different trails — like that old game show *Let's Make a Deal* — choosing between Door Number One and Door Number Two. She pulled out her cell phone. Of course. No service. She sighed loudly and tried Door Number Two. Walking up the path, she saw a clearing. It didn't look familiar, but it did look like it might be a parking lot. Yep. A parking lot. Nope. Not the right one. There were no vehicles. Maybe her motorcycle had been stolen. Likely not. She trudged back down the trail, back toward the beach, so she could start over and try Door Number One.

Pearl cursed herself for coming out here so early. She had walked to the nature preserve closest to her house this morning at first light. Her efforts bore fruit — she returned home with an impressive pile of shells and fragments. But no, she couldn't leave well enough alone. She jumped on her motorcycle and headed to another nature preserve, then from there, she came here. As she walked, a memory from her days as a high school guidance counselor flashed through her mind — a freshman girl had been murdered one year, walking alone on the Jersey Shore at dawn. Unthinkable. And then there was her daughter-in-law, Marina, who was raped in her own home. Every thirty seconds or so, a violent crime. Wasn't that the statistic you always heard? *What was I thinking? An old lady like me, wandering around like this on a deserted beach.* She studied the trees on her way back to the beach, careful to avoid the spot where the trail curved just slightly to the left, just enough that if you didn't pay attention, you would end up away from the beach instead of toward the shore. But if you veered to the right, you would end up, in short order, on the soft sand with the smallest, gentlest waves tickling your feet. A half-hour later, she was still in the woods.

"Shit. Fuck. Piss." She said it out loud. To the trees. To the birds. To the trail. "Shit. Fuck. Piss." John came home from school, proudly declaring these three words when he was eight or nine years old. *Shit. Fuck Piss.* How the hell did she miss the place where the trail curved? How did she end up walking left and not right? She should just turn around and backtrack — retrace her steps. She'd made a mental note of the fat palm tree, the one with bunches of those spiny, spiky plants — the devil's walking stick — growing around it. All she needed to do was find that tree. She turned around and walked back the way she came. Exhausted, she felt like she'd been walking in circles, the fat palm tree just a dream.

She plopped down on a stump, sitting on her hands to get them to stop shaking. She forced herself to breathe in, deeply, through her mouth, then exhale, slowly, through her nose. Just like in the meditation class Sally dragged her to. Unable to still her mind in the class, she'd gotten frustrated, and after the second session, never went back. The deep breathing was useful, though, and she employed the technique whenever necessary, like right now.

She pulled herself together and resumed walking. A familiar tree! Not the fat palm tree, but one that she hadn't seen in nearly two hours. With renewed confidence, she upped the tempo of her walking. She needed to get out of these woods and see something familiar.

She felt herself starting to hyperventilate. She tried to stifle the rising panic and pushed forward, determined to find her way.

Finally. Finally! The fat palm tree! The devil's walking stick! Pearl laughed out loud. She veered toward the right and eventually met the beach. Thank God! She walked up the path, determined, with every ounce of her being, to find the correct parking lot.

"Bubba, it's so good to see you." Her motorcycle! Door Number Two! Ding-ding-ding! She hugged the handlebars. With trembling hands, she lifted the seat and carefully decanted the shells from the bucket into the storage compartment. It took four tries to get the bungee cords around the bucket and the bucket secured to the back of the bike. Still shaking, she put on her helmet and rode home.

PEARL STUCK an English muffin in the toaster and poured herself a full glass of orange juice. When she walked through the door, she realized she hadn't eaten breakfast before going out on her expedition. She took a deep breath, wondering if that's what had caused the episode of confusion — her blood sugar had dipped too low. Of course. She smiled, happy to be home, glad to have come up with an explanation. Relieved to be in her house and not lost in the woods, not lost on the beach. She tried to laugh it off, and while tempted to call Sally, she felt too shaken to want to recount it.

Eating her breakfast in what seemed like one large inhale, Pearl called Marina's cell phone to see what time they'd be leaving Disney in the morning. When the call rolled over to voicemail, she gave up and didn't leave a message. They faced a four-hour drive from the Magic Kingdom, so if they left at ten like Marina said they probably would, then they should arrive tomorrow sometime after lunch. Pearl's fingers started dialing her son John's number. She quickly hung up before he could answer. She never did mention to him that Marina, Nester, and Luke were visiting for Christmas. Honestly, did it even matter? Still, she felt somewhat guilty, like she was hiding something from him.

Pearl had been so busy the past few weeks that she hadn't even thought to drag the Christmas tree out of the garage. She didn't think she could manage the bulky box, especially getting it up the two stairs that led into the kitchen. Maybe if she carried the tree, piece by piece. It would take a while, but at least it wouldn't be heavy that way.

Tumbleweed, the fat tabby that she adopted last year, brushed up against her leg and walked in a tight circle under the table. The cat curled at her feet, resting a paw on top of her foot. Pearl extracted her foot, slid her chair out from under the table, reached down, and scratched the cat's neck.

"Do you want to help me with the Christmas tree?" Pearl continued scratching, but the cat didn't respond. "Alright then, have it your way." She left the dishes on the table and made her way to the garage to deal with the tree.

First things first, she would need to move Bubba out of the way. She opened the garage and rolled the bike backward until it sat perched neatly on the driveway. She'd forgotten to remove the Home Depot bucket and undid the bungee cords, setting it against the wall in the garage. She opened the seat compartment and retrieved the shells, collecting them in her outstretched shirt and carefully carrying them into the kitchen. She set them in the sink and filled it with hot, soapy water. She had forgotten about the shells. True, she had arrived home with food fixation and rushed to the kitchen, anything and everything else secondary. But once she'd taken care of that and her blood sugar levels began to normalize, well, she should have remembered the shells. But she didn't. They never existed until she opened the seat and Bubba spit them out. She felt a sense of dread rising up from her gut.

"When you hear hoofbeats, think horses, not zebras," she said to the cat, who got up and padded to the garage as if reminding her that she still had not brought the Christmas tree in. "Screw the tree. We'll get a fresh one when the kids get here," she said, pleased with her new plan.

PEARL STOOD in the doorway to the main guest room and regarded it, wanting to make sure it felt elegant and homey, the way she knew Marina would like it. Yesterday afternoon, when she decided to eschew the fake Christmas tree, she ran over to Publix and bought three Orchids, Marina's favorite flower. She placed them strategically around the room — one on the dresser, one on the left-hand nightstand, and one on the bathroom vanity.

She walked in and ran her hand over the bedspread, smoothing wrinkles that didn't exist. She thought a few bars of good chocolate on the pillows would add a nice touch, and made a mental note to pick some up later.

She made her way a few steps down the hall and peered into the smaller of the two guest rooms — the one she set up for Luke. She'd seen him only twice in the last six years, the last time when he was just a toddler. She'd visited him in New Jersey that time, in her son's old house, the one Marina lived in with her new husband, Nester. It was odd, seeing Marina with another man in John's house. Pearl loved her son but believed he got what he deserved. She never, in her wildest imagination, would have thought she'd side with Marina on anything. Pearl had never cared for her. Never. Especially after the rape when Marina decided to follow through with the resultant pregnancy. God, she'd been mad at that woman and what she'd put John through. But somewhere along the way, something changed. John walked out on Marina, and Pearl felt sorry for her. She got to know her in a way she hadn't in the twenty years John had been married to her. She helped Marina during the last trimester of her pregnancy, and when Luke was born, well, she couldn't separate herself and draw a line in the sand, pretending the baby wasn't her flesh and blood. Oh, of course, he wasn't. And she knew it. But Luke felt like her flesh and blood.

Pearl walked into the room and picked up one of the three books she'd placed on Luke's pillow: *The Wind in the Willows*. She flipped through the pages, imagining sitting on the couch together, a plate of cookies on the coffee table, reading the book. She placed it back on the pillow with the others: *The Wonderful Wizard of Oz* and *Charlotte's Web*. Maybe she should wrap them. She had time to think about it.

She picked up the bag from Target that sat on the chair by the bed and pulled out the Christmas pajamas she'd picked up. She laid them out on the foot of the bed, hoping she got the right size.

On her way to the kitchen, she popped her head into the small bathroom that Luke would use. Everything was spotless, not that a six-year-old boy would care. She looked at her watch and noted that she still had several hours before they were due to arrive. She filled the cat's dish with dry kibble, topped off his water, and sat down to eat a bowl of Rice Chex.

The French doors leading to Pearl's lanai whispered that the morning clouds had parted. She grabbed her camera and an empty coffee can, then opened the doors and stepped out, still in her bare feet. She watched the winter ducks bobbing and diving in the estuary behind her house: canvasbacks, mergansers, pintails, buffleheads, and a common goldeneye. It had been Marina who taught her to appreciate birds.

Pearl filled a coffee can with cracked corn and carried it down to the water, her camera slung over her shoulder. She didn't have a boat dock, but did have two Adirondack chairs — painted the brightest turquoise she could find — at the water's edge. She sat down and tossed a handful of corn into the water, positioning her camera as the ducks sped toward this coveted treat, snapping several photos in succession. Toss, snap, toss, snap — until the coffee can was empty.

It was only ten by the time she returned to the kitchen. Four hours to burn before the kids arrived. To prove to herself that her mental faculties were intact, she headed out for a ride on Bubba.

PEARL BOUGHT her Harley-Davidson Road King (aka Bubba) two years ago — a present for her seventy-fifth birthday. Her son and everyone else she knew tried to talk her out of it. Even Marina, who usually encouraged her eccentricities. John's complaint: *Your balance isn't what it used to be.* She reminded him that she'd never had particularly good balance. She now knew that the kind of stability required for standing on one leg or traversing a balance beam was quite different from the type of balance needed for keeping Bubba upright when stopped. Strength was the critical thing. And if nothing else, Pearl had strength. Strong legs, in particular. Ham hocks, her late husband used to tease. She had no trouble at all straddling the bike and keeping it steady.

She pulled out of her subdivision and slowly made her way through the first few stop signs and traffic lights. Once on the open highway, she let it rip, enjoying the sunshine on her face and the wind swooshing over her body. She rarely rode Bubba without her leather jacket but decided to just go as is — pants and a light sweater. From behind, especially with the darker bottom bits of her hair sticking out from the helmet, she looked like a much younger woman. Sometimes other bikers came up from behind, and when they saw her up close, well, she guessed by their expressions and how quickly they rode away that they had not expected someone so...mature.

She took the long route to the nature preserve, enjoying the solitude. No need for a radio. Just Bubba and Pearl and a heightened sense of self. She loved the freedom of simply turning the key, putting on her helmet, and going — often with no particular destination in mind. And to the naysayers who ask why she rides? She's taken to answering semi sarcastically, alternating between *the same reason a dog sticks its head out the window, and it's damned exciting.*

She pulled into the parking lot — the same one as yesterday — and studied the landmarks. She'd been here hundreds of times before and swatted away her rising concern that she suddenly needed to be mindful of her surroundings. Still, the probability of losing her bike a second time in a little over twenty-four hours was not very high. Out of an abundance of caution, she paused at the foot of the trail and took in the parking lot one final time.

As she walked, Pearl marveled at the fungus that had sprung up overnight. The large, red and white, baseball-sized mushrooms had not been there yesterday. Now they seemed to be everywhere, with small craters all over their bulbous forms. She stooped down to get a better look, wishing she'd brought her camera. Wait, there was a camera built into her cell phone! She fished through her canvas tote and swooned when she realized she'd left her cell phone on the kitchen table. She didn't like to travel without her phone. Even with the spotty service out here, having her phone comforted like a soft blanket. She took a deep breath and let the fungus disappear behind her as she continued down the trail to the water.

HALLELUJAH, she'd found the right parking lot. Bubba beckoned, and by the position of the sun, she figured it was eleven or so, but without a watch or her cell phone, she had no idea. She started the bike up and was horrified to find that the digital clock on the dashboard declared it to be one-thirty! She took the most direct route home and was relieved that the kids' rental car was not in the driveway.

She opened the garage door and rolled Bubba inside, figuring she had just enough time for a quick shower. In the kitchen, her answering machine blinked wildly. Seven messages. She'd been having trouble with telemarketers lately and decided to deal with it later, after her shower. Oh, hell, better see who this is. Pearl supposed it could be Marina calling to alert her to a delay or some other such inconvenience. And right now, she would be grateful for a delay. Better check her cell phone too. She flipped it open. Dale? Four missed calls? She hadn't talked to her in months. She listened to the messages and grabbed the edge of the counter for balance. She inched her way across the kitchen to the answering machine. She didn't need to listen to those messages to know that they weren't from telemarketers. She pushed the button anyway. After the first message, she unplugged the machine and threw it on the floor. Her knees buckled. She clutched the counter for support, but even that was too much effort. She dropped to the floor. The cat worked his way into Pearl's lap. An hour passed before she stood up, unsure of what to do next.

4

John

The warmth of the pub felt good against John's skin. He peeled off his coat and draped it over the open office door. He fired up his computer and glanced at email. The building inspector was coming this afternoon to look at the fencing Shorty had installed in the alley, which was part of a larger plan to open a patio seating area in the spring. If they could get the fencing signed off — a necessary evil if they had any hope of expanding their liquor license to the patio — then, weather permitting, they could get to work right after Christmas. John was eager to unveil the patio at the first sign of a winter thaw, even if for just one day. There was always the possibility of a fluke seventy-degree day in the middle of February. Only two days ago it was in the sixties. He was tempted to pull the trigger on ordering the furniture now, to get it in the pipeline this week, before the supplier went into serious holiday mode. He and Shorty had narrowed the furniture choices to three types: traditional, rustic, and funky. John kept going back to the offbeat, mainly because it reminded him of Annie.

He scanned email, his mind drifting all over the place. He made a mental note to call his mother today before her holiday guests arrived. He was miffed that she hadn't mentioned the fact that she'd invited his ex-wife down for Christmas. Nester called last night and talked like it was the most natural thing in the world to go visit the mother of your wife's ex-husband. John had been nonchalant with Nester, but then stewed over it the rest of the night.

"What time is Inspector Gadget coming?" Shorty appeared in the doorway, holding a glass of beer. "Taste this." He handed John the glass.

"One. He's coming at one." John closed his eyes and took a slow sip of the beer. An IPA. Nicely bitter. Citra hops on the nose. He liked it, acknowledging that fact by nodding and handing the glass back to Shorty. "What is it?"

"That new microbrew," Shorty said. "You know, the place those three dudes opened over on Morris St." He took a swig and smacked his lips. "They want to do a tap takeover, maybe after the holidays."

John nodded, and Shorty sat down at his desk, which was pushed up against John's, nose to nose.

"Other than the building inspector, I don't think we have much going on today," John said, getting up. "I need to go check things out in the freezer, start thawing burgers." He slid the restaurant supply catalog from his desk to Shorty's, the pages with the three types of tables earmarked. "You have until close of business to figure this shit out." He smiled, gave Shorty the finger, and walked out.

JOHN STEPPED into the freezer and pulled out boxes of frozen hamburger patties, placing them on a worktable just outside the heavy double-door. He unpacked individual patties, setting them in rows on large metal sheets. He'd become an expert at predicting, down to the last patty, how many burgers they would need each Tuesday for their half-price burger special.

He looked forward to burger nights — always their busiest, no matter the season. He loved watching the regulars forget the cares of the day with burger juice dripping down their chins. He introduced several new burger masterpieces since becoming Shorty's partner. The Jersey Burger (with chili and jalapeños). The Quack Burger (fried in duck fat, topped with a duck egg). The Hudson Burger (with five different kinds of cheese). And finally, the Butterfield Burger (cooked in butter and garlic, topped with parmesan cheese). The Quack Burger turned out to be one of their biggest sellers, Shorty's harrumphing about it be damned.

He couldn't believe it — Marina and Nester, getting on a plane and taking the kid to Disney. He tried to wrap his head around that and couldn't. And then visiting his mother. His mother! He looked at his watch, sure they were already in his mother's living room, hugs and cheery greetings out of the way. It made him sick. He rarely talked to Marina anymore, their only connection being Nester, and even that had become a loose connection at best. John still considered Nester his closest friend — always would — but the guy was hopelessly devoted to playing the happy hubby and doting daddy role. They rarely saw each other anymore, but Ness called last night to ask if he'd found a ring for Annie.

He wondered how Ness even managed to get Marina to agree to fly. Florida wasn't such a haul, they could have driven. During their marriage, getting Marina to do anything outside of her comfort zone was like pulling teeth. Especially flying. She hated it, was afraid of it. Marina was full of surprises since the divorce, like embracing parenthood — something she fought against during their marriage — with her fucking rapist's kid. His wounds bled anew every time he thought about it.

Hot sweat rolled down his cheeks as he fumed over the happy reunion at his mother's house. He continued unpacking hamburger patties, cursing as he slapped them onto trays, yelling as he slammed the trays down on the rack. With an angry grunt, he shoved the whole fucking thing into the refrigeration unit to thaw in time for the dinner crowd.

. . .

"Yeah, everything is deliberate. Even the atmosphere." John found Shorty and the building inspector behind the bar, Shorty pointing to the CD player. "It's almost Christmas, so I'll intersperse a few poppy-type holiday tunes into the usual mix."

It wasn't clear to John why Shorty felt a need to discuss music with the inspector. His anger at his mother, unjustified as it was, for not telling him about Marina and Nester's visit was still close to the surface. He took a deep breath and tried to swallow it. The building inspector stood by engrossed in every word falling from Shorty's lips. John stuck in a CD, filling the pub with the Clancy Brothers.

"And, you're right," Shorty said. "This business gets into your blood. You can't escape it."

They made their way to the door leading to the proposed patio. Forty-five minutes later, the three of them stood at the bar again. The inspector shook their hands, telling them the patio, fence, proposed seating area, ingress, and egress all looked good. Still, he would need to review the plans to ensure they met building codes, local ordinances, zoning regulations, among other mundane details. With Christmas around the corner, it would likely be the second or third week in January before they'd hear back from him. John wished it could happen sooner, but, c'est la vie. At least things were moving.

John walked from table to table, straightening napkin holders, lifting ketchup and mustard bottles and shaking them. Shorty came up behind him and handed him a stack of burger flyers. One for each table. John went along with this, but really, everyone who came in on burger night already knew the menu by heart. Wouldn't a chalkboard listing the burger specials be better? John handed him an empty salt shaker and took the flyers, following orders like a good soldier. He walked around the pub and placed one at each table. Same as last week, same as the week before that. A complete waste of paper and time. His cell phone vibrated in his pocket. Annie wouldn't call this early — he hoped all was well.

"What's wrong with you?" Shorty plopped into the booth across from where John was slumped over the table, head in his hands. John slid his phone across the table, not remembering sitting down. Shorty opened it.

"Okay. So what?" He stared at John. "So, Dale is calling you. So what?"

"I haven't talked to her in two or three years. Not since I got her wedding invitation."

"Maybe the marriage didn't work out, and she wants to see if you're available."

"You suck," John said, trying not to laugh. He threw a bottle of mustard at him. Shorty caught it and tossed it back. The phone buzzed again, wobbling in a circle on the table like a dog chasing its tail. Dale again. *She can chase her tail all she wants.* John didn't answer. His phone buzzed again. "What the hell does she want with me?"

"I already told you," Shorty said.

"I have no interest in talking to her."

"And I'm sure she knows about Annie," Shorty said, a hint of sarcasm on his lips.

"Actually, she probably does, through Marina and Nester." The phone buzzed again, the third call in less than fifteen minutes. John put his hand over it. When it stopped, he picked it up and turned it off.

"Thank God," Shorty said. "Come on. Let half-price burger night begin."

John maneuvered himself out of the booth, astonished at the effort it required. He shuffled to the front door and unlocked it, flipping the switch on for the Christmas lights. He stepped outside and took a few steps into the street, cocking his head to admire them, the calls from Dale forgotten.

"You folks ready for Christmas?" John braced himself for the requisite small talk with his regular customers. It was one of the things about being a pub owner he hated. He set the drinks down and remembered the barrage of calls from Dale, wondering what the hell she wanted. He mentally reviewed the possibilities: she wanted to reconnect; she was pissed that Marina got invited to visit his mother in Florida; she wanted to reconnect — no, he already discounted that.

He slowly came back to the present moment and started processing the words and as the couple at the table answered his question about Christmas. *God, how long have I been standing here?* He hoped he at least looked like he was listening.

"...and the dog will be groomed," Bruce finished.

"Just the little one. And the glasses didn't fit," Irene added. John nodded and said it all sounded great, silently hoping the glasses weren't for the dog.

"The usual burgers?" He didn't wait for a response, because these people were as predictable as death and taxes. He made a graceful exit and walked over to the bar, where he punched in Jersey Burger (for Irene) and Quack Burger (for Bruce).

THE RESTAURANT SUPPLY catalog had been placed neatly on John's chair. He picked it up and saw that a sheet of paper marked the page. Shorty had circled the black metal square tables, and on the paper wrote: *order eight of them and get the green umbrellas.* Great. He would do that first thing tomorrow. Right now, he needed to order waffles, refried beans, eggs, and bacon for New Year's Day. Yeah, he was that confident that his brunch invention would be a hit.

John pulled his cell phone out of his pocket and set it on the desk next to his computer monitor. He flipped it open and turned it on, stunned by all the missed calls from Dale. He checked his voicemail and saw that Dale had left him a message. He pressed the button to listen but slammed the phone shut before he could hear the tenor of Dale's voice. She brought out the worst in him, he understood that now, but six years ago, when she had come to visit after Marina's rape, well, let's just say she brought out something in him that he thought had died. His biggest regret was that he'd chased after it and jumped in headfirst the minute his marriage was over. What a mistake it had been. What a huge, fucking mistake. Why doesn't anyone warn you about getting involved with the siblings of exes?

"There you are," Shorty stood in the doorway. "If you're not busy, I could use some help out front."

"Why didn't you warn me about getting involved with Dale?" John stood up but didn't move toward the door. "I mean, back then, why didn't you tell me not to get involved with Marina's sister?"

"Would you have listened?" Shorty raised an eyebrow. "No, I didn't think so."

"I hate you," John said.

"I hate you more," Shorty said. "Just call her back already. Put to rest whatever is going on in your head. I need you here, and I need you to be fully present, if you catch my drift."

"I don't have feelings for her anymore."

"I know," Shorty said. "And you're not afraid of how you might react hearing her voice."

"Actually, I'm not." The truth was, he felt like Dale calling him was an intrusion into his life. And he refused to get sucked into her drama.

He followed Shorty to the dining room, where the smell of sizzling burgers made his mouth water. He'd forgotten to eat lunch and suddenly felt starved. Revelry and merriment rang out from every booth, barstool, and table. For the first time ever, he worried they might run out of burgers. He disappeared into the supply room, opened the refrigeration unit, and counted patties.

Back in the dining room, John ordered a burger for himself — the one fried in duck fat. He saw that Bruce and Irene needed their drinks refilled and did so without asking. Two hours flew by: running food and drinks to the tables, asking about family and Christmas, shaking hands with friends of friends in for the holidays, cringing at some of Shorty's music choices, wiping down and resetting tables.

John snuck away to his office to call Annie. He hadn't planned to see her tonight but found himself wanting to crawl into bed beside her. The kitchen stayed open until ten, but it would be well after midnight by the time he'd get out of there.

Damn. His burger. Shorty must have run it to the office from the kitchen. He lifted the bun and touched his finger to the meat — cold, of course. He was so hungry that he took a bite anyway. *Blech*. He washed it down with a swig of water. He picked up three limp fries and shoved them into his mouth. He took several more bites of the burger and guzzled more water. Within minutes the burger was gone, and he eyed the remaining fries. He picked one up, twirled it around between his fingers, then put it back down on the plate. After pushing the plate to the side, he picked up his cell phone to call Annie. Crap. Four more missed calls from Dale. A sense of impending doom descended like a foot on his chest. This couldn't be Dale wanting to chat or Dale feeling out his relationship status. She simply didn't operate that way. Something had happened.

He pushed the button on his cell phone and set the voicemail on speaker. Dale's voice sounded muffled, far away, small, and uncharacteristically high pitched, so he took it off the speaker and held the phone to his ear. He still couldn't make out anything she said. He turned the volume all the way up and played it again. He listened to the message several more times. Still unable to decode her gibberish, he checked to see if she'd left any other messages. She hadn't. He played the voicemail again, wishing he could slow the cadence of her voice, like on a tape recorder or a VHS. The pub phone on his desk rang, startling him. *Shorty will pick it up,* he thought. When John saw the blinking light, he knew that Shorty had. *Screw it.* He dialed Dale's number, which rolled directly to voicemail. Shorty walked in, looking pale and shaken. He stood in front of the desk. John closed his phone.

"Um, I could be wrong, but," Shorty said, trying to choose his words. "From what I understand," he continued, then hesitated. "Here's the thing."

"What? What?" John suddenly wondered if Annie was okay. "What's going on?"

"I just talked to your mother."

"My mother?" John blinked. "When? How?"

"Well, she called the pub."

"She didn't want to talk to me?"

"She did, but I didn't know where you were." Shorty paused. "She was hysterical."

"Hysterical funny, or hysterical-hysterical?" Of course, John knew the answer, but his brain couldn't process the words. He stood up and paced the room.

"Hysterical-hysterical."

"What the hell is going on? Is my mother okay? I'm calling her." He walked back to his desk and grabbed his phone, frantically punching his mother's number. No answer. *Voicemail box full.* "Oh, for fuck's sake, this is ridiculous." He sat, trying to get his pounding heart to settle down.

"Listen, John, your mother is fine," Shorty said.

"What then?"

"It's Nester." Shorty cleared his throat. "The three of them. Nester, Marina, and the kid. They were in a car accident this afternoon. On their way to visit your mother."

John felt relief wash over him. That's what Dale had wanted to tell him. He pictured the family bruised and battered but otherwise in good spirits. His mother at the hospital, yelling at the doctors, trying to figure out how to get the little family back to her place. Bummer that this happened on their vacation. Bummer that now his mother had to nurse two adults and a child back to health. Bummer.

"It's not good," Shorty said, throwing cold water onto John's *everything will be okay* scenario. Shorty filled in the details. John ran out the back door and retched. When nothing happened, he fell to his knees. He heaved, this time causing the undigested contents of his stomach to spill into the night.

5

Annie

Annie ran out of her apartment, not wearing a coat and now sat shivering in the back seat of a cab. She frantically patted the empty seat next to her, sure she'd forgotten her purse, sighing with great relief when she looked down and saw it sitting in her lap. She took a deep breath and held it, feeling the sharp edges of misery creeping up her spine as her last dose of pain pills wore off. Just that afternoon, her oncologist called and suggested something he deemed a bit unconventional but effective, he'd assured her. It amounted to a single, mega-dose of radiation. Not her favorite prospect, but she was willing to try anything and scheduled the procedure for the day after tomorrow. She wanted to talk to John about it later, but now, well, her cancer had slipped off the priority list.

She felt terrible leaving Henry home alone, not because she didn't feel like he could handle it — at thirteen (almost fourteen, as he often reminded her) he was quite capable of taking care of himself

— but because they'd been having such a quiet, pleasant evening. Each in their respective chairs in the living room, Henry reading *Harry Potter and the Order of the Phoenix* and she reading *The Five People You Meet in Heaven*. She had just settled in with her heating pad when Shorty called. She didn't go into the gory details with Henry but simply told him that John's best friend had died, and she needed to go over and comfort him. Henry practically shoved her out the door, assuring her that she could stay out as late as she needed, even spend the night. The child parenting the parent. Henry loved John, and that made her happy.

The cab driver let Annie out in front of Shorty's, which looked uncharacteristically mobbed, even for this time of year. She paid, made sure she had cash for the return trip, and stood in front of the door, cursing herself for not grabbing her coat. The festive lights around the door made a mockery of John's situation. She hesitated, remembering the first time she'd stood at this very door, three years ago, the night after the towers fell. She'd been afraid to go in then and was terrified to go in now. The door swung open, and several people spilled out, laughing and lamenting the cold. They would go home to their respective lives, unaware that inside the pub, probably in the back office, a man sat reeling in grief over his best friend's death. She caught the door just as it was about to slam shut and slipped inside.

She took in the bustle of the place, the joy, the laughter, the anticipation of the holidays. Under any other circumstance, she would have enjoyed the merriment. But her back — and her heart — hurt too severely. She'd only met Nester once or twice. But he and John were like brothers. She saw Shorty pouring beer and slowly made her way to the bar. A man offered her his seat, but she declined.

"Hey, Kirk, take over for a few," Shorty yelled. A young man with tattoos on the backs of his hands brushed past Annie. Kirk and Shorty do-se-do'd around each other, as if part of a choreographed dance recital, Kirk sliding behind the bar and Shorty sliding out. He gave Annie a quick hug and motioned toward the back of the pub, to the door leading into the office.

"How is he?" Annie followed a few steps behind — anything to prolong the time between now and a few seconds from now. She and John had known each other for three years, two really, if you didn't count the time between 9/11 and when he found her a year later. Two years. Such a short amount of time, yet they'd seen each other at their best, and at their worst. They'd even had to face the reality of her dying young, which often resulted in inconsolable sobs, from both of them. But never, ever, had they been faced with something like this. She had no idea what to expect, what she would find, how John would be.

"Sucky." Shorty gently opened the office door, and they stepped inside.

"Hey," John said. He leaned back in his chair, feet on his desk. He had the phone receiver tucked between his ear and his chin, its long, curly cord carrying the sound waves of despair. He put his hand over the mouthpiece and softly said: "I have Dale on the line." He went back to his conversation, eyes wet with tears, murmuring things Annie couldn't make out. She knew about Dale — it was one of the first things John shared when they were getting to know each other, spilling his guts about Dale, bit by bit, over a several-day period. At the time, she told him she understood. But Annie didn't understand, not really. There had never been a time in her marriage that she'd felt like she'd married the wrong man or pined for another. Even given Alec's foibles — his incessant list-making and holier-than-thou arrogance — she'd never once looked longingly and wistfully at another man. Until John, of course. But by the time she realized she'd fallen hard, well, Alec had already checked out.

"You want a beer?" Shorty looked at Annie, then at John on the phone. "We might be here a while."

"No, thanks." Annie looked at John, who was softly laughing at something Dale said. Her heart sank a little. "On second thought, yes, I'd love one." Shorty got up, and Annie called after him: "You'd better bring one for John."

"I think he needs something stronger," he said, walking toward the door.

Annie stood behind John and kissed the top of his head — her way of peeing on the rosebushes, although she felt ridiculous for the gesture and the meaning behind it. Dale had not a clue that the rosebushes even existed. Nor could she see Annie peeing on them. Annie rubbed John's shoulders as he talked. She heard Dale's voice coming from the earpiece, but couldn't decipher the broken, high-pitched tones. It sounded very far away.

"Okay. Talk later." John let his legs fall from the desktop. He sat up straight in his chair, scooted closer to the desk, and set the phone back down on the receiver. "That was Dale," he said to Annie, strangely calm, wet eyes now dry.

Having been married to a shrink had its benefits — free advice and psychological principals, doled out spoonful by spoonful throughout their twelve-year union. A mistake she'd made often with Alec was to bombard him with questions during times of crisis or when he'd been upset about one thing or another. It took many times of screwing up, of not being able to control her impulse to badger him, of him shutting her out — leading to a vicious cycle of continued badgering — before it finally sunk in. She needed to let John come to her. She needed to follow his lead.

"Nester was killed in a car accident," John said, matter-of-factly, as if he were reporting that Nester had chosen the salmon and wild rice for dinner. He opened his arms, and she hugged him, releasing the tight hold he'd had on his emotions for the past few minutes. He sobbed into her neck for what seemed like a very long time.

SHORTY RETURNED, balancing a tray containing Annie's beer, two glasses filled with ice, and a bottle of scotch. He set the tray down on the desk, handed Annie a beer, and poured scotch into the two glasses. Annie took a sip of her beer, wishing she'd asked for something stronger. She didn't like scotch, but figured it would take the edge off her pain better than beer. Either that or she would get so drunk that she would no longer care about or even notice how much pain she was in. Shorty raised his glass as if to make some sort of toast. Annie gently clicked her beer against his scotch, and both waited for John to pick up his glass, but he sat staring into space. She gently placed his hand around his glass. Going through the motions, John slowly brought the glass up to his lips. Clinking his glass against anyone else's seemed like it was more than he could bear. He set the drink back down, put his elbows on the desk, and buried his face in his hands.

"It's bad," John said through his fingers. "Marina is in critical condition." He hesitated, then moved his hands out of the way. "The kid, he's okay. I think just a broken arm or something like that."

"Fuck." Shorty reached across the desk and patted John's arm. "I'm so sorry, man." And then: "Listen, take all the time you need. I've got it covered. Don't worry about anything here. Do what you need to do." John sat, unresponsive, unmoving, cradling his head as if it were too heavy to hold up on its own.

Annie tugged at her turtleneck, choking on the heat. If she'd been cold earlier, she now felt like she was cooking from the inside. She pulled the collar away from her skin and held it out, willing a cool breeze down her shirt. The air in John and Shorty's office sat stagnant, unmoving, stale, and suddenly the smell and taste of the beer turned her stomach. She grabbed John's glass and took a long sip of scotch, shuddering as it slid down her throat. When the burn subsided, she let go of her collar and let it bounce back against her neck. She took another swig, thinking about her newest art therapy patient, Mel, and his odd request for scotch when she'd offered him coffee or tea. She imagined her face looked something like Henry's did the first time she and Alec fed him smooshed peas.

"The kid wanted a milkshake." John lifted his head with great effort, the lines on his forehead deeper and more defined than Annie had ever noticed. He was only fifty-six, but at that moment, looked seventy. "I'm not even sure how Dale could possibly know all those details already. But that's what she said. They stopped to get the kid a milkshake." John pounded the desk with his fist. "A fucking milkshake."

"They got hit coming out of McDonald's," Annie said, filling in the blanks for Shorty, who had been out getting their drinks when John rattled off the facts of the accident, as recounted to him by Dale. "Their car apparently spun out of control and ended up in a lane of oncoming traffic. Then another car hit them. Dale didn't say what happened to the other drivers."

"The car didn't *apparently* spin out of control," John said, lifting his head, emphasizing *apparently*. "It flat-out spun out of control."

Had this been Alec, four or five years ago, Annie would have pushed back. No matter the logic of whatever might have been going on with him and causing him to be short, she would have fought for her right to use whatever terminology she damn well chose. Sometimes days would go by before Alec came to her, sheepishly, humbly, apologizing. A symptom of more important things at play, she now understood. Now, Annie only pushed back when it truly mattered. Tonight she wanted to give John space and to make allowances for him in his grief.

"I need to go to Florida." John sat straight up and looked around the room as if seeing it and the people in it for the first time. "Fuck. I need to call the police department about Ness. I'm not even sure if they've been notified yet. Fuck. Fuck. Fuck!" He lifted the handle off the phone on his desk and dialed.

"Captain Murdoch. This is John. John Butterfield. Yeah. I'm sorry to call you at home. It's about Quinn. Yep. Yes. I'm going to try to fly down tomorrow, the next day at the latest. Yep, I can do it. Thanks. Goodnight." He looked at Annie. "They'd already heard." He choked back a sob. "I told the captain I'll ID the body. Ness was alone. No next of kin. Except for Marina."

"So, what's going on with her," Shorty asked.

"I don't know. My mother is there." John picked up his drink as if seeing it for the first time. He sucked it down in one quick gulp. "I really don't know. From what Dale said, she's not aware, or not conscious, or something." He stuck his finger in his glass and swirled the remaining ice. "My mother is a mess." He lifted the glass to his lips and used his tongue to scoop out a mostly melted, nubby ice cube, crushing it between his teeth. "Dale made some sort of arrangements with the hospital so my mother could take the kid home. That will happen in a few days." He retrieved another ice cube, this time with his fingers, and swallowed it without chewing. "Dale is in Australia and can't get a flight until later this week."

Tired of her hair falling in her eyes, Annie adjusted her headband, repositioning it closer to her hairline. She reached behind her back and rubbed. Shorty must have noticed this, must have seen that she'd helped John with his scotch and barely touched her beer. He must have noticed the empty scotch glass. He took the tray and quietly disappeared as John studied his computer screen, scrolling through a list of flights.

"I'll go with you," she said.

"I don't know. You have Henry to worry about. I don't want to burden you with this."

"This is not a burden." She wanted to be with him, help him, support him, love him. "I want to."

"I don't know," he said. "I just don't know."

Annie got up from her chair and sat on the desk, looking over his shoulder at the flights. She needed to call Henry and let him know she wouldn't be home tonight. She felt like a horrible parent, but she knew he'd get himself up, make himself breakfast, and take the bus to school. She needed to call Alec, too. Maybe he'd be willing to go over there and stay the night with Henry. She hopped off the desk and walked toward the back of the office, leaving John alone with his flight list.

"Alec." She didn't expect him to answer on the first ring. "I need a favor. A huge favor." She explained what had happened and that she wanted to fly out with John tomorrow or the day after. "Could Henry stay with you for a few days, maybe until Christmas?" Ten minutes later, they'd decided that while Henry would be okay by himself for tonight, Alec would go over and keep him company. Then Henry would stay with Alec through Christmas. She ended the call feeling tender toward her ex-husband, a rare occurrence. He'd been quite vocal over the past few years in his dislike for John, but, Annie supposed, he could sense the depth of their relationship. She felt especially grateful tonight for his support and accommodation. So grateful.

Shorty returned with fresh drinks. He handed Annie her own glass of scotch, then set one before John and once again, raised his glass. This time John raised his too.

AT FIRST GLANCE, John's kitchen appeared well-stocked for a man who ate most of his meals at the pub or at Annie's place. Upon closer inspection, though, most of the items in his fridge were either expired or opened and moldy. The same in the pantry. Annie rummaged through both, looking for something, anything, to throw together.

They'd walked the four blocks from the pub to John's house after Shorty kicked them out of the pub a little before nine. She'd wanted to call a cab, but that seemed too hard at the time. At the second traffic light with two blocks to go, Annie felt hot tears streaming down her face. She ignored them in an attempt to hold it together for John. It was now after ten. She'd encouraged him to take a long, hot shower, promising him he'd feel better for it, if not emotionally, then definitely physically. She also promised him something to eat, although he wrinkled his nose at the thought.

The plumbing gurgled and moaned as if clearing its throat. A minute later a pop, then a hiss, and finally water trickling out of the old showerhead, hitting the bottom of the tub, taking its time, building up to a crescendo, struggling as if running uphill, never quite reaching its full water pressure potential. A gentle rain rather than a monsoon. The sound — a calming white noise — echoed through the old plaster walls.

Annie stood at the counter, chopping limp carrots and celery. Limp was okay. Salvageable. She found a single, misshapen onion on the pantry floor, sprouting a green neck. Thank goodness, no slime. Along with the carrots and celery, the onion perfected an already aromatic sauté. An opportunity presented itself in the form of a roll of Jimmy Dean hot sausage, which she'd found in the freezer. She watched as it slowly rotated around and around in the microwave.

The main water pipe bucked, and then the silence of an ended shower. Annie stuck her head in the pantry again, moved a few random items out of the way, and pulled out a can of chicken broth and a can of garbanzo beans. Feeling like she won the lottery, she poured them into the pot with the vegetables.

John's footsteps thumped across the ceiling, his bedroom directly above the tiny kitchen. She threw the sausage in a pan and browned it, then added it to the large pot. There. Spicy sausage and garbanzo bean soup. Not quite the way her sister made it, but close. The only thing missing, a handful of kale. Somehow, she didn't think John would care.

"Yes, right. Tomorrow afternoon," John shuffled into the kitchen wearing a pair of striped pajama bottoms and a sweatshirt. He had his cell phone in one hand, and a sheet of paper in the other. "My mother," he said to Annie.

She nodded and turned back to the pot, swirling the wooden spoon and watching bits of carrots, celery, garbanzo beans, and chunks of sausage come to the surface. Careful to avoid the solids, she let the broth fill the spoon. She lifted it to her lips and tasted it. Not bad.

Still on the phone, John walked out of the kitchen. Annie picked up the sheet of paper he dropped on the table. A flight confirmation. One. *Seat fourteen-C, aisle.* One. One seat. One. She fought back tears as she set the paper down and resumed mindlessly stirring the soup. She jumped when she felt John come up behind her at the stove and put his arms around her. She was so upset she felt her body go stiff.

"It smells good," he said. "I don't know how much I'll be able to eat, but I'll try." He squeezed her, but she stood, unresponsive, stirring the soup. "What's wrong?"

"Nothing." Annie lied. "My back is killing me." At least that part was genuine.

"Let me rub it for you."

"No, no, that won't help." She turned off the burner and ladled the soup into two bowls. John picked them up and carried them to the table.

"This is bullshit." He set the bowls on the table a little too aggressively, soup splashing over the rims. "I thought they gave you new meds. They need to do something different."

"They are, they are," she said, happy for a distraction — a topic not related to the day's tragic event or the fact that he didn't want her to go to Florida with him. "I never got a chance to tell you today. I'm getting a mega-dose of radiation." She couldn't recall the day or time. "They say it will feel like a miracle." She reached for a napkin and wiped the spilled soup. She sat down, no additional words necessary. At least not for a bit.

"I'm leaving tomorrow afternoon," John said, raking the soup with his spoon. "I have to be at the airport by one-thirty."

Annie stared at the calendar, hanging on the wall behind John's chair. He'd never turned the month from November to December. Her ex-husband couldn't stand to look at a calendar that didn't have a big line through each day gone by. She felt the walls of John's tiny kitchen closing in around her. Was she mad or just hurt that he didn't invite her to go to Florida with him? She kept her eyes fixed on the calendar. She sensed him struggling with the soup — still too emotionally distraught to eat. She knew he felt responsible for all that had gone wrong in his ex-wife's life, the rape mainly — feeling like he should have protected her. Annie wanted to jump up and down and scream and beg him to take her to Florida with him. But she sat stoic, looking past John at the calendar on the wall, resolving to give him space. She wouldn't go to Florida with him now if he begged her.

"Oh, I have something for you." John stood and walked out of the kitchen, shouting over his shoulder. "Don't go away." He returned a minute later with a sheet of paper. He sat down and slid it across the table. Annie looked at the airline confirmation. One. *Seat fourteen-B, middle.* One. One seat. One. She fought back tears as she set the paper back down. "I tried to get you a window seat, but that would mean we couldn't sit together." He smiled, then his eyes filled. He blinked, and fresh tears streamed down his cheeks.

"Thank you," was all she could squeak out. John used his feet for leverage and pushed his chair away from the table, pulling Annie into his lap. She put her arms around him and buried her face in his neck, her tears mingling with his.

"What about Henry?" John pushed his soup away. "I'm sorry, I can't eat this right now."

"It freezes well," she said. "Alec is taking him." She looked deep into his eyes and wiped away the wet spots underneath them with her finger. "I didn't think you wanted me to come."

"I don't." He laughed. "My mother is a royal pain in the ass. I love her dearly, but she could be a bitch on wheels. Did I ever tell you she rides a motorcycle?" Annie raised an eyebrow and smiled. "I don't want you to be the unlucky recipient of her unfiltered angst." His eyes filled again. "Fuck. I can't believe it. I can't believe he's dead. I just can't believe it." Annie held him while he sobbed. "So, no, I don't want you to come." He pulled away and locked his eyes on hers. "But I can't imagine going down there to deal with this mess without you."

"A very selfish request," she said. "But I accept. I can't imagine you dealing with this alone. I was quite hurt when I thought you didn't want me to go."

"I know," he said. "I could feel it in the air."

"You're very perceptive."

"It's why they used to call me Hawk." John got up from the table carrying the two untouched bowls of soup.

And as if tonight were just any ordinary night, they stood at the sink, side by side, decanting soup into plastic containers, labeling them, and setting them neatly in the freezer. They left the stockpot and dirty bowls in the sink and climbed the stairs, dancing around each other in John's tiny bathroom with moves that looked perfectly natural and unscripted, as if they'd been doing life together for years and years.

6

John

John stared at the mountain of clean laundry on his bed, fresh from the dryer and still warm. He picked up a tee-shirt and pressed it into his forehead to soothe the sinus pressure he feared would only get worse the minute the plane took off. It had been a long night of fitful bursts of sleep, punctuated by his swirling mind and Annie's inability to find a comfortable position for her back. At some point, just before dawn, he'd plunged into a deep sleep, the type of sleep that strips memory. A deceptive sleep. The type of sleep that ends in a shocking wake-up where reality hits — the nightmare is real.

When he was a cop, John kept the soft, squishy part of his personality under wraps. Nester was the only other cop who'd seen it. The only person he wept in front of when Marina was raped and during the long months after. None of that compared to how much he cried during the past twelve hours. He hated the cliché, but honestly, he cried an ocean.

Trying to think about how to pack for this trip paralyzed him. His mother told him to pack for summer. But then he envisioned cold hospital rooms and figured he'd better pack a few long sleeve shirts and his fleece jacket. A sweatshirt too. Oh, and his striped pajama bottoms. He plucked items out of the laundry pile and tossed them into his duffle bag. He moved a few inches to the left to grab his jeans and stepped on something hard, cold, and sharp. The offending keychain that had slipped off the bed mocked him from its position on the floor.

"Fuck, that hurt," he groaned, leaning against his dresser and rubbing the bottom of his foot. He picked up the keys and threw them across the room. They bounced off the wall and slid across the hardwood floor, and, like a boomerang, landed right back at John's feet. He picked up the keychain and held out the third key — the one with the blue rubber cap over it. His old key. The key to his old house, his former life. The life he had before the rape. He changed the locks a few days later, but he never threw away the old key. Next on the keychain: the healing key — the key that represented the way forward after the rape. He could never have predicted it to be the key that would unlock all the doors to everything that had been broken in his and Marina's marriage.

John plopped on the bed and curled into a fetal position, feeling gut-punched — like he heard the news all over again. All the air seemed to escape his lungs. His cell phone buzzed. Annie. He didn't want to talk to anyone right now, not even her. He'd sent her home a few hours ago to do her own packing and planned to meet her at the airport later. Damn. Should he pack the ring? Take it on the trip? Give it to her on Christmas Eve? Or Christmas morning? Or a random Wednesday? He'd promised Henry Christmas morning and felt like he needed to honor that. He hoped they'd be back before then.

He looked out the window and caught the tail end of a firetruck roaring down the street. An ambulance followed. His imagination played tricks on him as he tried to envision what the scene outside of the McDonald's in Florida had been like. *They fucking had to stop to get the kid a milkshake.* John felt anger rising in his throat like bile. *Once again, the kid takes precedence.* The kid that Marina had to have, at the expense of their marriage. The kid that had to have a milkshake, at the cost of his daddy. And possibly his mommy. Fuck. Marina. He hadn't yet come to terms with the fact that she might die. When he talked to his mother last night, she said Marina was critical but stable. Whatever the hell that meant. He didn't know the details, but he did know that she was in a coma or some other such state of not being conscious. He wasn't sure if she had a head injury or what. Probably a head injury. Fuck. He didn't know. The bottom line, though, was that she's alive now. And Nester's dead. And the kid, once again, at the center of a cosmic shift. He picked up his phone.

"Hey. Sorry I didn't answer when you called." He paused. "I'm basically a mess." He smiled, hearing her voice. "Yep. See you soon." And then: "I love you."

He picked up the keychain again and looked at the other keys — much happier keys, the keys to his future. The key to his boat. After Annie had gone away, it was on his boat that he realized he loved her. The key to this house — the first house he owned as a divorced man, bought with the money he received from Marina buying him out of the house they'd lived in for almost all twenty years of their marriage. And finally, perhaps the happiest key of all — the key to Annie's apartment. She'd given it to him reluctantly, maybe a year or so ago. He hadn't asked for it. She'd simply said, *it probably makes sense that you have this.* He kissed her key and tossed the keychain in his bag.

He put on a black tee-shirt, and over that, his red flannel shirt. He picked up his duffle and carried it downstairs, leaving the remaining laundry untouched on his bed. He turned on the water at the sink and let it fill up with soap bubbles. He'd never dealt with the dishes from Annie's soup last night, and now the crust on the inside of the bowls was hard as concrete. They'll have to soak for a while. He called the morgue to let them know he would be there first thing in the morning to identify Nester. Then he called Captain Murdoch again. The department planned to wait for Marina to recover before laying Nester to rest with full honors.

He hung up the phone after talking to the captain, incredulous that he had to make such a call in the first place. The world was still turning. How could that be? How could the world keep turning when one of the best men he'd ever known was no longer in it? And here was John — a bona fide dick in many ways — alive and well and living a good life. Ness didn't deserve this. He'd been a good dad to Luke. A great husband to Marina. John knew he would lose Annie someday, too. But until then, they had moments: great moments on exceptional days, great moments on bad days, bad moments on good days, mundane moments filling in the gaps. All the moments, when added up, equaled a life of bliss, just knowing that the person who meant everything to you was still breathing.

He ran up the stairs and into the spare bedroom where he some-times lifted weights, sometimes took care of pub business on his computer, and mostly threw things that didn't otherwise have a proper place — unseasonal clothes, a ten-year-old pair of boots he never wore, stacks of papers and books, and Annie's ring. He'd hid it in the pocket of his dress blues which hung in the back of the closet, pressed between a suit that had come back from the dry cleaners four years ago and was still in the plastic, and his father's Army fatigues. He pulled out the box and opened it. The tiny diamond sparkled in the compass, more brilliant than he'd realized. Annie — his North Star.

He carried the box downstairs. He wasn't one to stock gift wrap for unexpected occasions but did have a pile of newspapers set aside for recycling. He pulled one out and unfolded it, placing the box in the middle. As carefully as he could, he wrapped the box with the newspaper, then secured it with duct tape. He opened his duffle bag, made a small burrow in the clothes, and tucked it in.

PART II

7

____

Luke

His arm hurt. Bad. Real bad. Luke studied it, looking for blood, but didn't see any. His hand hurt too. He felt grit in his eyes and rubbed at them with his other hand. And he was hot. He remembered asking Daddy if Grammy's house had a pool. Mommy would have told him if it had a pool, but Mommy liked to surprise him sometimes. She surprised him with this trip. He loved the plane ride but felt a little scared when it got bumpy. Daddy started singing his favorite song every time it got rough. *I've got friends in low places*. Mommy told Daddy to be quiet. But she laughed. Luke really liked the plane ride. He loved it when the plane took off and when it landed. He was excited to ride the plane again next week.

He was asking Daddy if Grammy's house had a pool when he heard a loud noise. The car crashed. And spun around. And crashed again. And now they were stopped. His arm hurt. His hand too. He heard sirens and looked out the window. No smoke. He saw a car crash on TV once, and there was smoke. And fire. *I've got friends in low places*. He started singing it, and Daddy opened his eyes.

"Hey Lukey," Daddy said.

"My arm hurts."

"I know." Daddy closed his eyes.

"Daddy. Dad. Daddy?" Luke put his hand on Daddy's shoulder and shook it. "Daddy, you're bleeding," Luke yelled. "Daddy, you're bleeding." He found the napkins from McDonald's and held one to Daddy's head.

"Lukey, it's okay. I'm okay. Try to be quiet. Mommy's sleeping." And then: "I've got friends in low places, where the whiskey drowns, and the beer chases my blues away, and I'll be okay." Daddy smiled and closed his eyes again.

Luke eased his body through the opening between the two front seats and patted Mommy's arm. She looked okay, not bloody like Daddy. He snuggled up between them and cried with his mouth closed, careful to be quiet.

8

Pearl

Pearl hurried down the hallway and stopped. She turned back toward the children's surgical prep area, where she had just, minutes ago, held Luke's hand and told him to be brave. He'd struggled against the sedation mask and within seconds, slipped into a peaceful sleep under the imposing surgical apparatus. Possibly the last peaceful sleep he would have in a long time.

She found the waiting area and sat down, unsure how long it would take to fix a badly broken arm. Luke had not yet been told about his dad's death or how badly his mom had been hurt. Pearl had often delivered difficult news during her career: A parent who'd been rushed to the hospital during school hours. Or a divorce in the making. Not to the principal's office, these kids would be sent. Nope. *Go see Mrs. Butterfield.* These kids would show up, hall pass in hand. Pearl would sit them down and just tell it. Directly. No euphemisms. *Your father had a heart attack, and your mother is at the hospital with him, and I will drive you there. Boom. I understand your parents are divorcing.*

Boom. *Your fourth-period science teacher says you're falling behind. Boom. I'm here to help...always here to help.* These were teenagers standing on the precipice between childhood and adulthood. Strong and resilient. Her grandson, as a six-year-old, had different needs. So young and innocent and baby-like. How in the name of God would she break the news to this precious little boy?

"Our social worker wants to wait until tomorrow before telling him about his parents." Pearl jumped. Dear God, had she been talking to herself? Out loud? The nurse squeezed her shoulder. "They're taking him to the operating room now."

"Yes, of course," Pearl said.

"He's in good hands."

PEARL'S CLOGS squeaked obnoxiously as she hurried through the hospital toward the ICU to see Marina. The squeaking echoed and seemed to bounce off the walls like laughter during a solemn church service. She pushed open the doors and stood, out of breath, in front of the desk.

"Marina Butter..." Pearl caught herself and corrected her error. She often forgot that Marina was now married to someone other than her son. "Marina Quinn." She tried to take a deep breath but seemed only able to fill a fraction of her lungs. "I'm her mother-in-law," she said, her voice a raspy whisper.

The nurse came out from behind the desk and took Pearl's elbow, leading her to a bank of chairs against the wall.

"Sit here. You can't go in yet. Would you like some coffee, in the meantime?"

"No, I don't want coffee." Pearl scowled and felt ready to burst. The nurse looked at her kindly, immune to hysterical family members. "I'm sorry," she said, letting her face relax. "No, thank you. I'd just like to see my daughter-in-law. Please"

"It will just be a little bit." The nurse smiled a practiced smile. "I'll fetch you the minute I get the green light."

Fetch you? Who talks like that? Pearl nodded and pulled her cell phone out of her purse. She knew the use of cell phones wasn't allowed in here, but she desperately needed to talk to someone. Anyone. Maybe she should call John. She looked around to make sure no one was within eyeshot and dialed his number. When he didn't answer, she wondered if maybe he was already in the plane on his way down. She didn't like the idea of his girlfriend tagging along. Didn't like it one bit. She simply wasn't up to putting on a face and making nice-nice to someone who she hoped was just a fleeting thing in John's life. She had far too much on her mind for that.

She took a deep breath, relieved that the air actually went all the way in and filled her lungs. Thank God John would soon be here to help her sort out this mess, deal with the coroner, deal with Marina's doctors, help her with Luke. And wait for Dale to come in from Australia. What a mess.

"Ah, Neal," she said to the ceiling. "If only you were here." She shook her head, missing her husband after all these years. How many? Fifty-two? Could it possibly be that many? She counted on her fingers, shaking her head. She still pictured him the way he looked the last time she saw him, sending him off to fight in Korea. So handsome. So young. John looked a lot like him, especially when he laughed, light dancing in his eyes. Maybe she should have remarried. John had been only four when Neal died. Not that much different from Luke. Oh sure, she'd enjoyed her share of flings over the years. But every time the trajectory turned serious, she panicked.

"I wonder what John's girlfriend is like." She waited for an answer. When one didn't come, she admitted to herself, a bit sheepishly, that a part of her hoped this tragedy might make John come to his senses and maybe, with Nester gone, well, maybe, just maybe rekindle things with Marina. Pearl let the thought trail off. She looked at her feet, then the floor. What would be so wrong if John and Marina got back together? She wanted this to happen more than anything. And yet. She shook her head. The very fact that John hasn't shared much about Annie was telling. So telling. She suspected this one was serious. Damn. Well, she could hope, couldn't she? What would be the harm in that?

"Mrs. Butterfield?" Nurse I'll-Fetch-You was back, again with a smile plastered on her face. "Would you like to see your daughter-in-law now?" Pearl nodded and followed the nurse through the door. "Stepping into an ICU room can be quite jarring." She looked at Pearl. "It's going to be scary. Just know that Marina is getting the best care possible." She deposited Pearl in a chair next to Marina's bed.

Pearl felt like she was trespassing on someone else's property. And it wasn't like any property she'd ever set foot on. The ICU did not emit a warm and fuzzy vibe. It felt more like a house of horrors, with its high-tech noises and flashing monitors everywhere. Poles, IV pumps, and wires galore. Sure, she'd been in the hospital with John bunches of times. But nothing like this. He'd had his tonsils out at eight and his appendix at thirteen. Not to mention his torn calf in high school. Or the time he had a serious case of pneumonia during his first year in college. And let's not forget the major surgery on his leg six years ago, and the extended rehabilitation it entailed. None of those scenes came close to the scene in front of her. She looked at everything in the room. Everything except Marina. She couldn't bring herself to do it.

"Mrs. Butterfield, I'm Julie, your daughter-in-law's critical care nurse for the next twelve hours." Pearl whipped her head around and saw a new nurse standing in the room. She held out a shaky hand, and the nurse took it and squeezed. Pearl's chest tightened with fear.

"Marina has severe trauma to her head. We're monitoring the swelling. Dr. Vargas, the trauma surgeon, should be here in a few minutes." She nodded as if anticipating a question, and continued. "He's probably going to want to surgically insert a device to monitor the intracranial pressure. There is bleeding in the skull cavity, so he will also want to see if any of the vessels need to be repaired."

"She's going to be okay though, right?"

"I want to tell you, yes, but it's too soon to say. We need to let Dr. Vargas assess what's going on in her brain. The next twenty-four hours will be quite telling."

"My son, her husband, I'm sorry, her ex-husband is flying down from New York." Pearl wasn't sure why she felt the need to mention this. Maybe to reassure herself that she had family, that she wasn't alone in the world.

The nurse didn't respond to Pearl's statement and instead hovered over one of the many monitors flanking Marina's bed. She pushed a button, then walked over to the IV drip and made an adjustment.

Pearl finally allowed her eyes to settle on Marina. She looked peaceful, despite all the tubes running in and out of her. And while her face had some swelling, there were no cuts or gashes or large zippers of stitches. She didn't look at all like someone with a traumatic brain injury. She looked like a woman taking a nap.

9

John

John stood on his mother's porch as if fighting against being pulled on stage by a magician. *Any volunteers from the audience?* He didn't raise his hand. He'd been dropped into this situation against his will. If the past six years had taught him anything, it was that life does its own thing. It doesn't ask for your permission or blessing. It doesn't even ask for your opinion. If it wants to toss you around like a pair of dirty socks in a washing machine, it does it whether you like it or not. Life does as it damn well pleases.

He pulled the keychain out of his pocket and shuffled keys out of the way until he found the one to his mother's door. She had given it to him two years ago when he brought his boat down, trying to get over Annie. It had been a sweet time between mother and son. Repayment for all the time she'd spent with him when he broke his leg. During the visit, he distracted himself by fixing things around his mother's house: the vent fan in the guest bathroom, damaged drywall on the ceiling, the leak on the lanai roof. He helped her pick out a new stainless steel fridge. And against his color sensibility, painted a turquoise accent wall in her small dining room.

He ran his hand over the porch railing and touched one of the support columns. During that visit, his mother complained about the peeling paint on hers and several of her neighbors' railings. So, what did he do? He spent the better part of a week painting porch railings up and down his mother's street. When he loaded up his boat for the return home, his mother and her neighbors presented him with several cases of beer. For as long as it lasted, it made damned good ballast.

He turned around when he heard Annie trudging up the walkway, her small suitcase rolling on two wheels behind her, click, click, clicking each time she ran over a crack in the slate pavers. He took the bag from her and carried it up the two steps, then stuck the key in the door and held it open for her.

"Well, here we are," he said, trying to keep his tone light. Annie followed him to the guest room and flung herself backward on the bed, splaying her body as if making a snow angel. "Your back bothering you?"

"Yeah, and I can't take my pills until around ten." She sat up and pulled him down next to her. "Do you mind if I just lay here for a while?"

"Yes. I mean, no. I don't mind." John felt relieved to have a few minutes to himself. "Get comfy. Do you need anything? Water? Something to eat?"

"How about a scotch," she said, smiling.

"If you're serious, I'll have one in your hand before you can blink."

"Right. That's all I need. Meeting your mother for the first time smelling like a distillery." She laughed.

"Fine. Have it your way." He kissed her forehead. "I might just have one myself." He winked and left her there.

The scent of his mother's sage candles overwhelmed him as he walked through the living room toward the kitchen. She had them all over the house and burned them incessantly during his last visit. It surprised him that he didn't notice the smell when he first walked in. He sat down and picked up the candle on the coffee table. *Wax and Wane Candle Company. Apothecary Collection. Purifying Sage.* He held it to his nose and breathed it in, remembering his walkabout two years ago to get over Annie. Let her live her life, he'd told himself. He didn't, at that time, even know if she were alive or dead. He'd spent the better part of that year pining for her. Yet, at the time, he couldn't bring himself to tell his mother about her. He'd simply focused on playing the role of handyman son, chalking it up to occupational therapy. Only problem: it didn't work, and he'd headed back home full of Annie, not void of her as he'd hoped.

He put the candle down and went into the kitchen, pleased to see that his mother had replaced the rest of the appliances — excellent complements to the fridge he'd helped her pick out. It looked like she painted the cabinets too — turquoise, of course. He couldn't say he liked the look but realized that there wasn't much else one could do with metal cabinets sporting a wood-look wallpaper. He sat down at the table and pulled the morgue's phone number out of his wallet. He got so lost in the candle that he forgot why he was here. It all came rushing back, the boulder he'd set down by the couch now threatened to crush him. He didn't remember picking the huge rock back up. The truth was, he never actually set it down. The gravity of the situation loomed as he pushed buttons on his cell phone. At almost five, chances of the morgue still being open were slim. No answer. He closed his phone and sighed, a bit relieved that he could put this task off until tomorrow.

"Hi." He looked up to find Annie standing next to him. A happy distraction. "What time do you think your mother will be home?" She scanned the kitchen. "We should make something for dinner, so she doesn't have to fuss."

"I have a better idea," he said, getting up from the table and opening the pantry door. His mother kept a folder on the top shelf. He pulled it down. "Let's order Chinese." Without waiting for a response, he rummaged through the folder and found the carry-out menu. "How's your back?" Annie glanced up at the ceiling, then shrugged, holding up her palms.

"Not great." Tears shimmered in her eyes. "I rescheduled my radiation for the twenty-seventh." She took a deep, shaky breath. "I'll be okay." He reached across the table and grabbed her hands, pulling her toward him. She moved her chair next to his and laid her head on his chest.

"Maybe you should have stayed home and had your procedure, then you could have come down."

"Yeah, maybe," she said. "But I didn't. And I'm here. And I'll just have to do the best I can."

"You can fly home, have it done, then come back."

"No. No way." She smiled, a little too forcefully, a little too broken. John knew that smile and knew what it meant. She'd smiled that smile a lot on what ended up being their last hours together, on his boat, a few days after 9/11.

John pulled her closer and squeezed her. He didn't stop to think that he might be hurting her ribs. He just wanted to melt into her, sitting here, in his mother's kitchen. Heart to heart. Body to body. To transfer all that was strong in him into her. To infuse her with his love. To take away her pain. He would give anything to be able to do that right now. She eased back.

"Is a glass of scotch still an option?" Annie's eyes pleaded, and John jumped up from the table and rummaged through cabinets without luck. He found a folded step ladder tucked away in the gap between the fridge and the wall. He pulled it out, stood on it, and found the elixir in the cabinet above the refrigerator. He grabbed two glasses, filled them with ice, and poured. Then he went back to the first cabinet he'd opened — the one next to the dishwasher. So, he hadn't imagined it. He pulled out his mother's butter dish and opened the lid. Sure enough, a stick of butter so soft you could frost a cake. He held it out to show Annie, whose arms were on the table, her head resting on them, the glass of scotch untouched. He set the butter dish on the counter and helped her up, walking with her to their room.

"Lay down," he whispered as he helped her onto the bed.

"Don't forget to ask for extra packets of hot mustard," she said.

"Don't worry." He spread a blanket over her and kissed her forehead.

"Wake me when the food gets here." She propped herself up on her elbows.

"I will," he said, backing out of the room, gently closing the door, thinking about the butter dish.

He stood at the edge of the kitchen, puzzled about the butter. Strange. Yes, he knew butter didn't need to be refrigerated. He had a friend growing up whose mother kept butter in a crock — with a tight lid — on the kitchen counter. But John's mother never did. He supposed she might have decided that she likes soft butter for her toast. He walked over to the cabinet where he'd found the butter and opened it, thinking it an odd place to store butter. Why would she store something that she used almost daily in such an inconvenient place? Not to mention the odd category of things she kept in there: dish towels, empty coffee cans, boxes of ant traps, a broken rolling pin, and Miracle Grow plant food. It didn't make sense. He put the butter away in the fridge and sat down at the table.

John polished off his scotch and started working on Annie's when he heard the garage door open. He got up and greeted his mother as she hung her purse on the hook in the mudroom with one hand, and held the door open for the cat with the other. He noticed a foul odor and wondered if it could be the cat. It smelled more like mildew. He scanned the room and didn't see a basket of forgotten laundry nearby.

"Mom." He embraced her. She stood in his arms. Slowly, she pulled away and regarded him. The cat nuzzled her leg, and she bent down to scratch behind his ears. She stood up and looked hard at John.

"Found the scotch, did you?"

"As a matter of fact." Her tone rankled him. "I also found your butter dish." He paused. "In your junk cabinet."

"And your point?"

"It had butter in it, Mom."

"And. Your. Point?" She let out a long, slow, loud breath.

"Never mind." He followed her into the kitchen. She plopped into a chair, fanning herself with the carry-out menu.

"You just won't believe it." She looked at him, eyes wild. "Marina is having surgery tomorrow to reduce swelling around her brain."

"Holy shit. What time?"

"First thing." Her eyes flickered with confusion. "No, not first thing. That's something with Luke. Ten. Yes. I believe her surgery is at ten."

"You hungry?" John couldn't process all this information. Not right now. He needed a distraction and fast.

"No," she said. "Not in the least." She stopped fanning herself and looked at the menu. "But I know I should eat. I hope you got Won Ton Soup."

"I did. And I got you some crispy egg rolls." John's mother got up and fixed herself a gin and tonic. Then she poured some kibble into the cat's bowl and refreshed his water.

"You just won't believe it," she said, again.

"I know," he said. "I've shed all the tears I can shed right now. I really need to put this in a box. At least until tomorrow."

"Where's Anna? When am I going to meet her?"

"It's Annie. And she's resting."

"Oh?" She raised an eyebrow.

"It's complicated, Mother." He wasn't ready to lay it all out on the table. He wasn't prepared to share the details about Annie's history and health. He knew that the minute he opened Pandora's box, his mother would probe. He felt too emotionally drained to answer the barrage of questions he knew would follow. He simply couldn't handle that tonight. Maybe never.

10
———

Annie

Annie stood, her back plastered against the wall outside the kitchen, straining to hear the conversation. She made out certain words — *trauma, gallery, surgery, Henry, morgue, Brooklyn*.

"It's nice to meet you, Mrs. Butterfield." Annie walked into the kitchen and extended her hand. Pearl stood up and hugged her instead, moving backward and holding Annie at arm's length to study her. She realized then that she hadn't bothered to look in the mirror after rolling off the bed. She touched her hair and cringed.

"You look fine, dear," John's mother said as she sat back down. "Call me Pearl."

"You doing okay?" John held out a chair and touched Annie's hand. She nodded.

"I'm so sorry about what happened to your, ex, your, um ex-daughter-in-law," Annie offered.

"Marina," Pearl said. "Marina is very dear to me, no matter how

76

she is related or not related." She glared at Annie, her tone stern and clipped. Direct, as Alec would say.

"Mother." John inflected his voice as he might when trying to redirect a child from the beginnings of a meltdown. "How about we eat?"

"I saw Luke right before I came home," Pearl said, her voice softer. "He had a serious break in his left arm. Elbow and everything. But he'll be okay. They're keeping him in the hospital for a few days." She looked at John. "They haven't told him yet."

Annie couldn't begin to imagine how to tell a young child that his father was dead and that his mother was very badly hurt and might not make it. She just couldn't imagine. Maybe she would call Alec to get some professional advice on what to expect with Luke from the emotional trauma surrounding the accident...and guilt. She could undoubtedly imagine Henry internalizing and blaming himself for something like this. Even at Luke's age, Henry would have felt responsible. He would have driven himself (and everyone else within earshot) crazy with the what-ifs. *What if I didn't want a milkshake? What if they didn't take me to Disney? What if I had been quieter in the car?* Her heart ached for this little boy.

"My ex is a psychologist," she said. "I'd be happy to call him. He could maybe give us tips on how Luke might grieve and what to watch for. You know, so we could help him."

"That's a great idea," John said.

"I was a high school guidance counselor," Pearl said. "I don't need any help with this." She fished the lime out of her glass and sucked on it, then got up and dumped the rind and the rest of the detritus from her drink down the garbage disposal. She returned to the table with a bottle of gin, her glass, and an ice bucket. But no lime.

"That is a great idea," John said again, directing the statement, louder this time, at Annie, while he turned his face, complete with knitted brows, toward his mother. He got up and pulled a baking sheet from the oven, the cartons of Chinese food occupying the space like buildings in a planned urban development. Annie jumped up from the table — any excuse to distance herself from The Judge — and started opening cabinets in search of plates.

"Just use the paper ones," Pearl said. "In the laundry room. The cabinet above the washer." She pointed toward the mudroom. "In there."

Annie stepped into the mudroom, grateful to be away from John's mother. A horrible smell distracted her from her task of getting plates. She covered her nose with the top of her shirt, biting it to keep it from falling, and recalled the time when a niggling odor turned into a gag-inducing olfactory nightmare. She and Alec had turned their apartment upside-down, searching for its origin. They'd even called an exterminator, thinking a mouse or a squirrel had somehow gotten into the building and died in the ceiling or a wall. *This is no dead animal*, the exterminator told them. A day or so later, Annie tripped over the source of the smell. Henry found a bottle — thick green, fuzzy, sludge at the bottom — in his toy box. He put the nipple in his mouth, then tossed the bottle across his room just as Annie entered. He ran toward her and gave her a wet-squishy toddler-kiss. Who knew spoiled orange juice could smell so bad?

The search for paper plates forgotten, Annie moved through Pearl's laundry room in a haphazard, hurried way. She found a wad of chopsticks from prior Chinese carry-out dinners and grabbed them, sticking them in the back pocket of her jeans. Deeper into the laundry room, Annie opened the top of a bench that had built-in cubbies, hooks, and baskets for storage. She found gardening tools, boots, an umbrella, and random grocery store tote bags. She shrugged and started back toward the kitchen. And then, as an afterthought, opened the top of the washing machine. Empty. When she opened the drier, she gasped, pressing her hand over her shirt-draped nose. She reached in and pulled out a package of frozen broc-coli, very much no longer frozen. She was about to grab a trash bag when John walked in.

"There you are, I was wondering..." He stopped mid-sentence and mimicked her gesture, pulling his shirt over his nose. "Damn. I thought I smelled something earlier." He shook his head. "You know, I found butter in a random cabinet in the kitchen."

"This was in the dryer," she said, holding the bag of broccoli at arm's length. "I don't think we should bring this up with your mother." Annie didn't want to make a bad situation worse. "You can talk to her about it privately, in a few days. Or never. Let's not pile anything else on her right now."

"You're right," he said, reluctantly taking the broccoli. "I'll put this in the garbage can outside."

"WHAT, EXACTLY, ARE YOU DOING?" Pearl's question startled Annie back to the present moment. She'd been playing with her food, mindlessly designing a mandala of rice, peas, chunks of chicken, bits of carrot, and a few strands of noodles, wondering what the hell she was doing here. John had been right in his initial apprehension — she should have stayed home. They were sitting at the table, the three of them, eating everything in sight. The conversation stayed superficial, each of them unwilling to bare even a tiny piece of their souls. The atmosphere remained charged with the electricity of tragedy — the smallest spark would engulf them in flames. John and his mother bantered about household minutia and the pub, tiptoeing around the topic of hospitals and car crashes and death.

"Oh, this." Annie glanced at her plate and looked at John, who was smiling. Her tendency to play with her food was a quirk he found endearing — something the two of them held close. An inside joke. A piece of the world uniquely theirs and theirs alone. "It's something I do. I don't even realize I'm doing it half the time." She got up and carried her plate to the sink. "Can I get anyone anything?"

"I'll take a beer," John said.

Annie came back to the table with two beers. Her loose sweatshirt, the one she napped in earlier, slipped off her shoulder — *Flashdance* in all its 80's glory. She pulled it back up and sat up straight, slowly sipping her beer.

"What is that?" Pearl leaned across the table to get a better look, the food-art apparently forgotten. She craned her neck toward Annie and pointed at her shoulder. "On your arm, a minute ago." She narrowed her eyes. "When your shirt slipped, I saw something. A tattoo?"

"Yep. It's a compass." Annie pulled the collar down to reveal the tattoo, which started on her upper arm and crawled around her shoulder and partially onto her rear deltoid. She'd gotten it as a celebration of survival: surviving 9/11, surviving Alec walking out on her, and surviving (at least so far) a terminal cancer diagnosis. Really, she should be dead by now. But she wasn't. She was alive.

"Interesting," Pearl said, examining it. "Did you design it yourself?" She fixed Annie's shirt and went back to her side of the table.

"Yes, she did," John said.

Annie reached under the table and put her hand in John's, interlacing their fingers. He squeezed. Another look, this one not as subtle, passed between them. She'd initially planned for her tattoo to be a luna moth. Until one day, while thinking about something else entirely, John's boat popped into her head. He'd taken her sailing amid the 9/11 aftermath, teaching her about the wind. He had an antique compass on the boat. When she went home, back to Brooklyn, well, she hadn't realized it at the time, but she'd been holding onto John. And the first time he saw the tattoo — six months after she'd gotten it and a year after she'd last seen him — he gasped. *My compass* was all he'd said. She knew then that it wasn't her brain that remembered the intricacies of the compass, it was her heart.

"Can I interest anyone in some ice cream? I have cookies and cream. And vanilla." Pearl, who seemed to have lost interest in Annie's tattoo, got up and opened the freezer. "I have a carton of mint chocolate chip, too." Annie shook her head, and John patted his stomach, indicating fullness beyond the reach of ice cream.

"Damn," Pearl said, sitting back down. "I bought the cookies and cream for Luke." The color drained from her face. From tiptoeing to stomping — just like that.

"Listen," Annie said. "I know tomorrow is going to be a rough day." She looked directly at Pearl. "Why don't you two do what you need to do at the hospital. I can tidy up here and go to the store and get whatever you need for the next few days."

"I did a small amount of food shopping, two days ago," Pearl said. "But there are still some things I need. I hadn't planned too far ahead." She reached across the table and patted Annie's hand. A breakthrough! "I'll make you a list." And then: "Back to the tattoo." Pearl had an uncanny talent for interrupting tender moments. "Why a compass?"

"It's complicated." Annie didn't know where to begin, how to explain what to say. Such a long, meandering story. Her emotional energy had waned long ago, leaving the pain in her back at the forefront of her consciousness.

"I'm so sick of everyone telling me things are complicated." Pearl banged the bottom of her glass on the table. Annie jumped.

"Okay, Mother," John said. "Okay."

"I'm sick of it." Pearl started to get up but stopped halfway out of her chair. She put her palms on the table for support. "What's so complicated? I'll tell you what's complicated. Your wife is in a coma, about to have brain surgery. My grandson's arm is badly injured, and he doesn't know his father is dead. So please stop telling me that everything else is complicated." She pushed herself away from the table, got up, and stomped out of the room. Stomp. Stomp. Stomp.

"I'm sorry about that," John said, but Annie barely heard him. The only sound that reverberated in her ears was the slip of Pearl's tongue, describing Marina as John's wife.

ANNIE SLOWLY PEELED the covers back and slid out of bed, stepping onto the floor quietly, careful of any movement or noise that might wake John. He'd finally fallen asleep after a long night of troubled discussion about his mother and anxiety about what promised to be a long, tense day. The sun wasn't yet up, and the house was hers and hers alone, at least for now.

She walked into a battle-weary kitchen — the dishes and carry-out cartons from last night littered the counter and table like wounded soldiers. After a quick assessment, she triaged the scene and got to work, pausing only long enough to make a pot of coffee and peek in the fridge for quick breakfast options. She pulled out a carton of blueberries and set them aside.

She poured herself a cup of coffee and sat down at the table. Pearl's words from last night circled her brain — *your wife is in a coma*. Annie hated that she felt a sliver of potential displacement. And she hated that she felt a bit — dare she admit this to herself — jealous. She pushed the unhelpful thoughts aside and sipped her coffee, contemplating the blueberries. She got up and opened the pantry, collecting cooking utensils and laying them out on the counter, frustrated that she would have yet more dishes to wash, but pleased at her ingenuity.

"WHAT IS ALL THIS?" Pearl entered the kitchen wearing a garish, lime-green robe with daisies sewn on each pocket. Annie loved it. "Scones?"

"I hope you don't mind, but I used the blueberries you had in the fridge." Pearl picked up a scone and examined it, sniffed it, then took a bite.

"This will do," Pearl said, carrying the scone with her to the coffee pot, nibbling on one corner as she opened the cabinet to get a mug. "Very nice," she said between bites.

Annie felt hopeful. A new day. Fresh, like opening the cover of a crispy new book, or, maybe more accurately in this case, turning the page to a new chapter — a chapter where all of the previous chapter's transgressions would be forgotten. All of yesterday's harsh words, spoken not out of hatred but out of the mouth of a very stressed and upset person. Or, she supposed, Pearl was simply on her best behavior this morning. Because that's what adults do, isn't it? Or could there be a connection forming? A real sense of working together to get through the next few stressful days. Because, after all, they were all, to one degree or another, in this together.

11

———

John

Rarely prone to panic, John's heart pounded, and his legs felt rubbery. In his more than twenty years as a police officer, he'd never been called or asked to identify a body. Never. His only experience with morgues was from what he'd seen on television and in movies: *The decedent's relative or friend is led into a cold, gray room where a robotic person in a white coat pulls out a drawer, then the relative or friend whispers "that's him" and collapses in grief.*

He checked in with the receptionist and sat down on a long, leather sofa — something you might find in someone's weekend mountain cabin. The only thing missing was a stone fireplace with a ten-point buck hanging above the mantle.

"Mr. Butterfield?" John looked up and realized he'd been breathing into his cupped hands. He stood. "I'm Irene Moss." She held out her hand. Reluctantly he held out his. She shook his hand briefly and placed her other hand over his, shaking it again, like people do in an attempt to make one feel at ease. This did nothing of the sort. "I'm so sorry for your loss."

John sat and resumed breathing into his hands. He stood up quickly and paced from one end of the sofa to the other, anything to get the darkness to recede. He blinked as hard as he could, shaking his head in an attempt to fling the darkness out of his eyes. He hung his head between his legs, willing the room to stop spinning. After a few deep breaths, his blood started circulating again, and points of light began piercing the darkness. He gingerly lifted his head, suddenly awash in sympathy and tenderness for his ex-wife, who'd spent much of her life battling anxiety. He felt horrible for dismissing her concerns as illogical and vowed that when she came out of her coma, he would apologize for the years of his insensitivity.

Irene Moss became visible, sitting in a chair kitty-corner to the mountain cabin sofa. He made eye contact with her and immediately regretted it.

"I wish I could take away your pain," she said.

"Who are you?" John's temples throbbed. He wanted to be left alone to do what he needed to do. He wanted to get the hell out of there.

"I'm your grief coordinator," she said. "I'll be helping you through the identification process."

"I think I can handle it." He rubbed his forehead.

"Well, you may think that." She raised an eyebrow. "Why don't you just trust me on this." She searched his eyes. "Okay?"

"Can we go in now?" He glared at her. "I just want to get this over with."

"Mr. Quinn was a friend?"

"My closest friend." John felt his voice crack. He swallowed. "We were partners on the police force for many years. New Jersey. Maplewood."

"I understand that his wife is here in the hospital?"

"Yes, in the ICU. She's in surgery as we speak." John bolted upright and resumed pacing. "You see, that's the problem. I can identify him, yes, but I don't want him moved until she gets the chance to say goodbye." He stopped and stood in front of Irene Moss. "Is that possible? Please tell me you can keep him here until then." He started pacing again. "She was in a coma yesterday. She's in a coma today and will probably be in a coma tomorrow. And the next day. It could be a while." He fell onto the sofa. "Can someone assure me he won't be moved," he shouted. "Please?"

"Of course. Arrangements have already been made to keep Mr. Quinn here." She was unflappable, this Irene Moss. The result of years and years and years of doing this, he figured, as she looked to be just a bit younger than his mother. "I understand there's a child involved as well."

"Marina's sister is traveling here from Australia. She has a good relationship with the kid."

"And you don't?"

"I don't what?"

"You don't have a good relationship with your friend's son?"

"I barely know him." John's face burned with shame. "It's a long story."

Irene Moss nodded and motioned for John to move in closer. He slid himself from one end of the sofa to the end closest to her chair. A man came out from behind a glass window and handed her a clipboard, which she placed facedown in her lap.

"I want you to know that everything we're going to do, we'll do right here." She clutched the clipboard. "There's no need for you to go into the holding room. There's no pulling back a curtain and looking at an actual corpse." She gently tapped the clipboard with her hand. "I have a photo here. It's going to just show Mr. Quinn's face."

"Please call him Nester." John's chin fell to his chest. "His name is Nester."

"Nester's face will be visible in the picture," she continued. "It will be framed by a blue paper sheet like you would put on during a physical exam at a doctor's office." She paused. "You won't see any of his injuries or evidence of medical intervention. Just his face."

Bile rose up in John's throat. He jumped up, frantically scanning the room for a trash can. He saw the door to the restroom near the other end of the room. In four long strides, he was hunched over the toilet — a cauldron of last night's Chinese food with a scotch and beer reduction. He vomited and heaved until only a trickle of clear drool dangled from his mouth. He stood, his legs still shaky, and flushed the toilet. He rinsed his mouth in the sink and splashed cold water on his face. Without bothering to dab himself dry with a paper towel, he returned to Irene Moss and the clipboard.

"Take all the time you need," she said, careful not to acknowledge any stench that may have followed him out of the restroom. "There is absolutely no reason to rush." She placed the clipboard facedown on the coffee table. "You can turn it over and look whenever you're ready." She made a steeple with her fingers. "There is absolutely no reason to rush."

John stared at the clipboard, willing it to remain facedown on the table. Ms. Grief Coordinator said he could take all the time he needed. He wondered who would try to out-stubborn who. He was dammed good at digging his heals in the sand. Nope, he wouldn't let Irene Moss out-stubborn him. He would sit here for the rest of the morning. And into the afternoon. Surely Ms. Grief Coordinator would get hungry. Or thirsty. Or would want to go home at the end of the day. He had nothing but time on his hands.

He tilted his head back and closed his eyes, indulging in an illogical fantasy that a mistake had been made. That it hadn't been Ness in the car with Marina. She could have been carjacked when they stopped at McDonald's. Maybe Ness took the kid to the restroom while Marina, drink holder with a milkshake and two Diet Cokes in hand, climbed into the car, only to be carjacked. Then the crash. And the dead man was the carjacker and not Ness. That could have happened. Couldn't it have? Of course, it could have. Or maybe Marina and Nester argued about some stupid thing. Perhaps the argument was just one more drip in the bucket that finally overflowed. And Marina scribbled a note, left it on the bed while Nester happily crooned in the shower, packed the kid in the car, and took off. Then, of course, Marina picked up a hitchhiker. Yeah. That's what happened. She picked up a hitchhiker and stopped at McDonald's.

John's mother had clearly misunderstood the details: It wasn't the kid who wanted the milkshake. It was Marina's kind heart that offered to take the hitchhiker to McDonald's and buy him a milkshake and whatever else he wanted. Then the crash. And the dead man was the hitchhiker and not Ness. That could have happened. Couldn't it have? Of course, it could have. There were hundreds of other possibilities that could turn the man in the picture into someone other than Nester. Hundreds. Thousands maybe.

John's hand, without his consent, worked its way toward the clipboard and hovered, mid-air until he jerked it back and clutched it with his other hand. He looked at Irene Moss sitting kitty-corner, oh so practiced and patient. She nodded as if to say, *go on*. Eyes closed, he lifted the clipboard and held it against his chest, chanting to himself: *carjacker, hitchhiker, carjacker, hitchhiker*. He counted to ten and opened his eyes. No carjacker. No hitchhiker. He handed the clipboard back to Irene Moss.

"It's Nester."

12

Pearl

The lounge in the children's ward, decorated with faux greenery and brightly colored bells, felt too happy, too cheerful for such a melancholy place. Peppy holiday music gushed in from somewhere. Pearl craned her neck toward the ceiling to try and hear it better, to try and figure out its source. She eyed an abandoned umbrella, closed tightly and propped against the wall. If she could only find the source of the music, she would whack it with the umbrella. Over and over again until the music stopped. How dare someone play happy music when down the hall a little boy was in bed with screws in his elbow and would soon learn of his father's death and mother's grave condition? *The hospital administrators will hear about this, mark my word.* She covered her ears to block out the sound.

Pearl had woven her way across the hospital to visit Luke as a distraction until Marina came out of surgery. The same trek from the ICU as yesterday, and, wouldn't you know it, she got lost. Despite the clearly labeled signs and colored arrows on the floor. The hospital architects and designers made it very difficult to get lost. Yet she got lost anyway. The only person going to Oz to ever veer off the yellow brick road.

She fingered two empty coffee cups that sat side by side on the small table next to her chair. Why would someone walk away and not dispose of their trash? Pearl had no tolerance for slobs, even if said slobs were disguised as distraught parents. She swallowed the last of her own coffee and placed the empty cup on top of the two cups, like a pyramid, then wearily scooped up all three cups and tossed them in the trash.

A nurse had interrupted Pearl's visit with Luke. They needed to help him go to the bathroom and asked her to give them some privacy. She kissed her grandson on the forehead and told him she'd be back later. Maybe with a present. He smiled halfheartedly and waved. He seemed to be in okay spirits. In a lot of pain still, and a bit subdued from the medication, but okay given the situation. She couldn't imagine being a six-year-old boy in a hospital without his parents sitting vigil over him. Luke seemed brave beyond his years. The only problem: he hadn't yet been told that his father was killed in the crash. Damn, she wished John hadn't divorced Marina, wished it were John who Luke called Daddy. She'd been quite vocal in sharing her less than shining opinion of Marina with him over the years. Especially in the beginning. She now wondered if all the mocking, all the little jabs over the years, all the negativity she espoused may have somehow poisoned John's heart toward Marina. Little by little. A slow boil. She will regret this to her dying day.

"There you are." John stooped down and gave her a perfunctory hug. "She's out of surgery, but it will be a while before we can see her."

"Did they say anything?" Pearl's eyes grew big.

"She has extensive swelling and some damaged brain tissue." He took a deep breath. "The surgeon had to remove some of the damaged tissue to make room for the living, undamaged tissue."

"They gave her a lobotomy?" Pearl stood up, then sat back down and let her head fall between her knees.

"Lobotomy's are not a thing these days, Mother." John shook his head, clearly frustrated. "The next forty-eight hours are crucial." He shrugged. "It's a waiting game now."

Pearl sat up and looked at her son. He looked like he'd aged a hundred years overnight. She wanted to support him but was furious that he walked out on Marina six years ago. If they hadn't divorced, maybe everyone would be okay, and she would be on her way to visit them in New Jersey for the holidays. Damn him.

"What are you doing with that woman?" Pearl glanced at the ceiling so John wouldn't see her rolling her eyes. "I mean, first of all, she's a bit too young for you. Wouldn't you say?" She couldn't fathom John and Annie being together longterm. She simply couldn't.

"Mother, I am not having this conversation." John threw his hands into the air. "She's forty-one."

"Oh, for God's sake, you know what I'm talking about." Pearl pursed her lips and exhaled through her nose.

"No, Mother. I don't know what you're talking about." He slumped in his chair. "Please enlighten me."

"You're acting like the thief with the burning hat." She glared at her son, ashamed of what she was doing, but unable to stop.

"Yeah, yeah. Enough with the idioms." He shook his head. "Just say what you need to say."

"It means you have an uneasy conscience that betrays itself."

"Well, of course, I do," he said, his voice a squeak. "You don't think I feel like the biggest piece of shit in the world?" He drew in a shaky breath. "Marina doesn't deserve this." And then the sobs came.

Pearl reached for his hand and held it. He made guttural noises: heaves, captured breaths, moans, and whimpers of pain. She felt her own eyes getting wet and dabbed at them with her free hand. She couldn't keep up and let the tears trickle, then stream down her cheeks, feeling grateful that she never wore makeup, or if she did, it was only a swipe of lipstick. No mascara streaks to concern herself with. She shook her head to rid it of these mundane things and instead thought about the days, weeks, and months ahead. She didn't know what Dale's plans were or how long she would stay. She knew John couldn't stay forever. She simply didn't know what she was going to do. And with that thought, she started sobbing in harmony with John. *What a sight we must be*, she thought. *What a sight.*

PEARL DIDN'T KNOW how long they'd been sitting there — mother and son — arguing and crying. She squinted at the large wall clock and simultaneously tapped on her wristwatch.

"We should go see Marina," she said to John, who slouched in his chair with his feet on the magazine table. He lifted his head, which had been tilted back, and tipped it side to side, massaging his neck with his hand. He looked at the clock.

"She's not going to be ready." He reached under his bad leg and gently helped it to the floor. His good leg followed on its own. "The surgeon said late afternoon, maybe after three."

"What time is it now?" She wanted to assure herself that she could, indeed, tell time.

"One-thirty." John stood and looked around. "I think I need something to eat. Maybe a yogurt or something light. But something." He looked at Pearl. "I'll get you something. What do you want?"

"I'll go with you," she said. "I need to stop at the gift shop. I promised Luke I'd bring him a present." She looked into John's eyes. "You should come with me to see him. He really is adorable." John ignored her. She knew that she needed to apologize for her comments about Annie. She searched for words that didn't come and wished she had some Play-Doh or modeling clay. If she had something to mold and mush in her hands, she could start to unravel all of the feelings and emotions and fears competing for her attention. She'd always kept a few cans of Play-Doh in her desk drawer for students to fiddle with, finding that it helped distract them enough to open up. Damn, she missed the feel of Play-Doh slithering through her fingers. She would have to buy some. She needed a few Christmas presents for Luke. She and Marina had planned to shop together when they got to Florida. She rubbed her hands together, suddenly weary.

"I'm sorry for what I said about Annie." She looked at the floor. "I'm truly sorry. I have a lot on my mind, not just this stuff." She decided to be honest, at least to the degree that she was willing to admit how frightened she was about the state of her mind. "I'm devastated that your best friend was killed, and Marina is in the ICU. I'm devastated that Luke will soon have to be told." She took a deep breath. "On top of all that, I've got some stuff going on with me. It's probably nothing." She looked at him harshly. "And I don't want to talk about it. I'm just telling you so that you might give me a little grace."

"I will give you grace," he said, seemingly unmoved by her babbling. "But I'm expecting you to be kind to Annie. There's no excuse for how you treated her last night."

She took in his cold stare, wondering what it must have been like for people he arrested, getting that stare. It was a doozy. She backtracked. "Okay. Maybe I was a little short. It was a tense situation." She paused. "Look, I just met her. Amid horrible circumstances, no less." She wiped away a rogue tear. "Annie and I had a nice morning. You saw that. We made our peace. Sort of." And then: "I really wish you didn't bring her."

"Well, I did." He locked her eyes in his cross-hairs.

"I'll try harder," Pearl said, hanging her head.

13

John

John walked alone from the cafeteria to the elevator. The tub of yogurt he'd eaten seemed to settle in his gut like a rock, and he didn't like the way his tongue felt — like it was coated in slime. He pushed the button for the elevator and waited, feeling like a camel had taken a shit in his mouth. When the doors finally opened, he made an about-face and jogged back to the cafeteria. He found the soda station and made himself an extra-large cup of Diet Coke — lots of ice. He stood in front of the fountain and sipped, letting the cold, sparkly, crispness fill his mouth. He took another gulp and added more soda to fill the gap.

The woman working the cash register was dressed in a festive — ahem — ugly Christmas sweater and wore a purple Santa hat. When he got closer, he could see that her feet were clad in red Doc Martins. The shoes made him think of Annie, whose footwear of choice was a beat-up old pair of black ones. She'd been wearing them when he found her on 9/11, and again when he found her a year later. His mother's words — *what are you doing with that woman* — tried to invade his headspace, but he flung them out into the stratosphere.

John got on the elevator, thinking about his mother again. They'd walked to the cafeteria together, but then she turned left and went to the gift shop instead. She was probably sitting next to the kid's bed by now, doling out ridiculously overpriced gifts. The one time John went back to his old house to visit Ness, the kid was a toddler playing with extra-large Legos. He lifted the kid up to place the final Lego atop a tower that was too tall for him to reach. And that was that. He pushed the thought from his head, reminding himself that Marina never wanted to have kids with him, yet chose to give birth to (and keep!) a baby conceived in rape. He shook his head, letting the memory of the kid's smile fall to the floor.

The elevator door opened, and John found himself standing in the vestibule of the ICU, wondering why he was there. Oh, he knew. It was just one of those moments of unreality, unbelief. An improv routine that had gone horribly wrong. This wasn't supposed to be part of his life's script. Not at all.

"Marina Quinn?" He laid his inquiry on the desk, in front of the serious-looking man sitting behind it. The multi-colored Christmas lights strung the length of the desk seemed incongruous with the sickness, injury, and misery that lay just beyond the double-doors. Maybe the brightly colored lights were supposed to be a reminder that in disease and injury, there was also healing and hope. He held onto that.

"I'll need you to wait over there." He pointed to a small lounge area — far enough away as to not be a distraction to the serious work that went on at the desk, yet close enough so Desk Man could come and get him if need be. "Someone will be over to talk to you momentarily."

John's and Desk Man's idea of momentarily were in two completely different realities. Nearly a half-hour had gone by, and no one came to talk to him. He got up, stiff from sitting, and approached the desk.

"I'm just checking on Marina Quinn," he said, addressing a new desk person. "I was told someone would come to get me." He looked at his watch. "It's been a half-hour." The woman behind the desk tippy-tapped on her keyboard and looked up.

"Wait right here. Dr. Vargas is consulting with another family. He'll be out momentarily."

Momentarily. That vague word again. John rolled his eyes and nodded. He moved a little to the left of the desk and leaned against the wall. Worry snaked through him. He had a sinking feeling that his mother's optimism was misplaced. After identifying Nester, the medical examiner came out and offered his condolences and a more detailed description of what had happened. Nester died of hemorrhagic shock. Plain and simple. Internal injuries caused by blunt force trauma — a crush injury from the car accident. John hoped he could leverage his past professional connections and get a copy of all the reports. He wanted to know exactly what happened, what caused the accident. He tried to visualize it, to ponder it. John figured Ness knew death was imminent. They'd both been through the training. Many times over. First signs of hemorrhagic shock: dizziness, sweating, fatigue, nausea, headache. The medical examiner had explained to John that the injuries were internal. Nester had nothing to pinpoint, no blood visible, except the cut on his forehead, minor in the grand scheme of things, something he likely didn't even notice. Then would have come the clammy skin, rapid heart rate, weak pulse, shallow breathing, confusion, and finally...*Oh, Ness. You fucking asshole. You just had to stop and get the kid a milkshake. Damn you.*

"Mr. Butterfield?" Dr. Vargas extended his hand. "Let's go sit over there." He cocked his head toward the lounge. John followed, wiping his eyes. They sat down. "I'm not going to sugarcoat anything. She's in pretty bad shape." John listened as fresh tears streamed down his cheeks. "I'm not saying it's dire. At least not yet." The doctor continued. "We'll have a better assessment in the next few days — the next two being the most critical. Our immediate goal, of course, is to reduce pressure in her skull and get the swelling to go down."

. . .

JOHN CLASPED his hands behind his head and clenched his teeth. Anything to control his impulse to grab the blinking Grinch brooch — pinned festively to the nurse's scrubs — and throw it on the floor. Then he'd stomp on it a few times for good measure. A blinking Grinch brooch! He glared at her as she spoke in a technical language laced with medical jargon that he didn't understand. Anything to avoid looking at Marina. And as long as he was glaring at the nurse, he was safe.

"It's okay," the nurse said, ignoring John's ire. "You can go up to her. You can even hold her hand if you want." She patted John's arm. He bit down on his tongue to avoid saying something that would likely get him thrown out of the hospital. Not that getting thrown out would be a bad thing. He could drive back to his mother's house, burst through the door, grab Annie, get back in their rental car, retrace their path to the airport, reverse their steps, rewind the tape, call in Superman to rewind the earth, all the way back to the moment when the kid asked for a milkshake. Nester would say *no, no milkshake, no McDonald's.* No accident. John would be doing his thing at Shorty's, Annie would be working on paintings for her spring exhibit, and Florida would be something that he would think about later after he proposed and Annie said yes.

Keeping his eyes fixed on the floor, he took a step toward Marina's bed. Then another. And another. He kept inching his way toward her until his knee banged up against the bedrail. He stood there, still looking at the floor, counting down from ten. When he reached one, he would look. Like the ball in Times Square on New Year's Eve. *Ten, nine, eight.* Watching the ball drop on TV had been one of his and Marina's corny traditions. *Seven, six, five, four.* During the last good year of their marriage — the year before the rape — she said she wanted to *stand among the throng at the crossroads of the world and experience the ball dropping live and up close.* John laughed at her. Reminded her of how much she hated crowds. What a fucking asshole he'd been. Why couldn't he have just said *yeah, that would be cool.* Still looking at the floor, he backed away from the bed — *three, two...one* — all the way out of the room. He inched away from the door and stood in the hall, unable to breathe, suddenly face to face with the blinking Grinch.

"I'm sorry, but I can't go back in there."

"I can't tell you what to do," she said. "But it's essential for her to feel her loved ones' presence."

"I'm not one of her loved ones," John said, almost inaudibly. The nurse leaned in closer. The blinking Grinch created a strobe effect. "Could you turn that damned thing off?" He pointed to the brooch, his voice audible now, reverberating down the hall. A pair of nurses walking by stopped and asked if everything was okay. Marina's nurse nodded and turned off the Grinch.

"WHY AREN'T YOU IN THERE?" John's mother stood over him like a police officer might stand over a suspect. Where had she learned that?

"I don't know," he said, which was the truth. He simply didn't know why he couldn't face what had happened. "I just can't. I can't look at her."

"Well, get over it and get in there." She started walking away, then turned around. "Come on. She needs you."

"She doesn't even know we're here. She's a vegetable."

"She's certainly not a vegetable," his mother said. "She's in a coma. Very different. Very, very different." She scrutinized him. "And it's temporary."

"Mother." John's patience had worn thin. "Perhaps you didn't talk to Dr. Vargas, her surgeon." He didn't wait for a response. "He said she's in bad shape. He didn't give me any warm and fuzzy feelings." He took a deep breath. "None."

"All the more reason to go in there." She pinched the bridge of her nose. "You're the closest person she has right now. At least until Dale comes." She paused. "She needs you. You belong in there with her." John's face hardened like a slab of granite. He stood.

"Do you know how many times I've talked to her in the last three years?" When his mother didn't respond, he shouted. "Do you?"

Cowering, she shook her head. "Maybe four times. That's essentially once a year." He threw his hands in the air and let them plummet to his thighs. "She is no longer mine. The one thing that held us together, by a thread, was Nester. That's it. If it hadn't been for Ness, I would have had even less contact with her."

"Go in there, John." His mother, defeated, was now the one who was slumped in a chair. "I held her hand for the past hour. I talked to her. The nurse said it's good for her." She drew a long, slow breath. "Go in there. You loved each other. You were married for a long time. Go in there."

John's mother might as well have been pointing a gun at him. Cocked and ready to fire, right between his eyes. She knew his guilt streams: having been dead asleep in the basement when Marina was raped upstairs in their bedroom and later berating her for not yelling louder or fighting back soon enough. And then, the coup de grâce — walking out on her for keeping the rapist's baby.

THE SHIFT MUST HAVE CHANGED — Marina's new nurse kept her distance. The atmospheric pressure in the room felt different too — less judgment, more detached compassion. John sat as far away from the bed as possible and fiddled with a paper clip that he'd picked up off the floor in the lounge. He twirled it between his fingers as he alternately shifted eyes from the wall on the other side of the room to the paper clip, to the door, to the dry erase board already filled with medical shorthand and instructions, to the window with the blinds drawn, to the monitors flashing and beeping, and then back to the wall. The nurse left him alone. For that, he was grateful.

His mother wanted to go in with him, but he waved her off, suggesting that she go downstairs to the lobby and wait for him there. Or spend a few more minutes with the kid. Or go to the cafeteria and pick lint off of her sweater. Or wander the halls. He didn't care. He needed to do this alone and alone meant that his mother needed to be on a different floor, or a separate wing, or on a different planet. Her whereabouts didn't matter, except when it came time to head home. He warned that if she wasn't in the lobby in an hour, he would leave without her.

John put the paper clip down and willed himself to just look at his ex-wife. He slowly let his eyes adjust to this new version of her: laying still and covered in sheets, blankets, tubes, and wires. Her feet almost reached the bottom of the bed, and he wondered how hospitals accommodated the ultra-tall, like the six-foot-six Michael Jordans of the world.

He envisioned Marina the way she might have looked three days ago, before the accident: her freckles, her bright orange hair, her long legs — all of the attributes that had initially attracted him. He'd wanted to spend his life with her, at least that was what he'd told himself. He'd saved up for a ring and then found himself walking up and down her street the day he planned to propose, hand in his pocket, worrying the ring between his fingers — a stalling tactic as he weighed the pros and cons of breaking up. What he really wanted to do was date her sister. He mentally made two columns: genuine Marina; wild and unpredictable Dale; sensible and agreeable Marina; argumentative Dale; reserved Marina; outspoken Dale. And many more. The list grew as he walked. And yet he found himself in Marina's apartment, the ring outstretched, believing that he loved her. He felt a sense of impending doom when she squealed *YES* and jumped into his arms, wrapping her long legs around him. Wanting to vomit, yet caught up in her excitement, he threw his head back and laughed with her, resolving to commit his life to her, determined to make her happy. He dabbed at his eyes. The quiet nurse, as if she'd been waiting for this moment, handed him a box of tissues.

"Thanks," he said, without looking at her.

"I'll step out for a few minutes," she said. "Give you some privacy." She paused in the doorway. "I'll be right outside the door." And then, "Ten minutes. Tops."

John nodded, thankful to be alone with Marina. He blew his nose and set the tissue box down in his lap. He unfolded the paper clip until it resembled a long, crooked, boney finger, then attempted to bend it back into some semblance of its original shape. It looked more like a pretzel than a paper clip. He set it down and looked at his watch — seven minutes before the nurse came back in. He picked up the paper clip again, then put it right back down. It was no use. He was stalling. He moved his chair all the way up to the bed and let his eyes travel from the tips of her feet — two lumps, the shape of which he could barely make out — up to her knees, then her middle. He stopped when he reached her arms. Both of them were pierced with the tips of IV needles, tubes traveling this way and that. He picked up her hand and held it. The ventilator apparatus in her mouth taped down with breathing tubes running hither and yon, concealed much of her face. He stared at her, unbelieving.

"Are you okay in there?" At the sound of the nurse's voice, he released Marina's hand and stood. She walked in.

"She has a son, you know," he said.

"Yes, I'm aware that he's a patient in the children's ward."

"Can I bring him here to visit her?" He paused and looked into the nurse's face for the first time. "I mean, later, when he's better, and when he's been told. I don't think he knows about any of this." He waved his arms around the room.

"Closely supervised." She smiled. "But yes."

JOHN TOOK his time walking to the lobby. He'd been in Florida for a little less than twenty-four hours, and already it felt like he'd been here much longer. His brain couldn't process what Marina looked like in the ICU. Until he saw her, he hung onto the false hope that he'd walk into her room and find her sitting up in bed, puzzled and asking: *what are you doing here?* What did he find instead? A woman on life support. A woman with a swollen face and a motionless body. A woman who looked less alive than her husband, who he identified just that morning as being very dead.

His head spun out of control as he tried all of his usual tricks to get it to stop, to no avail. He needed to sit. He wandered down a random corridor and plopped in a chair. He closed his eyes and took a few deep breaths, then got up and continued toward the lobby.

A ruckus greeted him as he approached the lobby. Laugher? And a lot of chatter. A gaggle of people standing in the vestibule near the restrooms came into view. His mother, among them, her voice, the loudest. *A lizard in the bathroom*, he heard her say. The door to the ladies' room burst open and out walked two security guards. A young man in scrubs came out behind them carrying a Styrofoam sandwich box. As the processional passed by, John could see small holes all over the lid. Whatever lurked inside — the lizard, he presumed, — banged and scratched inside the box, trying to escape.

"We got him," the guy in scrubs said. Cheering and high-fives erupted. Over a lizard. "He's a pretty good-sized one, too," he added. With the excitement over, the crowd dispersed, and John worked his way toward his mother, who seemed surprised to see him.

"There was a lizard in the bathroom," she said. "Can you believe it?" She pantomimed the size, surely an exaggeration, as something that big couldn't possibly fit inside a Styrofoam sandwich box. Ordinarily, John might have chosen to argue the point of the lizard's size. But he felt drained and just wanted to get the hell out of there. He needed to feel Annie in his arms and put this day behind him. That's all he wanted. All he needed.

"Ready to hit it?" He didn't wait for an answer and started toward the elevator — a straight shot from the restrooms. Two floors down and they'd be in the parking garage. And two minutes after that, in the car on the way home.

"I have to pee." His mother, still standing where he'd left her, pleaded with her eyes.

"Didn't you do that already?"

"No," she said. "There was a lizard in the bathroom." She laughed. "I'll just be a minute."

JOHN HELD the car door open for his mother.

"Buckle up," he said.

"I am buckled."

"Are you?" He raised an eyebrow and let his gaze slide down toward the seat belt buckle that dangled near her shoulder.

"Well, it must have popped out." She grabbed the buckle and brought it all the way down and into the waiting receptacle, where it clicked. "There."

John shook his head and held the steering wheel with both hands, staring out the window, straight ahead, looking mindlessly through the glass doors at the bank of elevators. His jaw hurt from clenching his teeth. He felt tired, cranky, and probably a little bit hungry. Over the years he'd perfected this dance with his mother, knowing when to let her lead, knowing when to let her barbs bounce off his suit of armor. Sometimes, and he believed now was one of those times, he needed to lead. To be the first to bring up a difficult topic. And today, many difficult topics loomed. The logical choices being Nester, Marina, and the kid. Logistics. The next steps. But none of those topics seemed to be as urgent as the topic he really needed to address. Still staring straight ahead, he sighed, then released the grip on the steering wheel.

"Mother, we need to talk."

"Can't we do it in the car?"

"We are in the car."

"You know what I mean." She opened the glove compartment and pulled out a brochure. "It's hot in here," she said, fanning herself. "Can't we talk while we're driving?"

"Your house is only a mile away."

"Actually, it's more like a mile and three-quarters."

"Mother!"

"Okay, then." She stopped fanning herself and put the brochure back in the glove compartment. She unbuckled her seat belt and opened the door.

"Where are you going?" John ran his fingers through his hair. His mother had one foot in the car, the other foot out. Hand on the door. Looking confused and a little bit frightened. He softened. "Mother, please get back in the car." She seemed frail and unsure of herself.

Could she have aged this much in two years? She got back in and closed the door, but didn't put on her seat belt.

"There. Happy?" She slouched in her seat.

John didn't quite know how to start the conversation he wanted to have. He didn't want to minimize the toll the past two days had taken on his mother. Still, the way she treated Annie last night upset him. He decided to dive right in.

"I know I don't have the best track record with women," he began, "but Annie is very important to me." Staring straight ahead, he waited for a response. When none came, he continued. "I should have told you about her when I brought the boat down two years ago." He took a deep breath, not expecting his mother to understand, yet feeling good to be getting this out in the open. "The thing is, I wasn't with her then. Yet I knew I loved her. Let's just say she entered my life for a very short time on 9/11, then she disappeared, and it took me a whole year to find her — I found her on the first anniversary of the attacks."

"I told you before that Annie and I had a nice morning. You saw it yourself. I was perfectly respectable."

"She was in the North Tower that morning," he said, ignoring her comment. John's mother gasped and put her hand over her mouth. "It's not like that." He shook his head and held out his hand in a mock stop-sign. "She had business there in the morning but was already outside when the first plane hit. She'd walked down to Battery Park and sat on a bench, apparently fell asleep, and woke up to a swarm of people running. She got caught up in the chaos and found herself standing by my boat. I took her hand and helped her aboard. When we got to Jersey City, well, it was clear to me that she had nowhere else to go, so I let her stay on the boat. She stayed for four days. Then she went home."

"She wasn't homeless?"

"Homeless?" John looked at his mother, incredulous. "Why would you think she was homeless? That's illogical."

"She was sleeping on a park bench. And you said she had nowhere to go."

"She'd been in the Bermuda Triangle." He sighed. "Not literally."

Detecting the first hints of a headache, he rubbed his forehead. "A few days before, she'd had a miscarriage, was diagnosed with cancer and found out her husband was cheating." He searched his mother's eyes and found nothing there but confusion. "I didn't know about any of it. Except for the cancer. She shared that, but not the rest. Her sister came into the pub three or four days later with a stack of missing person flyers. That's when the rest of the story came out." His chin dropped to his chest. "I went to the boat later that day to talk to her. But she was already gone."

"Did you sleep with her?"

"Mother!" Flames of anger shot through him. "What the fuck? That's none of your damned business." He glared at her. "There was nothing physical between us at that time." He took a deep breath. "The minute I realized she was gone was the minute I realized I loved her."

"Then why the hell didn't you go after her? You knew how to contact her, apparently, by the flyer."

"She was married. And had a ten-year-old son. And was dealing with a horrible diagnosis." Tears filled his eyes, remembering. His mother reached into her purse and produced a mini pack of tissues and handed it to him. "The last thing she needed was some old doofus like me swooping in and stirring things up." He blew his nose, becoming aware of people entering and exiting the building and vehicles pulling in and out of the parking garage.

John had enough for now. He would let the rest of the details reveal themselves in bits and pieces. He didn't even have the strength to tell his mother what he'd initially set out to say to her: To stop being rude to Annie — her earlier contrition be dammed. He started the car. Out of the corner of his eye, he saw his mother struggling with the seat belt. He reached over and helped her without a word.

14

Annie

Humidity, palm trees, and temperatures in the eighty's seemed incongruent with Tchaikovsky — *The Dance of the Sugar Plum Fairy*, to be exact. The staccato sounds of Christmas bellowed from the neighbor's window and bounced like ping-pong balls on the slate pavers of Pearl's lanai, where Annie was at the grill, scraping what looked like a few meals' worth of crusted meat. Scrape, scrape, scrape — mindlessly and in time with the music. She and Alec had taken Henry to the Brooklyn Ballet's performance of *The Nutcracker* when he was five — it seemed like yesterday. How in the world did her son become a teenager? She'd called Alec and talked to Henry this afternoon, and all seemed well. She figured she'd be home next week and told Alec not to cancel any of her art therapy appointments, especially Mel, who seemed skittish. One wrong move on her part and he'd vanish like a feral cat.

She stopped scraping, stepped off the lanai, and walked toward the water. She sat down and stretched her legs out in front of her and tilted her head back, letting the sun's warmth engulf her. She tried to imagine a lifetime of balmy Christmases. Never knowing snow, or the hope of snow. Wondering how Santa could stand the wool garb and thick beard. She couldn't hear the music from here but heard it in her head. Palm trees and *The Nutcracker*. As incongruent as two things could possibly be.

The gentle breeze felt like silk against her cheek. *This is why retirees move here or at least spend winters here*, she thought. This is why people vacation here. This is why depressed people are sometimes prescribed a healthy dose of sunshine. Impossible in New York in winter. Given her situation, Annie had every logical reason to be depressed. She never viewed herself as depressed, but often found herself on the verge of spiraling into a dark place.

She exhaled slowly, imagining what it might have been like to meet Pearl under any other conditions but these. Perhaps they would have gotten off to a better start. She imagined cutting down a palm tree, and setting it up in the living room. They'd string multi-colored lights on it, and she'd be prepared to argue with Pearl: colored lights versus white lights. She suspected Pearl was a white light kind of woman. *Shit!* She sat straight up. *Christmas tree. My Christmas tree.* She ran up the slope of the yard and back onto the lanai where her cell phone rested on the table.

"Ted...thank God you picked up." Annie grabbed a paper towel and wiped the back of her neck, which was suddenly drenched. "Do you still have that key I gave you?" She fiddled with the wet paper towel while he put the phone down to check. "Yep...that's the one...it's a long story...I'm in Florida with John...I'll fill you in next week... anyway, could you go into my apartment and water my Christmas tree?" She sighed, relieved to have such a good friend and neighbor in the building across the street. "Yep...just once a day." And then: "Ted... thank you...yep, I will...love you too." She didn't want to come home to a dried-out, dead tree.

ANNIE PULLED a package of chicken breasts out of the fridge and set it on the counter. Pearl's grocery list had been oddly specific and contained boldly written and underlined instructions: *Publix brand toilet paper — eight double rolls — if no double rolls, then Charmin extra-soft will do, but only if they have a twelve-pack.* And on and on and on. She figured Pearl must think she's a nincompoop who needs to be handheld — as if she were too incompetent to buy the right kind of half-and-half. The cat scratched at the back door and looked like he wanted to come in.

"I'm sorry little guy, but no." Another of Pearl's explicit instruc-tions: *The cat doesn't come in until dinnertime. No exceptions.*

She'd found most of the items on the list, all except the specific oranges Pearl wanted. The store had none. So strange that a major grocery chain like Publix would be out of oranges — in Florida! She asked a man unloading crates of bananas if she'd somehow missed them. *Lady, we never got our shipment today, come back tomorrow.* He shrugged, and that was that. She thought about stopping at a different store on the way back to the house, but Pearl had made a point to ask for a bag of Publix oranges. There must be some reason for the explicit request. Feeling adventurous, she took the liberty of buying a few things not listed, such as the chicken breasts and a bottle of red wine. She ignored Pearl's comment about keeping dinner simple tonight and decided to surprise them with grilled kabobs.

She cut the chicken into chunks, then did the same with a red pepper, an onion, a pineapple, two zucchinis, and a yellow squash. As artistically as she knew how, she crafted each skewer as a masterpiece unto itself. All six together on the tray formed a colorful motif — magazine-worthy. She opened her cell phone and took a picture, then doused the kabobs in Italian dressing. She covered the whole thing with foil and stuck it in the fridge.

She looked down at the floor and remembered that she'd wanted to tidy it up a bit. She found Pearl's vacuum and gave the floor a quick once-over. She noticed a mop and bucket in the closet where the vacuum had been and decided to really spiffy the place up. She quickly mopped the floor, leaving puddles of water in her wake. She found towels in a linen closet at the end of the hall and pulled out a couple of the rattiest ones. Through the living room on her way back to the kitchen, she saw a stereo system and thought some music might be nice. She popped open the CD carousel and found five Christmas CDs already racked and ready to go. She hit play and turned up the volume.

15

———

Pearl

Traffic always crawled this time of year in her neighborhood. Those damned snowbirds and other part-time residents created congestion everywhere. What would ordinarily have been a five-minute drive had turned into fifteen.

Pearl's stomach growled, and she had to pee again. Her eyes stung with with the dryness from having depleted every tear. Her tear ducts had gone on strike. Nothing left but dust and a few tumbleweeds. And, to be put upon by her son. Oh, he didn't say as much, but Pearl knew him well enough to know that she'd been scolded. A mother scolded by her son. Go figure. And for what? Asking his girlfriend about her tattoo? She couldn't fathom what she'd said to Annie that was so terrible. If she couldn't just be herself around people, then what was the point? She'd tried, really, she did, to treat Annie as normally as possible. And despite what John said, she didn't think this relationship would last. She hoped it wouldn't. The two of them didn't seem to fit. She honestly didn't know what he was doing with this young woman. Or not so young woman. Still, a baby compared to John.

"Thank God," she said when they finally turned the corner onto her street. She sighed in relief and looked at John, who clutched the steering wheel and looked straight ahead. "I hope she let the cat in." Pearl caught a glimpse of something shiny as John pulled into the driveway. "What is that?"

"What is what?" John turned off the car and looked at her.

"That shiny thing on the door."

"Well, it looks an awful lot like a wreath, Mother."

"You can lose the sarcasm. I can see that it's a wreath."

"Then why did you ask what it is?"

"It's not my wreath." Pearl got out of the car and walked across the paving stones to the front door. Sure enough. A wreath. It looked handmade, out of aluminum foil, of all things. With shiny red bells dangling from it. And green ribbon on the bottom. So that woman had gone through her garage and found the red bells. And the ribbon. Pearl pursed her lips, fuming. She took a deep breath and admitted to herself that the thing was quite creative. Retro, even, and reminded her of something her mother used to put out at Christmastime. Only it had been a centerpiece. Shaped like a bell. In fact, she thought it was something John made at school. A present for his grandmother. She touched the wreath, remembering her son as a little boy and wishing her husband were alive.

"Looks like something Annie might have made." John came up behind her, reaching around her to open the door. "I kind of like it."

"Well, I don't." She crossed her arms. "It's garish."

He held the door open, and she took a few steps into the living room and stopped. Music? She bent down and squinted at her stereo. Yep. The soundtrack from *Elf*. She had reluctantly accompanied her friend Sally to see the movie when it came out last year and surprised herself by liking it. Laughed out loud even. Liked it enough to buy the DVD and the CD soundtrack. Against her will, she found herself bobbing her head to the jazzy, peppy music as she walked toward the kitchen, annoyed that Annie would make herself so at home.

What the hell? That damned woman was skating around the kitchen floor, literally, a towel under each foot, unaware of the Olympic judge's scrutiny. Will she score a perfect ten? Hardly. Pearl let her handbag drop onto the table.

"What is this?" She shouted, and Annie turned around, bending down and quickly gathering up the towels.

"The floor looks great," John said, hugging Annie. Pearl drummed her fingers on the tabletop, and John turned around, mouthing the word *behave*.

"Yes, it looks great," Pearl said, forcing gratitude in her tone. "Something smells good. What are you making?" It took every bit of her resolve to not make a snide comment.

"I noticed your grill out back and thought chicken kababs would be nice. I probably should go check on them." She paused, remembering the wet towels in her arms. "I'll put these in the washing machine on my way outside." She paused again. "If that's okay." Pearl nodded and waved her hand in the universal gesture of *go ahead*.

"I'll help you," John said and followed her.

Pearl slouched at the table, unable to muster the energy or gumption to get up and hang her handbag on the peg in the mudroom. She closed her eyes and let herself drift into an almost hypnotic state, then slowly regained her bearings to the sound of meowing and the feel of a small body rubbing against her leg. She reflexively reached down and patted the top of the cat's head.

"Did she feed you? Yeah, I know. She fed you, didn't she? You're just manipulating me, aren't you?" Of course, the cat didn't answer. She pushed herself out of her chair and shuffled outside. The smell of the chicken made her mouth water.

"You shouldn't have gone to all this trouble," she said to Annie, who was brushing some sort of marinade over the kababs. "What are you basting with?"

"A rare, secret ingredient." She smiled. "It's just plain, old Italian dressing."

"Very interesting," Pearl said. "You didn't happen to feed the cat, did you?"

"Actually, I didn't. I'm sorry. I didn't think to."

"But you thought to mop my floors?" She glanced at John, who threw darts at her with his eyes. Again, with his damned stare. "I was just wondering," she said, defensive. "I didn't want the cat to eat twice." She softened when she saw Annie press a finger to the corner of her eye. "Look, the cat is a con artist. He would make me think he was starving to death." She winked at Annie. "In this case, I guess he'd be right."

It's been a rough day, she heard John say to Annie as they came back into the kitchen. Annie opened the oven and looked inside, then pulled out three baked potatoes.

"John said you like your spuds crispy on the outside," she said to Pearl. "I hope I didn't overdo it." Pearl got up, the cat trailing closely behind, and in a show of solidarity, tapped on a potato with her fingernails and nodded in approval.

"I'm sorry kitty, but I keep forgetting to feed you," Pearl said to the cat.

"Mom, I got it." John poked around in the cabinets until he found the kibble and filled the cat's bowl.

Pearl went to the refrigerator and opened the fruit bin to get a lime. She noticed that there were six of them, and suddenly remembered that she had accepted Annie's offer to do the shopping today. Wow, could it really have been just that morning that she'd penned her list? It seemed like an eternity ago.

"Did you get the oranges I asked for? I don't see them in here." She closed the fridge and quickly opened it back up again. *Well, I'll be dammed.* Right there, behind the limes, sat the earring she thought she'd lost. Marina had sent them to her for her birthday that past summer, and she wanted to have them on when they arrived for their visit. The tumbleweeds in her eyes blew away, and her tear ducts ended their strike. She cried anew. Not wanting to be the subject of anyone's pity or fussing, she shoved the earring in her pocket and wiped her eyes with the back of her hand.

"They didn't have any oranges," Annie said. "I even asked the produce guy. He said they never received their shipment and to come back tomorrow. She shrugged. "So that's what I'll do."

"Was it an older guy, with a bit of a paunch?" Pearl sighed a little too loudly and immediately regretted it.

"Yep. And he had black hair with a streak of gray on either side." Annie chuckled. "He reminded me of Al Lewis."

"Who's that?" Pearl didn't know anyone named Al Lewis.

"He played Grandpa on *The Munsters*," John said. Pearl couldn't make the connection. Perhaps it should register with her, but it didn't. She shook her head.

"Mom, you used to watch that show with me sometimes when I was a kid. It would come on in the late afternoon. You'd watch it with me and then go make dinner."

"Okay, now I remember," she lied. She had absolutely no memory of such a character in a show. "That was Leo," she said, addressing Annie. "He always says that. You have to stand there and call bullshit, and he'll reluctantly go to the back to get you what you want." She'd been looking forward to having fresh-squeezed orange juice in the morning. "Leo is a lazy bum." She stood. "I'm making myself a gin and tonic. Help yourselves to whatever you want." As if they needed to be told. Annie had certainly made herself at home, helping herself to the Christmas decorations and her precious blueberries. Pearl bit her tongue and proceeded to make her drink. She couldn't hold it in any longer. "I see you made a wreath."

"Yes, it's beautiful," John chimed in, rather loudly, Pearl thought.

"I hope you like it," Annie said to Pearl. "I just wanted something happy to greet you when you pulled up." She looked at the floor. "I'm sure today was hellish."

"You don't know the half of it," Pearl said, trying, unsuccessfully, to keep the tone out of her voice. What the hell was this woman doing in her house, in her kitchen, with her son? At a time like this? She picked up a knife and whacked the lime, launching half of it into the air. John leaped toward the counter and caught it as the other half slid off the cutting board, hitting the floor with a thud. He put his arm around his mother and walked her to the table.

"Sit down," he said. When Pearl didn't budge, he pulled out the chair and gently pushed her into it.

"I don't want to sit. If I wanted to sit, I'd have sat." In a fit of pique, she stood up but didn't move away from the table. Defeated, she sat.

"I'll make your drink. One jigger, right?"

"Two," she said, making a pillow on the table with her arms. She laid her head down, feeling very much like a pre-schooler at rest time.

PEARL PICKED up her napkin and wiped her eye, not because of tears, thank goodness, but because the juicy chunk of chicken she'd just removed from her skewer squirted her. She silently cut into it and took a bite, sensing Annie's eyes on her, probably waiting for some effusive praise for her efforts. She cut off another piece and slowly brought the fork up to her mouth, then tried a bit of zucchini. Not too firm, but certainly not mushy. Very, very good. She nodded at Annie, who seemed to let out a breath and relax her shoulders. Feeling proud of herself for keeping her mouth shut, she put a heap of butter on her potato and mashed it until the insides turned to liquid. She put a forkful in her mouth.

"This is delicious." In spite of herself, Pearl complimented the chef. She acquiesced when Annie and John said that they'd like to eat out on the lanai. Pearl wanted no part of it and said as much. All she wanted to do, really, was curl up on the couch in the fetal position and watch mindless TV. The pomp and circumstance of this dinner felt exhausting. "You really didn't have to go to all this trouble," she said. Yes, this meal was lovely. And tasty. But, dammit, it wasn't what she'd wanted. She wanted to keep things simple. Really simple. "None of this stuff was on my grocery list. You could have just heated up the frozen lasagna."

"Mother, Annie knows she could have made the lasagna." Of

course, John jumping to Annie's defense. It's the way it should be. She knew this but felt ornery and sorry for herself and generally worried about her own health and well-being — the earring she'd found in the fruit bin was one more reminder.

"John, it's okay," Annie said. "Pearl, I wanted to make things easy for you." She smiled. "As long as I'm here." She reached across the table and patted her hand.

"Fine." Pearl wanted to gag. This woman was too dammed cute. And too dammed nice. She didn't want to like her. Against every fiber of her being, she left her hand in place while Annie placated her. "Just let me be involved in the meal planning, please." She waved her arm around the lanai. "This is too much. You went to too much trouble." She let her chin drop to her chest. "This is too much." She noticed Annie's face reddening and immediately regretted the tone she'd tried, unsuccessfully, to conceal. "Please don't be so sensitive. I'm grateful for this. But it's too much."

"I've had enough of this." John got out of his chair and crouched down beside his mother. "Can we please be civil?"

"I am civil."

"John, it's okay." Annie jumped out of her seat.

"No. It's not okay." John held her in his arms. "It's not okay."

"It was a long, upsetting day for you both," Annie said. "I get that. I really do." She took her plate, mostly uneaten, and headed toward the kitchen. John got up to follow her, but she shook her head and waved him away. He followed her anyway.

Pearl played with her food, pushing it around her plate the way she'd seen Annie do last night. Feeling neither creative nor inspired, she fished the earring out of her pocket and held it up to the light, thinking about Marina, wondering what things would look like tomorrow. Maybe the doctor would burst through the door to let them know that Marina would be back to normal in a jiffy. Then, of course, was the delicate, oh so painful bit about Nester. Who would be the one to tell her? The doctor? A nurse? John? Maybe she would tell Marina herself.

Pearl arranged the items on her plate by color — green zucchini, red peppers. Without realizing it, she'd made a face. A happy, smiling face. She rearranged the smile into a frown. Pearl had always prided herself for feeling — both mentally and physically — much younger than her chronological age. She rode a motorcycle, for goodness sake! However, right now, sitting here on her own lanai, in her own house, playing with her food, she felt downright elderly. She moved two pieces of chicken to either side of her plate and made ears, pressing the earring into one of them. One earring. Like Mr. Clean.

"Where's Annie," Pearl said when John returned from the kitchen. He set a gin and tonic down in front of her.

"Her back is bothering her," he said. "She's in our room lying on the floor." He shrugged. "It helps, at least temporarily." He pointed to the gin and tonic and looked at his mother with a raised eyebrow. "Only one jigger this time."

"What did she do to her back?" Pearl ignored his comment about how much gin he put in her drink.

"Mother, don't you remember our conversation in the car?"

"Of course, I remember it. What do you think? I'm losing my mind?" She stiffened. "We talked about a lot of things."

"Didn't I tell you she has cancer?"

Pearl did, indeed, remember that cancer had been mentioned. In the past tense. Not once did John say that Annie still had it. She may be a bit scatterbrained at the moment, but she's not going senile. This revelation came as a huge relief. She glanced at Mr. Clean and his earring.

"You said she was diagnosed three years ago. I just assumed...So, she's not cured?" John's expression sobered. He nibbled on his lower lip. Pearl braced herself to be told it's complicated or that he didn't want to talk about it.

"It's terminal."

"I don't understand." This was not among the things she had braced herself for. She would never have looked at Annie and thought of terminal cancer. Annie looked healthy. She didn't look like she was knocking on death's door, like other people she knew who had cancer.

"Yes, she was diagnosed with an aggressive form of breast cancer a few years ago." John leaned in closer and spoke in low tones, taking a sip of the scotch he had brought in from the kitchen. "She chose a different route than most people." He leaned back in his chair, then leaned in toward Pearl again. "No chemo, no mastectomy. No radiation. At least not yet on the radiation."

"Why isn't she dead yet?" Pearl put her hand over her mouth and squeezed her cheeks, determined to work on her poor impulse control. But at seventy-seven years old, it was a lost cause. "I'm sorry, that came out wrong," she said through her fingers.

"Statistically, she should have died a while ago." He put his drink down. "Don't you think I've researched this? The median survival rate for people with stage four breast cancer is about twenty-one months." Pearl's eyes widened. "When she was diagnosed, the cancer had already spread into her spine. It's in two ribs now."

Pearl noticed her son's lower lip start to quiver, ever so slightly. As a toddler, this was the harbinger of a full-on wail. In anticipation, she handed him a tissue but was a beat too late. He cried as if his heart was being shredded from the inside. He didn't wail like a child, but his shoulders shook, and the small sounds that made their way out of his mouth were primal. She stood and hugged him from behind — a futile attempt to quiet his shoulders. She was afraid his convulsions would result in him having a seizure or a stroke or a heart attack. She had no idea what this kind of hysteria would do to him.

She held onto him as he shook, insightful enough to remain silent. His heaves eventually settled, and Pearl took a step back. She placed the tissue box in front of him. Finally, he looked up at her, his eyes swollen almost shut, like the time he and his friend Bobby had gotten into that poison ivy. How could she remember something from so long ago, and in such vivid detail, then forget her way back to the parking lot from the beach trail? And then do something as nutty as put an earring in the fruit bin. Absurd. She shuddered.

"So, yeah," he finally said, blowing his nose. "Annie should be dead by now."

"I just don't understand." Pearl's skepticism bubbled to the surface. Sally's sister had breast cancer and died a year after being diagnosed. And it was only stage two when they found it. "How can she look so normal? Why didn't she have chemo? None of it makes sense." She knew she couldn't say what she really wanted to, that Annie was faking.

"She decided, early on, to focus on the quality of her life, not the number of her days."

"But what about her son? Doesn't she want to live as long as she can for him?"

"That's just it," John said, taking another tissue and pressing it into his eyes. "She didn't want her remaining time to be spent sick from toxins in the chemo."

"So, she's a tree-hugging hippie?" Pearl couldn't help herself. Annie looked a bit hippie-dippie. John removed the tissue from his eyes and glared at her.

"It's not the toxins for toxins' sake," he said. "Annie doesn't want to spend the time she has left puking her guts out from chemo. She wants to feel good. To be productive."

"Okay, that makes sense," Pearl said, her tone laced with skepticism. "But how is it that she's still alive? How?" She hung on the word, then repeated it. "How?"

"Some sort of hormonal treatment. It's not a cure. But it's slowing the growth of the original tumor." His breath shook. "It's grown very little in the last three years. But the one in her back, at the base of her spine, well, that one has grown recently. And the spots on her ribs are new, but surprisingly, they're not giving her much trouble."

"Lord, I'm so sorry, John." She patted her son's hand. "What happens next?"

"After Christmas, she'll get radiation for her spine. Her oncologist believes it will take the pain away." And then: "Please go easy on her. I'm not sure what all the animosity is about."

"What animosity?" Pearl feigned surprise and insult. She knew she'd been hard on the woman, but couldn't help herself. And now, knowing of Annie's terminal prognosis, she was even more puzzled by this relationship. Why in the world would her son want to get tangled up with a dying woman? And as if reading her mind, John glared at her for what seemed like the hundredth time today. "Okay, okay. I'll do better." She reached for his hand. "I promise."

"This may not be the best time to bring this up," John said, pulling his hand away, "but there's something I need to ask you."

"If it's not a good time to bring it up, then don't bring it up."

"It needs to be addressed." He sighed. "I want to revisit something you said. About not being yourself, or something's not right with you...I don't recall your exact words."

"I don't know what you're talking about." She stood up. "You're confusing the hell out of me." She stood up. "I'm going to bed."

"Please sit back down," he said. "I guess that's just it. You seem confused lately."

"Do you hear that?" Pearl grasped at the opportunity for a diversion and silently thanked her neighbor's dog for howling like a coyote. She knew exactly what her son was getting at, and she didn't want to discuss it with him. She would play dumb and even lie to him if necessary, promising herself that she would talk to her doctor after the holidays. But she wasn't going to, under any circumstances, discuss her concerns with her son.

"Mother, you're changing the subject."

"Am I?" The dog howled again, this time decibels louder. "Don't you hear that?"

"Yes, Mother, I hear the damned dog." John leaned back in his chair and stretched his legs out in front of him. They were so long that the tops of his feet peeked out from the other side of the table. He folded his arms across his chest.

"Bracing yourself for a fight, are you?" She laughed, feeling a tiny bit tipsy from the gin. "I'm telling you there's nothing to discuss."

"At the hospital, just this morning, you said you have some stuff going on with you." He sat up, arms still folded. "I'm worried about you."

"Oh, that." Pearl needed a subterfuge, and she needed it fast. "Yes. I'm having some issues with my neighbor." She lied. "But I don't want to do anything about it and potentially ruin his holiday." She was proud of herself for thinking on her feet. "It's that obnoxious dog. Howling all through the day and night." She smiled to herself. She could be crafty when necessary. And felt no guilt or shame in lying.

"Funny, this is the first time I've heard the dog. And we've been sitting here for a long time." He moved his chair around toward his mother and put his hand on her shoulder. "Look, I won't pry into your private business."

"Thank God," she said with affectation and eye rolls. She stood. "It's getting warm in here." She took a few steps toward the wall and flipped the switch for the ceiling fan.

"Why is there an earring stuck in your chicken?" John studied her plate. "You didn't eat much."

"Can't you see?" With her finger hovering above the food, she traced the outline. "It's a smiley face." She cocked her had. "No, wait. It's a sad face."

"You didn't answer my question." He picked up the evidence and held it out to her. "Why is there an earring in your chicken."

"Because I put it there." This, at least, wasn't a lie. "I was making food art. Like Annie did the other night."

"Mom, I'm worried about you." John put the chicken back on the plate and shook his head. He flashed a hint of a smile but then grew serious.

"I can see that." She looked at her nails. She was supposed to get a manicure the other day. Yes. The day she got lost in the woods. The day she couldn't find her way back to the parking lot, back to Bubba. She could certainly blame it on that. She'd completely forgotten about the manicure. Until now. "I just don't understand why you're worried." Once again, a lie. She felt very much like she was being interrogated by the police. Which, in a way, she was. She braced herself for a lecture about the butter dish.

"You put your butter dish away in your junk cabinet, Mother. Why did you do that?" Bingo, she was right. He had to bring up the damned butter dish.

"I was distracted." When did she last have butter? Two days ago? Three? The day she lost Bubba! That's right! She came home and had an English muffin. With butter. She'd been quite distracted that day. It had to explain the butter dish. And the manicure. She would give herself grace on this one and immediately felt better. She was distracted! Hardly a reason to think she has Alzheimer's. *When you hear hoofbeats, think horses, not zebras.* She laughed out loud. She decided to tell him the truth about Bubba. "You know. I was quite distracted a few days ago, maybe the day before the accident. I took Bubba out to the nature preserve. I wanted to collect shells and sea glass. I veered off the trail in search of a special fungus I'd heard about (this was only partially true) and then had a hell of a time finding my way back to the bike." She threw her head back and laughed. "I came home and had an English muffin, and by golly, I put the butter away in the wrong place. I also forgot about my manicure appointment." She rapped the side of her head with her knuckles. "Scatterbrained old lady."

John listened, taking her in, seeming to consider her side of the story. She realized then that she must sound like a person pulled over for drunk driving, trying to explain — with passion and fervor — why she couldn't walk a straight line or recite the alphabet backward. Every reason except the real reason: that she was, indeed, driving while intoxicated. She sat up straight in her chair, readying herself for John's rebuttal.

"That actually makes sense." John sighed. "I don't suppose you were making something involving frozen broccoli that day too?"

"Broccoli?" Pearl knit her brows and tried to think of when she last had broccoli. She came up with nothing. "I don't believe so. No. I haven't had broccoli in quite some time."

"You didn't notice a bad smell in the mudroom yesterday?"

"Yes, of course. It was musty clothes. My laundry cycle was blown to hell when I got the call about the accident."

"There were no clothes in either the washer or the dryer," he said.

"But, there was a bag of frozen broccoli." He looked at her. "In the dryer."

"Oh, bullshit." She said, clutching either side of her chair. "Bullshit!"

"No, Mother, no bullshit." His face softened. "Annie found it last night when you sent her in there to look for paper plates."

"She's lying," Pearl said, suddenly remembering. When had Sally come for dinner? Was it last week? She wracked her brain, trying to remember the exact day. She'd planned to sauté some fresh broccoli but forgot to pick some up from the store. Then she pulled the bag of florets from the freezer and went out to the lanai to check on something. Still carrying the bag of broccoli, she set it down on the dryer door, which had been left open from when she unloaded it that morning. Then something else demanded her attention. She forgot about the broccoli and mindlessly closed the dryer door. Then Sally called and said she would bring a green salad. No need for broccoli. Damn. She never returned the bag to the freezer.

"Why would Annie lie about something like that?" John's frustration was evident in his voice. "I saw it with my own two eyes. The smell inside the dryer was overwhelming."

"Then why didn't you mention this at the time?" Pearl was on the verge of tears. She had no excuse, really, to account for her distraction with the broccoli. None. She didn't even want to begin to think about the earring but held tightly to her belief that this was nothing and that she was just a bit scatterbrained. Suddenly. With no real explanation. Panic engulfed her. She stoically put on her best face.

"I wanted to, but Annie talked me out of it." John covered his eyes with his hands. He loosened his fingers and peeked through them. "I'm sorry I brought this up. I'm worried about you, that's all." He let his hands drop. "You're right. A lot is going on. Let's drop this for now, and when you're up to it, we can revisit it down the road." He held out his hands.

"Thank you," she said, letting her hands fall into his.

.   .   .

ANNIE RETURNED to the lanai with fortune cookies and after-dinner drinks on a tray. Pearl was annoyed that this woman she hardly knew had managed to make herself right at home. Isn't that what any good host wants? For their guests to feel at home? *Make yourself at home. My house is your house. Mi casa, es tu casa. Home is where the heart is. Blah, blah, blah.* Annie apparently felt at home enough to rummage through her cabinets and closets, picking this and choosing that. *The nerve, helping herself to my liquor stash.* On the other hand, Pearl was grateful for the help, thankful for the things that Annie did in the background. She must remember to properly thank her at some point before they fly home.

"We never opened these fortune cookies last night," Annie said. "Plus, one of my favorite traditions of the holiday season is a glass of Baileys."

"Wow, this looks great," John said.

Yeah, yeah, just make yourselves at home, she wanted to say but bit her tongue instead.

"Anyway," Annie continued, raising her glass, "to the holidays and family and fortune cookies."

"It doesn't feel much like the holidays," Pearl said.

"I know it doesn't, Mother. Let's have a toast anyway." John raised his glass. "Here's to a restful night of recovery, because tomorrow promises to be just as stressful as today."

Pearl reluctantly picked up her glass and gently tapped it against John's, then Annie's.

"And here's to Marina and Luke. God help them both." Pearl looked at Annie, who turned away.

"Here's to fortune cookies," Annie said, barely a whisper. She took a sip of her drink, then put her glass down and shuffled the cookies. "Please, take one." She slid the tray closer to John, who picked up two cookies. He gave one of them to Pearl.

"I want to pick my own cookie," Pearl said, putting her little cellophane package back on the tray. "I want to get the fortune that is meant to find me. If you hand me a fortune, it might actually be meant for someone else."

"What do you do when you're at a Chinese restaurant, and the waiter hands you a cookie?" Annie asked.

"Yeah, what do you do, demand to see the entire stash of cookies so you can pick one out?" John drank half of his Baileys in one, long, slow sip. He laughed, his eyes crinkling genuinely for the first time since their arrival.

"Oh, go fuck yourselves," Pearl said, laughing. She liked to see the glint in her son's eyes. She hadn't seen it in a long time. Obviously not since he's been here. But even two years ago, when he'd spent a month with her, even then, no glint. She used the f-word just now because she knew it would bring their relationship back to baseline, even if only temporarily. It was a tactic she'd used with the students who came to see her. It leveled the playing field. If she dropped a four-letter word into the conversation, the student saw her in a more relatable light. She used it with care, and when she did, it always yielded good results. If nothing else, a relaxing of the shoulders would ensue. And soon after, the student would begin to open up. She was notorious among John's high school friends: *Mrs. Butterfield, the f-word lady*.

Annie gasped, feigning shock. She pointed to the tray, and the three of them dutifully put their fortune cookies in the middle of it. Annie closed her eyes and made a great show of mixing them up. Pearl selected first, hugging her cookie to her chest. Annie nodded at John, and motioned for him to make his selection. He shook his head and silently gestured *after you* with his hand. She grabbed the one closest and placed it next to her glass of Baileys.

"Pearl, you open yours first," Annie said.

"Nope. Youngest to oldest. I'll go last." Pearl countered, wanting to hold onto her untold fortune for as long as possible. Not that she believed any of it, of course, she didn't. But opening a fortune cookie held anticipation. A strip of paper claiming that you'll soon be rich, or around the next corner you'll meet the love of your life well, why not hold onto the anticipation. More often than not, the message would be uninventive and obvious.

"I guess that's you," John said, caressing Annie's shoulder.

She pulled the cellophane apart, extracted the cookie, and cracked it open in one graceful move. Pearl studied Annie's fingers and noted that they were long and lithe, like John's. She imagined her son extending his hand from out of the smoke and soot of 9/11 and meeting this young woman's hand. She recalled the first time she'd met Neal. He held the door of a New York deli, and as she walked in, her arm, bare in the summer heat, touched his. She'd been only eighteen, fresh out of high school. Life as she knew it had changed that day. When Neal was killed in Korea, well, they might as well have killed her too. But she soldiered on, for John.

Annie extracted the fortune, holding the paper up for everyone to see. Then she read it out loud. "Enjoy yourself while you can."

"Hear-hear," Pearl said, raising her glass. As the three glasses came together, she noticed a wistful look pass between John and Annie. Of course. *Enjoy yourself while you can.* What a cruel twist of fate for a woman with terminal cancer. Pearl felt shame and embarrassment seeping through her pores. "Okay, moving on. John, it's your turn." Choking back tears, John crushed the cookie right in the package.

"Avoid taking unnecessary gambles." He cleared his throat, a squeak of laughter escaping, incongruous with the gravity of their lives. It grew larger and filled the room, bouncing off the ceiling and flying through the window, traveling far and wide, drowning out the neighbor's howling dog. "Avoid taking unnecessary gambles," he repeated through fits of laughter. Annie pulled the paper from his hand and held it out for Pearl to see.

"Lucky numbers 12, 14, 17, 20, 28, 36."

Pearl was confused. An inside joke, maybe? And then, a lightbulb amidst the laughter. She got it. *Avoid taking unnecessary gambles,* and, oh, by the way, here are your lucky numbers. It didn't strike Pearl as funny at all. She ignored the laughter.

"Okay, it's my turn," Pearl said. She held either side of the cellophane and tried to pry it apart like Annie had done. Only it didn't come apart very quickly. Her damned arthritic fingers. In part frustration and part playfulness, she threw the cookie down on the table and hit it hard with her fist. Her almost empty glass jumped and teetered on its base, nearly toppling over. She deftly (thank goodness her hand-eye coordination seemed to still be intact) grabbed the glass and drank the remaining Baileys, suddenly wanting more. She picked up the crumbled cookie by the corner of the wrapper and ripped it with her teeth, launching fortune cookie shards across the table. She fished for the fortune, and when she found it, she moaned. "I got hornswoggled," she said, holding up a thin strip of white paper, half the size that it should be as if it got cut prematurely, quality control at its worst. She crumbled it and tossed it among the pile of cookie bits.

"After all that hocus-pocus bullshit!" John winked at Annie and looked at his mother.

"Wait, what's this?" Pearl spotted another strip of white, inside the tattered wrapper. "Yes!" She stuck her tongue out at John and began to read. "If you look back, you'll soon be going that way." She put the paper down and lifted her empty glass. "Any chance for another one of these?"

"Absolutely!" Annie collected the three glasses. She brushed the uneaten fortune cookie bits and empty wrappers onto the tray. John got up and followed her into the kitchen.

Pearl spread her fortune on the table before her, ironing the small, white strip flat with her finger. *If you look back, you'll soon be going that way.* She knew what this meant, obviously. Look forward, not back. Keep moving into the future, don't get hung up in the past. She had to do this after Neal was killed or she wouldn't have survived single parenthood. She had to keep trudging forward. One day at a time. She couldn't look back, couldn't let herself wallow. *If you look back, you'll soon be going that way.* She never believed in God. While she felt strongly that there was something or someone out there, she didn't buy into what the Bible said. Sitting alone on her lanai, she took the chance that maybe, just maybe she'd been wrong all these years and that there was, indeed, a God who listened to prayer. She tilted her eyes upward and whispered into the air.

"Let this be a dream. Let this be just one big nightmare. Let me wake up tomorrow as if it were two days before, but with no car accident. No death. No catastrophic injuries."

If you look back, you'll soon be going that way. So, she looked back. All the way back. All the way back to 1952, when Neal was killed. All the way back to the day before he deployed when she cried like a baby and begged him to stay. All the way back to that day at the deli when he held the door and their arms touched. *If you look back, you'll soon be going that way.*

16

John

The night was stagnant, the darkness thick. For the past hour, John had been on the bed listening to Annie quietly sob as he rubbed her back. He didn't know if it was the physical pain of a growing tumor or the emotional toll of her disease manifesting as it sometimes did under periods of duress. And his mother won the *Let's Cause Duress* award for her performance the past two days. He admittedly had grown blind to the way she'd treated Marina over the years. Maybe not as acutely scalding as she was with Annie, but more like a slow boil. A slow, and steady boil. Never missing an opportunity to find fault with something Marina had done. And never missing a chance to let him know that he could have chosen better.

He pulled the curtains back, hoping to see fireflies, but knowing they wouldn't show up for another few months. He hadn't thought much about Marina since they'd left the hospital, and he felt a twinge of guilt for that. Dinner had been a diversion, a place to let loose and decompress. But of course, his mother had ruined it for everyone. Annie seemed to take it in stride and made the proverbial lemonade out of lemons. The fortune cookies and after dinner drinks were a nice touch — something he wouldn't have thought of — and it made him feel especially tender toward her.

He opened the window a crack. A warm breeze blew the curtains into his face. He pushed them aside and opened the window all the way, and rested his elbows on the sill. He closed his eyes and forced himself to recall the image of Marina lying on the hospital bed with wires and tubes linking her to life. The nurse emphasized how important it was for the unconscious patient to hear the voices of loved ones. If talking to a vegetable wasn't bad enough, he didn't consider himself among her loved ones. They'd had so little to do with each other since the divorce. If it hadn't been for his relationship with Ness, he seldom would have seen Marina. Hearing his voice would be discomfiting — the stress of his voice in her ears might delay her recovery rather than accelerate it.

He picked up his cell phone to call Shorty. It was after eleven, and the pub was closed, but Shorty would still be there, shooing out the stragglers and going through his closing checklist: dating newly opened wine bottles, rinsing taps, and swishing a mop around the floor behind the bar. He felt terrible being away during one of their busiest weeks of the year. Shorty picked up on the first ring, spewing all kinds of obscenities at him for not calling sooner.

"A hello would have been nice," John said, smiling into the phone, Shorty's ornery voice a soothing balm for his soul. "Yeah, I know...it's been crazy here...my mother is being her pain-in-the-ass self...I'm sorry I'm not there...was it busy tonight? Marina's in bad shape... worse than I thought...no, the kid doesn't know...yep...okay, man... thanks...I promise I'll check in tomorrow."

Annie stirred, and John winced, sorry that he'd woken her. He'd tried to speak quietly but was so happy to talk to Shorty that the volume of his voice probably rose without his knowledge. She rolled over and propped herself up on the pillows. Her outstretched arms, he knew, was an invitation to snuggle, most often requested in times like this. Times when emotions bubbled close to the surface and threatened to eat you alive. All he wanted to do was continue sitting by the open window with his thoughts, but he got up and propped two pillows against the headboard and settled in, half sitting, half lying, still fully clothed and not at all sleepy. She wiggled herself into the crook of his arm and closed her eyes.

"Coming here seemed like a good idea at the time," she said. "But now I wonder if everyone would be better off if I left."

"Everyone who?"

"You and your mom." She sat up and looked at him. Her hair was matted, and her eyes wet and swollen. Perhaps she hadn't been asleep after all. "She clearly doesn't want me here."

"I agree that she's been difficult," he said. "But I think we may have had a breakthrough tonight." He thought about their conversation in the parking garage. But their follow-on conversation during dinner, when Annie had gone into the kitchen, may very well have been a chrysalis. His mother's demeanor and countenance changed when they talked about Annie's diagnosis and the reality of a shortened life. He honestly believed things would be different going forward. Like dry, cracked earth in a draught suddenly besieged with rain. He had a feeling that Annie wouldn't be pleased to find out that her life was now an open book before his mother. Well, not really an open book. More like a novella or short story. He'd given his mother the highlights, and it seemed to soften her a bit. Maybe a lot. "We had an interesting discussion when you left the room." He chose his words carefully. "I think she understands how important you are to me. How much I love you."

"You didn't tell her that I have cancer, did you?" Annie's body became rigid, and he could feel the heat rising in her cheeks — a tell-tale harbinger of tears.

"I had to."

"No, you didn't." Her voice cracked. "Now, she's just going to pity me."

"I promise you, she won't." He sighed. "We had a long discussion today. In the hospital parking garage, of all places." He pulled her in closer. "Our story is so complex, Annie. The how and why, and the deep bond we both felt, after only a few days when we hardly knew each other." He paused. "There really aren't words, but I tried. And I only told her that you had cancer when we met." He kissed her on the mouth, and, thank God, she kissed him back. "When she started in on you tonight, I couldn't stand it. She was horrified to hear that you still have cancer. I think she feels ashamed of how she's been behaving."

"I get why you told her. Sort of." Annie wiped her eyes with John's shirt. "It's just that sometimes I like to be anonymous. You know, pretend to be a normal, healthy person."

"I get it. Really, I do." He looked into her eyes. "For the longest time, people I knew looked at me with disgust in their eyes for leaving Marina. She was the victim. And I left her. Maybe I shouldn't have. But I did."

"You were a victim too," she said.

"Well, nobody, and I mean nobody looked at it that way." Damned tears. He used his shirt, as Annie had a moment ago, to wipe them away. "So, I know what you mean about wanting to be anonymous."

They sat silent. Annie's breathing became rhythmic, almost imperceptible. He kissed the top of her head and slowly, carefully inched her toward her side of the bed. He got up and pulled the covers over her bare shoulders. Then he went into the bathroom to brush his teeth. Such a mundane thing to do. Something most people do without thinking, almost Pavlovian. Wake up, brush teeth. Ready for bed, brush teeth. Ness had no way of knowing that when he brushed his teeth two mornings ago, it would the last time.

John undressed and slipped into bed. He laid down on his back and let his leg gently make contact with Annie's leg. Wide awake and staring at the ceiling, he tried to calculate how many times he'd brushed his teeth up to this point in his life. He started from his first memory of the act, before his father was killed. John would stand on his little stool and his father would dab some shaving cream on his face and let him scrape it off with a plastic knife. And then they would brush their teeth. Father and son at the sink. So, he started there, at age three. He got to twenty-seven before sleep overtook him.

PART III

17

Luke

A lady came in and told Luke that Mommy got hurt in the crash. Mommy didn't look hurt — she didn't even have any blood. The lady also said that Daddy got hurt in the crash. And that he's dead. That stupid lady had red hair like his and like Mommy's. Luke hated his hair. He wished he had black hair like Daddy. The stupid lady who said Daddy died has a stupid name: Candy. He wanted to see Mommy soon. Candy said she would come back and take him to see Mommy. Grammy came yesterday and gave him a sock monkey because he had surgery. He used to have a sock monkey at home, but it fell apart. The one at home was Abe. He would call this one George. Like Curious George. His favorite book was *Curious George Goes to the Hospital*. He was in the hospital too. Yesterday he got ice cream and ate it first. He didn't eat the disgusting green beans. Grammy said she would come and get him when it was time to go home. He didn't want Grammy to take him to her house. He wanted to go to his house with Mommy and Daddy. He wanted to get on the plane and go home. He wanted his own bed and his other toys. And he wanted to show his friend Jake his cast.

Luke sat in the chair next to the hospital bed, holding George tight against his chest. He wanted Mommy and Daddy. The tears came then, but he didn't want to cry. Candy said it was okay to cry. But he didn't want to. He just wanted to see Mommy and Daddy. But Daddy is dead. Candy said Daddy is dead. Candy is wrong. Daddy is okay. He's at the hotel. Or at Grammy's. Because Daddy sang to him in the car right after the crash. Daddy sang to him. Daddy is okay. Candy is wrong.

"Hey, sweetie, I need to take your temperature." The nurse crouched down beside him. "Lift your tongue up, sweetie." Luke did as he was told. The nurse stuck the thermometer in and told him to bite down, but it wiggled and fell out. "It's okay. Let's try again." The thermometer wiggled again, but he held it down as hard as he could. He blinked, and tears streamed down his face. "Now, now, what's this?" The nurse pulled a tissue out of her pocket and gently wiped his cheeks. "Here, you hold onto this in case you need it." She handed him the tissue. There was a beep, and the nurse took the ther-mometer out of his mouth. "Perfect. Good job, sweetie." She patted his arm.

"I want my mom." Luke's face burned. "And my dad." He pressed the tissue into his eyes.

"I'll see what we can do," she said. "Let's get you settled in bed for a bit. Candy will be here at two o'clock to take you to see your mom." She helped him onto the bed and turned on the TV. "Let's see. How about *Sponge Bob*?"

"*Animal Planet*," he said.

"Okay, then!" She picked up the remote and clicked through the channels until she found it. "*Animal Planet* it is!" On her way out the door, she turned around. "Lunch should be here soon. See you later, sweetie." She waved.

Luke didn't wave back. He just sat on his bed with his sock monkey. He stared at the screen but didn't want to watch TV. He looked at the door and closed his eyes. He made a wish.

"Come on, Daddy," he whispered. "Come on. My room is right here. I'm right here. Come on, Daddy." He decided to count, and when he got to fifty, Daddy would walk through the door. He would probably even bring him a present. *One, two, three, four...seventeen, eighteen, nineteen...thirty-three, thirty-four...*

Luke woke up to the lunch man tapping him on the shoulder. He sat up and looked at the door. No Daddy. "Was my dad just here? Did you see him?"

"Nope. Afraid not." The lunch man settled the rolling lunch table next to the bed. "Grilled cheese and tomato soup. And a brownie for dessert." The lunch man held out his hand for a high-five. Luke half-heartedly let his hand meet the lunch man's hand. "Enjoy your lunch, little man." As soon as the lunch man was out of sight, Luke pushed the rolling lunch table away.

"My sock monkey," he whispered. "George?" He looked under the covers. In a panic, he looked on the floor by the rolling lunch table. "George?" Luke held his breath to keep from crying and climbed off the bed. He walked around to the other side and found the monkey sprawled out on the floor. He picked it up and climbed back onto the bed, drawing in a deep, shaky breath.

With George settled on his lap and his eyes glued to the door, he counted, starting over from one. *One, two, three...fourteen, fifteen, sixteen...twenty...twenty-nine, thirty, thirty-one, thirty-two...forty-nine.* He closed his eyes hard and smiled. *Fifty.* He opened them. No Daddy. *Fifty-one, fifty-two, fifty-three...sixty-seven, sixty-eight...seventy-four, seventy-five, seventy-six...eighty-three, eighty-four.* He peeked at the doorway, which was just as it had been before — empty. He let the tears come freely now. *Eighty-five, eighty-six...ninety-eight, ninety-nine...*He didn't even bother with the final number. *Daddy isn't coming. Daddy is dead.*

LUKE KNEW how to read old-time clocks. Daddy taught him. Jake wanted to learn too, because there were only digital clocks in his house. Daddy taught Jake to read the old-time clocks. Mommy loved old-time clocks. The only digital clock in Luke's house was in Mommy and Daddy's room.

Holding George against his chest, Luke stared at the old-time clock on the wall. The second hand made its way around, the big hand on the eleven, and the little hand on the two. Daddy said when the big hand is on the twelve, whatever number the little hand is on is what time it is. Candy said she would come to get him at two o'clock and take him to see Mommy. He couldn't wait to show Mommy his sock monkey. He closed his eyes for a few seconds and opened them, hoping the big hand would be closer to the twelve. It was a little closer. He closed his eyes again. And this time when he opened them, the big hand was all the way on the twelve! But Candy didn't come. He sat up straight and looked around. He got out of bed and put his slippers on, then sat down in the chair by his bed.

"Hey there, sweetie." It was the nurse, not Candy.

"Where is Candy?" He felt his eyes fill with tears. "I want to see my mom."

"She'll be here soon." The nurse handed him a pair of shorts and a tee-shirt. "I thought you might be more comfortable wearing clothes to see your mom."

Luke looked at the clothes — his red shorts and his *Incredibles* shirt. He was saving these clothes for Grammy's house. Mommy said she would wash his other clothes when they got there.

"Why don't you take these into the bathroom. I want you to pee for me, and when you're finished, you can put these on. I'll wait right here."

Luke closed the bathroom door behind him and peed like the nurse told him. He flushed the toilet and washed his hands. It took him a long time to get dressed. The cast on his arm kept getting in the way. He finally walked out with his shorts on backward and his shirt dangling around his neck.

"Let's see about this," the nurse steaid. "Here we go, lift up your good arm and slip it right in here." She guided his arm with the cast through the other sleeve, careful to not hurt him. "There we go. You're all set."

"My shorts are on backward."

"Oh, that's alright. Nobody will notice."

"I don't want Mommy to see me with my shorts on backward." He choked back a sob. The nurse lifted him onto the bed, and in one quick motion, pulled off his shorts, righted them, and slipped them back on.

"Yoo-hoo!" Candy knocked on the door jamb before walking into the room. "Hey, Luke, there you are! You look all cleaned up and ready to go see your mom." She had a wheelchair.

Luke pulled away from the nurse and sat up, his legs dangling over the edge of the bed. He sniffled. "I need my shoes."

"You sure do!" The nurse got up, opened a cabinet, and pulled out his sneakers. "Let's get these on!" She slipped his feet in and started to tie them for him.

"I can do it myself."

"You sure can!" She took a step back and watched as he struggled to tie his shoes, using both hands and the limited mobility that his cast created. She raised an eyebrow. "Are you sure you don't want help?"

"Okay, you can do it." He extended both feet and let the nurse tie his shoes. He jumped off the bed and climbed into the wheelchair. "I'm ready."

"Okay, sweetie," the nurse said. "I've got to go see the little girl down the hall. I'll check in on you later." She patted the top of his head and walked out the door. Candy crouched down and looked into Luke's eyes. She took both of his hands.

"You had surgery on your arm, right?"

"The doctor put a screw in my elbow."

"Well, your mom had surgery too."

"She broke her arm in the car crash?"

"No. She bumped her head very hard. She had to have surgery on her head."

"Did they put a screw in her head?"

"No." Candy smiled. "They didn't do that. But they had to fix some things in her head." She squeezed his hands. "Your mom is still sleeping from the surgery."

"Can I wake her up?"

"She can't wake up yet, she has to sleep so her head can heal. You can hug her and talk to her and sing to her — whatever you want. She will be asleep, but she can hear you. She just won't be able to talk to you or see you. But she will know you're there." Candy wheeled Luke out the door and started down the hall.

"George!" Luke yelled.

"Shhh." She crouched down to Luke's level. "George?"

"My sock monkey." Luke pointed toward his room.

"Oh, yes, George! I can't believe we forgot George!" She turned the chair around so fast that Luke laughed. She pushed him, pretending to run, panting when they reached his room.

"He's on my pillow," Luke said. Candy left him in the doorway and jogged over to the bed, grabbed the doll, and deposited him into Luke's waiting arms. They rolled back out into the hall.

"Are you a football fan?"

"I like the Eagles."

"The Eagles? You don't like the Giants or the Jets?"

"I hate the Giants." Luke got quiet. Then: "My dad hates the Giants. He was born in Philadelphia. He loves the Eagles."

LUKE CLOSED his eyes as they approached the noisy and scary ICU. He didn't like it and didn't want to see it. Candy stopped pushing the wheelchair but didn't say anything. He was afraid to open his eyes. She tapped him gently on the shoulder, crouched down, and peeled his hand away from his eyes.

"Here we are," she said. "I want you and George to sit right here for a few minutes." She patted the cushion of a couch. "I need to have a chat with the doctor and make sure your mom is ready for you."

"She's awake?" His eyes grew big, and he smiled at the prospect.

"No, but like I said before, she'll be able to hear you and feel you."

He climbed out of the wheelchair and onto the couch, clutching

George. He looked at the clock. The big hand on the six, the little hand still sort of near the two. He remembered Daddy's words: *If the big hand is on the six, it means it's whatever-thirty.* Luke stared at the numbers. Yes, the little hand was pretty much on the two. So, it's two-thirty. He heard footsteps and thought Candy might be coming back to get him.

"Grammy!" He jumped off the couch, forgetting Candy, forgetting George. He ran to Grammy and hugged her hard. He wanted her to pick him up and carry him, but in the car, before the crash, Mommy told him that he had to be careful because he was getting big and Grammy was getting old, and if Grammy tried to pick him up it would hurt her back. He finally let go and led Grammy to the couch. They sat down, and he put George in her lap. A big man sat down with them.

"Do you remember your Uncle John?" Grammy said, looking at the big man.

Luke stared at the big man. He didn't really remember him. Maybe he saw him once when he was little. Daddy talked about Uncle John. And showed him pictures. Yeah, that's Uncle John.

"You're a policeman," Luke said. "Like my dad."

"Yes. That's right," Uncle John said. "I was a policeman. But I broke my leg and couldn't be a policeman anymore after that."

"Did you have surgery? I had surgery." Luke held up his cast. "They put a screw in my elbow."

"Wow. That's a cool looking cast. It's the same green as the Eagles." Uncle John smiled. "Your dad's favorite team."

"It's my favorite team, too," Luke said. "Did you have surgery when you broke your leg?"

"Yes. And they put six screws in."

"Where are the screws?"

Uncle John showed him his scars and pointed to the places where his bones were screwed together.

"My mom had surgery on her head," Luke said. "And she's still sleeping. I'm going to visit her pretty soon."

Grammy put her arm around him and kissed the top of his head.

He plucked George out of her lap and held him to his chest with his good arm. He settled himself next to Grammy and laid his head against her chest.

"How did you break your leg?"

"When I was a policeman, I got into a fight with a bad guy." Uncle John pointed to the sock monkey. "What is his name?"

"George." He handed the monkey to Uncle John.

"Hello, George." Uncle John pretended to be a bad guy fighting with George. He bent George's leg into a twist. "The bad guy fell on my leg and broke it. It was twisted just like that." His voice grew soft. "Your dad was with me the whole time. He even rode in the ambulance with me. And he stayed with me when I had surgery."

"My daddy is dead," Luke said, burying his head into Grammy's chest.

"I know," Uncle John whispered. He picked up the monkey and placed it on Luke's lap. "I know."

LUKE STOOD in the doorway to his mother's room, afraid to go in. He wanted his sock monkey but left him with Uncle John, who said George would have surgery on his leg and would be healed by the time he was done visiting his mom. He knew Uncle John was only pretending. He knew George's leg wasn't really broken.

"It's okay. You can go in. Your mom is comfortable." Candy stood in the doorway with her hand on Luke's shoulder. She moved toward the bed and picked up Mommy's hand. "You see. I can hold her hand." She bent down and put her cheek next to Mommy's face. "And I can hug her too."

"Can I sit on her bed?"

"Yes, of course, you can," she said. "We have to let the nurse make some adjustments to the bed, just to make sure all the lines and tubes don't get disturbed." Luke stepped slowly toward the bed, watching the nurse push buttons. Mommy's head moved, but it was just the bed going up.

"Hi Mommy," he said, touching her hand. He looked back at

Candy, who nodded. He sat in the big chair next to Mommy's bed. Candy came over and said she needed to talk to Grammy and Uncle John and would be back in a few minutes.

"Hi Luke," Mommy's nurse held out her hand, and Luke shook it, just the way Daddy taught him when Daddy got that police award. He'd followed Daddy around and shook hands with all the police officers. "My name is Donna. I'll be right outside the door, so you can have some special time with your mom." She smiled at him. "You can sit on her bed, but please be careful of her breathing tube, okay?" Luke nodded, and his lip quivered.

"Why does she have a breathing tube?" Only very sick people need breathing tubes. Daddy let him watch a movie once, and it had a hospital and a very sick lady with a breathing tube. Daddy told him only very sick people need breathing tubes. He tried to think of the movie but couldn't remember anything except for the breathing tube. His eyes filled with tears.

"Everyone has a breathing tube after surgery," the nurse said. "I'm sure you had a breathing tube after your surgery."

"I didn't have one," he protested. "When I woke up, I didn't have that." He pointed to his mother's face.

"Well, I'm sure you did, honey. You just don't remember."

Luke did remember. He knew he didn't have a tube. He just knew it. He turned away from the nurse.

"Your mom's breathing tube is nothing to worry about." She touched his shoulder. "I promise." She turned around to leave. "Remember, I'll be right outside the door. Please come and get me if you need anything." Luke nodded, waiting for Donna to go away.

"Mommy. Mommy? Can you hear me?" He knelt on the chair and leaned over the bed rail to get a closer look. Mommy's eyes were closed. He reached his good arm up and touched her hair, which felt greasy, like when she didn't shampoo for a few days. "Mommy. It's me. It's Luke. Lukey." He whispered because he didn't want the nurse to hear him. "Mommy?"

Luke stroked Mommy's hair. He wanted to sing her favorite song, the one that has his name, but he felt shy, so he just kept saying her name over and over. When his arm got tired, he climbed off the chair and found the place where he could climb onto Mommy's bed. He inched his way up toward her head and carefully laid his head next to hers on the pillow. He closed his eyes, trying to think of something to talk about.

"Grammy gave me a new sock monkey," he said, his voice barely a whisper. "His name is George." He turned his head and studied her face. She didn't have a cut like Daddy. Where did she hurt her head? He didn't see any blood on her after the car crash. "I had grilled cheese and tomato soup for lunch. I only took a few bites. Your grilled cheese is better. Maybe Grammy will make grilled cheese when we get to her house." He didn't like the way she smelled and sat up. Mommy always smelled like flowers. He didn't like this smell and started to cry. He didn't want the nurse to come in, so he laid back down and cried into Mommy's pillow. "I want Daddy," he said, between sobs.

"Are you okay, honey?" It was Donna. He lifted his head off the pillow and sniffled. She handed him a box of tissues. "It's okay to feel sad, you know." Luke nodded. "Have you had enough? I can bring you back out to the lounge."

"I want to stay here."

"Just five more minutes, okay?" She walked toward the door, looking over her shoulder at Luke before she disappeared.

"Lukey's boat is painted green, ha, me boys! Lukey's boat is painted green, the prettiest boat that you've ever seen. A-ha, me boys a-riddle-i-day! A-ha, me boys a-riddle-i-day!" He bobbed his head to the beat of the drums in his mind, just like on Mommy's Great Big Sea CD. Mommy loved this song so much. He hoped it would make her happy. He sang the verse again. And again.

"Lukey's boat is painted green, ha, me boys! Lukey's boat is painted green, the prettiest boat that you've ever seen. A-ha, me boys a-riddle-i-day! A-ha, me boys a-riddle-i-day!"

He climbed off the bed and danced around the room, singing his favorite part of the song.

"Lukey's rolling out his grub, ha, me boys! Lukey's rolling out his grub, one split pea, and a ten-pound tub." As always, he laughed at the thought of a single pea in a big bathtub, then continued. "A-ha, me boys a-riddle-i-day! A-ha, me boys a-riddle-i-day!" When he was little, every time this part of the song came on, Mommy would say, in a loud, silly voice, *one split pea and a ten-pound tub*, and he would laugh and laugh and laugh.

18

John

John held the kid's sock monkey in his lap and watched his mother mindlessly and silently flip through the pages of a magazine. As was the case yesterday, they had the whole ICU lounge to themselves. Marina couldn't possibly be the only patient in the entire unit. Maybe the only one with visitors? And then, as if on cue, a young couple walked in and sat down on the sofa opposite him, holding hands, but not looking particularly distraught. Probably here visiting an elderly relative, he figured. He wondered now what deceptions his countenance might be hiding. Did he look distraught? Were there dark circles under his eyes from sleepless nights? Did his expression hang like *Droopy Dog*? Or did he simply look like a guy making an obligatory visit to his comatose ex-wife?

"Mr. Butterfield?" The woman who brought the kid here stood in front of him, holding out her hand. He stood and looked at his mother, who put down the magazine and also stood. "I'm Candace Furman. The children call me Candy." John and Pearl took turns shaking her hand. Candace sat, and following her lead, John and Pearl sat too. "I'm the hospital social worker assigned to Luke's case. Tell me a little bit about your relationship to Luke."

"I'm his grandmother." Pearl sat up straight, making her position in the pecking order known.

"It's a complicated situation," John said. "How much time do you have?"

"I'd like to talk while Luke is out of earshot. Ordinarily, I'd talk to you in my office, but I want to be available if he comes out of his mother's room agitated or upset." She got up and walked toward Marina's room, peeked in the door, and returned, smiling. "I think we have plenty of time to talk."

"There's nothing complicated about this," Pearl chimed in. "I'm his grandmother, plain and simple. Maybe not by blood, but it might as well be by blood."

John studied the social worker's face, which showed no sign of confusion or surprise. The three of them sat silent for a moment, until John, still holding the sock monkey, spoke up.

"The kid is my ex-wife's son. Conceived in rape. Our marriage crumbled when she was still pregnant with him. She married my best friend, the man the kid calls Daddy." Why the hell did he tell her all this? He sunk deep into the cushions and tried hard to disappear.

"Your marriage only crumbled, because you let it," Pearl snarled.

"Mother now is not the time or place."

"Let's stay focused on the here and now," Candace said. "I understand there was no guardian named, in the event of something like this.

"What do you mean?" John looked from Candace to his mother. "It's not like she's dead. They're letting the kid visit her. He's probably climbing all over her. They wouldn't let him do that if they thought she was going to die. Or would they?" John wondered if that was why they were letting the kid visit like that. He looked at his watch — the kid has been in there for a half-hour already. His body stiffened, the blood draining from his face. He put his head between his knees.

"It's okay," Candace said. "This is a lot to absorb." She waited until

John sat up again before continuing. "I'm assuming you and your mother will be in temporary guardianship of Luke until more permanent arrangements can be made."

"That's just it," John said. "You're talking like Marina is already dead."

"Whether she lives or dies is immaterial right now." She looked at John, then at Pearl, then back at John. "The fact is, if she pulls through, it's going to be a long road and a long time before she will be capable of caring for Luke."

"I can't believe this." John stood up and paced the perimeter of the small lounge, muttering. "I can't believe this. I have to go back up north. I can't stay here until she recovers. I can't do this. I barely know the kid." He stopped in front of the couch, where he'd left the sock monkey. "George." He picked up the doll and sat down, settling it on his lap.

"Luke can stay with me as long as necessary," Pearl said, looking sideways at John. "Marina's sister is coming in from Australia in a few days. She's an attorney. She'll know what to do."

"How could they have not named a guardian?" John was incredulous. The thought of being stuck in Florida for any longer than necessary unnerved him. His best-case scenario had Marina stumbling out of her coma in the next day or two, Dale arriving, and he and Annie leaving. He hadn't stopped to consider a longer-term requirement. Nor had he stopped to consider a sock monkey named George or the fact that he had suddenly become *Uncle John*.

"This is a common situation," Candace said, with a practiced kindness. "Unlike in movies, the number of couples who actually have those kinds of legal documents drawn up is small."

"Most people don't like to think about dying, John." Pearl, always chiming in.

"Well, they should," he said, shaking his head.

"Let's regroup here," Candace said. "Luke's surgeon feels he should be well enough to be discharged Thursday. He'll need follow-up on his arm. And physical therapy. But that can all be taken care of out-patient from wherever he ends up staying."

"He'll come home with us Thursday," Pearl said. "That's two days from now. They were on their way to my house for the holidays when the accident happened."

"Luke may seem fine right now, but, as you know, he's been through a lot of trauma. I don't think he fully understands that he will never see his father again."

"He knows his dad is dead." John sighed. "He sat here and told us."

"You have to understand the six-year-old mind," Candace said. "He may understand what death is, but he's really only on the cusp of being mature enough to understand its permanence."

"How can we help him?" Pearl pulled a notepad and pen out of her purse and sat poised, ready to transcribe whatever came out of this social worker's mouth.

"He needs continuity and normal activities."

"How?" John's head throbbed. "The kid is far away from home, his father is dead, and his mother is a vegetable."

"John!" Pearl whacked his arm with her notepad. "Marina is not a vegetable. I've always hated that term. What is she, a carrot? For crying out loud. She's going to pull through."

"We all certainly hope that will be the case," Candace said. "I understand that Luke's routine will be a bit different for the next few days or a week, just like it would be under normal circumstances on vacation."

"I was hoping to take him to our water park," Pearl said, wistful. "But not now, of course." She wrote something down. "We'll find lots of fun things to do."

"Great, that will help tremendously," Candace agreed.

"What about the hard stuff?" John didn't want the next few days to be a fantasyland. Realism needed to be addressed and maintained — he didn't want to sugarcoat anything. He held the sock monkey up to his face and sniffed it, then looked into its beady eyes. He put it down next to him on the couch. "I mean, we can't just party-party-party and not address reality."

"You're right about that," Candace said. "Kids don't grieve the way we adults do. Their grief ebbs and flows. One minute they're happily playing, and the next minute they're crying." She looked at Pearl and patted her hand. "Just let him be. Let him talk if he wants to. Don't shy away from talking about his dad. Especially memories that you shared. Kids love to hear stuff like that."

"What about Marina?" Pearl set the notepad in her lap and fidgeted the pen between two fingers. "How do we begin to address that with him?"

"Don't give him false hope, but, he does need some hope. We should know more about her prognosis by the time we discharge him on Thursday. I think it would be great if you bring him here to visit her, maybe even once a day while he's here in Florida." Her beeper went off. She glanced at it and stood up. "Excuse me, I need to make a call. I'll collect Luke afterward and bring him back to you. I'll bet he'd be happy to have one of you wheel him back to his room."

What a fucking mess. John couldn't wrap his head around the who, what, where. The kid had to go back to school after the holidays. How the hell would that happen? Did Dale plan to take him to live with her in DC? Pearl was in no shape to take care of a six-year-old long term. Especially now, with her mental capacity in question. He held the thread of logic between his fingers — that his mother's odd behavior had been triggered by this tragedy. But he held another thread of logic — loosely because he didn't want it to be so — that his mother, at seventy-seven years old, had begun a natural, mental decline. Most of the time, he enjoyed his mother's company. Especially when they debated about benign issues or world events. It saddened him to imagine her intelligence turning into incoherent babbling.

John got up and walked toward Marina's room. He looked back at his mother, shook his head, and motioned with his hand for her to sit tight. *I'll be right back*, he mouthed. The nurse sitting outside Marina's door glanced at him but said nothing. The door stood partially open, just enough for the nurse to respond quickly should she hear an odd beep or the yelps of the little boy who was laying on his back in Marina's bed, his head on her pillow, the color of his hair youthfully bright compared to Marina's hair, which had faded to a pale orange over the years. The kid was singing. Singing!

Marina had never wanted kids, and with each passing year, the discussions grew more serious — longing on his part, interspersed with reluctance on hers. And the more he brought it up, the deeper she dug her heels into the ground. Nester's words from so long ago pierced his heart: *Just get a vasectomy already, she doesn't want kids.* He'd convinced himself it was all for the best. Busied himself with life and moved on. Until Marina got raped and became pregnant. And decided to keep the baby. He still felt the betrayal of that as if it had happened yesterday. Time and distance (and more than a few sessions with a counselor) allowed him to accept that Marina's intensely complex decision had not been made to punch him in the gut. Logically, he knew this. Emotionally, well, that was a different matter entirely.

The kid's song grew louder as he lifted Marina's hands and swayed them as if dancing with her. John inched his body away from the door while still maintaining a line of sight into the room. He didn't want to embarrass the kid with his watching. And suddenly, the kid was off the bed, singing and dancing around the room like a dervish. And then the kid laughed. And laughed. And laughed.

Like a wave crashing on the beach, the reality of Nester's death and the reality of Marina's condition hit him hard. The whirling, laughing kid who Nester raised as his own. A sob lodged itself in John's throat. He tried to stall its escape by swallowing and holding his breath. He shuffled back to the lounge, holding it in as best he could, trying to compose himself for his mother's sake. All of his efforts failed him. He sat down on the couch and wept.

"Mommy is sleeping, but you and Grammy can go see her now." The kid came barreling across the floor and plopped himself between John and Pearl. "Uncle John?" The kid patted his arm. "Why are you crying?" Without a word, John's arm, of its own volition, with no input or approval from his brain, found itself around the kid's shoulder. He picked up the sock monkey and held it out to him. He took a deep breath and tried to steady his voice.

"George's leg is all better," he said through tears, "and he's so happy to see you." The kid took the doll and snuggled in closer, burying his head in John's chest.

"I think I'll go in and say hi to your mom," Pearl said to the kid. "You'll probably be in your room when I get back."

"Will you come to see me later?"

"Maybe, but Uncle John and I need to get a Christmas tree because you're coming to my house on Thursday. That's the day after tomorrow."

"Okay. Bye Grammy. See you Thursday."

"Bye-bye."

John watched his mother wipe her eyes as she walked away. The kid danced the sock monkey in the air. Afraid to move, afraid to disrupt this moment that he couldn't quite define, he sat as motionless as he could. He kept his arm around the kid's shoulder, apprehensive of this strange impulse to nurture. He rationalized, telling himself that he simply felt sorry for the kid. He hardened his heart and pretended that the kid's little voice calling him Uncle John didn't tug at him. He reminded himself: the very existence of this kid launched the marble that knocked over the first domino in a string of dominos — the beginning of the end of his marriage. Yet he sat there, arm around the kid, the kid's head on his chest, feeling something that bordered on fatherly affection.

"I'm here to take Mr. Luke back to his room." A woman in scrubs standing next to the sofa with an empty wheelchair broke into his thoughts.

"Actually, I'd be happy to take him," John said. The kid slid off the sofa and climbed into the wheelchair.

"I'm ready," he said, looking at John.

"Off you go then," the woman said.

"Off we go!" John pushed the wheelchair down the hall and to the elevator doors. "I have a slight problem," he said, crouching down to look into the kid's eyes. "I don't know where we're going."

"Children's ward. On the fourth floor," the kid said.

When the elevator doors opened, John wheeled the kid in, sliding the wheelchair close to the buttons. The kid pushed the button for the fourth floor, and John watched the doors close, wondering how he ended up here.

19

Annie

The absolute worst place in the world to be, three days before Christmas: Toys R Us. The line of cars from the traffic light, around the corner, and into the parking lot moved slower than ketchup oozing out of a just-opened bottle. Annie hadn't anticipated this sojourn to Toys R Us. Pearl had come home from the hospital yesterday and announced that Luke would be discharged on Thursday, suggesting in her most accomplished, you're a lifesaver voice, that Annie might just want to pick out a few things to put under the tree. She thought she saw Pearl batting her eyelashes. It made Annie want to gag or laugh — she wasn't sure which.

So here she sat, stopped in traffic, anticipating tomorrow. *Tomorrow, tomorrow, I love ya, tomorrow, you're only a day away.* She turned off the radio and sang to herself, having seen that play on Broadway as a teenager. And unlike in the song, she didn't love tomorrow. Tomorrow represented one less day she had on earth. Right, everyone was just passing through, so to speak, but Annie acutely felt the absence of a string of tomorrows. She brushed the thought away in favor of more immediate concerns: Thursday — tomorrow — represented a disruption in the casual threesome that she, John, and his mother had become over the past few days. She held no unrealistic expectation that Pearl would come to adore her, yet maybe, just maybe they could become friends.

Annie sat up straight and gripped the steering wheel. Cars honked all around her. She looked out the window — had she done something stupid? Nobody had moved in the past three or four minutes. She relaxed, convinced of her innocence. The car in front of her shifted, ever so slightly. Keeping her eyes glued to the road, she thought about Luke — the mere fact of whom had caused John so much angst. How could she relate to this child in ways that wouldn't make Pearl interpret any gesture as trying to usurp her role as the madam of the house? John's description of his mother as being a pain in the ass didn't come close. Pain in the ass described her on her best days.

"Just be yourself," she said out loud. She turned the radio back on. "If Pearl gets upset, that's her problem to deal with. Just be yourself." She finally reached the traffic light into the shopping center. If she blinked, she'd miss the nano-second that the light turned green — letting only one or two cars through at a time. The clock on the dashboard taunted, reminding her of how little time she had to accomplish this mission. She craned her neck, finally close enough to see a police officer standing in the parking lot, directing traffic. A police officer! Never in her life had she seen pre-Christmas chaos quite like this — not even on Black Friday.

Poised and ready, finally at the head of the line, the light turned green. Pressing her foot on the gas pedal, she accelerated forward, but instead of going straight through into the parking lot, she made an illegal U-turn to get the hell out of there.

THE PARKING LOT at Target felt eerily calm. More crowded than on an ordinary day? Probably. But mobbed? No. Not at all. Annie found a row of parking spots toward the back of the lot, and was glad she'd decided to come here instead of battling the crowd at Toys R Us. By the time she escaped the Salvation Army bell ringer (she didn't have any cash or loose coins) and walked through the double doors, she was drenched in sweat. An anachronism of a different sort — the oddity of a hot, muggy morning, a sweaty neck, palm trees, convertibles, and now, people walking around Target in shorts and flip-flops, amid the sound of Christmas music. She grabbed a cart and stopped in front of a display of gift-wrap. *Better get some.* She threw four rolls of the glitziest gift-wrap into her cart.

At Luke's age, Henry was obsessed with Legos. Nothing but Legos. So many Legos. She'd said as much last night, and John became wistful, recounting one of the few times he'd seen Luke, maybe three or four years ago — there had been Legos all over the house. Big Legos, for toddlers, John explained. Well, Luke was six now, and that meant he could have the more challenging sets. As much as she wanted John to soften to this little boy, she felt an irrational fear that it might pave the road back to Marina. If that were to happen, well, she couldn't compete. Annie took a deep breath and swallowed the thought whole, imagining it plopping into her stomach with her breakfast. Enzymes and acid breaking it down until it turned into goop, the nutrients fueling her and the ugly thoughts coming out the other end where she could flush them away.

Annie spotted some cute Christmas-themed dish towels and picked them up for Pearl. In the frenzied rush to get to Florida, buying a hostess gift had been unimportant. She brought Pearl a bouquet of cut flowers the other day, but couldn't imagine not having a box to put in her hand on Christmas morning. She needed a token gift for John as well. Her real gift to him — a painting of his boat on the river — sat hidden in her studio. She plucked a schmaltzy Christmas tee-shirt off the rack. Hopefully, it would at least make him laugh.

She trudged the perimeter of the store and parked her cart on the outskirts of the toy department, careful to not block the endcap, and found the Lego aisle. Dodging frantic shoppers, she elbowed her way between an older couple arguing over Spider-Man versus Star Wars.

"Just buy both," Annie said.

"I suppose we can do that," the woman mumbled.

"But these damned things are so expensive," the man said, holding up the Star Wars box and waving it around in the air. "It's robbery, what they're getting for these things." The woman grumbled and placed Spider-Man back on the shelf. Annie grabbed it and two other sets. Years of buying them for Henry inoculated her from the shock of their cost. She'd always thought of them as an investment — they lasted forever and were played with often. Henry still fiddled with his Legos from time to time.

She dashed through the other isles to see if anything jumped out at her. Some ideas hit her, ones that she hadn't previously thought of. She found her cart and dropped the Legos in, then went back for the rest of her items by category. Random toys: a set of all five original Power Rangers action figures and a set of six matchbox hot rods. Games: *Uno, Jenga,* and *Pictionary Junior.* Books: *Harry Potter and the Sorcerer's Stone.* Creative: Construction paper, plain white drawing paper, a sketch pad, a large box of crayons, markers, colored pencils, and a four-pack of Play-Doh — primary colors, and a can of white.

Annie took a quick look at the Christmas decorations and found a display of garlands in contemporary colors — fuchsia, lime, aqua, and purple. She knew Pearl would object to her funkifying Christmas, but she didn't care. And then the gem of all gems — oversized shiny, plastic balls in the same colors. Like a rebel, she grabbed ten of them and headed in the direction of the checkout, selecting the shortest of the long, meandering lines. Everyone in the store seemed to be on the same schedule. She braced herself for a long wait.

20

———

John

J ohn jumped in the truck he borrowed from his mother's neighbor and pulled into the street in search of Christmas trees. Not sure which direction to go, he turned left and drove several miles, pushing buttons on the radio until he found one playing holiday music. He felt better after yesterday's breakdown in the hospital lounge. After wheeling the kid back to his room, he stayed for a bit, sitting next to him and talking about random things — John couldn't remember what — and finally, saved by the nurse, extracted himself. He'd gone back to the ICU and replaced his mother at Marina's bedside. It felt strange, but he talked to her a little, telling her about the kid. John thought he saw her eyes blink. He wasn't qualified to make such a judgment call, but it sure looked like her eyes flickered. Probably an involuntary twitch. It could be the beginning of her long, slow recovery. Or it could be the beginning of the end. He hoped that the kid's visit — his singing and snuggling —

somehow penetrated the blood-brain barrier and entered her soul, giving her hope and a reason to hang on.

He wondered if Marina sensed Nester's absence. A visceral reaction, even in her coma, that Nester wasn't just out running an errand — that he no longer existed in the flesh. If Marina and Ness had a connection like the one he had with Annie, well, there was no way Marina didn't sense the void.

A hand-scribbled sign pointing toward a Christmas tree lot caught John off guard. He slowed the truck to get his bearings, and as he approached the lot, he could see the remaining trees in a pile on the ground — castaways. He kept going and made a U-turn at the next light.

During dinner last night, John suggested taking the kid to the tree lots to help pick out the tree. Annie loved the idea. But no, his mother wanted everything perfect before the kid's arrival. She wanted him to walk into a Christmas wonderland. *If you want it perfect, then let's just drag your fake tree out of the garage*, he'd said. *But the smell of pine*, his mother argued. John muttered something about buying pine scented spray, but the matter was settled, and his marching orders issued.

He noticed a Home Depot out of the corner of his eye. *And what's that? Christmas trees*! He quickly put on his turn signal and moved over and into the parking lot. Why hadn't he thought of this in the first place? The Home Depot near his house in Jersey City had Christmas trees — and much cheaper than the inflated prices you paid for the privilege and romance of walking through a pop-up lot.

He parked the truck and jogged toward the store, bypassing the entrance and heading straight to the outdoor garden section, the front of which had been converted into a mini-tree lot. Douglas fir, Balsam fir, Fraser fir. Okay. Just Fraser fir. He grabbed the first decent looking tree and lugged it to the wrapping station. He rubbed his bare leg. Scratched by a branch. Pine needles like little spears. Now he knew why Christmas was ordained to be a winter holiday in much of the world. Long pants would have protected his leg.

Back on the highway, he wondered how Annie made out shopping for the kid. *Crap.* He didn't have anything to give her for Christmas. *Crap, crap, crap.* He pounded the steering wheel and thought about the ring at the bottom of his duffle bag. Proposing on bended knee in Florida and in front of this strange, new audience seemed somehow wrong. Plus, he'd promised Henry that they'd do it together. He hadn't planned to stay through Christmas, but now it looked like he was stuck. Dale's travel schedule kept changing — Monday now, maybe Tuesday. He couldn't leave his mother alone to take care of the kid. He and Annie discussed it last night and agreed to stay at least until Dale got there.

John pulled into a strip mall halfway between Home Depot and his mother's house. He scanned the stores, looking for a unicorn among the usual suspects: CVS, Subway, a Hallmark store, Modell's Sporting Goods, Hunan Hollywood, LensCrafters. A used bookstore caught his eye — he would go back to it if need be. Maybe something from Modell's? He walked into the Hallmark store and wandered the aisles, picking up ornaments and putting them back down. He looked at a display of coffee mugs and laughed when he saw one that would be perfect for his mother: *she who must be obeyed.* He didn't have anything for her, either. He grabbed it, happy to have found something. Hopefully, it would make her laugh. Deeper in the store, an ornament — a father and son on a sailboat — stopped John in his tracks. His breath caught in his throat as he picked it up and examined it. The little boy looked to be the kid's age. With red hair sticking out from under a blue baseball cap.

The grief that triggered his weep-fest in the hospital yesterday threatened to revisit in the middle of this crowded store. He put the ornament and mug down and charged toward the door, sidestepping several people to avoid crushing them. Once outside, he paced the strip mall, forcing himself to take deep breaths. The surgeon told him yesterday that Marina's status had not changed. John mentioned the blinking eyes, but the surgeon said it was common and didn't account for progress. *Just put one foot in front of the other. Where the hell is the truck? One foot in front of the other.* He found the truck, and with a shaky hand, struggled to unlock the door. Once inside, he put his head on the steering wheel and fought another cresting wave of hysteria.

21

Annie

Annie craned her neck to peek around the woman in front of her. Assessing her position in line — still quite deep with no end in sight — she shrugged and eased her way out, berating herself for not thinking to get a jigsaw puzzle for Luke. She looked at her watch and decided that the delay would be worth it. Alec used puzzles with children in his practice. A somewhat challenging one might provide a nice distraction for Luke. Something to focus on and do with his hands while processing, and maybe even talking about, his feelings.

She trudged back to the toy department, all the way on the opposite end of the store. Quickly scanning the rows of puzzles, she picked up Mount Rushmore — two thousand pieces. Ages twelve and up. Probably too advanced for a six-year-old. Impossible to finish. And drab colors to boot. Her eye caught a smaller box with a colorful scene: hot air balloons flying over a glassy lake, the reflections as colorful as the balloons themselves. Bright green rolling hills in the

162

background, topped with a cloudless sky. A peaceful scene that made her smile. She put her foot on the bottom shelf and hoisted herself, stretching her arm to reach the box. Ages eight and up, with a thousand pieces. Close enough. She would teach him how to separate the end pieces first, then how to group pieces with similar colors and patterns. All of the green ones for the grass would be easy to separate. Then the sky.

"Oh, for God's sake." Pearl's voice cut like a chainsaw through Annie's thoughts. "I thought you went to Toys R Us."

"It was mobbed. I couldn't even get into the parking lot." Annie dropped the jigsaw puzzle into her cart. Pearl's tone had unnerved her, and she decided then and there that she wouldn't fan the flame. So, in her calmest voice, she said: "I aborted and came here." Pearl picked up the puzzle and shook the box.

"This won't do." She handed it to Annie. "Put it back." Annie shook her head and threw the box back into her cart. "Put that puzzle back," Pearl spat. "He doesn't like puzzles." She peered into the cart, cocked her head, and pulled out the Power Rangers set. "Nope, not this either. He's into Ninja Turtles." Annie stood, incredulous, unmoving, and mute. Pearl touched the rolls of wrapping paper and shook her head. "We don't need all this paper. I have some from last year." She took the rolls from Annie's cart and tossed them into her own, empty cart. "I'll put these back on my way to the registers."

"No!" Annie found her voice and grabbed the rolls of paper. "I'm buying these. And I'm buying the puzzle. And the Power Rangers." She felt her face go hot, fully expecting it to turn red. She willed herself to not cry. She gripped the cart's handle and walked away.

"Now, where are you going?" Pearl followed. "Don't you walk away from me!"

Annie turned on her heels. She took a deep breath but said nothing. What could she say? She simply couldn't win. And apparently, she couldn't hold her tears in either. She let them fall freely.

"Oh, now, enough with the crying." Pearl sighed audibly. "You've got to stop taking things so personally."

"Really? You think so?" Annie didn't look back and kept moving forward, plodding along with a tight grip on the cart, wincing in pain. By the time she reached the checkout area, all twenty-five registers were open, the lines five or six people deep. She couldn't face standing there, wide open and unprotected from Pearl. She held tighter to the cart, worried that her legs would buckle under the weight of her back pain. She didn't know how she was going to survive the next few minutes, let alone the next few days.

Instead of getting in line, Annie parked her cart in front of Starbucks and ordered a Gingerbread Latte. She found an empty table near the window and sat down. She pulled out her cell phone and dialed her sister's number. No answer. She sipped her drink and watched people in the parking lot, loading bags into their cars. She turned away from the window and saw Pearl standing at the counter. She slunk down in her chair, wishing she were home in Brooklyn, hoping Pearl wouldn't notice her. She sat back up and braced herself as Pearl walked toward the table, a steamy drink in her hand, pointing at the empty chair. Annie looked out the window again, feeling her eyes grow heavy, silently cursing the reaction this woman had on her. She slowly turned around and looked Pearl in the eye and nodded toward the chair.

"You don't have to like me," Annie said, suddenly brave. "But for the sake of John and now Luke, we need to find an equilibrium." She tried to mimic John's intimidating stare but feared she looked comical.

"I don't dislike you," Pearl said. "It's just that my son is a complex person. And with everything that's happened, I feel like he doesn't need distractions." She blew on her latte and took a dainty sip. "Look, I think he needs to focus on Marina and my grandson."

"That's just it," Annie said, her composure once again, regained. "I think it's noble of him to be here until Marina's sister comes. My ex-husband pledged to take care of me if and when I need it. But you see, I don't want my ex-husband taking care of me. I'm not even sure I want John taking care of me." She took a deep breath. "John has had nothing to do with Marina for many years now. Nothing. It would be different if they'd had children together."

"They have Luke."

"You're delusional." Annie immediately regretted her choice of words, especially in light of some of John's concerns about his mother's mental health. "I'm sorry, I didn't mean it like that."

"How, exactly, did you mean it?" Pearl glared at her.

"Never mind." Annie let her head hang. She held her drink with both hands and breathed in the steam. "No, I take that back. It seems like you're living in the past, pretending Marina, John, and Luke are a happy family. They aren't. They weren't." She took a sip. "According to John, you didn't even like Marina."

"You're absolutely right. I didn't like Marina. I didn't like her at all." She shook her head. "But I was wrong about her. She's a good person. And she was good for John." Annie wanted to scream. She wanted to pitch an adult-sized hissy fit. *I'm good for John, too*, is what she wanted to say, but the words wouldn't form.

"Nobody knows what goes on inside anyone else's marriage. If things were as good as you say, they'd still be together."

"My son is stubborn to a fault. Once he made up his mind to leave her, there was no talking him out of it. She was the bad guy in his mind." Pearl reached across the table. Annie recoiled from the feel of Pearl's boney, papery hands, and felt immediately ashamed of her reaction. She hung her head and let her hands slowly creep across the table. "I'm trying to apologize." Pearl cleared her throat. "I know we got off to a shitty start. I'm sorry, and I hope you can forgive me."

"Let's just move on," Annie said. "What do you say we get in line and get the hell out of this place. We have a lot of wrapping to do."

"Okay," Pearl said. "But not with that garish paper you're buying."

Annie shook her head and felt the first hints of laughter bubbling up. She walked to her cart and removed the offending rolls of giftwrap, standing them against a display of plastic wreaths.

22

———

John

John pulled into the neighbor's driveway, left the key under the doormat as instructed, and lifted the Christmas tree out of the truck's bed. He hoisted it onto his shoulder and carried it across the neighbor's lawn to his mother's house. If he hadn't been so damned distracted, he would have driven up his mother's driveway, unloaded the tree, then returned the truck.

Shit. Annie and his mother were both at home. He'd hoped for some alone time to wallow in self-pity. At least the garage was already open, allowing him a stealthy entry. He carried the tree in and leaned it against the wall. He unfolded his mother's gardening bench and sat down. He made a few cuts in the netting that held the tree in an unnaturally thin, conical shape, imagining it sighing in relief as it popped out and expanded into its natural beauty.

He thought about the kid — wondered what he was doing right now. Maybe eating lunch? The kid talked incessantly yesterday about the hospital grilled cheese and how his mom's grilled cheese was the best. John lied, telling him that before too long, his mom would be out of the hospital and making all the grilled cheese he wanted. *Dammit.* He pushed the kid out of his mind. The wave of panic that he'd been riding all day threatened to swell and knock him off the bench. He took a deep breath, reminding himself that this wasn't forever; it was only for a few more days. But not knowing how long left him feeling unsettled. He fished his cell phone out of his pocket and frantically dialed.

"Dale...I didn't wake you, did I? It's me...John...Very funny...Oh, three in the morning...sorry...I'm reaching my breaking point and want to know when you'll be here...What about Bill? I'll let my mother know...Annie? She's dealing...Thanks."

John closed the lid on his phone and slid it back into his pocket. Dale seemed a bit ambiguous about her long-term plans but said she would, indeed, be there Monday to help figure out the next steps. It wasn't exactly what he'd wanted to hear, but at least it was something. He heard the door to the mudroom open and turned around, smiling when he saw Annie, tenderness toward her melting his heart.

"You're home," she said, wearing an apron and covered in flour. "I'd hug you, but I don't want to get this gunk all over you."

"I don't care about the gunk." He wrapped her in his arms and buried his head in her neck. He kissed her and pulled a blob of cookie dough out of her hair. "You smell like a gingerbread house."

"Well, you may not believe this, but your mother and I have been in the kitchen for the past couple of hours making cookies."

"Holy shit!" John raised an eyebrow and smiled. "I just talked to Dale. She'll definitely be here on Monday."

"Thank goodness," Annie said, pressing her hand into her back. "Now, I can reschedule my radiation."

"She said Monday evening." He pulled her onto his lap. "I don't think it would be fair to leave the minute she gets here."

"I know," Annie said. "You want a carefully orchestrated transition."

"Something like that. How about we book our flight for

Wednesday morning? You could schedule your radiation for later that day or Thursday." He searched her eyes. "How does that sound?"

"That will work." She pushed her hair out of her eyes. "I talked to Alec a little while ago. He'll keep Henry through New Year's Day."

John liked the idea of having Annie all to himself on New Year's Eve. Maybe he would propose then. And do it again the next day with Henry present. He made a mental note to call Shorty and let him know that he'd be back at work on the third.

"Come on," Annie said, standing up. "I'll help you with the tree." She lifted the top, and John grabbed the bottom, and together, they carried it up the steps and through the door that Pearl held open.

"Thanks, Mom," he said. "Could you grab the tree stand and preservative? I left it over there by your bench." John stood with his back against the door, holding it open. Pearl grabbed the items and followed John and Annie, letting the door slam behind her.

His mother, covered in flour, set the tree stand in front of the living room window. She looked at the label on the tree preservative and squirted the requisite amount into the well. John and Annie lifted the tree and gently placed it in the stand. John tightened the screws holding it in place and backed up to look at it.

"I think it needs to tilt a little bit more toward the left," Annie said. John made the adjustments, and Annie gave him a thumbs-up. "Perfect," she said, putting her arm around him. "It's been an amazingly interesting day." Annie's voice was so soft that John had to move closer to hear her. "Your mother and I called a truce." She laughed. "Or something like that." She laughed louder. "We're having fun in the kitchen," she said, even louder, as Pearl approached with a watering can.

"We sure are," Pearl said. She poured water into the tree stand, careful to not let it overflow. "We're making gingerbread walls and roofs for when Luke comes."

"That's a great idea," John said, wondering if Marina and Nester had ever built gingerbread houses with the kid. He fluffed up the branches on the tree.

"It looks very fresh," Pearl said, nodding her head in approval.

"It was slim pickings pretty much everywhere," he said.

"Pearl, where do you keep the lights?" Annie took off her apron and rolled it into a ball, careful to not drop dried pieces of gingerbread on the floor.

"In the garage with the rest of the decorations," Pearl said. "There should be one box of lights. The crappy, generic ornaments are in the red, plastic tub. The good ornaments are in the green one. Bring everything."

"Aye-aye," Annie said, disappearing into the garage.

"I can't believe it." John shook his head and laughed. "If I didn't know better, I would think you two have known each other for years." Pearl rolled her eyes and started for the kitchen. John followed her. "I talked to Dale a little while ago. She'll be here Monday, probably after dinner."

"Hopefully, she'll have a brilliant idea or two about where we go from here." Pearl pulled out a roll of plastic wrap and large Ziploc bags. "Help me with this, would you?" She gestured toward the stacks of gingerbread house pieces. "We need to wrap all of these and then stick them in the bags."

"Wouldn't it be better to let the gingerbread sit on the counter to harden?"

"Actually, Pearl, he's right." Annie emerged from the garage carrying the box of lights. "I used to do this with my son. The first year we put the pieces in baggies, and when it came time to make the houses, let's just say the walls caved in." She laughed and continued to the living room.

"C'est la vie," Pearl said, putting the plastic wrap and Ziploc bags back in the drawer.

JOHN AND ANNIE walked into the living room carrying the two plastic tubs of ornaments and placed them gently on the couch. He lifted the lid off the red container — cheap, plastic, generic ornaments — and let it drop to the floor. Next, he opened the green tub — his mother's special ornaments. He couldn't remember the last time he'd spent Christmas at his mother's house. Certainly not since she moved here.

He stuck his hand into the tub and ran it over the topmost ornaments, reacquainting himself with the tub's hibernating contents. They seemed to yawn and force their eyes open, begging him to let them sleep for just a little while longer. The bulk of the ornaments dated back to the seventies, when his mother became obsessed with collecting them. It certainly made gift-buying easy — he used to buy her two or three each year. At some point, Dale started sending her White House ornaments. The oldest ornament in the box was a tarnished metal circle with a rocking horse in the center and 1948 engraved on the horse's saddle — the year he was born — a gift from his father. He pulled ornaments out of the box, one-by-one, noting the variety in shape, size, fragility, color, whimsy, and sentimentality. Many were made by him, as a young boy. Some of them were never meant to be ornaments, like the stained-glass cookies he and his mother made when he was, oh, maybe six or so — the same age as the kid. They came out of the oven and then cooled to a texture so hard that only a hammer could break them. Eating them was out of the question, so the best looking ones adorned his mother's tree for years. And of course, the bird ornaments that Marina had given her.

Annie sat down next to him as he held the stained-glass cookie ornament to the light. The stained glass — basically a melted hard candy — was shaped like a star and pressed in the middle of a round sugar cookie.

"This thing has been around for, let's see, probably fifty years." He sniffed it to see if it still had a cookie smell. Nope. Smelled musty. "It's amazing the mice never discovered it." He passed the ornament to Annie. "I've seen mice chew through plastic tubs like this to get at birdseed." He shook his head and took the ornament from her, carefully placing it back in the box. He stood up and studied the rows of lights Annie had untangled and laid out across the living room floor. She handed him an extension cord, and, one-by-one, plugged in the lights. They all worked.

Silently, he and Annie strung the lights. She disappeared down the hall and reemerged carrying a bag from Target. She dumped the contents on the floor and rummaged through them, producing several strands of garland in bright, non-traditional colors.

"My mother is going to go ballistic when she sees this," he said, as Annie strung the first strand. "She's a Christmas purest."

"I showed them to her earlier, and, believe it or not, she said I could use them."

"And all this too?" John picked up the large, similarly colored plastic balls.

"Yep." Annie put one on the tree. "I got them for the window side. We can intersperse these with some of your mother's generic ones. We'll save the special ones for the front."

"Brilliant," he said.

"Fresh from the oven." Pearl strolled into the living room and handed John and Annie each a chocolate chip cookie. She regarded the tree, now adorned with Annie's colorful garland. "I won't go so far as to say that I like it, but it has a certain something."

"I have an idea," John said, feeling bold. "What if we hold off on hanging the good ornaments until the kid gets here. Don't you think he might enjoy trimming the tree?" John startled himself by wanting to include the kid. Three days ago, he would have said to just sit the kid down with some crayons or in front of the TV.

"I really want the house in order before he gets here," Pearl said, swallowing the last of her cookie.

"It will be in order," John countered. He scratched his head. "We'll put the box over there, out of the way. Everything else will be all set, including presents under the tree."

"Yep, in fact, I'd better start wrapping," Annie said. "See you in a bit. If you want to help, I'll be in the bedroom."

"I really would like to get these things hung today," Pearl said.

"Look, Mom, I think it would be a good distraction for him. It might make him feel useful or something like that." He raked his fingers through his hair. "I don't know."

"How about I hang the delicate ones. I'll leave a few for him to hang." Pearl rummaged through the box and pulled out three glass snowmen. She hung them toward the top of the tree.

John silently helped his mother trim the tree, leaving a few ornaments for the kid to hang. The ornament he'd seen in the Hallmark store — the one with the father and son sailing — came back to haunt him. He ate his cookie slowly, thinking that he should just go back and buy the damned thing.

23

Pearl

She sat in the passenger seat of her car, fanning herself while John drove. The air conditioner exhaled cold air, but she felt hot as if cooking from the inside. Pearl honestly didn't know what came over her the past few days, treating Annie like a rat in the pantry. She found it hard to admit to herself, let alone to John, what an ass she'd been. But it was right there in plain sight — no admission of guilt was necessary. She found it exceedingly difficult apologize to Annie yesterday. Her blind spot, she supposed, was that she judged too quickly and too harshly. She promised herself to get better acquainted with Annie and to put any residual feelings of animosity aside, at least for the time being. She would keep her secret hope of reconciliation between John and Marina to herself.

"You're awfully quiet this morning," John said, gripping the steering wheel with both hands. He glanced at his mother.

"Just calculating a million things to do, preparing for the road ahead."

"Everything's pretty much done," he said, skepticism in his voice. "All we need to do now is get the kid and get home." Pearl put the brochure she'd been using to fan herself back in the glove box. She was no longer hot. As a matter of fact, she was freezing. She closed the air conditioning vent and squeezed her arms against her chest.

"It's a beautiful morning, is all. That's really all I was thinking about."

"Okay, whatever you say."

"Why don't you believe me?"

"Because I know you too well."

"What do you think Luke will want to do when we get home?" She sighed loudly, ignoring her son's statement, which was only partially true.

"How should I know?" John put on his signal and merged into the right-hand turn lane to the hospital. "Let's just see how things play out naturally."

"Fine."

John pulled up to the curb and unlocked the doors. She hated it when he did things like this. She may be on the upper end of the senior citizen spectrum, but she was no invalid. She could certainly unlock her own damned door. She didn't need her son to molly-coddle her like this. She looked at him, fury in her eyes.

"What?" He shrugged and threw his hands in the air. "Why are you looking at me like that?

"Park the car. I will walk with you." She crossed her arms.

"Mother, I'm not having this conversation." He gestured toward the door. "Please get out of the car. I will meet you in the lobby."

"Why are you in such a bad mood?" She sat stiffly in her seat, still belted in.

"Bad mood?" John put both hands on the steering wheel, then lowered his head until it was resting on his hands. "I'm sorry, Mom. This is all just so fucking overwhelming."

Pearl unbuckled her seatbelt, reached across the car and squeezed his hand, then opened the door and got out. She watched the car roll away from the building and disappear into a sea of other cars. Sweat formed on her forehead and the back of her neck. *Too damned hot. Why did I ever move to Florida?*

She walked through the revolving door to wait for John inside. She ignored the huge Christmas tree in the middle of the lobby and instead walked over to a display of colorful abstract paintings, in colors similar to the hideous garland Annie bought. She walked along the perimeter of the lobby, looking at the odd pictures and made a mental note to ask Annie about her work. All of her work. She was truly curious, even if she didn't care to ever have the woman as a daughter-in-law.

The art extended around the corner and down a wide hallway. She went from painting to painting, cursing John for taking so long. She had no idea how long she'd been waiting, but it felt like forever. He must be having a hell of a time finding a spot. She should have just told him to use the valet service. She looked at her watch. She forgot what time the social worker said to be here. She opened her purse and fished for the room number but couldn't find it. Maybe they should just go to Luke's room instead of the social worker's office. And what was that woman's name? Cathy? Cindy? Caroline? It started with a *C*, of that she was sure. Or was it a *K*?

Pearl wandered down the hall and back to the lobby, or at least that's what she thought. *This is odd.* She looked at the sign on a door. Outpatient Surgical Center. *How the hell did I get here?* Too embarrassed to ask, she backed out, retracing her steps, down the hall, past the artwork. *Wait a minute. These paintings are different.* Then, like a band of guiding angels, three doctors emerged from around the corner, chatting amicably. She followed them. Thank God. The cafeteria. *Exactly where John told me to meet him.* She stood in line for a coffee, not entirely sure she even wanted one. With shaking hands, Pearl handed money to the cashier and told him to keep the change. She picked a table nearest the entrance and sat down, wanting to be sure John saw her when he came in.

24

John

Annoyance and frustration rose from the bottom of John's feet and traveled the length of his legs, consumed his midsection, burned his face, and threatened to make his head explode. He stood near the Christmas tree and scanned the lobby, but his mother was nowhere in sight. Four corridors jutted out like spokes on a wheel. He took a few steps into each one, and when he didn't see her, he calmly approached the front desk.

"I dropped my mother off a few minutes ago and went to park the car," he explained. "She didn't stay put like I asked her to, and now I can't seem to find her." John twisted his neck to quickly look around the lobby again. "Have you seen her?"

"Is she tall with a silver, chin-length bob?"

"Yes!" He nearly toppled over with relief. "Did she stop here to get her visitor's badge?"

"No, she didn't. I saw her heading toward the cafeteria." She shrugged. "I figured she was meeting someone."

John walked quickly to the cafeteria and spotted her right away, sitting with her back toward the door, seemingly lost in thought. He lightly tapped her on the shoulder. She jumped.

"You scared the living daylights out of me." She scowled. "Where the hell have you been? I've been waiting here for ages."

"You know, you could have at least gotten me a cup of coffee." John tried to hold his frustration in but felt it seeping out through his nostrils. He sat down.

"It would be ice cold by now, you took so long," she said and started to get up. "Let's go."

"Not so fast. Sit back down for a minute." He took a deep breath as he tried to snort his frustration back up his nose. "I thought we agreed that you would wait for me in the lobby." He sighed.

"No, we didn't. You told me to get coffee and wait for you here."

"Mother."

"I did exactly what you told me to do." She removed the lid from her coffee and swirled the cup around as if it were a good cabernet. She took a slow sip, then put the top back on.

He rewound the scene all the way back to when he pulled up to the entrance. She had refused to get out of the car, and they argued. He knew he didn't tell her to wait in the cafeteria. Or to get coffee. They had an appointment with the kid's social worker. He looked at his watch. They were already five minutes late. He decided then and there that arguing with his mother about where she was supposed to meet him wouldn't be the least bit productive.

"Okay, Mother. You're right. My bad. Let's go. We're already late for the social worker."

"I have to pee," she said.

"Can't you hold it? We're already late."

"If we're already late, then it won't matter if we're two minutes later." She got up and shuffled toward the bathroom.

John shook his head, incredulous. After witnessing his mother's odd behavior over the past few days, and now this, he was convinced that she had no business caring for the kid by herself, and was relieved anew that Dale would soon be here. The quicker he could get out of here and back to his life with Annie, the better. He missed Shorty and the daily minutia of running the pub more than he cared to admit. Three days until Monday. And another day and a half until he and Annie would be soaring above the clouds, heading home.

His mother's escapade concerned him. A bit illogical, he knew, to worry that she had somehow wandered away from the hospital, or, gotten abducted. It wasn't like him to let his imagination plunge him headfirst into the deep end like that. He couldn't shake the image of his mother standing on the curb under the awning, another car pulling up, and her getting in. And given her mental state lately, such a scenario wasn't beyond the realm of possibility. Did she really believe that he'd told her to wait in the cafeteria? Or was it a cover-up — a way to save face because she knew she had screwed up?

"All set?" John stood up and took his mother by the arm, gently leading her out of the cafeteria and toward the desk to sign in and get their visitor badges.

"We're taking my Grandson home today," she told the woman at the desk as if the woman actually cared.

Pearl walked ahead of John and pushed the button for the elevator, getting in and letting the door close before he could get there and wave his arm around to keep it open. *Dammit, Mother*! He pushed the button several times in rapid succession, hoping to find her on the right floor.

JOHN SLID out of the elevator before the doors fully opened and jogged a few steps toward the social worker's office. He stopped abruptly when he saw his mother and Candace standing in the hallway, laughing. He slowed his pace to a brisk walk, and when he reached them, apologized profusely for being late, protecting his mother by taking the blame.

"You're okay," Candace said, assuring them that their tardiness would not create a cascading spiral of bumped appointments and unavailable beds. "Let's sit in my office for a minute. They're getting Luke ready. The nurse will bring him to us." She led them to a tiny room, cluttered with books and papers. John and his mother sat in chairs opposite the desk. "We've arranged for his cast removal six weeks from now."

"Six weeks?" John looked at Candace, then at his mother. "I don't know where we'll be in six weeks." His heart pounded.

"Don't worry about any of that now," Candace reassured. "Just let us know if you move him up north. We'll make arrangements with your local hospital."

John wiped his head with the back of his hand. He hadn't considered this logistical maelstrom. He doubted Marina would be up and about in six weeks. He couldn't stay here until then. Simply couldn't. Wouldn't. No way, no how. He took a deep breath.

"Any special instructions, for now?" John needed to know what to expect. He hoped that focusing on the here and now would take his mind off the future unknowns.

"Just love him. That's all I can say. Let him talk. Let him ask questions. Place no expectations on his grief. Take it second by second. Oh, and don't let him get his cast wet. An empty bread bag works great. Just secure it at the top of his arm with a rubber band."

"So that's it then?" Pearl sat up straight in her chair. "We've prepared quite the Christmas for him."

"That's wonderful," Candace said. "Just try not to overwhelm him, though. If he doesn't take favorably to anything, just let him be. For example, don't force him to eat. Don't force him to participate in any activity that he doesn't want to participate in."

"What about pain management?" John remembered, too vividly, his post-surgical pain. He rubbed his leg, thinking about it.

"I believe they've weaned him off the heavy stuff and have him on Children's Tylenol." She handed John a piece of paper. "No aspirin. Everything is spelled out pretty succinctly on here."

"Can I come in?" John turned toward the muffled voice outside the door, then turned back to Candace, who nodded. He got up and opened the door. Luke jumped out of the wheelchair and flung himself at John. The nurse, still standing in the doorway with the wheelchair, laughed. "I'll just leave this here. Swing by the nurse's station on your way out. I'll need to walk down with you."

"Hi, sweetheart," Pearl said. She held out her arms. Luke peeled his arms from John's waist and walked over to his grandmother. He hesitated, then went back to John and handed him his sock monkey.

"Hello, George," John said. He held out the monkey, but the kid wouldn't take it.

"He wants you to hold him." With the matter of who would hold the sock monkey settled, the kid climbed in Pearl's lap. He picked up a Rubik's Cube from the corner of Candace's desk and started mindlessly fiddling with it, his little fingers sticking out from the bottom of the cast. He held the cube with that hand and turned the sides with the fingers on his other hand. Almost like he knew what he was doing. John had a Rubik's Cube during the height of the craze in the early 80's and had gotten quite good at solving it. Nothing like the twenty-two or so second record, but a satisfying ten minutes...ish. Okay, maybe the first time took him a bit longer — a half hour? An hour? He didn't remember, nor did he give a shit. "Can we go now?" The kid set the Rubik's cube down on the desk. He slid off Pearl's lap and took John's hand. "Let's go, Uncle John. Let's go to Grammy's house."

"Not so fast, buddy," John said. "Let's see if Candy needs to tell us anything more."

"No, I think you're all set. You've got the paperwork." Candace looked at the kid and pointed to his cast. "No getting your cast wet. Okay?"

"Come on, Uncle John." The kid took the sock monkey and climbed into the wheelchair. "I want Uncle John to push me." John looked at Candace and shrugged.

"Mom, do you have any questions for Candace?"

"Nope."

"My cell phone number is in the paperwork," Candace said. "Please call me if anything comes up."

"Thank you," John said. "We really appreciate everything you've done."

Candace got up and crouched down next to Luke. She held out the Rubik's Cube, and he took it. Then she extended one hand, and he took that too, shaking it like a little man.

"Goodbye, Luke. Merry Christmas."

"Bye, Candy."

"Aren't you going to thank her for the toy?" Pearl tapped on the Rubik's Cube.

"Grammy, it's not a toy, it's a puzzle." He held it up as if Pearl had never seen one before. "It's a hard puzzle. Thanks, Candy."

25

Luke

Luke had forgotten all about Christmas. Then he saw the big tree in the lobby, and he remembered. After Thanksgiving, he (with Mommy's help) wrote a list for Santa. He forgot what he put on the list. Legos, definitely! And video games for his Nintendo. He also asked for Philadelphia Eagles stuff. Uncle John stopped the wheelchair in front of the tree.

"What does that sign say?" Luke pointed to a mailbox next to the tree.

"Ah, it says *Letters to Santa*. Did you write a letter to Santa?"

"Yes. Daddy took it to the post office. Can I get out?" Luke didn't wait for an answer and jumped out of the wheelchair, letting the Rubik's Cube and his sock monkey slide off his lap and onto the floor. The nurse said goodbye and took the wheelchair away. Luke watched as she disappeared down the hall. His lower lip quivered. He started to run after her, but Uncle John stopped him.

"I have your treasures," Uncle John said. "Right here, see?" He held out his hand, revealing George and the Rubik's Cube. "You and Grammy stay here and look at the tree. I'll go get the car."

"Can I go with you?"

"I need you to watch Grammy and make sure she doesn't get lost." Uncle John crouched down to be eye-level with Luke. "It's an important job. Don't let her leave this Christmas tree." He looked around. "Actually, you can let her sit down in one of those chairs." He pointed. "You can sit there too if you want."

Luke watched Uncle John get swallowed by the revolving door, then disappear. He took Grammy's hand and led her to the chairs. They both sat. His legs didn't reach the floor. He leaned into Grammy's arm, and she hugged him.

"Can we see my mom before we go to your house?"

"Sweetie, she needs to rest. Uncle John will take you to see her tomorrow." Luke didn't want Grammy to see him cry, so he buried his face in her arm.

"I need a piece of paper," he finally said. "And a pencil." Grammy opened her purse and shook her head.

"Nope, I don't have any."

"But, I need to write a letter to Santa."

"Now?" Grammy looked confused. "I thought you said you wrote one, and your dad mailed it."

"I have to write another one. A different one."

"Uncle John will be here with the car any minute. Can't this wait until we get home? Uncle John can take it to the post office later."

"I need to put it in that box over there by the tree. It says *Letters to Santa* on it."

"You can write a letter tonight and when Uncle John brings you back here tomorrow —"

"No! I need to do it now." He couldn't stop himself from crying. His shoulders shook, and hot tears dripped down his face. His nose was runny. Grammy handed him a tissue from her purse and patted his leg.

"You sit here. I'll go see if they have paper at the desk." Luke took a deep breath, relieved. He didn't know how to spell what he needed to write and would need to ask Grammy to help him. "Look at this," Grammy said when she returned. "They have special paper just for letters to Santa." She handed him a red pencil. He took the paper and positioned it on his lap. Grammy picked up a magazine and gave it to him. "Put this under the paper. It will be easier to write."

Luke knew how to spell *Dear Santa*. He pressed down hard with the pencil, trying not to break the point.

"How do you spell *please*?"

"P. L. E. A. S. E."

Luke transcribed. He continued. *Please make my mommy get...*

"How do you spell *healed*?"

"Healed?"

"Yes. Healed."

"H. E. A. L. E. D."

Healed.

He continued. *Her name is Marina Quinn.* He knew how to spell all the names in his family. He needed to learn how to spell Uncle John. *Love, Luke Quinn.* He folded the letter and handed it to Grammy.

"May I?"

"I'll read it to you," he said. Grammy gave the letter back. "Dear Santa. Please make my mommy get healed. Her name is Marina Quinn. Love, Luke Quinn."

"That's beautiful, Luke." Grammy sniffled and got another tissue out of her purse. She wiped her eyes. "Go put it in the box."

Luke ran to the box and when he got there stood in front of it. He unfolded the paper and read it to himself. It was neat and tidy — his best handwriting. Santa would be proud of his spelling, even though Grammy helped him. He folded it back up and kissed it. Then he held it over the box and slowly lowered it until he had no choice but to drop it in. He skipped back to Grammy, excited that Santa would make Mommy healed.

"Look," Grammy said, pointing at the window. "There's Uncle John. Let's go, shall we?" Luke skipped, and Grammy walked.

.　.　.

UNCLE JOHN HELD the rear door open, but Luke didn't immediately get in. In fact, his first thought was to turn around and run far away from the car. It was hot outside. He didn't want to get in the car.

"Come on now," Uncle John said. "The faster we get on the road, the faster we can get to Grammy's house."

Luke didn't move. He felt his legs starting to shake, then a trickle of warmth. He crossed one leg over the other and covered his private area with his hands. He didn't know what to do. Grammy was already in the car. She was reading something and not looking at him. He didn't want to cry again but couldn't help it.

"What all this?" Uncle John crouched down, but Luke turned his head away, not wanting him to see the tears. "Ah, I see. You had a little accident." He reached into the car and pulled out the little rolling suitcase that had been retrieved from the crash and had, miraculously — save a few scrapes and scratches — survived intact. "No big deal. We'll go inside side and change." He opened the front passenger door. "Mom, we'll be right back." And then: "It's okay, buddy. Let's go hit the restroom." They padded back into the hospital. Uncle John paused in the waiting area and lifted the suitcase onto a chair.

"Those are all my dirty clothes," Luke said, sniffling and wiping his eyes. "We were going to wash them at Grammy's house."

"Let's see what we have here." Uncle John pulled out a pair of shorts. He held them up and inspected the front and back, then held them to his nose and sniffed. He made a face and pinched his nose together with two fingers. "Yikes!" Uncle John made a crinkly face. "I'm just kidding. They don't smell. I think these are clean."

"I need underpants," Luke whispered. Uncle John dug around and found a pair that looked clean.

"Here you go." Uncle John closed the suitcase and stood. "I'll go with you and wait right outside the door." Luke nodded and went in.

After a few minutes, Uncle John knocked on the door. "Everything okay in there?"

Without answering, Luke flung the door open and walked out, looking dry but no less forlorn. He handed the soiled clothes to Uncle John as they walked back to the car.

"Uncle John?" Luke couldn't keep his voice steady. "I don't want to go to Grammy's house. I'll stay here with Mommy."

"I don't think that's an option, buddy." He opened the car door. "Climb in, and we'll hit the road."

"I don't want to go."

"Let's not do this, okay?" Uncle John sighed. "I promise to bring you back here to visit your mom tomorrow."

"I want to see her today." He yelled. "I want to see her now." Uncle John tried to open Grammy's door, but it was locked. He tapped on the window, and she rolled it down.

"We have a bit of a situation here. Luke won't get in the car. Can you talk to him, please?" Grammy stepped out, and Luke flung his arms around her, sobbing.

"I want Mommy."

"I know, I know." She cooed. "Mommy needs to rest. She's in a special part of the hospital. They can only allow visitors for short periods."

"I want my mom!" Luke shrieked.

"I don't know what to do." Grammy looked at Uncle John. "Should we call Candace?"

"Let me try getting him into the car." Uncle John turned to Luke. "We need to go, buddy. We can't leave the car here any longer." Uncle John moved out of the way. "Go on, get in."

"My arm hurts."

"We'll stop at the drugstore on the way to Grammy's house and get you some Children's Tylenol like Candy said. It will help."

Luke didn't want to get in the car. Uncle John tried to lift him up, but he stiffened. Uncle John was strong, like Daddy. He kicked his feet and couldn't stop crying. Uncle John somehow got the seatbelt buckled, but Luke undid it.

"I. Don't. Want. To. Go."

"Luke, stop this!" Grammy turned around and yelled at him. "Just stop. Let Uncle John buckle you in."

Luke wiggled and wiggled and wiggled, but Uncle John never

yelled. He just kept buckling the seatbelt. And Luke kept unbuckling it.

"Did you know that if I get pulled over by a police officer and you're not in your seatbelt, I could go to jail?" Luke stopped wiggling. He didn't take off the seatbelt this time but started crying again. Quiet sobs.

"What if we crash?" Luke's voice was barely a whisper. Uncle John leaned in closer.

"What was that? I couldn't hear you."

"What if we crash?"

"Crash?"

"What if we crash?" Uncle John climbed in the back seat.

"Buddy, I can't promise you that we won't crash. But I do promise to drive very, very carefully."

"Daddy drove carefully."

"Your dad was a very safe driver." Uncle John paused. "But sometimes accidents happen. I promise to drive carefully." He looked deep into Luke's eyes. "I promise."

26

Annie

It felt like meeting a blind date. Not that Annie had any experience along those lines, but she imagined it might be like this. She knew a little bit about Luke. Basic attributes like his age and history. But she'd never talked to him, never even saw a picture. She imagined a tiny version of Marina, who she'd met, quite by accident one day when she stopped by Shorty's on a Wednesday afternoon, maybe a year or so ago. Nester had been there too, she doesn't remember why. She remembered feeling strange talking to the woman who John had once loved. Sizing her up, trying hard to imagine John with a woman so elegant and refined. Not beautiful, but handsomely natural. An *Ivory Girl* like in the old TV commercials. In comparison, Annie felt like a ragamuffin, or, as her mother used to say, *Sally off the pickle boat.*

She stepped onto Pearl's front porch with a cup of tea, a modest pile of magazines, and scissors. She'd called Alec for tips on how best to interact with a six-year-old boy who had, in an instant, lost so much. Alec's simple advice — just be yourself. Imagine that. Coming from a man who, despite twelve years of marriage, never really accepted her as just herself. Before they finished their call, he suggested that she try to integrate art therapy into the natural setting, meaning, don't make a show of it. Just draw and color with Luke. After talking with Alec, Annie rummaged through Pearl's mudroom in search of old magazines, plucking several out of the recycle bin and hoping she wouldn't take offense.

Annie quickly worked her way through the magazines, cutting out almost every image, even ones she didn't think would resonate with a six-year-old. When she was finished, she carried the clippings into the house and tucked them among the pages of her sketchbook. Then she went back out to the porch to enjoy the rest of her tea and wait. The sound of a vehicle put her on high alert. She walked down the porch steps to get a better look, and the sight of Pearl's car caused her pulse to skyrocket. *Okay, this is it.* She took a deep breath. *Like meeting a blind date.*

She retreated up the steps and into the house. She didn't want to overwhelm Luke and feared her very presence on the porch might do just that. Although knowing John, they would probably come into the house through the garage. She ran into her room and grabbed her sketchpad and a pencil, letting the magazine clippings drift to the floor.

Annie positioned herself at the kitchen table like a stage actor waiting for the curtain to go up. She opened her sketchbook to a work-in-progress and pretended to be thoroughly engrossed in making the pencil move across the page. She didn't want to look like she'd been waiting. Plus, the open sketchbook might be an excellent conversation starter. What six-year-old boy wouldn't enjoy talking about a picture of a sailboat on the river. She could use that as a springboard to talk about John's boat, and, to feel him out to see if he likes to draw or color. *Integrate art therapy into the natural setting,* Alec's voice ringing in her ears.

Annie jumped when the garage door went up — the noise loud and rumbly in the quiet of the kitchen. Among the muffled voices and footsteps were a childlike high octave and sneakers hitting the floor in double-time. Luke, with a dirty, tear-streaked face and puffy eyes, stopped in front of her. He didn't say anything, didn't glance down at her sketchbook. He just stood.

"Luke, this is Annie." John walked into the room, dragging a miniature suitcase behind him.

"Hi, Luke." Annie smiled and extended her hand. Reluctantly and a bit shyly, he put his hand in hers and pumped it up and down. "It's great to finally meet you."

"Can I go to my room, Uncle John?"

"Of course. Let me show you where it is." John looked at Annie and shrugged, then disappeared down the hall.

So, this would be harder than she thought. She hated that she scripted such a scene. How stupid of her. She imagined curling up in a ball and hiding at his age. Even Henry, at that age, was never Mr. Inquisitive or Mr. Charming when she and Alec had people over. She put down her pencil and closed the sketchbook, deflated, and feeling utterly ridiculous.

Pearl hadn't come into the kitchen yet, and the mudroom seemed strangely quiet — Annie heard no banging around, no activity. She got up and found Pearl standing at the washing machine, her finger poised near the buttons, hovering and moving over them like a blind person reading brail. Annie stood just inside the doorway and watched, wondering if she should invade Pearl's private world. When she saw Pearl's shoulders starting to shake, she decided it was time.

"Is everything okay in here?"

"I'm doing a small load of laundry." Pearl seemed distracted and confused. "The damned machine is acting up."

"Let me have a look." Annie moved in closer. Small load, indeed. A pair of shorts and underpants. That was it. She looked around. "Do you have any other laundry we could throw in with this? We could kill two birds with one stone."

"No, I don't think I do. I'm all caught up."

"I'll be right back. I have some things that could be washed."

Annie left Pearl standing at the machine. She paused in front of

Luke's open door. John and Luke were sitting on the bed — Luke holding a Rubik's Cube and John quietly discussing formulas for solving the puzzle. Luke seemed attentive but still a bit far away. Images of John teaching Henry to sail flooded her mind. The ache in her back reminded her of the fleeting nature of her life. She didn't feel afraid of dying — at least that's what she told herself on her good days. But she didn't want to leave this life. She simply didn't want to. And if she let herself think about it too much, she would spiral into the darkness. And that would help no one right now. She took a deep breath, not surprised at the tears streaming down her face. She gathered up her and John's dirty clothes and carried them back to the mudroom, surprised that Pearl had not moved.

"Here we go." Annie opened her arms and let the clothes fall into the drum of the washing machine. "Pearl, are you okay?" Annie squeezed her forearm. Pearl's trance broken, she looked at Annie.

"I think my washer is broken."

"Let's see. It doesn't look like you put the soap in yet." Annie grabbed the detergent, pouring it into the well. "What setting are you trying to use?"

"That's just it," Pearl said. "None of the buttons work."

Annie pushed the button for a regular load with hot water. Everything seemed to work as it should. She had a feeling that Pearl had simply gotten overwhelmed. Or worse, had a stroke. She glanced at her face, without seeming obvious, and noted that she looked fine. No droopiness, although she wouldn't be able to tell unless she could get Pearl to smile. One thing was sure — her speech wasn't slurred. What about arm weakness?

"Great news! It looks like I fixed it!" Annie held out her arms to give Pearl a hug. A subterfuge to assess her arm strength. A smile! No drooping mouth. Pearl returned the hug. Okay, not a stroke. Probably the same confusion that caused her to put the frozen broccoli in the dryer. She would talk to John about it later. She put her hand on the small of Pearl's back and led her into the kitchen. "How about a nice cup of tea?"

"A gin and tonic would be better." Okay, so Pearl was back to her old self. Annie wagged her finger.

"Nope, not until dinnertime. Speaking of which, what do you want to do for dinner? I was thinking of the frozen lasagna."

"Fine." Pearl looked around the room. "Where is John?"

"Oh, it's so cute." Annie accessed her most chipper voice. "They're both sitting on Luke's bed, doing a Rubik's Cube puzzle." She smiled. "They're very engrossed in it." She didn't mention that Luke still looked somewhat shell-shocked. A perfectly normal reaction. She once again felt silly for thinking any of this would be easy.

"Thank God," Pearl said. "You have no idea what we went through getting him here." She exhaled and then put her head in her hands. "You would think we were kidnapping him." She looked at Annie. "He didn't want to get in the car. He was deathly afraid of getting into another car accident."

27

John

The kid didn't say a word about the Rubik's Cube or John's skill at solving it. And now he was stuck — literally — sitting against the headboard, a flimsy pillow under the small of his back, and the kid's head on his arm, which had officially gone numb. He desperately wanted to move the kid but didn't want to wake him. He wanted to see Annie, and willed her to walk by. He felt trapped by the kid, in more ways than one. At the same time, he felt sorry for him. How could he not? Losing both parents. Coming home to a strange house filled with unknown people, except, of course, for his *Grammy*. Still, the kid hadn't seen her since he was three or four. Candace's number was written down somewhere. He planned to call her later this afternoon and tell her about the incident in the parking lot — Luke wetting himself and his visceral fear of riding in the car.

A minute ago, the late afternoon sun poured into the room in an almost blinding way. Of course, trapped like this with the sleeping kid's head on his arm, John couldn't get up to close the curtains. But now, all of a sudden, the bright glare disappeared — the harbinger of an impending storm. Flash. Lightning. And a low, thunderous growl, like an angry animal ready to pounce on its prey. And now, a deluge. Nothing impending here — the harbinger had failed to give enough notice to react. Unless John had been so lost in thought that he hadn't noticed the fading light. This was entirely possible. He closed his eyes and let his senses get lost in the sound of the rain. It was the kind of rain that made people outside scatter like cockroaches. The type of rain that would drench you in an instant. A brighter flash, a louder roar. He saw yellow behind his eyelids like the after-effect of a vintage flashbulb. Another flash. An earsplitting crack. John jumped. The kid stirred but didn't open his eyes. The kid was out cold.

John gently eased his arm out from under the kid's head and lowered him down onto the pillow. He slipped one shoe off, then the other, and since they'd been sitting on top of the bedspread, he simply folded it over and covered him.

Shaking out his prickly arm, he sat down in the chair beside the bed and watched the kid sleep. So, this is what it was like to have a kid: watching him sleep, being careful not to wake him, worrying about thunder scaring him, wanting him to be happy, wanting him to not hurt. He had absolutely no ties to this kid. No ties at all. Except for the fact that his ex-wife carried the kid in her womb. He couldn't get past the fact that Marina never agreed to have kids with him. That was what hurt the most — that the idea of having kids had been closed to him, yet when her rapist impregnated her, well...

John tossed the memory out the window and into the rain, which had slowed from cats and dogs to just cats. He could see a hint of blue on the horizon and almost wished it wouldn't clear. He didn't want the sun to shine, or the blades of grass to sparkle or the humidity to be visible, touchable. He wanted a gray, gloomy, coldish night. He wanted to curl up on the couch with Annie. That's all he wanted. He supposed he could do that, no matter the weather outside. Christmas was two days away, and he longed, suddenly, to be back in the cold grime of Brooklyn, or on the windy docks in Jersey City. He wanted to be behind the bar with Shorty. Anywhere but here. Anywhere but in this room with the sleeping kid. Anywhere.

He got up, closed the curtains, and slowly backed out of the room.

28

Luke

Luke climbed off the bed and looked out the window. It was still light outside, and everything looked wet. Where did Uncle John go? The Rubik's cube sat on the nightstand, just where Uncle John left it. He picked it up and tried to remember what Uncle John said. *Make a criss-cross with the white ones. Then do all the white corners.* Beyond that, he didn't remember. He threw it down on the bed and ran out the door, calling for Uncle John and Grammy. He found everyone in the living room watching TV — an old-time movie, like Mommy watches. Mommy loves old-time movies. He ran back into his room, got the Rubik's Cube, and ran back to the couch, wedging himself between Uncle John and the lady. He couldn't remember her name.

"Uncle John, who is she?" Luke whispered in his ear.

"This is Annie."

"Hi, Luke," Annie said. "I hope you had a good nap."

Luke shrugged, then held the Rubik's Cube out to Uncle John. "I don't remember what to do next."

"Okay, let's see." Uncle John took the cube and examined it. "I see you started the white ones."

"You started them. Remember?"

"Ah, yes. Now I remember." Uncle John turned the cube over. "I like to do the yellow corners and edges after I get all the white ones." He handed it back to Luke. "You give it a go."

"Maybe later." He looked at Grammy, who was sitting in a chair watching the movie. He was hungry and smelled something good. He climbed onto Grammy's lap. "When can we eat dinner?"

"The lasagna should be ready by the time this movie is over."

"What is this movie called?"

"Oh, fiddlesticks. I can't remember." Grammy laughed. "It's on the tip of my tongue, really."

"It's called *White Christmas*," the lady, Annie said. "It's my all-time, favorite Christmas movie."

"What are they doing?" He pointed to the screen.

"They're practicing dance moves. They're going to put on a Christmas show at a beautiful country inn. Those two men, see them there on the screen? They were in the Army during World War II."

Luke slid off Grammy's lap and ran to his room. He rummaged around the bed until he found his sock monkey. He carried it back to the living room and plopped back on the couch. He held George tight against his chest and watched the singers and dancers.

"Here you go." Grammy handed him a little bowl of pretzels. "This should tide you over until dinner."

"Grammy?"

"Yes, Luke?"

"I love you."

LUKE ENJOYED THE MOVIE. He didn't really understand it, but he liked the music. He loved the beautiful tree at the end and all the red costumes. He ate a lot of pretzels but still felt very hungry. He followed Grammy into the kitchen. She opened the oven and bent down to stick a knife into the lasagna. Then she licked the blade. She stood up and pushed a button on the stove. Then she bent down again and stuck her finger in the lasagna.

"Oh Lord," she said. "This is still frozen in the middle." She looked at Luke. "It looks like dinner will be delayed. How about you open the freezer for Grammy and pull out the garlic bread."

Luke found the frozen bread and set it on the counter. Uncle John and the lady, Annie, came in.

"How can I help," the lady, Annie, said.

"You can make a salad."

"Dinner's not ready," Luke said. "It's still frozen."

The lady, Annie, approached the oven and pushed some buttons. She said something in Uncle John's ear, but Luke couldn't hear it.

"Should be ready in about a half-hour," the lady, Annie said. "How about we put on some Christmas music. The three of you can finish decorating the tree. There's a box of ornaments next to the TV. I'll stay here and make the salad."

"Great idea." Uncle John looked at Luke. "How about it, buddy?"

"Come on, Grammy. Let's go." He grabbed her arm and tugged.

Uncle John kissed the lady, Annie, on the lips. Like Daddy kissed Mommy. It made him sad, but he didn't know why. He wondered if Mommy was awake yet. Uncle John said he would take him to see Mommy tomorrow. He wanted to make a Christmas present for her. But his coloring stuff wasn't here. He felt himself starting to cry as he followed Grammy and Uncle John out of the kitchen.

Grammy turned off the TV and put on Christmas songs. There was no fireplace like at home. He wanted a fireplace. Daddy always made a fire in the fireplace when they decorated the tree. And Mommy made hot cocoa.

"Can we have hot cocoa?"

"Oh, my goodness. I don't have any hot cocoa."

"But Grammy, we always have hot cocoa at home when we decorate the tree."

"I'm sorry sweetie, I don't have any."

Uncle John brought the box of ornaments to the couch. Luke peered inside and pulled out a metal ball with a bell inside. He shook it and put it back in the box.

"I heard a rumor that you're going to make gingerbread houses tomorrow." Uncle John sat down on the couch. "You should have smelled it in here yesterday. The whole house smelled like gingerbread."

"I don't want to make gingerbread houses. I want to see my mom tomorrow."

"We can certainly do both," Grammy said.

"Is the lady, Annie, your wife?"

"No. Not yet, anyway. I hope to ask her to marry me soon." Uncle John put a finger to his mouth. "But please don't tell her. I want it to be a surprise."

"Why did you kiss her?"

"Because I love her very much."

Grammy stopped what she was doing and stared at Uncle John.

"My mom used to be your wife."

"Yes." Uncle John's eyes grew big. "A long time ago. Before you were born."

"Did you love her very much."

"Yes, Luke, I did."

"I'll be in the kitchen," Grammy said. She looked nervous. "I'll yell when it's time for dinner."

"You're not going to decorate the tree with us?" Luke wanted Grammy to stay.

"No, sweetie. I'm not." She kissed the top of his head. "I'll be in the kitchen if you need anything."

Luke shrugged and pulled another ornament out of the box. This one was a bird made from a pinecone. He half-heartedly shuffled to the tree and hung it, then went back to the box, but instead of pulling out another ornament, he sat on the other end of the couch, away from the box.

"You've had enough of this already, I see." Uncle John pushed the box away and sat down. "No pressure," he said. "Sure, I could certainly use the help, but no pressure." Uncle John moved the box close to the tree and quietly hung ornaments.

Luke watched Uncle John and remembered him kissing the lady, Annie, in the kitchen. He wondered if Uncle John ever kissed his mom like that. He couldn't imagine his mom kissing Uncle John.

"I want to go see my mom right now." John dropped an ornament on the floor and returned to the couch.

"Buddy, we can't. It's not visiting hours anymore. We're going to have to wait until tomorrow."

Luke buried his head in the couch pillow. He could feel Uncle John rubbing his back, but he wiggled himself away. He didn't want anyone touching him. He wanted to go see his mom. That's all he wanted to do. He lifted his head.

"But I don't want to wait until tomorrow. I want to go now."

"Come on, sit up. I want to see your face."

"No." And then reluctantly, Luke rolled over and sat up. He wasn't crying. But he was sad. "I want to see my mom now."

"First of all, you're very special because usually, they don't let kids into the Intensive Care Unit, where your mom is, at all." He shifted his weight on the couch, then crossed his legs. "They don't let anyone, not even adults, in after a certain time." He glanced at his watch. "It's well past that time. No more visitors. If we just show up there, they will send us home, and we will miss dinner."

"I'm not hungry. I don't want dinner."

"Fair enough. But we still can't go to see your mom until tomorrow."

Luke put his head on the pillow again and turned away from Uncle John. He was sad. And he couldn't stop himself from crying. He didn't want Uncle John to hear him cry. He tried not to shake. The pillow was starting to get wet. He felt the couch bounce a little, and he peeked out from the pillow. Uncle John was back at the tree, hanging more decorations. Why did Uncle John stop being married to his mom? He didn't understand. He knew what divorce was. Jake's parents got divorced in the summer, and he saw his daddy on weekends. Luke would never see his daddy again. He buried his head in the pillow and sobbed, uncaring of how much noise he was making. He didn't care. He wanted his dad back. He wanted to see his mom. And then he remembered his letter to Santa, asking him to heal his mom. He felt a glimmer of hope. A tiny sliver. He needed to be good. He needed to be very good. That meant he needed to stop crying and help Uncle John finish decorating the tree. Jake said Santa isn't real. But Mommy told him Jake was wrong. Santa is real, and he is watching. He wanted Santa to make his mom better, so they could go home. All he wanted was to go home. He sat up and wiped his eyes with his shirt. Then he got up and hung the last few ornaments, while Uncle John stood by, smiling.

29

Pearl

Pearl stood at the kitchen counter and opened two packages of frozen garlic bread, which had thawed quite a bit in the past few minutes. She liked her garlic bread crunchy — to hell with how John and Annie wanted it — and placed the two loaves, naked, on a cookie sheet. She set the lasagna — bubbling and oozing with gooey cheese — on top of the stove. No need to insert a knife to test for doneness. Annie's salad sat on the table, prepped, and ready to be tossed.

"Anything else I could do?" Annie emerged from the mudroom.

"How about setting the table out on the lanai. It's cool enough now. I think it will be pleasant." Pearl lied. She would rather not make any pomp and circumstance out of dinner tonight. Why couldn't they, just once, keep things simple? She knew John and Annie would want to sit outside, so, what the hell. She didn't have the strength to argue, and the path of least resistance seemed to just suggest the damned lanai in the first place. She reached into the cupboard, pulled out four plates, and handed them to Annie. "We'll eat the salad on the same plate with the lasagna."

Pearl leaned against the counter, somewhat short of breath. She pressed two fingers into her neck, looked at the clock, and counted. Sixty-seven beats per minute. Relieved, she drew a deep breath. She had expected her heart rate to be much higher. John's words in the living room had startled her. *I hope to ask her to marry me soon. I love her very much.* Did he genuinely want to marry a woman with incurable cancer? It boggled her mind. Would she have married Neal if she'd somehow known he would be killed in the war? She honestly didn't know. She didn't know what she would have done. She didn't want to admit that yes, she would have married him anyway. Acknowledging that brought the reality of John marrying Annie a little bit closer. She thought about Neal — how she couldn't breathe without him. Would walking away have been any less painful than the gut-punch she felt when the men in their service dress uniforms ambled up the walkway? If it hadn't been for four-year-old John, she would have curled up in a ball and stayed that way for a very long time.

Pearl stepped onto the lanai to light the candles, but they were already lit. She noticed Annie sitting in one of the Adirondack chairs by the water, staring off into its vastness. She wondered what Annie was thinking about. She took a step forward, feeling tender toward her, wanting to sit down next to her and stare at the water too. No words. Just the two of them lost in their own thoughts. She moved quietly through the yard, but by the time Pearl reached the chairs, Annie was no longer sitting, but bending down, cupping her hands and splashing water on her face. Had she been crying? Why else would one splash water on their face but to wash away the evidence of having cried? Pearl knew she should go down there and comfort her. She started walking, then hesitated. No. She couldn't do it. She didn't want Annie to see her soft side. If she could keep Annie somehow on edge, well, maybe she wouldn't want to marry John.

Dammit, she wanted her son and Marina to get back together. Plain and simple. It was the only practical thing. The only thing that made any kind of sense at all.

She turned around and walked stealthily back toward the house, the smell of garlic bread growing stronger by the second. She increased her cadence, jogging through the lanai, and back into the kitchen. *Thank God, no smoke.* She pulled the bread out of the oven — perfectly golden, not a spec of char. She wrapped it in foil and set it on the kitchen table, then grasped both ends of the lasagna to carry it out onto the lanai. Halfway from the stove to the door, the foil pan holding the cheesy goodness buckled. Pearl, as if watching herself in a slow-motion film, tried to adjust the pan so that it rested on her forearms. But while the sides were cool enough to touch and carry, the bottom was not. She let out a yelp, and the pan tumbled to the floor, landing facedown. *Shit.* Red sauce oozed from the overturned pan like blood from a murder victim. She righted the pan, hoping the lasagna would still be intact, bonded by the thick layers of cheese. *Fuck.* The pan was empty, the beautiful lasagna spreading across the floor.

"Shit. Fuck. Piss." She yelled it to the walls. To the table. To the sink. "Shit. Fuck. Piss."

"Grammy, what happened?"

"Mom, are you okay?"

John and Luke joined Pearl in the middle of the kitchen. The three of them stared down at the mound of meat, cheese, noodles, and sauce on the floor. The concoction slowly flattened and expanded its girth, like a dropped ice cream cone. The sound of the door to the lanai opening and closing momentarily broke their trance. Annie appeared, creating a foursome. Mouth agape, she stared.

As if a drill sergeant blew a whistle, they sprang into action. John picked up the foil pan and put it in the sink, squirted it with soap, and filled it with hot water. Then he dumped the water, folded the pan in thirds, and tossed it into the recycle bin. Annie ran to the mudroom and returned with a dustpan. Using it as a shovel, she scooped up as much lasagna as she could and deposited it in the trash. Setting the cheese and sauce streaked dustpan in the sink, she grabbed a wad of paper towels and wiped the floor. Pearl reached into the cabinet under the sink and retrieved a bottle of Fantastik, sprayed the spot generously, and wiped it up with yet more paper towels. Luke sat at the kitchen table and watched, munching on a hunk of garlic bread.

30

―――――

Annie

Annie jumped up from the table to answer the door, insisting that she pay for the pizza. They'd eaten the salad and half of the garlic bread while they waited, and waited, and waited. It seemed like every household in this part of Florida had ordered out for pizza tonight, and Annie wondered how many did so because someone dropped the lasagna. She paid the delivery person and carried the box out to the lanai.

"I don't know what happened," Pearl was saying to John when she returned. "The thing just buckled."

Annie set the pizza box in the middle of the table and opened the lid. Steam rose from the box and permeated the lanai with an aroma that made her miss Henry and their cherished tradition of ordering out for pizza amid the hullabaloo of the approaching holidays.

She selected the smallest slice in the box, marveling at how something as simple as cutting a circle into eighths often yielded varying sized wedges. Luke stuck his hand in the box and pulled out one of the biggest slices. John selected a slice, then grabbed one for his mother, sliding it onto her plate while she had her head turned. He opened a bottle of red wine and filled three glasses. He looked at Luke.

"Sorry, buddy, but I don't think you'd like this stuff."

"My mom and dad drink wine." He looked down at his plate and mindlessly picked at his pizza.

"Anyway," Pearl said, "I don't know what happened. The thing just buckled."

"Mom, it's okay. We're past it. Let it go."

"I just don't know what's wrong with me lately."

"You're under a lot of stress right now," John said. "Let's move on and enjoy dinner. Tomorrow we'll visit Marina. And then it will be Christmas."

"I think I'm going to call my doctor in the morning," Pearl said.

"Are you sick, Grammy?"

"No, sweetie. I'm fine. I've just been a little scatterbrained lately." She reached for Luke's hand and squeezed.

Annie grimaced, her back telling her that if she didn't take her pain medication soon, she'd be in for a very long night. She didn't want to get up from the table and miss her pizza nostalgia. As much as she didn't miss being married to Alec, she did miss their pizza days. She lifted her slice, closed her eyes, and took a bite. She put the pizza down, chased it with a long sip of wine, then repeated the process.

"What are you doing?"

She opened her eyes to find Luke staring at her and John laughing.

"Annie is a pizza fanatic," John said. "She loves pizza almost as much as she loves me."

"I don't know, I might love pizza more." John feigned a hurt look, and she leaned over and kissed him. "It's true," she said to Luke. "I love pizza. I grew up in New Jersey and now I live in New York. There is no better pizza than New Jersey and New York pizza." She took another bite. "But Florida pizza is pretty good too."

"Florida pizza sucks," Pearl said, making Luke laugh.

"Luke, do you like to draw or paint?" Annie had been looking to ask him this question for hours, and now the moment seemed right. Careful to avoid any painful triggers, she sought to interest him in doing some crafts with her — a ploy to try a bit of art therapy. She'd tried to ease into the topic several times today, but could never quite find a non-awkward way to do it. To hell with it. Might as well just be direct and ask the question. She waited for an answer.

"I'm not good at it," he said. "My mom is a great painter."

"Annie is a great painter, too," John said. "But different from your mom."

"I thought we could make a Christmas present for your mom," she said, eager to dispense with the comparisons. "I have a bunch of art supplies here." After talking with Alec earlier, she decided to not wrap the art supplies for Christmas. She thought they might come in handy now.

"Okay."

Annie detected a hint of compliance in Luke's voice, like he wasn't all that fired up to make his mother a present, but wanted to be agreeable. Still, she felt cautiously optimistic.

"And don't forget," Pearl said, "we're making a gingerbread house tomorrow."

"Do you have Twizzlers to put on it?" Luke addressed his question to Annie, which gave her hope.

"As a matter of fact, we do!" She looked at him with exaggerated enthusiasm, the way you sometimes do with kids. "We have a lot of other things too. Did you know that Neccos, a candy from when I was a kid, make perfect shingles and excellent patio pavers?"

"I know about Neccos," he said. "I got some in my Halloween bucket. Mommy hates them."

"I'll tell you a secret: I hate them too," John said. "They taste like Tums."

"How do you like to use Twizzlers on gingerbread houses?" Annie waited for his answer. A clue into his psyche, perhaps.

"I use them to make the roof. We have a red roof on our house."

Annie smiled. So, he wants his gingerbread house to, in some small way, replicate his real-life home. His house before the tragedy. His house on the other side of the demarcation. His house as he will forever remember it. She picked up her plate and limped into the kitchen — the twinge in her back had turned into full-on pain.

"Everything okay?" John approached her from behind and whispered in her ear, kissing her neck along the way. When she turned to face him, tears streamed down her cheeks.

"My back feels like shit."

"Let me take you to the ER. They'll give you something stronger than what you have here."

"No way," she said sniffling. "I don't want to upset your mother or Luke."

"Go take your pills and lay down. I'll be in shortly."

She nodded and hugged him tightly, not wanting to let go.

31

Luke

Luke sat up in bed, and for a minute, didn't know where he was. None of his toys were here. And his bookshelf was missing. What about his desk, where he was working on his Lego pirate ship?

"Mommy?" His voice was hoarse. "Mommy?" And then he remembered. He wasn't home, wasn't in his room, wasn't in his bed. He looked down for his sock monkey. He couldn't find it. He looked under the covers, but it wasn't there.

"George, where are you?" He fought tears. As if George himself had heard Luke's cries, the monkey peeked out from under the pillow. Luke held it close and quietly cried. He didn't know the time. This room had didn't have a clock. He quietly climbed out of bed and pushed the curtain away from the window. It was a little bit light out, so it must be morning. His Rubik's Cube sat on the nightstand, on top of the books Grammy got for him. He didn't know if he would like those books, but he would try to read them because Santa was watching, and there was only one more day until Christmas. It was Christmas Eve! Santa would come tonight! Luke knew he had to be especially good today because, at midnight, Santa would fly over the hospital and make Mommy better. Today he will do everything Grammy tells him. He will be helpful to Uncle John and the lady, Annie. He will eat his cereal quietly and put his dishes in the sink. He knelt down and put his hands together. He knew about God. And he knew about Santa.

"Dear God, please make my mom better. Please remind Santa about my letter. Please." He didn't understand the connection between God and Santa, but he figured if God was the boss of everyone, then he was the boss of Santa too. And if God told Santa to read Luke's letter, then Santa would read it. Because Santa gets millions of letters. And Luke didn't want his letter to get lost or forgotten.

He grabbed George and slid off the bed. Still in his pajamas, he quietly padded down the hall. Uncle John's door was closed. So was Grammy's. He made his way to the kitchen and stopped when he saw the lady, Annie, sitting at the kitchen table, drinking coffee. He turned around to leave, but it was too late.

"Hi, Luke," the lady, Annie said. "Happy Christmas Eve." Luke stood silent, clutching George. And then he remembered that Santa was watching.

"Hi."

"What are you doing up so early?"

"I was just thirsty." The lady, Annie, got some orange juice out of the fridge, and a cup out of the cabinet. She brought the orange juice and cup to the table.

"Here, sit down and have some orange juice." She poured it into the cup. Luke didn't really like orange juice — apple was his favorite — but he sat down and took a sip. "I was thinking about making pancakes for breakfast. Would you like that?" Luke nodded. He wasn't hungry, but he wanted to be good. Because Santa was watching.

"When can we make a present for my mom?"

"Let's do it today. How about right after breakfast."

"Can we do it now?"

"Let's see." The lady, Annie, looked at the clock. "It's only seven. Uncle John and your grandmother were up late, so they're probably still happily asleep. Okay. Let's make something now."

Luke smiled. He was happy. Because he wanted to give his mom the present today. He knew it wasn't Christmas until tomorrow, but if he gave it to her today, maybe Santa would think he's a perfect boy.

"What do you think you want to make?"

"I don't know."

"Let's go in the garage and see what supplies your grandmother has. We'll use our imagination and see what we think of." Luke followed the lady, Annie into Grammy's garage. He saw some empty flower pots on the workbench and picked one up.

"My mom loves flowers. We could paint one of these and put flowers in it."

"That's a great idea. Let's put that aside. I have some acrylic paints in my room that would work perfectly." The lady, Annie, continued looking around the garage. Luke put the flower pot on the steps and saw a bag of colorful stones and pieces of broken glass. He picked it up and showed it to the lady Annie.

"Could we glue these on the flower pot?"

"We sure could. We'll need a hot glue gun."

"My mom has a hot glue gun!"

"They're handy." She pulled a shoebox off of a high shelf. "I can't believe it. Look what's in this box." She held it out for Luke to see. "A hot glue gun. And glue sticks. Today is our lucky day."

32

———

Annie

Last night had been impossible to sleep. At some point after midnight, Annie found herself crying hot, pathetic tears. Nothing offered relief. She came close, oh so close, to asking John to drive her to the hospital. She'd tried hard to not wake him but became so desperate that she couldn't help herself. He held her as she cried. Held her as she writhed in pain. And rubbed her back — something that usually made the pain worse — until his hands threatened to fall off. The warmth from his fingers soothed, if not her pain, then her soul as she tried to push away the reality of what this new level of pain meant.

She left Luke in the kitchen with his orange juice and flower pot, and slowly opened the door to the guest room. John had finally fallen asleep, and she didn't want to wake him. She tiptoed around the bed and picked up her bag of art supplies — the one she always carried with her — then crept silently out of the room.

She felt excited about her project with Luke and looked forward to seeing what he would create. If nothing else, it would be a pleasant diversion. She felt punch-drunk tired, but her pain level was only a three instead of an eight — a significant improvement. At least for now.

Luke covered the kitchen table with newspapers like she'd asked, and surrounded the flower pot with the stones and glass that he'd dumped out of the bag.

"Wow. You've done a lot to get ready. This is great." She looked at his piles, then at him, and smiled. If she didn't know better, she would think this was John's son — they shared the same droopy, sleepy eyes. She opened her bag and laid out her supplies — brushes, paint tubes, a pallet, some mixing utensils, an old rag, and a pencil. She covered a baking sheet with a piece of newspaper and set the flower pot on top. "Have you given any thought to your design?"

"I don't know," he said. "My mom loves purple. Do you have purple paint?"

"No, but we can make it. Do you know which two colors, when mixed together, make purple?" Luke shrugged and shook his head. She fully expected him to know, and was surprised that he didn't, particularly with an artist for a mother. "Can you try and guess?" Luke picked up each tube of paint and examined it, then shook his head again. "Let's experiment," she said. "Let's take some yellow and some blue and mix them together." She squeezed a tiny bit of each color onto the pallet. "Go ahead. Take that little plastic knife and mix the two colors together." He did. And he looked at her with wide eyes.

"It's green," he said.

"Yep. It is. So now you know: yellow and blue make green. What do you think yellow and red make?"

"I don't know." He grabbed the yellow and red tubes and squeezed out more paint than Annie would have liked.

"Here, let's wipe off your knife before you mix those," she said, wiping the tip of the knife with the rag.

"Orange!" He seemed pleased with himself. He picked up the blue tube and the red tube and squirted paint on the pallet. He held out his knife, and Annie wiped it. He swirled the two colors together, and then, in amazement, said: "Purple."

"Good job." Annie got up and put the pallet in the sink. She let hot water run on it until it was clear of paint. She dried it with a paper towel and brought it back to the table. "Are you thinking of painting the whole flower pot purple? Or some sort of purple design?"

"The whole thing."

"Okay, then we'll need two big blobs of paint. Go ahead and squeeze out big blobs of red and blue."

Luke mixed the blobs together and seemed pleased with the results. Annie explained that by adding a dab of white, he could make the purple a bit lighter, like lavender. And that by adding more red or more blue, he could find the precise shade. He tried some white but didn't like what it did. Annie sat back and watched as he added a bit of red, then a bit of blue, then more white. He swirled the knife around, not thoroughly blending the colors.

"I like this. I like the swirls."

"That's so pretty. How about we do this." She took a brush and gently ran it through the paint, showing Luke how to lightly brush the pot. "You don't want to brush too hard, or the swirls will go away," she said. She watched him work, watched him concentrate, thinking of Henry at that age. Henry had given her a sun-catcher — hand made out of melted Jolly Ranchers — for Christmas the year he was six. She'd hung it in the window Christmas morning, and by afternoon, it had melted in the sun. They'd laughed at how its lovely circular shape morphed into something indefinable.

"Can I paint the little tray too?"

"The saucer?" She picked it up. "Yes, definitely. But let's sign your name on the bottom first." She pulled a black Sharpie out of her bag and handed it to him. "How about you put your first name and the year. Then you can paint the top."

When Luke finished, Annie put the baking sheet with the flower pot on the counter to dry, explaining that it would take a few hours, then they would apply a coat of clear varnish, to make it shiny and to protect it. When that was all dry, they could glue the stones and find flowers from his grandmother's garden.

"How about those pancakes now?" She smiled at Luke as she collected her supplies and put them back into her bag. She looked up and saw John standing in the doorway. He approached Annie and her apprentice.

"It's my turn to cook," he said yawning. "Cinnamon pancakes coming right up."

33

John

John stood at the sink, rinsing the breakfast dishes, soaking up the quiet like the sponge soaked up the soapy water. He had the kitchen to himself — his mother had just left for her doctor's appointment, and Annie had gone outside with the kid. He looked out the window, hands still in the water, and watched Annie dig up flowers for the kid's hand-painted pot. His mother had brought out a bowl of shells she'd been collecting, and the three of them sat after breakfast, gluing them all over the pot. John liked it better before all the embellishments — unadorned and straightforward. Shouldn't the flowers be the star of the show? The kid's flower pot seemed over-the-top gaudy, but, he supposed, the kid knew better what Marina would like than John ever did. Plus, it was the kid's gift, not his, and not his to orchestrate or dislike. If Marina had any semblance of awareness, she would be deeply touched.

He dried his hands, poured himself a third cup of coffee, and stood at the window, watching Annie and the kid. Seeing her with his ex-wife's kid seemed strange. A kid with absolutely no connection to him. *No connection. None whatsoever.*

The warmth of the coffee mug felt comforting on his hands — not as achy as they'd been earlier, but still somewhat stiff. God, he'd felt helpless last night. All he wanted to do was fix Annie's pain, and he failed miserably. If nothing else, he hoped that rubbing her back all night comforted her, because he knew it did nothing for her pain. His hands were numb by the time he climbed out of bed. A small price to pay. Her whimpers broke his heart, and if rubbing her back all night helped, yeah, a small price to pay. He set reminders on her phone, so she wouldn't forget to keep on top of her medication. He hoped that the radiation treatment next week would, as her oncologist said, be like a miracle.

He dreaded taking the kid to see Marina. Dreaded it. Dreaded getting an update from the surgeon. Dreaded being away from Annie. If last night did anything, it highlighted the fact that although Annie seemed fine most of the time, she was, in reality, quite sick. He yawned uncontrollably, unable to consume enough caffeine to make up for the sleepless night.

Voices in the mudroom, faint at first, grew increasingly loud, as natural as two voices could be — as if he had been *Uncle John* forever and Annie had always been his Annie.

"Irises!" John tried to hide the incongruence between his overly joyful voice and the weariness in his eyes. The iris was one of Marina's favorite flowers, second only to orchids.

"They're the same color as my mom and dad's room," the kid said.

It never occurred to John that Marina wouldn't redecorate their bedroom once Ness entered the picture. John had painted it purple (Marina's choice, not his) a few days after the rape. Rearranged the furniture, bought new bedding, and a new rug. It had all happened in a day — before and after. Like one of those home renovations shows on TV.

"I hope your mother doesn't mind that we dug out some of her bulbs," Annie said.

"You know she'll be pissed," John said, laughing. "I'm going to tell her."

"Please don't."

"Grammy won't care," the kid said. "It's for Mommy. She loves Mommy."

"She does indeed," John said, putting his arm around the kid. He pulled him in and kissed the top of his head. Annie looked on with something in her eyes, something he couldn't define. He let go of the kid and took her into his arms.

JOHN CALLED CANDACE before leaving the house, and thank goodness, she had time to meet. The kid willingly got in the car this time. He'd tried to be brave, but it was clear to John that he was still scared. The kid sat in the back seat, clutching his potted plant, insisting that John check and recheck to make sure his seat belt was locked and tight enough. *You'll explode if we make it any tighter*, John said. But the kid had been on the verge of tears. So, John made a show of tightening the belt, tugging on it, and proclaiming it was as tight as it would go. They made it to the hospital without a meltdown. Hallelujah.

Several small clusters of people flanked John in the ICU lounge — more people than he'd seen here yet. He sat with his head back against the top of the chair and closed his eyes. The kid wanted John to go in with him to give Marina the flower pot. John declined, and then, for effect, gave the kid a kid-sized version of his death-stare. It worked — the kid and the flowerpot went in without him.

He opened his eyes and looked at his watch. Candace had collected Luke a half-hour before. He picked up a magazine, flipped it over, and put it back down — he'd read it cover to cover two days ago.

"Mr. Butterfield?"

"Yes." John stood.

"I'm Dr. Baldwin, the physician on duty." They shook hands and moved away from the lounge. "That's quite the kid you have. He obviously loves his mother very much."

"He's not my kid."

"No?" The doctor looked confused.

"No."

"The patient isn't your wife?"

"My ex-wife."

"Oh. I see." The doctor jotted something down on his notepad. "So, he's not your kid?"

"This is not rocket science," John said, annoyed. "Luke is my ex-wife's son. Not my son."

"Okay. Ah. Yes." He flipped through Marina's chart. "Now, I see. Her husband was killed in the accident."

"Ding-ding-ding-ding."

The doctor stared at him for a moment, apparently not well versed in sarcasm. John made a mental note to revisit with Dr. Vargas, anything this imbecile told him. Damned holiday staffing. And it wasn't even the holiday, or the weekend, yet.

"So, let's talk about your wife," he cleared his throat, "excuse me, ex-wife." He turned the page on her chart and studied it, mumbling while running his finger over the surface of the paper.

"Have you even examined her?"

"Yes. This morning."

"No offense, but you're acting like you've just been handed her chart and know little to nothing about her or her condition." John's last remaining teaspoon of patience evaporated.

"You're right. I'm making the rounds for her surgeon. And I don't know her stats as intimately, but I can tell you where she is at the moment. I doubt it will change much between now and Monday."

John stood straight, ready to listen. He needed something to hang his hat on, some glimmer of hope. He promised Dale he'd call with an update.

"Mrs. Quinn is showing signs that she is slowly progressing from total unresponsiveness to early responses. Meaning, she is beginning to respond to things around her. For example, when I examined her this morning, she had a slight response to touch and light, but not to sound. She'll get there, though. Which is why visiting her is so important."

"So, she's improving?" John's heart raced. "She's going to come out of this and recover?" He searched the doctor's eyes. "She'll be okay?"

"We're not exactly out of the woods yet, but these are all promising signs of progress."

"Thank you, Dr. —"

"Baldwin."

"Thank you, Dr. Baldwin." He held out his hand. Instead of shaking it, the doctor gave him a little hug.

"Don't be alarmed if every three steps forward, she takes two steps back. That's basically how it goes in these cases."

John nodded as the doctor walked away, then paced the length of the lounge, back and forth, running his hands through his hair. He didn't hear his mother approach from behind. She tapped him on the shoulder.

"I'm not losing my mind," she said, a huge grin encompassing the majority of her face. "I don't have Alzheimer's. I'm not dying."

"What are you talking about, Mother?"

"I have a urinary tract infection." She laughed. "A fucking UTI."

"I don't understand."

"Apparently in old farts like me, a UTI can cause confusion. The butter, the broccoli, blah, blah, blah." She laughed, pressing her hand against her mouth when she snorted.

"You're joking."

"Thank God, I'm not."

"Mom, that's wonderful," he said, embracing her. "I'm so relieved."

"Not as relieved as I am." She shook a pharmacy bag in front of his face. "Five days of these antibiotics shall have me back to my old crotchety self."

"Sit down," John said, riding his own wave of encouraging news. "Let me tell you what the doctor said about Marina." He relayed all of it, suddenly not wanting to follow up with Dr. Vargas. He wanted to hang onto the hope that Dr. Baldwin gave him.

"Mommy's getting better?" The kid ran to him, holding Candace by the hand, practically dragging her.

"Little by little," John said.

"That's good news," Candace said, sitting down. "Luke, if you want, you can go see your mom for a few more minutes before we leave. Nurse Maggie will take you in."

"Do you think he's going to be okay?" John looked at Candace expectantly.

"Yes, and no." She looked at John, then at Pearl. "The bottom line is he thinks he caused the accident because he wanted to stop at Mickey Dee's."

"Oh, dear God," Pearl said.

"He's going to need a lot of counseling for the next few years. A lot."

"That's an understatement," John said.

"For now, please bring him to me any time. I'll be out for the holidays until Monday. If things get bad between now and then, call my colleague." She handed John a card.

"Thank you," John said. "We're all very grateful."

34

Annie

Annie knew Henry would be up early. Even at thirteen, she suspected he'd be the first person up, quietly watching TV or sitting with a book until the rest of the house slowly emerged from sleep. It was strange, not being with her son on Christmas morning. After the divorce, she worried about how she and Alec would handle holidays, but it seems to work okay. The first year, Alec came over for Thanksgiving, but not Christmas. Over the past two years, it morphed into Alec taking Henry to Connecticut for Thanksgiving. This year, Alec's dad had a minor surgical procedure in mid-November, putting the kibosh on Thanksgiving. Alec took Henry for Christmas instead. As if the fates already knew. As if God had set the stage so that Annie would be free to support John during this upheaval.

Last night was better than the night before. Much, much better. She'd been diligent about her medication and, as a result, slept, if not soundly, at least less fitfully. Any sleep was better than no sleep. Two hours straight, without having to adjust her position — a real blessing.

There had been a general sense of relief hanging over the house last night: the anticipation of Christmas, coupled with the promising news of Marina making tiny bits of progress. And Pearl finally having identified the root cause of her confusion. Luke, though, still seemed on edge and talked incessantly about his letter to Santa, but wouldn't tell anyone what the letter contained. Pearl said she knew, because he'd written it in front of her. She'd promised to not out him. Somehow, Annie suspected that Luke's letter had little to do with toys.

The coffee maker's gurgling slowed to an occasional drip. Annie poured herself a cup and stood in front of the dining room table, which had been set for breakfast last night. They would open presents, then have a slow, leisurely breakfast. A tray of cinnamon buns that, like the Pillsbury Doughboy promised, would be *poppin' fresh good*, was racked and ready to go into the oven. Luke's gingerbread house sat proudly in the middle of the table. He'd made a half-hearted attempt to construct and decorate it, laying the Twizzlers on the roof and picking out candies for the exterior. Annie hoped that the presents she'd selected for him would at least offer some distraction. They could start the puzzle after breakfast, and maybe, after that, they could play some of the games she bought. She tried to let go of any expectations about how the day might play out.

There weren't a ton of presents under the tree, but enough to make things interesting. Annie liked to let Henry rip into the sea of colorful boxes the minute he rounded the corner into the room. Alec, on the other hand, preferred more structure and ceremony around the gift-giving. He would play Santa and hand out presents one at a time, with pauses to open, display, and *ooh and ah* over — like a grade-school game of *Show and Tell*. This could take hours. She and Henry, and now John, did Christmas differently. Back to basics. There was nothing more Christmassy to her than watching a kid dig into a pile of presents — wrapping paper flying in all directions. She intended for Luke's Christmas in Florida to be just as joyful. If not joyful, she could at least make it festive. Wouldn't it be fun to do a before and after photo — the calm of the early morning, versus the chaos of post-presents?

Annie made her way to the kitchen — her coffee mug needed refilling — and saw her sketchbook sitting on the counter where she'd left it two days before. Maybe she would just sketch the before and after, rather than take silly photos with her cell phone. She could do a quick watercolor later and present the two pictures to Pearl as keepsakes.

Back on the couch, Annie studied the tree, the presents, the competing items in the background — a faux mantle with four unstuffed stockings dangling haphazardly. A table with a TV, and a bookcase on either side. She'd take artistic liberties and not include those things in her finished product. With the sketchbook in her lap, she made the initial perspective markings, then set to work, drawing lightly, filling in shadows, making her pencil dance effortlessly across the page. She didn't hear the little boy approaching from the hall. Nor did she notice him climb up on the couch — close enough to watch, yet far enough to remain undetected. She looked up, and their eyes met. She handed him the sketchbook.

"I'm making this for your Grandmother," she said. "I'll paint it later. I'm also going to make one of all the wrapping paper after everyone opens presents."

"My mom draws really good."

"I know. Birds, right?" Luke nodded. He handed back the sketchbook, unimpressed.

"Can I go see my mom today?"

"I'm not sure. You'll have to ask Grammy or Uncle John." It was strange, referring to John as Uncle.

"I asked Santa to make her better." Annie didn't know how to respond. So that's what he'd written in his letter. She decided to say nothing, and instead just squeezed his hand. "Can I see your drawing book again?" She nodded and handed it to him. He flipped through the pages, then gave it back. "Can you make a picture of me in here? For Mommy." Annie thought about this. Maybe she'd sketch him opening presents. Or perhaps just sketch him sitting on the couch in his cute Christmas pajamas.

"Of course." She looked around the room. "I'll tell you what. Why don't you open one present now, and I'll draw a picture of you opening it." He seemed to like this idea — his smile being the clue. He climbed off the couch and sat among the presents. Unsure of what to do next, he looked up at Annie. "Go ahead and pick one with your name on it."

He selected one from the pile, confirmed that it was, indeed for him, and opened it. Annie knew by the size and shape that he'd chosen the Harry Potter book. She quickly sketched his form near the tree, hands ripping the paper.

"Look in this direction," she said, pointing toward the far wall. She continued sketching and nodded when she was finished. Luke climbed back on the couch, this time closer to her, his new book in his good hand.

"Harry Potter," he said, turning pages. "This book is too hard. Why would Santa bring me this?" *Think fast, Annie, think fast.* She took a deep breath.

"I'm guessing that Santa knows how smart you are and figured your mom or someone else would read this to you."

"Could you read it?"

"Right now?"

"Yeah."

She opened the book to the first page.

35

John

They say that these are not the best of times but they're the only times I've ever known. John stirred in bed, barely awake, with this Billy Joel song — Summer, Highland Falls, pounding in his head. As he gained lucidity, he wondered what deep part of his brain conjured this song in his sleep. John wasn't much of a musical person — he rarely hummed a tune or battled ear-worms. And if the definition of an ear-worm implied a catchy tune being stuck in one's head, this particular song was hardly catchy. Where the hell did that come from? Sure, he liked Billy Joel. But this song? Not one of his Top 40 hits, that's for sure. Yet John knew all the lyrics, and sung them quietly to himself as he lay there. Annie's spot next to him in bed was empty — the smell of coffee wafting through the house being the clue to her whereabouts. *For we are always what our situations hand us, it's either sadness or euphoria.*

He slowly got out of bed, feeling a glimmer of hope for the first time in nearly a week. The doctor he'd spoken with yesterday gave him that glimmer. Marina wasn't a vegetable. At least not at this point in time. And if she wasn't vegetable by now, she would only keep improving. Wouldn't she? He didn't know. But he felt, in his gut, that she would pull through this. And Dale would be here Monday — her arrival representing the demarcation between his responsibility and hers — a passing of the baton. *Now we are forced to recognize our inhumanity, our reason coexists with our insanity.* Dammit, this song. *I'm dreaming of a white Christmas.* The best way to thwart an ear-worm is to replace it with another song. It was Christmas morning, after all. *Where the treetops glisten, and children listen to hear sleigh bells in the snow.*

He pulled on a pair of shorts and a tee-shirt. His mother didn't have Alzheimer's. He was skeptical that a urinary tract infection could cause such a bizarre set of symptoms and be void of abdominal pain. He held his hope about that at bay, and would wait to see if she improved with the antibiotics. Still, the diagnosis buoyed his mother's spirits — there was levity in the house like he hadn't seen in a long time. Annie's night had been better too. She laughed with his mother and made a gingerbread house with the kid. And then later, much later, when the house was dark and quiet, John and Annie, snuggled up and half asleep, somehow ended up fully awake and making love, almost as if they'd been starved and were suddenly presented with a smorgasbord. Sweet sleep followed.

While John brushed his teeth, Bing Crosby and Billy Joel dueled. *I'm dreaming of a white Christmas. Now we are forced to recognize our inhumanity, our reason coexists with our insanity.* He spit toothpaste into the sink and bent down to rinse his mouth straight from the tap. He spit again. A quick glance in the mirror at his thinning hair, standing on end like a mad scientist, horrified him. His hair, still mostly dark, was laced with more gray than he'd noticed the last time he really looked. When the hell did he get so old? He splashed water on his face and ran his wet hands through his hair, taming the wild strands. His mother had asked him what he sees in Annie. Looking at himself in the mirror, he wondered now what Annie sees in him. Obviously not his looks. *May your days be merry and bright, and may all your Christmases be white*. Yeah Bing!

He straightened up the bed, smoothing the comforter and fluffing the pillows. Satisfied, he opened his duffle bag, reached in, and fished around for the box containing Annie's ring. When he found it, he tossed it on the bed, then quietly opened the bedroom door. He heard voices in the living room, but couldn't tell who, besides Annie, was up. He closed the door and tore at the newspaper and duct tape — he'd wrapped it more securely than he remembered — and lifted the ring out of the box. He slid it on his little finger — it barely went down to his first knuckle — imagining himself on bended knee, sliding it on Annie's finger. He was tempted to do it now. Walk right into the living room and declare his love for her in front of anyone who would listen. He didn't want to wait. He fumbled for his cell phone and called Henry.

"Merry Christmas, bud...you already talked to her, great...listen... I have the ring...I know I promised you I'd...what's that? You don't mind? Thanks bud...if you talk to her later, or tomorrow, don't say anything...just in case I chicken out...no...not chicken out forever... just chicken out here in Florida...one way or another, I promise to propose to your mother before New Year's...you too."

John let the ring fall into his pocket and stuffed the box and the wrapping into the bowels of his duffle bag, concealing any evidence with his remaining clean undershirts. *And though we choose between reality and madness it's either sadness or euphoria.* Damn Billy Joel. He shoved the singer into the closet, then tossed his duffle bag in there, imagining it hitting Billy in the head.

He followed the smell of coffee and found Annie and Luke sitting on the couch, Annie reading aloud in that animated way adults read to children. When he walked back into Annie's life, Henry was an older, fairly independent kid, not wanting or needing to be read to. Careful to not interrupt, he headed toward the kitchen for coffee and was almost knocked down by a rush of people exiting just as he was about to enter. A rush of people. Two people. His mother. And...

"Dale?"

"Merry Christmas, John." She burst into tears but didn't embrace him.

John slowly walked toward her and hugged her. He hadn't seen her since they'd called it quits six years ago. He let go and looked at her. Still the same.

"I gave her the update," Pearl said.

"It's good news, right?" Dale wiped her eyes. "I mean, it is, right?"

"I hope so," John said. "When did you get here? I thought you weren't coming until Monday."

"I was able to hop on a flight — long story, let's just say I pulled a lot of strings."

"Have you met Annie? Have you seen Luke?"

"Not yet, I just walked in though the garage a few minutes ago."

John's need for coffee forgotten, he led Dale into the living room.

"Aunt Dale!" Luke jumped up and flew into her arms.

Annie stood and introductions were made.

"Uncle John? Will you take me to see my mom now?"

John searched for his ear-worm, but it had left him for greener pastures. He suddenly missed Billy Joel and promised himself to let him out of the closet soon. He stuck his hand in his pocket and fiddled with the ring, cursing his abysmal timing and putting his idea of a spontaneous proposal on hold.

"In a little while, buddy. In a little while."

36

Pearl

The smell in the kitchen made Pearl gag. The coffee — an otherwise pleasant aroma — smelled acrid. She would have to teach Annie a thing or two about proper coffee-to-water ratios. She had a good mind to forego the coffee altogether and have a glass of orange juice instead, but she'd been up late and needed the caffeine. She poured herself half a cup and filled the rest with cream. She pressed the mug to her lips and took a slow, cautious sip. Her nose involuntarily wrinkled. She took the lid off the sugar canister, added two tablespoons to her coffee, and took another sip. Better, but still pretty horrid. She added a tablespoon more of sugar and carried it out to the living room, where she joined the others.

The scene outside the window did not exactly conjure a Currier and Ives vision: green grass instead of snow, palm trees instead of pine. A gentle breeze. The living room — now that could have come straight from Norman Rockwell. Ah, but a first glance was about as close to Rockwell as it went. While sweet in its own way, the scene was more reminiscent of the moments before or after the happy family photos are snapped: the child of John's ex-wife sitting next to his ex-lover, while his current lover sat on the floor, trying to coax the child into opening presents. The outtakes. Pearl sighed and sat down on the couch next to John.

"That social worker said not to force him," she whispered, careful not to let the others hear.

"She's not forcing him," John hissed.

"It sure looks like she is," Pearl hissed back.

"I guess this is for you, from Santa." Annie turned to Pearl and handed her a present. She looked at Dale. "I'm embarrassed, but Santa left your presents in Australia."

Luke swiveled his head toward Dale, and seemed upset that Santa could mess something up so epically.

"It's okay, sweetie," Pearl said. "It's an innocent mistake. Santa will make sure your Aunty gets her presents." How could Annie be so stupid? To say something like that. Something that would get the wheels turning in a six-year-old's head. He needed naivety and innocence right now. On the other hand, Pearl was astute enough to know that Annie was merely trying to cover up the fact that none of the presents under the tree were for Dale. Still, she was livid.

"Actually," Dale chimed in, "since I'm an adult, it's okay. Santa doesn't always bring presents for adults."

"But he has to," Luke said, his eyes filling with tears. "I asked Santa to make Mommy better. She's an adult. What if Santa made a mistake. What if he doesn't make Mommy better?"

John got up and crouched down beside him. He was about to whisper something in Luke's ear, but Luke flinched and ran to his room.

"Dammit Annie." Pearl couldn't keep the venom out of her voice. "How could you say something like that?"

"She said nothing wrong." John jumped to Annie's defense. "If anyone said something moronic it was Dale."

The room fell silent. Annie stood up, walked across the room, and sat down next to Dale. Pearl stared, awestruck, at the stark contrast in the two women. While Annie was certainly cute in a non-fussy sort of way, Dale was stunning. She hated to admit this, but, Dale had been wrong for John. She saw it when they dated, and she sees it now. And while her secret hope would always be for John and Marina to get back together, she knew that what he had with Annie was different. She saw it in his eyes. Felt it in the air around him. All this, despite her deep affection for her former daughter-in-law. Life was never easy.

"He's right." Dale stood up. "I have no filters, you know that." She looked around. "Since we're not doing presents now, how about we pop those cinnamon buns in the oven. I'm sure the smell will lure Luke out of his room." She went into the kitchen, Annie following close behind.

"I'll go check on him," John said.

Pearl sat in the empty living room, holding her coffee-sludge. She leaned back on the couch, letting her head fall against the back. Norman Rockwell. Definitely the outtakes. She wondered the back-story of his painting, *The Runaway*. The little boy at a lunch counter, his bindle containing all of his treasures — the things he couldn't possibly live without — on the floor. The friendly policeman sitting on a stool next to him. What little-boy problems were so big that running away seemed like a good alternative? A comatose mother and a dead father, perhaps? That, and the gut-wrenching feeling that he was somehow responsible.

37

Luke

Luke hated this house. He hated Christmas in this house. He didn't want the presents in this house — he knew they weren't from Santa. He hated the food in this house. He hated the people in this house. These were not his people. He wanted his mom and his dad. He wanted his own house, his own room. He hated this room. He hated this bed. He sat against the headboard with his knees pressed against his chest and his good arm squeezed tightly around them. Someone knocked on the door. He didn't want to talk to anyone. They knocked on the door again, then opened it a crack. Luke pressed himself harder against the headboard, pretending to escape through the wall. The door opened slowly. Uncle John. He buried his head in his hands and could hear Uncle John coming in. The bed bounced a little when Uncle John sat down.

"The thing about Santa," Uncle John said, "is that he's a human being. He's not God. He's not a doctor. He delivers presents, but he doesn't heal sick people."

Luke didn't want to hear these things. He didn't believe Uncle John. If Santa could fly a sleigh, he could do anything. He closed his eyes really tight.

"You heard what the doctor said yesterday." Uncle John shifted on the bed and made it bounce again. "Your mom is getting better. Little by little she will continue to get better. But she was hurt very badly in the accident. It will take a long time for her to get back to normal." He paused. "But she is getting better. That's the best Christmas present. She's getting better."

Uncle John got off the bed. Luke opened one eye — he didn't want Uncle John to see him looking — and watched him walk out of the room, closing the door gently behind him. He loosened the grip he had around his knees and slid down. He put his head on the pillow and held his broken arm in the air. He liked the color of his cast. Green. Like the Philadelphia Eagles. He thought about mixing paint with the lady, Annie. His green cast was made with yellow and blue. He couldn't wait until Mommy was better and he could show her that he knows how to mix colors to make other colors.

Something smelled good. He put his hand on his stomach to get it to stop rumbling. He didn't want to eat. He didn't want to see any of the people in this house. His sock monkey, George, was on the dresser. George wanted him. So, he got up to get George. He turned to get back on the bed, but ended up at the door instead. He opened it. And the next thing he knew, he was in the dining room eating cinnamon buns and bacon. Uncle John said they could go see Mommy after breakfast. He made sure to eat everything.

"We'll open presents when we get back," Grammy said.

"Okay." Luke played along but he didn't want to open presents. Because this wasn't his house. It wasn't his Christmas. It wasn't his people. He didn't want these presents. He wanted the ones at home. He wanted Mommy and Daddy. That's all he wanted. Mommy and Daddy.

38

John

The kid was standing in the shower, singing his head off, some silly, nonsensical song. John rolled his eyes and mindlessly twirled the squares on the kid's Rubik's Cube. He had no idea how to help a six-year-old take a shower. Annie said to just make sure the water didn't get too hot and to wait outside the door. Since he didn't want to sit on the floor in the hallway, he left the bathroom door open a crack and went into the kid's room to wait.

"Uncle John?"

John got off the bed and poked his head around the door into the bathroom.

"What do you need, buddy?"

"I'm done." The kid stuck his head out from behind the shower curtain.

"You didn't get your arm wet, did you?"

"No. Could you turn the water off?"

John kneeled next to the tub and reached behind the shower

curtain for the knobs. When the last of the water trickled out of the shower head, he wrapped a towel around the kid and lifted him out of the tub and onto the floor.

"Let me see your arm," he said, touching the plastic newspaper bag that he'd used as a cast protector. He took another towel and carefully wiped the kid's arm above the plastic, then stretched the rubber band wide enough to pull it down over the cast. Plastic gone, John felt the cast, tapped on it, and bent down to get a good look at it. "Dry as a bone! I think I did a pretty good job wrapping this thing!"

"Can we go see Mommy now? Hi Aunt Dale."

John stood up and opened the door wider, surprised to see Dale standing in the hall fidgeting.

"Lukey, can I borrow Uncle John for a few minutes?" Dale looked from Luke, to John, and then at the floor. "Go get dressed and when we're ready to go to the hospital, we'll come get you."

The kid nodded and skipped to his room, closing the door behind him. John looked quizzically at Dale.

"What's up?"

"He's a great kid, isn't he?" Dale looked at the floor, then square into John's eyes. "John, there's something I need to tell you. Can we go for a walk?" The last thing in the world John wanted to do was go walking with Dale. He was about to tell her to go pound sand, but something in her voice troubled him.

"Is everything okay?" He shifted from one foot to the other. "Between you and Bill?"

"Yes. Yes, of course. Nothing like that."

"Okay, good." He didn't want to go for a walk, didn't want to venture too far away from Annie, who was resting in their bedroom. "Can we just talk here, or out on the lanai?"

"It's personal. I really don't want your mother to hear this, although she'll find out soon enough. Annie too. But not yet. I need to talk to you privately first."

John's apprehensions sufficiently raised, he nodded toward the living room which was, thankfully, empty. He quietly and carefully opened the front door. They slipped outside and walked down the porch steps, across the paving stones, and onto the sidewalk. They turned left and walked until an easement between two houses presented itself. They sat down on the curb.

"Right after Bill and I got married, we started trying to have kids." Dale rested her head on her knees, which she'd pulled tightly into her chest. She peered at John sideways, through a curtain of hair. "It never worked. I just figured it was because I was older."

John stared at the minivan across the street and the family piling into it. A man balancing a stack of wrapped Christmas presents came out of the house and deposited them into the open tailgate. The man then made another trip to the house and John heard a woman say *go help your father*.

"It had nothing to do with my age." Dale stretched her legs out in front of her. John watched the family with the minivan drive away. He looked at Dale.

"Why are you telling me this?"

"Have you seen Luke's eyes?" Dale adjusted her legs and sat up straight. "Seriously. Have you really looked at his eyes?"

"What are you saying?"

"Turns out my body doesn't produce fertile-quality cervical mucus."

"I've heard enough." He covered his ears and stood. "I'll see you back at the house." Dale reached for his hand and pulled hard. His legs buckled and he nearly fell backward, catching the pavement with his hands.

"What are you trying to do, break my other leg?" He wiped bits of dirt off his hands.

"Just listen, please." Her eyes pleaded. John nodded, afraid of where this conversation was heading. "I'm pretty much infertile."

"What does any of this have to do with me?"

"You might want to consider suing the urologist who performed your vasectomy."

"Why the hell would I do that?"

"I'll just be blunt." She looked at him, incredulity in her eyes, apparently unable to comprehend his confusion. "Marina and I talked a lot during my emotional rollercoaster rides, you know, when Bill and I were trying."

"Dale, you're not being blunt. You're being cryptic. I'm out of here." He started to get up, but felt paralyzed by the topic. He sat back down.

"Marina and Nester wanted to start a family."

"Start a family? They have a family. Dale, I'm done. Seriously." He got up, and stayed up this time. He took a few steps back toward his mother's house, expecting Dale to be on his heals. He looked back and saw her still sitting on the curb, her shoulders shaking. He swallowed his frustration and walked back to the easement and stood in front of her. She looked up, tears rocketing down her cheeks like bobsleds. It occurred to him then that he'd never seen her cry like this. He sat down and put his arms around her and held her, rocking her like a child. Slowly, her trembling stopped and she peeled herself away.

"Marina and Nester tried." She wiped her eyes. "Nothing ever happened. When I started talking about my issues, Marina brought it up with her gynecologist. Turns out her issues are different than mine. She has a very small number of eggs, which causes sporadic ovulation, making it difficult to conceive." She pulled a tissue out of her pocket and blew her nose. "Difficult, but not impossible."

John remembered all of the times early in their marriage — before his vasectomy — when Marina panicked because her period didn't come.

"Her periods were always fluky," he said, his mind exploding over the implications of this topic. "Wait a minute." He looked at Dale. "Are you saying the kid might be mine?"

"When you got snipped, did the urologist give you the all-clear at some point?"

John reached into the depths of his internal file cabinet — fifteen years' worth of stuff — and remembered the urologist telling him it would take three months before he'd have no more sperm in his semen. Did he ever go back and have a sample analyzed? He didn't remember. He thought he did. Or did he?

"Honestly, I don't remember." He sighed. "She never got pregnant. So, I had no reason to think anything was amiss." He put his head in his hands and massaged his forehead. He looked at the sky, then at Dale. "So, is that what you're trying to tell me? That the kid could be mine?"

"He's definitely not Phil Riley's."

"How do you know that?"

"When Marina's fertility problems came to light, she started to wonder about Luke being Phil's." She looked at John. "I mean, really, Luke looks nothing like him." She sighed. "We had to jump through hoops, but we got the evidence file from the rape reopened." She paused. "The point is, the results were undeniable. Luke is not biologically related to the Riley family."

"Maybe Marina had an affair."

"Have you seen Luke's eyes?" Dale ignored his comment. She stood up and started walking back toward the house. John got up and followed. She turned around. "Look at his eyes."

"Why didn't she tell me any of this herself?" John yelled, jogging to catch up to Dale. "What about Ness? Did he know any of this?" Dale stopped walking and turned to face him.

"They just got the results last week, right before they left for their trip." Her breath caught in her throat. She pinched the corners of her eyes at the bridge of her nose, but the tears flowed freely. "They planned to tell you after the holidays."

JOHN COULDN'T THINK, couldn't breathe, couldn't get his heart rate to settle down. He sat on the chair beside his bed and inhaled. In. Out. In. Out. A jackhammer pounded in his head. *Have you seen his eyes? Look at his eyes.* He didn't believe it. Couldn't believe it. Wouldn't believe it. How the hell could his vasectomy have failed? It was supposed to be a permanent solution. Permanent! He's been with Annie for nearly three years and hasn't gotten her pregnant. As far as he knew, there was nothing wrong with her fertility. Even in the midst of her cancer, she's had no chemo, none of the kinds of drugs that might make it difficult to conceive. He hung onto a thread of hope that this was some sort of mistake. He planned to go straight to the urologist when he got home. He needed answers. If his vasectomy had somehow failed, he needed to know how and why. His head swirled in a sea of what-ifs. If he wasn't the kid's father, then who was? The thought of Marina having an affair seemed ludicrous, yet he supposed it was possible. Had they even made love in the days before the rape? Damn, that was long ago now and so fraught with stress and emotion that he barely remembered the before. He mined his brain. They'd had a pretty good sex life before the rape. Even if he couldn't recall the specifics, he was certain they'd made love.

The thought of Marina having had an affair suddenly seemed the better of the two options: His Kid or Not His Kid. Not His Kid appealed to his sensibilities. Not His Kid ensured that leaving Marina six years ago had been the right decision. His Kid, on the other hand, created a series of complex issues. If Marina lived but didn't regain consciousness, would he share custody with a vegetable? What about Dale? His Kid might mean that Dale walks away from any sense of obligation to stick around while Marina recovers. His Kid would reopen the wounds of that time in his life and would cause him to revisit every decision — the big ones as well as the insignificant ones — that he'd made in the days, weeks, and months following the rape. His Kid would mean just that: his kid. To care for, to raise, to...love?

"Uncle John?" Shit, the kid. Shit. Shit. Shit.

"Just a second." John got up and smoothed his hair, his shirt, his shorts. He took a deep breath, barely feeling it fill his lungs. He opened the door.

"It's time to go see my mom. Grammy said to get you."

"I think I'm going to stay here with Annie. You go with Grammy and Aunt Dale."

"But you promised to take me to see my mom." The kid's lip started to quiver. Dammit.

"Ah, yes. I did promise, didn't I?" He faked a smile. "Annie's in the shower. Let me at least wait until she's finished so I could let her know we're leaving."

"You could leave a note in the kitchen."

"I know I could leave a note," he said, "but I'd like to make sure she feels okay before we leave." He studied the kid's eyes, noting the way the outer corners drooped slightly. And the lids — protruding like hoods — covered much of his eyeballs. Green. The kid's eyes were green. Ah ha! John's were brown. A small hope to cling to.

"Is Annie sick?"

"She has a sore back."

"John, where are you?" His mother's voice penetrated the air between them. Her footsteps grew louder and closer. "There you are. What are you doing?"

"Give me ten minutes, tops." He stepped around his mother and walked into the kitchen, where he found Dale sitting at the table.

"You didn't say anything to my mother, did you?" He sat down next to her.

"Of course not. And I won't. It's not my business."

"Thank you." He stood up. "I don't know how to tell Annie."

"Why don't you see if you could talk to someone at the hospital today, maybe get tested. I'm sure there's a urology department. You could hold off telling her until you get the results."

"Now, that's a brilliant idea." He shook his head and didn't try to keep the sarcasm out of his voice. "I'm sure there's a urologist on duty Christmas Day just waiting for a crazed man to walk in and demand a semen analysis." He started to walk away, then turned around and stood in front of her. "I don't keep secrets from Annie. I need to tell her."

"Did you tell her about us?"

"Yes, I did. I told her everything."

JOHN STOOD in front of the mirror in the bathroom, wiping away the steam from Annie's shower with his hand. He opened his eyes wide, pushing the drooping corners up with his fingers. He opened them wider, telling himself that his lids didn't protrude and cover his eyeballs. He turned his head to view his eyes from the side. Nope, they didn't protrude. Or did they? And his lids didn't cover his eyeballs. Or did they?

"What are you doing?" Annie startled him and he jumped. He didn't hear her get out of the shower. He handed her a towel.

"I have something in my eye." He pulled a tissue from the dispenser, wet it with some cold water, then dabbed at his eye. He felt like a schmuck play-acting like this, but, as in comedy and also tragedy, timing is crucial. He heard his mother yelling through the house, *let's go John, I'm aging.* Annie brushed past him and went into the bedroom. Nope. This was not the right time to tell her. Not at all. He would tell her tonight. "There, got it," he said, mostly to himself. He crumbled the tissue and dropped it in the toilet.

"Go on, get out of here," Annie said. She was facedown on the bed. She turned her head. "Don't keep everyone waiting."

"Are you okay?" He sat down on the edge of the bed and touched her shoulders. She lay silent. "Is it your back?" She nodded.

"I'm staying here, they can go without me," he said.

"No, you're not." She sat up. "Go. Please. I'll be okay."

John brushed his finger across her face. Fresh tears. Of course. He held her. Her wet hair was plastered to her head. He ran his hands through it anyway. He didn't know how he would tell her about this new conundrum. He suddenly looked forward to discussing it with her, hearing her perspective, deciding next steps together.

"Are you sure you'll be okay here, by yourself?"

"Go."

"Call me if you need anything. Please."

"I'll be fine."

39

———————

Annie

The strangest of Christmases. The arrival of Dale jolted Annie to the core — she didn't realize until the moment the beautiful breeze blew into the house — how tense she had been about meeting her. She accepted the fact of Marina and the circumstances surrounding their break-up as part of who John was. But Dale seemed different. Early in their relationship, John had let everything that had happened between him and Dale come tumbling out. His time with Dale had been a short-lived, whirlwind romance that fizzled out to nothing before anything ever really began. Yet there was something about the way it all had transpired, the raw passion that John described (perhaps a bit too graphically) that had thrown Annie off a beat. This morning, seeing Dale for the first time — in technicolor and living sound — was like meeting a celebrity. And watching the two of them together, sitting on the curb wrapped in each other's arms shot like a bullet through her heart.

After breakfast, Annie slipped away to sit by the water, but had grown restless and started walking. When she saw them in the distance — indistinguishable from any random couple sitting outside away from the Christmas hullabaloo — she'd smiled. How cute, a couple escaping outside for a moment alone. Until it was no longer a random couple but John and Dale. She ducked behind a parked car and watched. Until she could no longer stand it. She turned around and ran as fast as she could back to the house.

They all piled into Pearl's car, leaving Annie behind, but only by her own insistence. She feigned fatigue and back pain, neither of which were a hundred percent true. She didn't want to join them on their road trip to the hospital — didn't want to be anywhere near John. She loaded the last of the breakfast dishes into the dishwasher and wandered into the living room, where she stared at the unopened presents under the tree. Her legs grew weak, and she let herself fall onto the couch. She buried her head in one of Pearl's throw pillows and sobbed.

ANNIE DIDN'T REMEMBER CONSCIOUSLY DECIDING to walk to the hospital. All she'd intended to do was take a short walk around the block — to the spot where she'd seen John holding Dale. Retrace her earlier steps, make sure she hadn't imagined it. Now she was standing in the lobby, enquiring about Marina Quinn, and getting a visitor badge.

Up the elevator, into the ICU, and then the lounge, where Pearl and Luke sat, talking about something that she wasn't quite close enough to hear. She had no intention of joining them. Her feet took her in the opposite direction, straight to Marina's room. She peeked inside and saw John and Dale in an embrace.

Annie stood in the doorway, unable to break herself away from this self-torture. She opened her eyes wide to keep the tears from rising above flood level. She could feel her face getting hot, turning red. She scratched at her hairline. She held onto the door jamb for support. Images from the past few years flooded her vision — a slide show looping through a series of freeze-frame moments: John and

Henry at Riverside Park acting silly. John at her art exhibits. Dinners at John's pub. John trying to rub her pain away. His talk of marriage. His attempts to build a cordial relationship with Alec. The laughter. The tears. The love. She watched as John pulled away from Dale and sat down on the chair beside Marina's bed. Dale stood behind him and put her hand on his shoulder. He cocked his head toward Dale, then picked up Marina's hand. Dale shifted, and Annie took a half-step to the right, plastering herself against the wall, her lower lip trembling like a child's, not wanting to be seen. She took a deep breath and inched her way back to the door. Go ahead and tell her, she heard Dale say. *Tell her, John. Tell her you'll get tested. Tell her you'll help take care of Luke, whether or not he's yours.*

Annie gasped, quickly covering her mouth, hoping nobody heard her. She clasped her hands in front of her, suddenly cold, despite the heat rising in her core. She rubbed her fingers against her palm — something she's done since childhood during times of stress. She tilted her head and studied the ceiling, anything to get her heart to stop pounding. She felt paralyzed, stuck in purgatory between the bustling corridor and the lounge, where she would have to face Pearl and Luke. She'd been right to feel off-kilter about Dale. It was apparent that John was still in love with her. And now Luke's paternity seemed in question. She felt a sudden urge to flee, but an unknown force had her in a stranglehold. She couldn't move. Simply couldn't lift one foot off the floor to be planted a mere six inches forward.

She pressed the heel of her hands under her eyes to halt her tears, but she couldn't hold the levee in place — the river too intense, too forceful. Her heart poured out of her eyes and she feared she would bleed to death. If she wanted to get back to the house before anyone else, she had to leave right then. She breathed deeply, chewing her lower lip, consumed with pain, both emotional and physical. She wiped her eyes, took a deep breath, and limped to the elevator.

ANNIE STAGGERED up the front steps, hot, sweaty, tired, and in severe pain. She held onto the porch rail with one hand and lifted her other hand to unlock the door. Thank God, the others weren't home yet. She shuffled to the guest room and swallowed two pain pills.

For the first time since seeing John sitting on the curb holding Dale in his arms this morning, she felt clear of head and knew what she had to do. She called a cab — it would be here within a half-hour — to take her to the airport. Changing her airline ticket could wait. All she knew was that she couldn't stay here.

She picked up her sketchbook and found the picture she'd drawn of Luke. Her blood rushed to her head — she could feel it swooshing in her ears. She laid down on the bed and curled up in a ball, letting a slow wail fill the room. She couldn't do this — she needed to leave now. There would be no second chances. She uncurled herself and sat up. She carefully tore out the drawing of Luke and laid it on John's pillow. Then she tore out an empty page, scribbled a short note, and placed it on the pillow next to the drawing. No *X's* or *O's*. No affectionate greeting or loving salutation. No name.

She lifted her suitcase onto the bed and hastily filled it, sure she would forget something, and not caring one bit. John was probably so full of Dale that it would be a while before he noticed her absence. She regretted coming on this trip with every ounce of her soul. She had no business coming here. None. And despite their truce, Annie was sure that Pearl would cheer the minute she realized she was gone.

Her suitcase and purse in hand, she took one quick glance around the room and saw John's keychain. She picked it up and let the keys dangle like wind chimes. She took a deep breath and for a second, considered staying. She tried to conjure a logical explanation for what she'd seen, and one came instantly to mind: John and Dale had been comforting each other. Yet she couldn't erase what she'd seen and the way it made her relive the day she found Alec's book of poetry — the one in which he'd earmarked an erotic love poem for someone other than her. That discovery had sucked the breath from her lungs. Seeing John and Dale together today sucked the life from her soul. She picked up the note she'd written and tore it up. She pulled the sketchbook out of her bag and sat down on the bed. In a less hurried pen, she wrote a gentler note.

Her cell phone buzzed. The cab. Before putting John's keychain back on the dresser, she removed the key to her apartment — the one she'd given him — and slid it into her purse, hurrying out the door and into the rain.

40

John

The first drops of rain fell just as they pulled into the driveway. In the time it took John to open the door to let his mother out of the car, the sky went from sunny to dark. Dale and the kid jumped out of the backseat, laughing and running into the garage, missing the deluge by seconds. John followed, closing the garage door behind him.

"I don't know," he heard his mother say to Dale. "I thought she said she'd put the roast in the oven." She yelled into the mudroom where John was taking off his shoes. "John? Did you talk to Annie? She said she would start dinner."

"Can we open presents now, Uncle John?" The kid poked his head into the mudroom. John stood and followed him into an eerily empty kitchen. That void he'd wondered about the other day — the void Marina certainly felt in Nester's absence — well, he felt a similar void now. *Where is Annie?* A sense of illogical, impending doom based on nothing concrete. Just a trail of tiny breadcrumbs leading to this empty house. He knew Annie wasn't here — felt it in his bones.

"How about we do that later, after dinner? I'll put the TV on for you. Let's see if there's a Christmas movie you'd enjoy." The last thing he felt capable of doing was playing the role of chipper Uncle John.

"I'll do that, John." Dale took the kid's hand and went into the living room.

"John? Where is Annie?" His mother was at the kitchen table, looking bewildered. "Did she come up with some alternate dinner plan?"

"How the hell should I know?"

"Didn't you see her? She was in the hospital. I saw her walking toward —"

"John?" Dale ran into the kitchen. "The front door was open. I looked out and saw a taxi pulling away."

He ran to the door and stood paralyzed, mouth agape. *You're joking me.* He took the porch steps two at a time and ran into the rain — after a cab he couldn't see — and only stopped running when he came to the easement, the place where he and Dale had talked that morning. Out of breath, he bent down and put his hands on his knees, then sat on the curb and pulled out his cell phone. No missed calls. No messages. He should have known. When he'd called a little while ago to check on Annie, the phone rolled straight to voicemail. And again, when he called to tell her they were on their way back. He maintained his composure both times by telling himself she was resting or out picking up some last-minute item that she needed for their Christmas dinner. But he knew better, knew something was up. He had a sinking feeling he'd get back to the house and find her gone. He only wished he knew why. John sat and stared at the house across the street, watching for the return of the minivan. Wherever that family went, they weren't home yet. As he sat and watched, he felt the first crushing sob burst out of his mouth. He sat on the curb until the rain stopped.

He hobbled back to the house, his leg sore from chasing the vapors of a long-gone taxi, his eyes sore from crying. He walked in, right past Dale and the kid who seemed engrossed in whatever the hell they were watching. He felt Dale's eyes follow him down the hall, but smartly on her part, she didn't get up. He went straight to the guest room and right away saw what he knew he would find. He picked up the two sheets of paper and carried them to the kitchen, folding one of them and sticking it in his back pocket.

"She made this for you." John handed his mother the drawing of Luke. She ran her fingers over it and set it down.

"What happened?" She searched his eyes.

"She went home."

"But why?" He didn't want to discuss it with his mother but felt like he owed her some explanation. He made one up.

"She needs to see her oncologist first thing on Monday. She's been in a lot of pain."

"She couldn't wait and say goodbye?" She raised an eyebrow, then knitted her brow in confusion or anger — he couldn't figure out which.

"She said in her note to tell you goodbye and to thank you for everything and that it was great meeting you." He lied. "She was able to get a flight out tonight. If she didn't take it, she'd be stuck here another day." He lied again.

"I don't believe a word of it." His mother sat up straight. "She came to the hospital and didn't tell you she was leaving?"

"I don't care what you believe." John's brain didn't register what his mother had just said.

"Are you okay? You're soaking wet."

"Dammit, Mother!" He got up and pulled a beer out of the fridge. He popped the top and drank half of it in a frantic gulp. "I'm not okay." He put his head in his hands. "I'm not okay."

"So, she's gone home. She went home." She rubbed his forearm, trying to get him to look at her. He didn't budge. "She could get in to see her doctor first thing Monday, instead of waiting three more days. It's all very sensible."

"Mother, that's not the point." He let his hands fall to the table and looked at her. "She didn't answer her phone all day. She left you in a lurch with dinner. This is not like her." He drew a shaky breath and cried, audibly, into his hands.

"Didn't you talk to her this afternoon, at the hospital?" His mother wrapped a towel around his shoulders. He hadn't even heard her get up. "Luke and I saw her. She got off the elevator, then disappeared down the hall, toward Marina's room. I just figured you saw her and talked to her."

"And you didn't think to mention this at any point after that? Like in the car, when I tried to call her?" He couldn't keep the anger out of his voice.

"I've mentioned it three times already — you haven't been listening." His mother got up and made herself a gin and tonic. "I won't claim that I'm not a scatterbrained old lady, but I will say that she just wasn't at the forefront of my mind today."

"Right, until you walked in and dinner wasn't ready." John got up, swallowed the rest of his beer, took another one out of the fridge, and, like a sullen child, went to his room.

JOHN TURNED on the water and let it get hot. When the bathroom turned into a steam chamber, he climbed in the shower and let the water scald his head. He stood like that for a long time. It was only when he felt woozy from the heat that he stepped out.

He sat down on the edge of the bed, wondering how he could have been so stupid. It all seemed so obvious now. His walk with Dale, and then Annie's odd coldness when he returned. What had she seen? What had she heard? In all likelihood, she saw them embrace in Marina's room. Innocent in every way, and yet without context, the two scenes combined, well, Annie must have fallen into an emotional lava pit. He needed to talk to her. Needed to explain. What he should have done was jump in the car and driven to the airport. How could he have been so stupid? He redialed her number. He couldn't even leave messages — her voicemail was full.

John got dressed, then opened the door a crack. He heard the sounds of clanking and cooking, laughter and the TV. He felt like a ghost crashing someone else's life. He closed the door with his foot and fell onto the bed, landing facedown. He rolled over onto his side and saw his airline ticket on the dresser. He got up and brought it to the bed. He called the customer service number to change his flight, then hung up before the automated voice recited the list of options. She didn't want him to follow her home — she'd made it damned clear. He unfolded the note, which he'd practically memorized:

J*OHN,*

Please know that I love you with all my heart. I also know that you love me and that there is a trust between us that makes what I'm about to say seem illogical. I saw you and Dale sitting outside, then later in the hospital. Watching you hold her in your arms was disquieting — an emotional shock. My head and heart are in a battle. My head knows that your embraces were of the comforting kind amid the tragedy that brought us here; my heart simply can't be consoled.

Add to that the news that Luke might be your child. I'm having a hard time processing what it means or how it even happened. I trust you'll get tested soon and not take Dale's word for it. Wow. A son. Your dream has come true.

I know I'm cowardly for running away from painful things. I want to stay, but can't face you, can't face Dale, can't face Luke. And your mother — there's no way I could face her knowing Luke might be yours. I'm sure she'll try and push you and Marina back together. God, you left her because of the child, and now he might be yours. I don't even know how you'll deal with that, but I do know that I'd just be in the way. You need to figure it out.

I don't know where we go from here. I need to clear my head. I think you need to clear yours too. I don't see how I could possibly fit into this complicated situation, no matter what path you end up taking. Please don't come after me. Stay here and sort this out.

Love,

Annie

P.S. I left some of my art supplies and the art stuff I bought for Luke. It's in the top dresser drawer. Maybe you could help him color the drawing that I made of him. I thought it might be nice for him to give it to your mother.

DAMMIT, *Annie.* John was so mad at her that he couldn't see straight. How could an accomplished, intelligent, insightful woman be so fucking illogical and impulsive? He wanted to defend himself. To stand in front of the gate at the airport and demand that she give him at least five minutes to explain, to talk, to reassure her that he loves her more than life. As if that were even a possibility in these heightened airport security days.

He sat against the headboard and sipped his beer. He'd read Annie's note several times. More if he counted the quick skim just before going into the kitchen. He tilted his head back and sighed. Everything she'd written was spot on. She was too insightful for her own good. Yet so fucking illogical. If she was perceptive enough to know that he and Dale had no feelings left between them, then why would she allow herself to self-destruct? Why? He knew that the heart couldn't be trusted — it had a mind of its own. Why couldn't she just let her heart feel hurt for a bit, then settle back into reality? Just deal with the pain, then move past it.

He tilted the bottle and let the last little bit of beer trickle down his throat. He craved another but didn't know how to walk through the house without having to talk to anyone. He didn't want to talk to anyone. Not his mother, not Dale, and not the kid. Especially not the kid. He closed his eyes and imagined walking in on Annie, sitting on the curb with Alec's arms wrapped around her. He couldn't picture it. He only knew her as his Annie, not Alec's "Brenda," and simply could not imagine her with that dweeb of a husband. But what would he think if he'd encountered such a scene? He hoped he'd see it for what it was — two exes hugging over some issue, maybe something to do with Henry. More than likely, Alec would be comforting her over some aspect of her illness. Just as he comforted Dale when she cried over her infertility.

He squinted into the beer bottle to see if there was one last drop he could extract. Empty. Just the way he felt. Completely empty. He didn't know how he would get through the rest of this day, this night, and the string of days and nights to follow. He didn't know how he could live without Annie. Yeah, feelings override logic. And right now, his feelings dictated going after her. He slid down the headboard until his head was on the pillow. He took the other pillow — her pillow — and buried his face in it.

"Can I come in?" John sat up but didn't answer. "John, come on. Open the door."

"Hold on, just hold the fuck on." He got up and threw on a pair of shorts and a tee-shirt. He opened the door.

"Luke is asking for you," Dale said. "Your mother and I roasted some chicken breasts." John didn't respond. "Can we put this away for just a few hours, get through Christmas, let Luke open presents. Then you can wallow all you want."

"Wallow?" John was incredulous. "Is that what you think I'm doing? I'm fucking distraught is what I am." His breath caught in his throat. He covered his eyes.

"Your mother said she went home for treatment." Dale took his hands and peeled them from his eyes. "Look at me. You'll call her in the morning. You can even fly home tomorrow and come back in a few days. I don't care. But tonight, for the sake of your son, please take a deep breath and come eat with us."

"That's just it. We don't know for sure that Luke is my son."

"We both know that in all likelihood, you're a father."

John folded Annie's note and tossed it at Dale, a little too hard, and it brushed past her face. She scooped it up from the floor and opened it.

"I made up the bit about Annie going home for treatment," he said, but Dale seemed already engrossed in reading the note. "Not a word of any of this to my mother."

"Has your mother really been pushing you to get back with Marina?"

"That's all you're getting out of this note?"

"No, but that strikes me as strange."

"My mother is strange." He shook his head and sighed, feeling a ball of yet more sobs forming in his throat. He let them escape.

"I'm sorry." Dale patted his leg.

"Please don't touch me."

"Come on, John. Really? I'm happily married. And I'm sorry Annie saw what she saw, but really, I think she's being a bit dramatic." She looked at John. "Don't you?"

"No, actually, I don't." He drew in a shaky breath. "I flip-flop from being madder than hell, and kind of knowing what she felt when she saw us." He rubbed his temples. "So, no, I don't think she's being dramatic at all. She's being human."

"What are you going to do, then?"

"I don't know. I called the airline about a hundred times already, but keep hanging up." He wiped his eyes. "I want to run after her, but at the same time, I want to respect her wishes."

"I'm not sure what to tell you," Dale said.

"Don't tell me anything." He got up and smoothed his hair. "I'll try to put on a face. But it won't be easy." He took the note out of Dale's hands, folded it, and tossed it on the dresser next to his keychain.

JOHN DID WHAT ANNIE SAID. After dinner, while Dale and his mother cleared the table — an attempt, most likely, to give John some leeway to nurse his aching heart — he took the kid aside and together, furtively, added color to Annie's sketch. The kid wanted to wrap it in Christmas paper, so John dug around and found his mother's stash. He laid out a large piece and rolled the picture in the wrapping paper like a scroll, securing it with ribbon on either end — a far cry from his newspaper and duct tape masterpiece. He fluctuated between swallowing the near-constant lump in his throat and feigning excitement for the sake of the kid.

"Where do you want to put it, buddy?" John stood in front of the tree, the presents untouched from this morning. "How about right on top." He pointed to the top of the tallest pile.

"I just want to give it to her," the kid said. He started toward the kitchen with the scroll.

"How about we wait here until they're finished with the dishes, then you could give it to her." The kid seemed satisfied with this plan and sat on the couch with the scroll in his lap. "I have a great idea," John said. "Let me go get George, so he can watch you open your presents." He didn't wait for a response and headed to the kitchen to tell his mother to act surprised when she saw the drawing. He returned with the monkey and set it down on the couch next to the kid. John sat on the other side.

"When is the lady, Annie, coming back?" This question startled John. He'd already told the kid that Annie had to go home to New York.

"She's not coming back," John said, avoiding eye contact. "She has to see the doctor about her sore back. And she needs to go back to work." A sob caught in his throat. "Plus, she has her own son to take care of." Henry. Damn. He wasn't just losing Annie, he was losing Henry too. He turned his head so the kid wouldn't see him wiping his eyes.

"How old is he?"

"Who?"

"The lady, Annie's son," the kid said. John sniffed and turned to face him.

"Henry is thirteen."

John's mother came in and set a plate of cookies on the coffee table. Dale followed with a tray containing a bowl of ice cream for the kid, and three steaming mugs of Irish coffee.

"Let Christmas present-opening begin," Dale said, a little too cheery for John's taste.

He sat in a fog, cupping his warm drink, wondering if Annie was home yet and what she was doing. He put his mug down and snuck away, disappearing into the kitchen. He stood against the counter and, as if torturing himself yet again would do any good, he dialed her cell phone. When it rolled to voicemail, just like he knew it would, he prepared to snap the phone shut the second he heard the *voicemail box full* message. His legs almost buckled when he listened to her voice, her recording that he knew by heart. She must have cleared out her messages. *Beeeeeeeeep.*

"Annie. It's me." His voice cracked — he couldn't keep his anguish out of it. There was so much he wanted to say, so much he wanted to clear up, but he couldn't find the words. "I love you. I love you so much. Merry Christmas." It was all he was able to squeak out. He hung up and returned to the living room, sitting down just as the kid handed him a present from under the tree.

"Uncle John! This is for you. Santa brought you a present. Open it."

John tore into the paper and held out a silly tee-shirt with a Christmas penguin on it. *Annie.* He shook his head and smiled, setting the shirt aside, clenching his teeth, shoving the ache down his throat.

PART IV

41

Annie

Annie slowly opened her eyes and rubbed the back of her neck. Not fully awake, she sat up and mumbled, *since when is your chest so boney*, and looked up expecting to see John, convinced she had fallen asleep sitting up — he with his back against the headboard and she next to him with her head on his chest. Instead, she saw the dirty backseat window of a taxi and snow slowly dancing around an unusually dark sky. She looked at her watch — one in the morning — and then at the ticking meter. She tapped on the plexiglass, separating her from the driver. He glanced over his shoulder.

"Where are we?" She pointed at the backs of row houses in a neighborhood she didn't recognize. They'd just driven under a single lightbulb dangling from a wire strung between two poles. She shuddered, suddenly afraid, and hoped she was dreaming. "Why aren't we on the parkway?"

"There was an accident two miles back there." He gestured with his head. "The cops diverted the traffic through here. We should pop back on the highway in a few."

Annie looked behind her and saw other cars. She exhaled, relief washing over her. She felt the hairs on the back of her neck fall back into place, after having stood at attention for the past few minutes.

"Thanks." She rested her head against the window and opened her purse, feeling for her cell phone. She closed her eyes and wondered how many more missed calls there would be from John. She'd had quite a few by the time she'd gotten to the airport and had been surprised and a little bit miffed that he hadn't left any messages until she realized that her mailbox was full. She cleaned it out just before boarding.

She opened her eyes and noticed that the landscape had drastically changed. Thank God, they were back on the parkway, not too far from her exit. The snow swirled in a wind that hadn't existed a half-hour ago. Without a thought, she opened her phone to call John and tell him about the snow. Call John. Something she'd done hundreds, maybe thousands of times. She closed it, determined to not cave in, thinking back to the note she'd left him, feeling confident that they both needed to clear their heads. Calling him about the snow would just lead to a million inquiries, explanations, and pleas. She opened her phone again. *One missed call. One new message.* She thought she'd imagined it, but apparently not. She listened. John's voice, so full of sadness, wishing her a Merry Christmas. Her breath caught in her throat. No inquiry, no plea. Just *Merry Christmas*, and *I love you* in a squeaky voice she didn't recognize. She'd done okay on the plane — full of adrenaline from her hasty departure — and didn't cry, not even a little bit. John's message jolted her into a new reality — she'd walked away from a man she loved so much that it sometimes hurt. What in God's name was she thinking?

"Lady, we're here." The driver craned his neck. "Lady, you okay back there?" Annie looked up through tear-clouded eyes but didn't answer his question. She looked at the meter and handed him her fare, plus an extra twenty for a tip.

"Merry Christmas," she said.

"Same to you." He got out of the cab and popped the trunk, lifting her suitcase out and depositing it at her feet.

She stood in front of her building, hand on her suitcase, and watched the taxi disappear. A layer of soft snow covered the sidewalk. Her breath — visible, cloudy puffs — rose in the cold air. Almost all the windows in the surrounding houses and apartment buildings were dark, a sure sign of deep, post-Christmas sleep. *God, I wish John were here.* She stood, paralyzed, unsure what to do next. She dug through her purse and found her keys. *Okay then, that's what I'll do. I'll open the door and go in.*

A SOFT, colorful glow beckoned. Annie noticed it when she opened the door to her apartment and wondered if she'd left a light on. But the color didn't make sense. A warm conglomeration of pinks and reds and greens and blues emanated from the living room. John had taught her enough about crime prevention and listening to that quiet voice of intuition to know that she probably shouldn't blindly walk into the living room. Being aware of her surroundings dictated being wary of this new and different glow, yet she didn't feel any of the fight or flight signals — no fear, none whatsoever.

She left her suitcase on the landing and followed the light, almost knowing its source before she saw it — intuition at its best — a fully decorated tree. She laughed and cried and fell to her knees. Before she boarded the plane, she called Ted to let him know she'd be home in a few hours and that he wouldn't need to water her tree anymore. She imagined him corralling Donald and Elijah, stringing the popcorn that they'd been eating in front of *A Christmas Story* and marching over to trim her tree. Elves.

She touched a branch, soft and supple, then stood up and found the spot, pushing popcorn garland out of the way. The pinecone. And the penguin. She stood staring at the penguin until her legs felt weak. She sat down on the floor and listened to John's voicemail again. And again. And again.

· · ·

THE HARDWOOD FLOOR dug into her hip. Annie rolled over, then sat straight up, momentarily unaware of her surroundings. Shooting pain radiated from her back all the way up to her neck. She stood, dizzy, and in agony. Sunlight pouring in through the window created a sharp line on the floor. She looked at her watch, fully expecting it to be afternoon, and was stunned to find it was just after nine. She shuffled to the door and retrieved her suitcase, using it as leverage — a walker of sorts — to help her into the kitchen. She sat down at the table, then opened the front zipper and pulled out her bottle of pain medication, swallowing two pills without water. She leaned back in the chair, letting her legs splay out in front of her, feeling her hair loosen from its headband and hang over the chair like a scarf. She gathered it up — a tangled mess — and tied it loosely on top of her head.

A sense of paralysis engulfed her, just as it had when the taxi dropped her off. She felt untethered, unsure of where to put herself, not knowing what her next move should be. She had people to call: Alec, Henry, Ted, her sister, her oncologist. John. No. Not John. She picked up her phone and listened to his message again: *Annie. It's me.* Pause. *I love you. I love you so much. Merry Christmas.* Wait. Another voicemail? She pressed the button without bothering to look at who had left it. Her heart dropped out of her chest when the first syllable told her it wasn't John. What came next took her breath away.

She called her oncologist back and scheduled an appointment for later that afternoon. The rapidity at which they were able to *squeeze her in* made her shudder. *I want to see you as soon as possible to discuss your scan.* She'd had the scan a few weeks ago. And they'd discussed it then. Perhaps this was an old message, left before the holidays, and just now showing up in her voicemail box. Technology, not to be trusted. She listened to the message again, paying careful attention to the date/time stamp. *December 26, 2004 at 8:17 a.m.* No ambiguity. And on a Sunday morning the day after Christmas! Why the hell was her oncologist working today?

The prospect of bad news from her oncologist filled her with a nervous energy that obliterated her earlier paralysis. She got up and moved around the kitchen, slowly at first, then with a false sense of purpose. She didn't really need to empty the dishwasher, but she did. Then she wiped down the already clean counters, made a pot of coffee, took a quick shower, changed into fresh clothes, then returned to the kitchen with a blank sheet of paper and a set of colored pens. Her next mission: make a list. Because if she filled the paper with things she needed to do, she could maybe, just maybe thwart the evil spirits dancing around in her spine. She crumbled the paper and threw it hard against the wall. If her ex-husband found solace and comfort in making lists, well, it wasn't working for her. She opened her phone and called Alec.

"Oh, Henry...hi, sweetie...well, I'm actually home...late last night... still down there...I'm not sure when he'll be back...how was Christmas? I said I don't know when he'll be back...it's a complicated situation down there...I don't know...I need to talk to your dad."

Annie waited while Henry got Alec. She hadn't expected the barrage of questions about John and felt stupid for not anticipating this.

"Alec...please, don't start...yeah, the answer is the same...it's a mess down there...because my oncologist wants to see me today...yes, I realize it's Sunday...I know...it's probably bad...I promise to keep you informed...listen, I need to keep busy these next few days...I know you're out until next week...I was wondering if I could maybe see some of my patients? Yeah, Mel would be great...sure, just let me know when."

She hung up the phone and stood at the kitchen window. Last night's snow had all but melted, leaving the streets below wet, slick-looking, and sparkly in the sun. She sat back down, feeling the paralysis begin to wrap around her like a wet blanket. Unable to think clearly, she folded her arms on the table and laid her head down on them. *Annie. It's me.* Pause. *I love you. I love you so much. Merry Christmas.* She'd listened to John's message so many times that its words and tone and timber were burned into her brain. She wondered if this was what stage actors portraying real people did — listen to recordings or watch videos of their subject, over and over, until their voice, their tone, their mannerisms, their subtleties became a part of them. *Annie. It's me.* Pause. *I love you. I love you so much. Merry Christmas.*

Wanting to hear his voice in her ear, she lifted her head and reached across the table for her phone. *Annie. It's me.* Pause. *I love you. I love you so much. Merry Christmas.* Okay, she would listen just one more time, then delete it. *Annie. It's me.* Pause. *I love you. I love you so much. Merry Christmas.* Her finger hovered over the number two — press two to delete — but couldn't do it. Simply couldn't.

42

———

John

The first urologist John called wouldn't take him without a previously scheduled appointment, and oh, by the way, they were booked solid through New Year's. He pleaded: *How about another urologist in the area?* The man's voice on the other end of the line reluctantly recited a number. And when John called, the story was the same. Not wanting to drive all over town in search of someone to test his sperm, he finally thought to call the fertility clinic that just happened to be in the same hospital complex where Marina lay in limbo. He explained more than he probably should have to the receptionist. She seemed kind and told him to come right in. The only problem: producing the sample. He laughed out loud when she suggested that he bring his own, ahem, magazines. *We have some in the room then, if you need them.* God, this was going to be hard.

"See you all in a little while," he said to his passengers as he pulled the car up to the curb at the hospital's main entrance. He raised an eyebrow at his mother — a preventative measure against another hissy fit like the one she'd thrown the last time he tried to drop her off at the curb. He was relieved when she stepped out.

"Don't be too long," his mother said. "The meeting with Marina's surgeon is in an hour." She closed the door then leaned toward the car and tapped on the window. John lowered it. "Where are you going, anyway?" Dale knew where he was headed, his mother and the kid did not.

"I'm parking the car, Mother." He winked at the kid, who laughed at the silly question. "Then, I have a couple of errands to run."

"Come on, Pearl," he heard Dale say. He watched her link arms with his mother and lead her toward the revolving door, the kid trailing behind. He waited until they were inside before pulling away to look for a place to park.

JOHN FELT FOR HIS PHONE — a new habit born in Annie's absence. The new rhythm of his life: sleeplessness, a soul-crushing sense of loss, a compulsive need to check his phone, a dwindling amount of patience around his mother, and an aching face from forcing a smile around the kid for the past two days. *Holy shit. Has it only been two days since Annie left?* It felt more like two decades, with no end in sight. He'd nearly choked a few times, swallowing the angry words he'd been about to spew at Dale. Who did she think she was, waltzing in on Christmas Day, delivering this news about the kid? Couldn't she have just kept that to herself? What was he supposed to do with this information, anyway? The kid revered Nester. Daddy. John would never be able to replace the one true *Daddy* that the kid had ever known.

He looked at the date displayed on his watch — Monday — the day Dale originally planned to arrive. If she'd only stuck to her original plan, Annie would still be here, and he wouldn't be sitting in a cold, stark room, unable to perform on demand. He glanced at all four corners of the ceiling, convinced there were cameras, yet logically knowing that there weren't. Still, there were people on the other side of this door, walking up and down the hallway, going about their business, knowing fully that John was doing something usually done in private — something he hadn't felt the need to do in a very long time.

This is awkward and embarrassing. He closed his eyes hard and tried to think of Annie, as she was three days ago, as she was before the storm. He couldn't. For the past two days, his emotions undulated between the kind of grief that took his breath away, to hope, to despair, to anger. And right now, he was angry. Angry at her for reverting to her default of running away. When he tried to view the situation from her perspective, he calmed down a bit, at least long enough to agree with her sensibilities. Then he would get angry all over again. *Dammit, Annie. Why couldn't you have just talked to me?*

He picked up a magazine and flipped through it, uninspired. He shook his head and put the magazine down, closing his eyes, remembering the first time he and had Annie made love. He held his breath, feeling his body respond, finally. For a few blissful seconds, he and Annie were in Brooklyn, in her room, clothes strewn haphazardly across the floor, sheets a crumpled mess at the foot of the bed. He shuddered and released into the sterile cup, the blur of the moment gone, replaced abruptly by the reality of the cold, sterile room. He put the lid on the cup as he'd been instructed to do and got dressed.

JOHN DIDN'T KNOW how he managed to find his way back to the ICU lounge area. He plopped down onto the sofa next to his mother.

"Where the hell were you?" His mother knit her eyebrows together and stared at him. He stared back. "The surgeon is running late."

"Swell."

"Dale and Luke are visiting with Marina now. Do you want to see her?"

"I do not," he said, averting his eyes. He looked at the floor.

"What's the matter with you?" She put a hand under his chin and lifted it. John brushed his mother's hand away. He stood up and took a few steps away from the lounge, in the opposite direction from Marina's room. He didn't turn around to see if his mother had gotten up to follow him. A few steps more. He turned his head just enough to see that his mother was still seated and looking forlorn. Feeling guilty, he retraced his steps back to the lounge and sat next to her.

"What time will the surgeon be here," he said, trying to keep his tone as neutral as possible.

"I don't know. Soon, I hope."

John fought the sudden temptation to tell his mother where he had been and why he had been there. He still needed DNA proof, and until he had that, the chance that the kid wasn't his still existed. *Five million sperm per milliliter of semen*, the urologist at the fertility clinic told him. Good motility. *Yes, you could father a child*. John listened in shock when she explained that a vasectomy could fail if the vas were missed during the procedure or if the tube regrows. Both scenarios were rare but possible. Obviously possible — the proof was in the cup. He'd have to wait to talk to a urologist back home and get tested to find out what, exactly, had failed. It had been fifteen years since his procedure — he was sure his urologist was retired and playing golf somewhere in Florida, probably not too far from here.

"Uncle John!" The kid stood in front of him and tossed George into his lap. What had been just a stupid sock monkey yesterday was now the beloved toy of his son. His son. John reminded himself that he still needed DNA proof. Unless and until that came back positive, he could go on pretending that the kid was still just a kid who meant nothing to him. He set the monkey down and put it in a sitting position next to him on the couch.

"How is your mom doing today?" The kid shrugged. John looked at Dale, who had just come from around the corner. "How is she?" He noticed that Dale looked a bit unnerved.

"Is it my turn to go in?" John's mother stood.

"Can you sit with Luke for a minute?" Dale looked at Pearl. "I need to talk to John." John shrugged and followed Dale down the hall. "I don't know, but I overheard one of the nurses." Dale's eyes filled with tears. "I'm not expecting good news from the surgeon."

"What do you mean?" John pressed his shoulder against the wall for support.

"I don't know, it's just a feeling."

"What exactly did you hear?" He looked behind to make sure the kid had not followed them.

"The nurse stepped out of the room to talk to someone. Another nurse, I guess." She pulled a tissue out of her pocket and dabbed at her eyes. "Something about her response levels reverting."

"That could mean anything."

"I know. I'm trying to hold it together until we talk to the surgeon." She looked at her watch. "Who is very late."

"I had the test," John said, changing the subject.

"Oh, shit. I forgot all about that." She blew her nose. "And?"

"My sperm are alive and well."

"Thank God, you never got me pregnant."

John nodded in agreement, unprepared for how much her statement stung. He was glad too. Very glad. But had it happened, well, who knew where they would be now? This conversation made him wish he'd gotten Annie pregnant. Now that he knew he could, maybe, just maybe...he let the thought trail off, holding tightly to the illusion that Annie would wake up tomorrow and wonder why she'd left. He needed to be patient — a feat consuming all of his emotional energy. In his clear-headed moments, he knew that if he ever hoped to be in Annie's life again, he needed to give her space.

"I stopped by to talk to Candace." He looked at Dale. "She sent me to get my cheek swabbed."

"What about Luke."

"She plans to stop by the ICU." He looked at his watch. "Actually, she should be here any minute." He moved away from the wall and straightened his shirt. "The plan is to take him to pediatrics for a quick look at his arm and vitals. They'll tell him to open wide and say ahh. You know the drill." They took the first slow steps back to the lounge, to face whatever the surgeon had to say.

"John?" Dale stopped walking. "What are you going to tell Luke."

"I don't know. Maybe nothing."

"And your mother?" She crossed her arms. "She knows something is up."

"Yeah, well, there are many somethings up right now." He felt the all too familiar lump of despair rising in his throat. "She knows how distraught I am over Annie. Isn't that enough for now?"

"I think she deserves to know the truth."

"I'll tell her soon." He started walking, then stopped. "In my own way and in my own time." He looked at her, perhaps a bit too sternly. His mother needed to hear it from him, not Dale. He hoped his look, and his tone made that clear.

Dr. Vargas led John, his mother, and Dale into his office, taking off his white coat and draping it over the back of his chair. He sat behind his desk, removing his glasses and rubbing the bridge of his nose — the telltale sign of a doctor about to deliver unhappy news. The three of them sat in front of the desk. John, in the middle, extended his arms out to either side and took Dale's hand on his left and his mother's on his right. He reflexively squeezed their hands as the doctor spoke.

"She is no longer responding like she had been over the weekend. Testing indicates more swelling. I've cleared my schedule to do another surgery this afternoon. I want one last shot at this. I'm not hopeful about the outcome but want to try." And after a brief pause: "Realistically, I think you should prepare for the worst."

Dale ripped her hand away and ran out of the office. John's mother, still holding his hand, started to get up. John pushed her back down.

"Let her be," he said. Then to the doctor: "I'm confused. We called last night for an update and were told there'd been no change."

"Things can change on a dime in these cases," the doctor said, replacing his glasses.

"So, they can change for the better then, right?" Pearl looked expectantly at the doctor, who shook his head.

"No, I'm afraid, not in this case." He took off his glasses again. "Not without a miracle."

"Then why even bother with the surgery?" Pearl's tears flowed freely down her cheeks.

"Like I said, I wouldn't be doing my job if I didn't give it one last shot." He handed Pearl a tissue. "I've seen miraculous things happen." He looked at John. "But, I'm strongly suggesting that you come in here tomorrow prepared to say goodbye."

"Please don't say anything to her son," John said. "We need to be the ones to tell him." He ran his hand through his hair, grabbing a fistful and pulling it hard. He clenched his teeth. What the hell was he supposed to tell the kid? His head spun, and he felt himself start to hyperventilate. He squeezed his mother's hand so hard she winced.

JOHN SAT beside Marina's bed with his elbows on his knees and his head resting in his hands. She looked peaceful, utterly unaware of the sobering words that the surgeon had just a little while ago delivered. A ribbon of hair fell over her eye. He reached across the bedrail and gently lifted the hair away, smoothing it down with his fingers.

"I know he's mine," he said, barely audible even to his own ears. "He's ours." John let his head fall to his chest. He carefully picked up Marina's hand and interlaced his fingers through hers, like he used to do when they watched movies together or when they walked. He tried to remember the last time he'd held her hand, and couldn't. Like Luke feeling responsible for the accident, John felt responsible for the rape — the crime that caused the first domino to fall.

"I'm sorry." He picked up her hand and held it to his lips. "I'm sorry I didn't protect you. From the rape. From all this."

He tried to think of other things that eluded him, like the last time he'd treated her kindly. That had to have been when she'd promised to get an abortion. And now he wondered why he'd been so hell-bent on it. The kid had wormed his way into his heart on this trip, even when he still thought the kid's biological father was Marina's rapist. Yeah, he'd treated her kindly when he thought he was getting what he wanted. And when she didn't get the abortion, well, he basically treated her like dirt. And that didn't include trying to have an affair with her sister.

He imagined plunging into the depths of the Hudson in winter — the cold water of reality choked him. He'd been so angry at Marina and left her, for what? For what? Wanting to have a baby? He'd been too fucking proud to take a deep breath and consider that maybe she'd also been struggling. If he'd stayed, they might have discovered the truth about the kid earlier. Life would have continued. It wouldn't have been perfect, but he would have made it work. If he hadn't left her, then he wouldn't have lived on his boat, and if he hadn't lived on his boat, then he wouldn't have gotten into that brawl — the one responsible for his leg, the one that ended his career.

"I'm sorry, Marina." He tried to remember her face the last time he'd seen it before the accident, maybe a year ago. "I'm so fucking sorry. God, I'm sorry."

If he hadn't left her, he would have been Daddy, right from the start. And there would have been no fucking stop for a milkshake. No way. Never. What did he expect? That life after Marina's rape would be easy. He'd tried to accelerate her healing and had felt strongly at the time that aborting would be the first step. But he knew better now. He'd been thinking only of himself. Because how dare she have a kid that wasn't his.

John held her hand up to his eyes and let her feel his tears. He kissed her fingers and placed her hand back on the bed, knowing he would forever regret the steps he took that led him away from her. He was finally beginning to understand that loving someone didn't mean a string of happy feelings. Intimacy dictated taking it all — the good, the bad, the ugly. Which was precisely what he intended to do — with Annie. Because if he hadn't left Marina, the road he chose would never have led him to Annie. Good coming out of all his bad choices, if such a concept even existed. He bent down and let his forehead touch Marina's.

"I love Annie so much, Marina. It's different. I can't even explain it. Different than you and me." He let his tears fall freely. His heart was on the verge of exploding, and he needed to change the subject.

"Luke is a great kid." He looked at the hand-painted clay pot and cluster of wilting flowers. "I promise to take care of him. I promise to love him. I promise to never let him forget you or Ness." He kissed her forehead and sat up.

He pulled out his phone, desperate to hear Annie's voice. Before he'd found her at her gallery opening two years ago, she'd been a myth, untouchable, an etherial fantasy. Back then, she was like a timid cat — poised to flee at the first threat. He'd worked so hard to prove that her heart would be safe with him. It took a long time, but she gradually opened up and let him into the inner parts of her soul. His mind raced back to Christmas morning when Dale pulled him outside and told him about Luke. He'd only wanted to comfort her. How could he have been so stupid? Exes don't console each other like that. He envisioned Annie stumbling upon the scene. He might as well have handed her the bricks and mortar to rebuild the wall around her heart. It would be his mission to dismantle the wall, even if it took the rest of his life. Brick by brick, if that's what it took.

"Is Mommy still sleeping?" John turned and saw Luke approach the bed. Candace stood in the doorway, nodding. He closed his phone and set it on the table next to Marina's bed.

"Come on up here." He lifted Luke onto his lap, being careful to not bang his cast on the bedrail.

"Hi, Mommy." Luke held onto the rail and leaned in to kiss her. He looked at John. "Mommy is getting another operation later."

"Who told you that?"

"Grammy told me." Dammit, how could his mother be so stupid? Luke didn't need to know any of the details. He didn't need any false hope, either. John lifted him over the rail and deposited him onto the bed with Marina.

"You visit with your mom for a bit." He looked at the doorway. Candace was no longer standing in it. "I need to find Candy and talk to her for a minute."

He stood up to leave but stopped to watch Luke snuggle up to Marina. His good arm fell across her chest, and his head rested on her shoulder. John watched Luke close his eyes and sing his song.

Even with closed eyes, there was no mistaking that Luke's eyes were his eyes. Nester had to have known that Luke couldn't possibly share Phil Riley's genes, well before any testing took place. He wondered why Ness never said anything, never raised the possibility that John had been a fool. He shook his head and sighed. Simple: Ness wanted Marina for himself and probably feared that John would have a change of heart if he knew and would beg for forgiveness. With hindsight being what it was, he wondered if knowing Luke was his son would have made a difference. Yeah. It would have. Absolutely.

JOHN FOUND CANDACE walking toward the lounge, where his mother was sitting on the sofa with her arm around Dale. He jogged to catch up — he wanted to talk to Candace privately and feared losing the opportunity if she reached his mother and Dale first.

"Do you have a second?" He stood behind her, out of breath. "Let's go over there." He gestured toward two chairs near the window, just beyond the nurse's station. They sat. "How did it go earlier, with Luke?"

"He did great," she said. "I understand your ex is heading back into surgery soon." She looked into John's eyes. "I'm so sorry."

"I know, I know." John let his chin fall to his chest. "How long before the DNA results come in?"

"It should be about a week. They'll call you."

"When should I tell him?" John crossed his legs, uncrossed them, and sat up straight. "I mean if the test proves paternity." He searched her eyes. "Maybe I shouldn't tell him."

"I think you should tell him, but not now, not any time soon." She took a deep breath. "You're going to need to get him into therapy pronto. As soon as possible. The therapist will guide you."

"My mother doesn't know about this yet."

"I won't say a word," Candace said. John stood and held out his hand, then hugged her instead.

43

Annie

The wind, sharp and cold, froze the tops of her ears. Annie tugged on her useless hat, a size too small, stretching it all the way down past her earlobes. Futile. Spring-loaded, the hat rode back up until it sat on top of her head like a beanie. She tightened the scarf around her neck and shoved her bare hands into the pockets of her cobalt blue pea coat, which seemed to match the sky's brilliant blue.

She walked the promenade at Battery Park under a canopy of naked trees. Seagulls bobbed and weaved around her, competing for a chunk of the soft pretzel someone had dropped. The birds didn't seem to care that it still had mustard smeared across the lower loop. A group of children surrounded a man dressed as the Statue of Liberty. *God, he must be freezing*, she thought. Just looking at him made her feel colder. She pulled the hat down over her ears again, this time holding it in place as she walked, at least until her hands protested.

She stopped at a hot dog cart, the wind whipping its red umbrella around like a pinwheel. She bought a hot dog and hot tea. She hadn't intended to get anything to eat, but the pretzel on the ground caused her empty stomach to announce itself. She sat down on the steps behind the cart and devoured the hot dog. Now all she had to do was find the bench.

Annie's oncologist had been blunt: the hormone therapy that had served her well the past three years was no longer, on its own, enough. He recommended they start local treatment — radiation, namely — for symptom control right away. She'd been planning on that anyway, so her doctor upping its urgency didn't alarm her. His other recommendation — six rounds of chemo, every three weeks for six months — did frighten her. The chemo drugs would be delivered directly into the fluid around her spinal cord. They would address the spots on her ribs later, or not at all if they didn't grow any bigger. She'd planned to go straight to Alec's office after her oncology appointment to tidy up and organize the workspace in her art room for her session with Mel tomorrow. But when she climbed in the taxi, *Battery Park* tumbled out of her mouth.

She walked — shell-shocked about the chemo — until she found the spot. The benches by the water all looked the same. She walked the promenade, bending to examine the left-hand corner of each seat as she went. The cold temperature worked in her favor today — all the benches were empty. Ah, yes, finally. She sat down and touched the spot, tracing the tiny heart with her finger. She put the cup down and pressed her finger into the heart. She and John came here one spring morning a year or so into their relationship and sat down on the bench. *It probably makes sense that you have this,* she said when she handed him a key to her apartment, placing it in the middle of his palm, closing his fingers around it, raising his hand to her lips and kissing it. After a few silent minutes, he unfurled his hand and used the tip of the key to carve the heart.

Annie pulled her hat down over her ears. She shoved her hands in her pockets. And she sat on the bench in the cold, the wind twice as strong at the water's edge, trying to remember why she ran away from him like a coward two days ago. He hadn't tried to call her, not since Christmas night when he left the message. Did he realize she'd taken her key back? She pulled her left hand out of her pocket and touched the heart again, then studied the finger where Alec's ring once resided. She knew that John would have slipped a ring on that finger a long time ago if only she'd been open to the idea. Looking at her naked finger now, she wondered why she'd been so resistant.

She reached for her phone, tempted to call John. He had always been the first person she wanted to talk to after each doctor's appointment. Giddy excitement in her voice as she told him things were stable. Other times cautious optimism. And this last time, before the accident, before Florida, a bit of sobering pessimism. And now the real possibility that she was about to fall into the category of a cancer patient. Not that she wasn't already or hadn't been all along. But, up until now, it had been so damned easy to pretend at normalcy. If she agreed to chemo — and she wasn't yet sure, although her oncologist practically pleaded — she would have many more bad days than good ones. But if six months' worth of some bad days bought her more time, more good days down the road...maybe. She just didn't know.

Awash in new resolve, she closed her phone. She'd made the right decision to leave. The potential that John could be Luke's father — she simply couldn't grasp the enormity of it. It would be stressful enough for anyone to have a child suddenly fall out of the sky and into their lap. Add in the guilt that John must be feeling for walking out on Marina — because of Luke. Mix in three tablespoons of trauma — Marina's condition, Nester's death, Luke's grief. Yep, a recipe for disaster. She didn't want to ruin an already bitter stew by throwing in her problems.

Her cup, now empty, toppled over in the wind and fell to the ground. Annie chased it across the promenade, scooped it up, glanced back at the bench, and hurried to the nearest waiting taxi.

HER APARTMENT, usually a place of refuge and recharging, threatened to choke her. Annie unwrapped her scarf, unbuttoned her coat, plucked off her hat, and threw the whole ensemble on the floor. She shuffled to the living room, feeling like she was about to fall into a bottomless pit. She'd barely warmed up in the taxi and felt the raw, late-December chill as if she were still outside. The afternoon sun poured in through the living room window, partially blocked by the Christmas tree. She sat down in a patch of sun on the floor and hugged her knees. She needed to hear John's voice. She needed to listen to it like she needed to breathe. She got up and went back to the landing by the door and grabbed her phone from the entryway table, kicking her pile of outer garments across the floor. She needed to hear his voice. That was all. She wouldn't call him, she would simply listen to his message, the one that played on a continuous loop in her head.

She plucked the throw-blanket from the couch and wrapped it around her shoulders like a cape. Standing in front of the Christmas tree, she touched the branch with the pinecone and penguin and lost all composure. Crumbling into a heap on the floor, she dialed John's number, not at all sure what she was doing or why.

"Annie." The reality of him on the other end of the line spooked her, and she slammed the phone shut, horrified that she'd succumbed to her weakness. She stared at the phone, prepared to be startled when it rang. But it never did.

44

John

Out of a sense of duty — he was the father of Marina's son after all — John sent the others home. He would stand by during the surgery, get status from Dr. Vargas, then take a taxi back to the house. Mostly, he wanted Luke out of the way, just in case. *I'm strongly suggesting that you come in here tomorrow prepared to say goodbye.* John had a bad feeling. A horrible feeling. It wasn't just the surgeon's words, it was the look in his eyes.

He paced the lounge, unable to sit still. During the past week, he'd read most of the newspapers and magazines: *Time, People, Sport's Illustrated,* the *South Florida Sun-Sentinel, Reader's Digest, USA Today,* and *Consumer Reports.* On what seemed like his hundredth trip past the magazine rack, he spotted a *Good Housekeeping* magazine with a picture of a gingerbread house on the cover. He picked it up and sat down, running his fingers over the image. It had a red roof, like the one Luke had made just a few days ago. The magazine promised *hundreds of inspiring ideas.* He skimmed the pages: *Beautiful Trees and*

Trimmings, Dazzling (Easy) Cookies, Quick Crafts, Favorite Family Recipes, Great Gifts Under $10, Christmas Survival Guide, Tips on Tipping and *How to Stay Healthy and Stress Free*. This was supposed to be a typical December. He would have loved to flip through a magazine like this with Annie and plan activities with Henry, and now, possibly, Luke. He allowed himself to imagine what it might be like back home, under these new circumstances. Only if he still had Annie. Without her, none of the rest of it mattered.

John's phone vibrating in his pocket broke his reverie. Probably his mother again wanting a status check. The last time she'd called Marina had only been in surgery for two hours, and things looked okay. He looked at the clock on the wall — another two hours had gone by — and he realized that nobody had come out to update him in quite some time. He pulled out his phone, expecting to see his mother's number but saw Annie's instead. He stared at the phone like a zombie, paralyzed, and unable to move. Another vibration jolted him into reality.

"Annie." His heart pounded in his chest. Silence. A second later, dial tone. He closed his eyes and took several deep breaths, feeling his heart begin to return to a normal rhythm. He took another deep breath and opened his phone to call her back, fully expecting her to not answer. He took his eyes off the phone for a split-second and saw a figure trudging toward him, acting utterly defeated. John stared — he knew without being told. Dr. Vargas approached, pulled off his surgical mask, and shook his head. John put his phone down and partially stood, bent at the waist, and held onto the chair for support. He glanced down at the magazine, now on the floor, splayed open to *Miraculous Stories of Real-life Angels*. There would not be any miracles today.

THE TAXI DARTED through the early-evening traffic like a sprinter vying for position during the last hundred meters of the race. The driver deposited John in a wash of twilight — oranges, and purples — in front of his mother's house. He sat down on the porch steps, giving himself a minute to compose himself before going inside. Leaning on the stair rail, he tilted his head back until it met the composite wood. Not wanting to cause mass hysteria, he opened his phone and called Dale. She answered before it even rang.

"It's me, don't say anything, just listen. Please." He heard his mother and Luke talking in the background. Relief washed over him when Dale didn't respond. He pictured her holding a finger to her mouth and shaking her head, maybe even going into another room. "Make some excuse and come out to the front porch. Alone." He closed his phone and waited. He watched as the front door opened, one inch at a time. Not letting it open fully, she slipped out and sat down beside him.

"What's going on?" Dale searched his eyes. She stood up, then sat right back down. "Talk to me. What's going on?" She grabbed the front of his shirt, then collapsed in a heap at his knees.

"I'm sorry," he said. "I am so fucking sorry."

"I can't lose another sister. I already lost one sister. I can't lose Marina. I can't lose her." Dale grunted, hugging her knees and swaying from side to side.

"Shhh." John grabbed her shoulders to still her. "She's gone, Dale." He paused for a response, and when none came: "She's already gone." They sat in silence. John's leg had gone numb, sitting on the steps. He wasn't sure how much time had gone by. If he didn't act quickly, his mother and Luke would begin to wonder what happened to Dale.

"I need you to pull yourself together," he said. "I need to tell my mother, and I want to do it without Luke underfoot."

"He was about to watch something on TV." She rubbed her eyes with the back of her hands. "I'll watch it with him."

"Go in through the garage." He thought about the logistics involved. He felt protective of Luke and wanted to be the one to tell him. "Get my mother alone and ask her to come out here. Make sure Luke doesn't see her go out." Dale nodded, lifting herself off the steps, a hunched and crooked form disappearing around the corner of the house under a rapidly darkening sky. John waited for his mother, dreading the conversation, fully expecting a barrage of aspersions and guilt-tripping.

"What's all this about?" His mother stood at the base of the steps, hands on her hips, a frenzied fire in her eyes. John stood and hugged her, gathering momentum, preparing for the first round to be fired.

"She died, Mother."

"I know," she said, pulling away from him and looking at him as if he were a wounded animal. "I figured something had happened when we didn't hear from you." She dabbed at dry eyes as if she'd done all of her crying before this confirming moment.

"I need to tell you something." This hadn't been part of his plan, but his mother exuded strength. He'd long forgotten this facet of her. It was what he'd grown up with, but over the years she'd become less sure of herself, more easily flustered. He liked this strong version of her the best. They walked up the steps and sat down on the porch swing.

"Promise me you won't ask too many questions," he said. His mother nodded. "I didn't know this until a few days ago, but Marina and Nester tried to have a baby together." He decided not to share the things Dale had said about her own fertility issues.

"My God, she wasn't pregnant, was she?"

"You promised, Mother. No questions. Let me get it out. And no, she wasn't pregnant." Pearl nodded, taking his hand and squeezing it. John pushed the swing with his feet, letting the rattle of the chain links hypnotize him. "Turns out, she couldn't get pregnant, at least not easily." He laced his fingers behind his head and leaned back, the sensation of the swing transporting him to his boat. Annie floated in and out of his mind. "They did a DNA test with Phil Riley's daughter. Recently."

"Phil Riley, the rapist?"

"The one and only." He lifted his legs as the swing rocked. "Luke isn't biologically linked to that family."

"What are you saying?" She held onto the chain and stopped the swing with her feet. "He's Nester's son?"

"He's mine." John took a deep breath and didn't try to hold in his tears.

"But you had a vas—"

"It failed."

"How do you know that?"

"Because I got tested. Today." John ignored his mother's desire to stop the swing. He pushed hard with his foot and continued until the swing gained momentum. She held tightly to the chain, but didn't flinch, didn't argue, didn't attempt to get off. "I've been able to father a child all along. I also took a DNA test, and Candace got Luke swabbed. Those results will come back in a week or so." He looked at the sky, now completely dark and starless. He needed to move things along. Marina's body would be bathed and positioned in her room, so Luke and the others could say goodbye. The hospital said four hours but could hold her longer if necessary. John needed it to be soon.

"I always thought he had your eyes." Pearl put her hand under John's chin and turned his head to face her. "I don't need the results of a DNA test to believe it."

"I don't know how or when or even if ever to tell him." He stopped the swing and stood. "But, I do need to tell him about his mom." He held out his hands and helped his mother off the swing. "I'd like to do it alone if you don't mind."

JOHN HELD the front door open for his mother. He watched her plod through the living room and turn the corner toward the kitchen. The house smelled of beef and onions simmering in red wine — something that might be comforting on a cold December evening back home. Not on a muggy evening in Florida, where the grief hanging in the air would threaten to sop up the stew, like a piece of crusty sourdough bread.

Luke's legs jutted straight out in front of him, too short to even bend over the cushions at the knees. His broken arm rested on his thighs. John didn't recognize the cartoon that had captured all of Luke's attention.

"What are you watching?"

"*Rugrats*."

"I've never heard of that show." He feigned interest. "What are they doing?" The background music, a little too loud for John's taste, pierced his body like nails on a chalkboard

"Tommy is the baby in the diaper. He has a cut on his finger." Luke's eyes stayed glued to the TV. "The bigger kid is Chucky. He's helping Tommy be brave."

"Tommy looks kind of like you."

Luke turned to look at John. He crinkled his nose and laughed. "No, he doesn't."

"Yeah, he does." John tousled Luke's hair. "Okay, maybe only a little."

The show continued as John mentally rehearsed what to say and how to say it. He finally concluded that there was no easy way. None. John's watch inched toward the top of the hour when the cartoon would likely end. He picked up the remote, ready to turn the TV off the minute the credits started rolling. The show ended, and John, still lost in scripting what he would say, lost track of time. Another episode began. He decided to leave the show on for background noise.

"Luke, I need to talk to you about something serious." John turned to face him, but Luke's eyes remained glued on the TV. "I have an idea. Let's go outside and sit on Grammy's porch swing."

"I want to watch *Rugrats*."

"I'll tell you what." He picked up the remote and clicked the TV off. "Let's go outside."

Luke's lower lip curled — the harbinger of tears — as he hopped off the couch and followed John outside. John lifted him onto the swing and sat down beside him. He pushed with his foot to set the swing in motion, letting it undulate, slower and slower, until it stopped. He gave the swing another strong push.

"Your Mommy died today." The words tumbled out of John's mouth, betraying his eloquent and scripted speech. He waited for a response, a cry, a sob, a whimper. Luke sat silent, staring straight ahead. "Do you understand what I just said?" Luke nodded. John let the swing slow down, then pushed it again, prepared to do this for as long as it took. Not knowing exactly what he wanted for an outcome, he braced himself for a long night. "We need to go to the hospital pretty soon. You can say goodbye to her there."

"Where will I live?" John whipped his head around to look at Luke, this blunt and practical question, not what he'd expected to hear.

"I don't know." He didn't want to lie — he honestly didn't know. But he did know one thing and decided to say it out loud. "I promise to take care of you."

"Where do you live."

"Not too far from your house, buddy, not too far." John didn't want to hike into the jungle of details yet. The growth too thick, the canopy blocking out all the light. He would use a machete to clear a path, letting the details emerge over the next few weeks. Or however long it would take. "We'll stay here with Grammy for a bit. Okay? Until we figure things out."

Luke put his head on John's chest. John pushed the swing with his foot and leaned back, draping his arm around Luke's shoulders. It was only when they finally got up that he noticed the wet circle on his shirt where Luke's face had been.

AT MIDNIGHT, John found himself back on the porch swing. After the the hospital visitation, nobody wanted to eat dinner. The stew sat in the crockpot, untouched, for God knew how long. After settling Luke in bed and comforting him until he fell asleep, John found the stew — a coagulated mess, most of it plastered to the sides of the crock — and scraped it into the trash. He felt something brush against his leg and looked down to see the cat. He patted the swing.

"Come on up here." The cat jumped into John's lap. He held his glass of scotch out of the way and pushed the cat off to the side. "There you go. Sit anywhere but on me." The cat curled up on the opposite end of the swing.

John sipped his scotch and opened his phone. He'd wanted to call Annie earlier, but the torrent of events swept him away. He stared at the phone as if in doing so, Annie would feel the void of being apart and call. If he allowed himself to get technical and count beans, he could say that she left, and the ball was in her court to call him. He closed the phone and set it down in his lap, determined to not cave in.

The problem was, he didn't want to count beans. He wanted to count the number of years they could have together. He wanted to count the hairs on her head and the tiny freckles on her shoulders. He wanted to count the number of memories they could make together. Mostly, he wanted to climb inside her mind and understand, really understand what she was thinking.

In a fit of longing, he called her. Of course, straight to voicemail. Why would he think anything would be different? He closed the phone and gulped the rest of his drink. *Dammit, Annie.* He dialed again, this time, speaking after the beep.

"Annie." He took a deep breath. "She died." He closed his eyes. "Marina died." And then, barely audible, "I love you, Annie."

45

———

Annie

Annie left the radiology center with a bittersweet heart. Her oncologist had assured her that this one large dose would relieve the pain and other symptoms caused by her bone metastases. He emphasized the palliative nature of the treatment — it wouldn't wholly zap away the tumor on her spine. But he expected pain relief to come quickly — within a few days — and last as long as six months. If the pain returned sooner, the treatment could be repeated. The session had been quick and painless — in and out and on her way to Alec's office in less than forty minutes. Still, her doctor's blunt words caused real fear — *you've already lost the first battle, and you're going to lose this war unless you consider chemo.*

The cab driver took his time winding his way through midtown Manhattan back to Brooklyn. She sat stiff, expecting at any moment to be overcome with the radiation's side effects. *You probably won't have any,* the radiologist administering her treatment told her after the third time she'd pressed him about adverse reactions. *Maybe a little fatigue in a few days, but, probably nothing, don't worry, you will feel like a new person by New Year's.* A new person. Wouldn't that be wonderful? A person who didn't walk away from the love of her life. She swallowed the ever-present lump in her throat, looking out the window at the traffic, the storefronts, the people on the street — anything to distract herself.

"Stop!" Annie leaned forward in her seat. The cab driver whipped his head around, not attempting to hide his annoyance. He pulled up to the curb. "That record store across the street, behind us." She pointed. "I need to go in there for a minute."

"Make it quick," he said. "I'm not stopping the meter."

Annie nodded and stepped out of the cab, running to the record store, hoping beyond hope that they'd have what she wanted. She scanned the alphabetized CD bins and found it right away. Kajagoo-goo. The liquor store next door beckoned. *Why the hell not*, she thought. She bought a bottle of scotch and two cheap glasses. Pleased with herself for thinking quickly and creatively, she imagined Mel's delight when he walked into her art room and heard the band he'd asked her to play last time. The scotch, though, was a wildcard. She might pull it out if necessary. *Break glass in case of emergency.* Across the street, the cab driver leaned against the hood, smoking.

"I'm not paying for your smoke break," Annie said as she opened the back door. The driver took one last drag and climbed in, slowly exhaling a cloud of smoke. He tossed the butt out the window as he maneuvered back into the traffic.

Annie touched the spot on her back, where the beam of radiation had penetrated. Her original pain still existed, the meds she'd taken early this morning already wearing off. She took a deep breath, wondering when she would notice the *miraculous* benefits of the radiation. She felt impatient suddenly and didn't want to wait a few days. She wanted pain relief now. She wanted to feel like a new person now.

Traffic crawled. Annie leaned back against the seat, resting her head on the window. She fished through her purse for her phone and opened it, brushing her finger over the *new voicemail* indicator on the screen. She'd been asleep last night when John called. When she woke up, she'd been so anxious and distracted about the day that she never checked her phone, only to discover his message during her frenzied and disquieting morning at the radiology center. She hadn't wanted to listen to it then, so she'd tucked it away for later.

THE WAITING room in Alec's psychology practice smelled musty. Annie held the door open to let the wind rush in, freshening the air like a ghost wielding a bottle of Febreze. All buttoned up for the holidays, there'd been no one coming in and out, no pots of fresh coffee, no Alec with his too liberally applied Lagerfeld cologne — nothing to mask the natural bouquet of this old building.

Annie walked past Alec's private office and went directly to her art room, putting on a pot of coffee — for the aroma, mostly — and hiding the scotch behind it. She gathered the items from Mel's previous session and set them out on the art table, placing the Kajagoogoo CD among them. She picked up Mel's collage and plopped down in her corner chair — her perch — feeling apprehensive about this session. While it would give her something to think about other than her own problems, she feared she'd be distracted, and wished she'd never asked Alec to arrange it. She studied the pictures Mel had chosen for his collage — so many bananas, and the woman he'd seemed wistful about. Feeling wistful herself, she opened her phone. Like yanking a bandage off sensitive skin, she pushed the button and listened to John's voicemail: *Annie. She died. Marina died. I love you, Annie.* Her hand shot up to her mouth. She couldn't breathe, couldn't move, couldn't detect a heartbeat. She let her hand fall away from her face, and let her head fall between her knees.

"Hello?" A woman trailing behind Mel's motorized wheelchair entered. Annie jumped up from her chair, embarrassed that she hadn't been in the waiting room to greet them. Mel positioned himself in front of the art table. "Are you okay?"

"I'm so sorry," Annie said, utterly distracted, wondering how much time had gone by since she sat down. "You must be Mel's wife." They shook hands. "Forgive me, I, um, I just received some horrible news. I'm not sure I could do this today." Mel turned his head in her direction, looking deflated, and Annie back-peddled. "No, never mind. This will be good for me. I need to keep busy."

"Are you sure? We could come back another day this week. Or after the holidays."

"This will be good for me. Let's keep things as is."

"Do you want to talk about it?" Mel waited until his wife was out the door.

"Talk about what?" Annie looked at him, puzzled. Then it registered. He was asking about her unpleasant news. "Actually, no, I don't want to talk about me today." She smoothed her shirt with her hands and wiped imaginary lint off her pants. Mel picked up a green crayon and made circles all over a sheet of white paper.

"What is this?" Mel let the crayon fall from his hand. He picked up the new CD and waved it around like a flag.

"Kajagoogoo."

"I can see that." He put it down. "Why?"

"You asked if I had any of their music the last time we met."

"I never meant for you to go out and buy a CD.

"I'm always eager to add to my collection," she said, picking it up and ripping at the plastic wrapping. "They make these things so hard to open."

"You're not going to play it, are you?" Mel's eyes raged.

"I was, but if you —"

"I don't want to listen to that." He turned his chair back to the table. Mel's tone shot an arrow through her heart. She plopped down in her chair, her excitement at having acquired the CD extinguished. She fought tears as she slid a classical music CD into the player and turned up the volume. The scotch she'd bought teased from behind the coffee pot. She shuffled back to the art table, resisting the temptation to pour herself a glass.

"I upset you, I'm sorry." Mel turned to face her. "Thank you for the CD. The music brings back bad memories, that's all."

"Then why did you ask me to play it last week?"

Mel picked up a blue crayon and slashed the green circles, swishing it back and forth across the paper. He looked at her, his hand still pushing the crayon, the paper turning bluer and bluer by the second.

"I felt sorry for myself and wanted to wallow." He put the crayon down and picked up a red one, scribbling jagged, angry lines.

"Yeah, I know the feeling. I've been wallowing a lot lately." She felt her tears come to the surface again. "I think I'm going to pour myself a glass of scotch. Do you want one?" Annie walked over to the coffee pot and grabbed the scotch and two glasses. Without waiting for an answer, she set them on the art table.

"Do I have a choice?" Mel said as he watched her pour liquid gold into one of the glasses.

"I'm sorry, Mel. I never should have agreed to meet you today." She took a sip, relishing the warmth it produced in her. "I've had a hellish few days."

"Did you at least have a good Christmas?" He pointed to the other glass and nodded. "You don't need to twist my arm. I'll have one."

"I had the shittiest Christmas since the year my mother died." She filled his glass and lifted it into his hand, guessing that he might need help gripping it. He planted his fingers firmly around the glass, and she let go. She picked up her glass and clicked it against his. He lifted his glass in a shaky hand and brought it to his lips, tilting it and letting the scotch flow into his mouth. He held it there, then set the glass on the table, the scotch still pooling in his mouth. He swallowed it and shuddered.

"Damn, that's good." He sighed. Annie nodded, scanning the art table, focusing on Mel's crayon scribble, the jagged red lines undeniably representing his anger and upset over the Kajagoogoo CD. She didn't want to pry, but she did want to explore. She needed an inconspicuous way to enter the topic. Creative ideas alluded her, so she decided to be direct. She held her glass to the light and swirled it around like John sometimes did.

"Tell me about Kajagoogoo," she said, her voice craggy from the sudden onslaught of alcohol. She watched Mel pick up a crayon —

orange this time — and bang it into the paper, stabbing it in the heart. He picked up his glass and guzzled the remaining scotch. He slammed the empty glass on the table and jabbed his finger at it. Annie jumped.

"A refill, please." He barked.

"Not if you keep talking to me like I've killed your cat." Annie didn't care that this man was a quadriplegic. Simply didn't care. She was in no mood to be treated disrespectfully.

"I'll pay you to kill my cat." A hint of a smile fell across his face. "My wife's cat, actually. I hate the damned thing. He's too big to fit in the microwave."

Annie softened but didn't laugh.

"I've already been over all this stuff with Dr. Arnstein. I really don't want to rehash it." He maneuvered his wheelchair away from the table. "I'll just wait for my wife out there. I'm done with this kindergarten crap."

Annie shrugged, any fight she had in her quickly evaporating. She waited until he was out the door and out of sight before she poured herself a little more scotch. She picked up her glass and carried it to her corner chair. She lifted her legs onto the chair and tucked her feet under them, resting her elbow on the chair's bulbous armrest. She closed her eyes, letting the scotch undo her. Choking on the lump in her throat, she put her head in her hands and rocked back and forth. Her knees were wet by the time she looked up, sensing a presence. Mel sat in front of her, his empty glass in his lap. He held it out to her with a shaky hand.

"Please, Sir, I want some more." Mel, a middle-aged Oliver Twist, batted his eyelashes. "This time of year is hard for me," he said, rolling his chair back to the art table. Annie refilled his glass and sat down beside him.

"I'm sorry, Mel." She let her tears fall freely. "I'm kind of a mess today. Someone died. And my cancer is progressing. On top of all that, I walked away from the love of my life a few days ago." The laughter long forgotten, she felt exposed, laying her heart on the table like that.

"I'm sure you had a good reason to walk away," he said. She found it interesting that he chose to focus on her broken heart, rather than her broken body.

"I don't know anymore."

"I walked away from someone this time of year too. A long time ago."

"The woman in your collage?" She pointed to the poster board that she'd left propped against the wall next to her chair. Mel nodded and rolled across the room. He picked up the collage and brought it back to the art table. "Where is she now?"

"Dead."

"Ouch. I'm sorry."

"Dr. Arnstein didn't tell you about any of this?"

"No, he doesn't discuss those kinds of things with me." Annie wondered if Alec would tell her if she asked. She never asked. "He gives me background about the person, that's all." She sipped her scotch. "He told me about your suicide attempt and tragic accident." She put her glass down. "Nothing more than that."

"You might as well play the CD," he said, waving his arm toward her stereo system.

"I wouldn't play that CD now if you begged me." She raised her eyebrow at him.

"Please." He batted his eyelashes again. She laughed and shook her head.

"Do you promise to be nice?"

"Indeed."

Annie popped out the classical music CD and loaded Kajagoogoo. New wave 80's music filled the room. She made her way back to the table, careful to let Mel feed her whatever he was capable of. There would be more sessions, she hoped.

"I should have been on the plane," he said, his voice barely audible.

"What plane?" Annie wondered if he, too, had been so close, so very close to the attacks on 9/11.

"Lockerbie." Mel turned his head and stared at the collage. "I met Colleen in London. She went to school there."

"What about you? What were you doing in London?"

"A semester. Just one lousy semester." Mel sighed. "I'll say it quick: We fell head over heels. But then she wanted to get serious, you know meet the parents and all that." His hands seemed shakier as he lifted his glass to his lips. Annie resisted the urge to help him. He put his glass down and wiped a trickle of scotch from his chin with the back of his hand. "I agreed to fly home to Boston with her for Christmas, but I didn't really want to."

"Let me guess," Annie said. "She got on the plane, and you didn't."

"Bingo." He picked up his glass and held it out. Annie reluctantly touched her glass to his. "It gets worse. I went to her flat to break up with her, but she wasn't there. So, I left a note. And that was that. A *Dear Jane* letter." He shook his head. "She got on that plane with a broken heart. Her last few hours alive were lousy, because of me."

"I'm so sorry, Mel." Annie wanted to hug him but sat and stared at the wall behind him. She wiped fresh tears from her eyes. "I wish I could say something that would turn fifteen years' worth of guilt into something good. But I can't."

"Precisely why I'm in this predicament." He tapped on the arm of his wheelchair.

"I was in the North Tower on 9/11," she said, searching for anything in common between them. "I was there early that morning but left before anything happened. I could have easily been in there when the plane hit." She hung her head. "I don't know why I was allowed to escape if you know what I mean." She'd been wrestling with this for three years. "Just a few days before, I'd been diagnosed with incurable breast cancer. I'm alive now, but I will die from this, probably sooner rather than later." She choked back a sob. "Why not just let me die in the building? Why allow me to live for a few years only to die anyway?" She wiped her eyes. "Dying as a hero that day might have been better than this."

"Bullshit," Mel said. He slammed his empty glass down. "Look at what you've done for me, in less than an hour." He raised an eyebrow.

"I'm listening to this fucking CD and feel better than I have in a long time." He raised his glass. "You might very well have saved my life today."

Annie smiled and shook her head. He was right. She quite possibly had more time here than she knew. Maybe not. Whether she had an hour, a day, a few years, or a decade, she didn't want to waste another minute of it.

"And you might have just saved mine," she said, laughing. She didn't care, she got up and hugged him. Long and hard. She pulled away and looked at his crayon scribbles, the concept of art therapy set aside in favor of tilting back scotch and letting demons rise to the surface. "Will you excuse me for a few minutes?" She stood. "I need to book a flight to Florida." Mel knit his eyebrows together. "It's a terribly long story, but the love of my life is there, and I need to go to him."

"Don't let me get in your way," he said, waving his arm toward the door, surprisingly lucid after so much scotch. "I'll just sit here and color." He jabbed his finger in and out of his open mouth — the universal symbol for *gag me*. Annie rolled her eyes and laughed.

ANNIE SETTLED INTO HER SEAT, clutching her hastily filled backpack against her chest. The airplane's jet bridge seemed to spit two or three people into the cabin at a time, long minutes apart, a surprisingly empty vessel for the week between Christmas and New Year's. The two seats beside her were empty, and she hoped it stayed that way.

She didn't plan to stay in Florida very long, maybe a day, maybe two. Just long enough to offer her condolences to the family and talk to John. Perhaps this was a fool's errand — what was there left to talk about, anyway? She didn't know. Did she owe him an apology? Probably. She loved him, that's pretty much all she knew. Her heart — which had been slammed shut on Christmas morning — had softened during the past few days. She would tell him she loved him, that's all she would do. She had no expectations, and would let the day unfold into whatever shape it wanted. A wrinkled mess? A neat little package? An irreparable fracture? She reminded herself that she had no control over the outcome. She would tell him she loved him. That's all she would do.

"Ma'am? Excuse me, Ma'am?" The flight attendant pointed to Annie's backpack. "You need to stow that in an overhead bin or under the seat in front of you."

Annie reached inside and pulled out John's old sailing sweater. She slid the backpack under her seat and spread the sweater across her lap like a blanket. The cabin door closed, and the flight attendants performed their safety demonstrations. She looked out the window, the canned information droning on — an annoying buzz in the background — as the plane slowly pushed back from the gate onto the taxiway. The chill of the morning palpable outside the window, the Manhattan skyline barely visible on the gray horizon. A thin strip of pink shone through the clouds, the sun not quite ready to greet the day.

As the plane taxied toward the departure runway, the signs and numbers painted on the tarmac created a fuzzy illusion. A muffled voice came over the intercom: *flight attendants prepare for takeoff*. The plane slowed for barely a second before the engines roared, and the scene outside Annie's window blurred like an abstract painting of grays, whites, blacks, yellows, and more pink than had been visible a minute ago. Wheels lifting off the earth, the ground falling away, the headlights of morning rush-hour like yellow and red dots on snakes slithering across the island of Manhattan.

She wanted to surprise John, catch him off guard, not give him too much time to think about the myriad reasons — all valid — to be angry that she'd pushed him away. Out the window, the grid of the city, visible zoned demarcations, gave way to more fluid boundaries. Distinct buildings morphed into the browns of bare treetops and a frigid, dormant landscape.

Annie curled her legs under her and leaned her head against the window. With no seatmates to object, she pulled out her backpack and dropped it on the seat beside her. She fished for her sketchbook and a pencil and set them on her tray table, not knowing what she would sketch. The drink service cart bumped its way up the aisle. Prepared to wave it away it, she found herself ordering a hot tea. She set it on the tray next to her art supplies, then folded the sweater into a pillow and wedged it between the window and her head, pressing her nose into it, trying hard to inhale what little of John's scent was left — no longer John's but hers for the past three years. She sniffed. A little bit. Yes, she smelled a little bit of John. She closed her eyes, leaving her nose nestled in the scratchy wool.

"Ma'am? Excuse me, Ma'am?" Annie lifted her face off the sweater, rubbing the back of her neck, trying to get her head to stop throbbing. She dropped her tea — untouched and cold — into the waiting mouth of the trash bag in the flight attendant's hands. "You're going to need to stow those things," he said, pointing to the backpack and other items strewn about.

Annie rubbed her eyes and looked out the window. The grays of Manhattan had given way to the greens and blues of South Florida. Three hours and you're in another world. Tiny houses with tiny blue pools, growing bigger and closer by the second. Palm trees. So many palm trees. Four days ago, she hated Florida and never wanted to see it again. But now, as the plane floated toward the earth, it all looked different, more vibrant. A thud, the screeching brakes, the muffled voice on the intercom: *Welcome to Miami, sunny and eighty-two degrees.* She stuffed the sweater into her backpack and made her way off the plane.

46

———

John

They had no will, no guardian named. A natural detail to overlook, a concept easy to avoid. Who wants to talk about death, anyway? He and Annie skirted around the topic. And it rarely came up during his marriage to Marina. But at least he and Marina had a will. When they divorced, John had it nullified and drew up a new one for himself and his meager assets.

Dale had spent yesterday, between fits of hysteria and nostalgia, trying to fill in the blanks, find the missing pieces. The only conclusion she'd been able to come to was that Marina and Nester had no will, no guardian named. Luke was, at least, listed as a beneficiary on all of their bank accounts. There was also the issue of the house and all of its contents. What a mess. And now, Luke. Nester had adopted him. If the DNA test came back confirming what John already knew, then there would be other legal hurdles to jump over. What a pain in the ass it would be to unravel. John looked forward to none of it and was grateful for Dale's help and connections in the world of lawyers and judges.

"Uncle John, can we go now?" Luke flung open the door to the garage, the metal handle banging against the wall. John cringed at the noise. He stood up and examined the wall for damage. Just a few dents, no doubt from his mother's occasional carelessness. He made a mental note to fix the door, so it didn't swing so wildly before heading home to New Jersey. He planned to stay with his mother for another week, then take the kid back and fight on foot. He had absolutely no idea what he would do once there. Move into his old house so the kid could finish the school year? What about running the pub with Shorty? And damn, Maplewood was too far away from Annie. He still hadn't talked to her, had no idea what she was thinking or how she viewed the *us* in them. He didn't even know if there was still an *us*. His original airline ticket home still sat on the dresser in his mother's guest room, the flight leaving tomorrow morning. He toyed with the idea of flying home to try and talk to Annie but didn't want to upset Luke, who'd become especially clingy.

"Yep, I'm just about ready. I have gloves, a bucket, and a shovel. What else do we need?" Luke sat on the garage floor and examined the items that formed a semi-circle around his grandmother's gardening bench. He looked at John.

"What if we find something perfect? Can we take a plastic bag, so it doesn't get mixed in with the other stuff?"

"That's a brilliant idea." John pulled a grocery store bag out of his pocket. "But, I'm way ahead of you." He winked and patted Luke's head. "Let's go find some shells." He pushed the button, and the garage door went up. John squinted in the sun as he and Luke stepped onto the driveway.

"Can we take Grammy's motorcycle?"

"No, buddy, not with your arm in a cast. You need to be able to hold onto me with both arms."

"I can hold tight with my cast." He grabbed John around the waist, squeezing with his good arm, his broken arm half-heartedly resting against his torso. "See?"

"I'm sorry, buddy, it won't be safe." He peeled Luke's arm away. "We're taking the car."

"I want to ride on Grammy's motorcycle." Luke's voice rose, and John's patience plummeted.

"Do you want to collect shells or not?"

"Mommy said I could ride Grammy's motorcycle." Louder still. "Daddy was going to take me." Even louder.

John walked into the garage and sat down on his mother's gardening bench. Luke, still in the driveway, stomped his feet and danced around the motorcycle, yelling and crying. It had been like this since Monday — since Marina died. These meltdowns tried his patience. Big time. He had to force himself to take deep breaths and remember what Luke had been through. He wouldn't cow-tow, though. Particularly for something unsafe. The yelling ebbed, the crying grew quieter. Luke put his head on the motorcycle seat, his shoulders bobbing up and down. John got up and stood beside him.

"I'm sorry you're mad," he said, rubbing Luke's shoulders and back. "I'll be puttering around in the garage if you change your mind about collecting shells." He walked away, leaving Luke to get the ball of emotions out of his system.

JOHN STRUGGLED to wrap Luke's cast in plastic. *Just in case we get too close to the water*, he'd said. He finally won that battle, and Luke climbed in the car, his face still wet from crying, and settled himself in the back seat. John stole glances of him in the rearview mirror during the short drive to the nature preserve. Yesterday, John wanted quiet and longed for a cease-fire in the never-ending barrage of questions and chatter that came out of Luke's mouth. But now, Luke's mouth was clamped shut. John pulled onto the gravel drive and made his way into the parking lot.

"Hey buddy, we're here." John parked and turned to face Luke. "Listen, we don't have to do this if you don't want to." John turned back around and waited, for what, he wasn't sure. It had been his mother's idea to bring him here, and Luke's plan to find shells to bury with Marina. John wasn't even sure if Luke understood what that meant. Shit, he wasn't even sure when or where to bury Marina and Nester. The police department agreed to transport both bodies to a funeral home in Maplewood. *Fuck, was this really happening?* John clenched his teeth. He needed to hold it together for the kid.

"I want to." Luke unbuckled the seatbelt and pushed his whole body against the door to open it. He stumbled out and ran down the dirt path toward the water.

"Dammit, Luke." John ran after him, wincing each time his foot hit the ground. He glued his eyes to Luke's red tee-shirt and stumbled on a root, landing facedown in the dirt. "Fuck!" He picked himself up and continued running.

John was drenched in sweat by the time he reached the sand. Luke stood a little too close to the water for his comfort. They never discussed simple things, such as whether or not he knew how to swim or at least not drown. Damn, he had a lot to learn. He took off his shoes and carried them down the beach, tossing them in the sand a few feet from where Luke stood. He breathed deeply, trying to get his heart rate down. He was out of shape, no joke. He'd need to do something about that.

John plopped down on the hard, wet sand, pretending to not notice the waves marching toward him. Luke stared straight ahead, either unaware or uncaring of John's presence. The first wave hit. John jumped up, soaked, pretending to have been caught off guard, hoping to get a reaction — any reaction — out of Luke. Nothing. He sat back down. The next wave hit. More silence. As the third wave approached, Luke grabbed John's hand and tried, with all his might, to pull him up. John played along and let himself be pulled.

"Uncle John, you can't sit so close to the water."

"Why not? I know how to swim."

"You're all wet."

"So what?" John took off his shirt and tossed it in the direction of his shoes "It's hot out here. The water feels great." John smiled as relief washed over him like the waves. He didn't realize how much he'd missed hearing the kid talk.

"I wish I could go in." Luke held his plaster-encased arm up in the air. "But, I have this stupid cast." He sat down near John, his arm still in the air. A wave came, and in one swoop, John lifted him up and held him high above the water. Luke laughed as John swung him around and then gently placed him in the sand.

"Now we're both wet. Your shoes and my shirt. Your grandmother won't be happy."

"We could just put everything in the dryer when we get home. She'll never know."

"Brilliant."

Luke walked along the shore, jumping and leaping in the waves breaking at his feet, doing a lousy job of keeping his cast out of harm's way. John trailed behind, scanning the sand for shells. In the mad dash to run after Luke, he'd left their bucket and other supplies in the car. Luke bent down and swished his hand around in the foamy waves. He pulled it out and examined whatever treasures landed there, picking through them, tossing the rejects back, like a miner sifting for gold, clenching his fist to protect his plunder. John saw something sticking out of the sand. He bent down and pulled. A perfect, tiny conch shell. He put it in his pocket. Maybe he'd never give Annie a ring. But a seashell? Sure, he could give her a seashell. Neutral in every way. No strings attached. An unexpected and uninvited sob escaped his throat. Less than a week ago, she'd been nestled in the crook of his arm, their hearts beating in unison. Less than a week ago, he knew she loved him. He knew nothing now. How could so much distance have grown in such a short time? John wiped his eyes when he saw Luke turn around and walk toward him.

"What did you find, buddy?" John squatted down and examined the contents of Luke's outstretched hand. "A sand dollar?" John brushed his finger across the flattened sea urchin. "Can I hold it for a second?" Luke let him take it. John turned it over and felt for spines, grateful that he felt none, thankful that he didn't have to make the kid throw it back. "It's perfect."

"Mommy will love it."

"She will indeed, buddy. She will, indeed."

. . .

THE SCENE in the living room was a familiar one: a pop-up command center, Dale at the helm, Pearl's computer desk, and the four-by-four space around it strewn with papers.

"I got this for Mommy," Luke said to Dale. He held out his sand dollar for her to behold.

"That's gorgeous, sweetie," she said. "It will be with your mom forever and ever." She looked at John, then back at Luke. "Just like you will be in her heart forever and ever."

"Uncle John washed it. Now it needs to dry." Luke blew on the shell. "I'm going to put it on my windowsill." John watched as Luke skipped down the hall and into his room. He waited until he heard the door close, then sat down on the floor amid Dale's piles.

"I noticed my mother's motorcycle isn't on the driveway," he said. "When will she be back?"

"She didn't say." She picked up a handful of papers and waved them in front of John's face. "This shit gets more complicated by the second." She slammed the papers down. "Textbook case of why every adult over the age of eighteen should have a will." She shook her head, then wiped away tears.

"Listen, I know you need to head north to deal with all this stuff," John's eyes scanned the piles. "When are you planning to leave?"

"I hoped to be out of here by Friday."

"Okay, good." He ran his fingers through his hair. "That's good. Because I need to head north myself." His eyes pleaded. He needed Dale to be around, needed her to stay here while he begged Annie to take the wall down. "Just for a day or two." He looked at the ceiling, then back at Dale. "I never changed my ticket. I could be on the plane first thing in the morning." Dale said nothing, shuffling the same papers over and over again. "I need to talk to her, Dale. She's not answering her phone. I need to see Her. Need to get to the bottom of this."

"Your mother is going to have a cow when she hears this." Dale put the papers down. "She seemed glad that Annie left."

"I told you before, she had this strange notion that Marina and I would get back together."

"Not anymore." Dale burst into tears. "Not anymore." She took a deep breath and wiped her eyes. "How long will you be?"

"A day, maybe two." He counted days on his fingers. "I promise to be back no later than Friday, early." He looked at Dale. "My mother will be fine with Luke for a few hours if our times don't overlap."

"You really love her," Dale said, wistful.

"More than I ever thought possible."

"Just be careful." Dale hesitated. "She seems fragile."

"She's the strongest person I know."

"Not fragile like porcelain or crystal." She scratched her head. "More like a dandelion. The round puff."

"So, you're saying if I blow too hard, she'll scatter to the winds?"

"Not exactly," Dale said. "You don't even have to blow that hard."

"You don't know her." He stood up, annoyed. "Yeah, she spooks easily. So what?"

"I'm just saying, be careful. Don't go up there all macho and bravado. Be humble."

"Macho?" John laughed, genuinely laughed for the first time in what seemed like ages. "Since when am I macho?" He snorted, and Dale doubled over in fits of laughter. John shook his head, grateful. "Thanks, sis."

"Did you just call me sis?" Dale sat up, all evidence of the laughing fit gone. Poof.

"Why not? You were my sister-in-law once." He searched her eyes. "Now we're connected by Luke. So yeah, sis." He looked hard into her eyes and wondered what it would be like to lose a sibling. She'd lost two. As an only child, he'd never really know. Nester might very well be the closest he'd ever come to having and then losing a brother. "Do you really believe the bullshit we're feeding Luke?" John needed to change the subject, the touchy-feely stuff too overwhelming. "You know, telling him Marina will love a fucking shell that she'll never see or touch? Telling him that he will live in her heart forever?"

"I'm just trying to make him feel better." Dale's face turned three shades of red, darkening by the second. John felt like an ass for upsetting her. He took her hand.

"I know." He blinked away tears. "I'm guilty too. We're all doing it." He let the tears fall, he didn't care. He licked them as they fell toward his mouth, salty despair. "I guess there's no harm. He's just a little boy." Dale squeezed his hand, then let go and turned back to the papers.

PACKING AGAIN. This time with purpose and intent. John didn't need much — only the clothes on his back, the tiny conch shell he picked up on the beach, and the ring. He gathered his keychain and wallet, stuffing one in his front pocket and the other in his back. He placed the airline ticket itself — a harbinger of hope on flimsy cardboard — in the top compartment of his duffle bag.

Luke was still asleep, thank God. Last night he'd tried all manner of tactics to get John to let him come. *I want to go to my house and get my toys.* No, we'll do that after New Year's. *I want to tell my best friend Jake that my mom and dad died.* You can see Jake after New Year's. *I want to go to your house, Uncle John.* I'll take you to my house after New Year's. *I want to eat at your restaurant.* After New Year's. And then, the coup de grâce: *I want to show the lady, Annie my sand dollar.* John had no response to that, and just hugged Luke and told him he'd miss him and would see him Friday.

He sat down on the bed and unfolded Annie's note. He picked it apart, line by line, prepared to address each and every one of her concerns:

1. *Please know that I love you with all my heart.* Then why the hell did you leave me?

2. *I also know that you love me and that there is a trust between us that makes what I'm about to say seem illogical.* Then why did you say it?

3. *I saw you and Dale sitting outside, then later in the hospital. Watching you hold her in your arms was disquieting — an emotional shock. My head and heart are in a battle. My head knows that your embraces were of the comforting kind amid the tragedy that brought us*

here; my heart simply can't be consoled. There are no feelings between Dale and me. None. Zero. Zilch. Nada.

4. Add to that the news that Luke might be your child. I'm having a hard time processing what it means or how it even happened. I trust you'll get tested soon and not take Dale's word for it. Wow. A son. Your dream has come true. I did get tested. Yeah, I can father a child. And yeah, I'm probably Luke's father but won't know for sure for a week or so. How could my dream come true without you in it?

5. I know I'm cowardly for running away from painful things. I want to stay, but can't face you, can't face Dale, can't face Luke. And your mother — there's no way I could face her knowing Luke might be yours. I'm sure she'll try and push you and Marina back together. God, you left her because of the child, and now he might be yours. I don't even know how you'll deal with that, but I do know that I'd just be in the way. You need to figure it out. There's nothing to figure out. You're never in the way. Never. And yes, we need to work on this tendency of yours to flee.

6. I don't know where we go from here. I need to clear my head. I think you need to clear yours too. I don't see how I could possibly fit into this complicated situation, no matter what path you end up taking. Please don't come after me. Stay here and sort this out. There is nothing to sort out, nothing to clear up in my head. I love you. I want you in my life. It's that simple.

7. I left some of my art supplies and the art stuff I bought for Luke. It's in the top dresser drawer. Maybe you could help him color the drawing that I made of him. I thought it might be nice for him to give it to your mother. Watching the two of you together affected me in a way I didn't expect. And that was before I learned he might be mine.

John folded the note and slid it into his duffle bag with the airline ticket. He looked around the room and saw nothing else he needed. He tiptoed out, pulling his fleece jacket off the peg behind the door, on a mission to save his life.

47

Annie

Wet heat rushed into the cab as Annie opened the door to get out. She paid the driver and stood on the curb, the humidity engulfing her, dressed all wrong in her jeans and turtleneck. She'd asked the driver to drop her at the end of the street — she didn't want the attention that a cab pulling up in front of the house might bring — and stood paralyzed, suddenly unsure of why she came or what she intended to say. She took a step, then another, then another, stopping just shy of Pearl's driveway. She felt a wave of relief when she didn't see John's rental car. It would be easier to talk to Pearl alone first, then get settled, cleaned up, and mentally prepared to face him. The garage door was up, and she could see Pearl's motorcycle perched close to the wall, so she knew at least someone was home. Annie peeked around the palm tree at the bottom of the driveway — no one on the porch, thank God. Leaning against the tree for support, she wiped her face with her headband

and took a deep breath. Forcing her legs to move, she tentatively made her way up the walkway.

Annie rapped on the door with her knuckles and stood up straight, donning her most self-assured face. She knocked again, rapping harder, letting her backpack slide off her shoulders and catching it in the crook of her arm. She pressed the doorbell and looked into the house through the narrow windows on either side of the door. When no one appeared, she turned around and sat down on the first step, setting the backpack beside her. The cat came bounding up the steps and rubbed against her shin, then disappeared into the bushes, reappearing a second later with a small black snake in his mouth.

"Tumbleweed!" Annie stood up. "Put that down!" A rhythmic gymnastics routine ensued, the snake a fine stand-in for the ribbon. The cat, soon bored, dropped the snake and ran down the steps in search of more interesting shenanigans. Before Annie could blink, the snake slithered back into the bushes.

She picked up her backpack and walked across the lawn and into the garage. Her tapping on the glass door went unanswered. She stood, her face pressed against the glass. She tapped the glass again, sighing at how difficult this already was. In a fit of boldness, she opened the door and walked through the mudroom, stopping in the kitchen doorway. Pearl stood at the sink, her hands encased in bubbles, craning her neck at the sound of Annie knocking on the wall. She turned off the water and wiped her hands on her shorts.

"What the hell are you doing here?"

Annie stumbled backward, her hands shaking from the shock of Pearl's tone. Everything she'd rehearsed fell from her head and landed around her feet, splattered and broken, all over the floor. She took a deep breath and clenched her fists.

"Pearl, I'm so sorry for your loss." Annie hung her head.

"Is that what you came all the way back here to say?" Soapy water dripped from her elbow.

"Yes." She picked words up off the floor, one by one. "And to see John."

"He's not here." Pearl held up her hands, then let them fall. "He's not here. And even if he was —"

"Can I come in?" Annie searched Pearl's eyes. "Please."

"He doesn't want to see you," she said, her tone clipped. "It's best that you leave."

The two women stood — Pearl in the doorway, blocking the kitchen like a guard, and Annie leaning against the wall, heat creeping into her cheeks. She knew what it felt like to be punched in the gut. She'd felt it during her first cancer diagnosis, and again sitting in the oncologist's office three days ago. She'd felt it when Alec's infidelity came to light. She didn't think a gut punch could be any worse than when she saw John with his arms around Dale on the curb. But Pearl's words, *he doesn't want to see you*, hit her with the force of a battering ram. All of the air escaped her lungs. She slid down the wall and onto the floor.

"How dare you come waltzing back in here like you've done nothing," Pearl said, her voice barely audible. "You hurt him. I won't stand for it." She started yelling in anger. "He's grieving for Marina. He's dealing with Luke. He's dealing with the estate." She cleared her throat. "He doesn't need this from you now. He has enough to deal with."

Annie rocked back and forth on the floor, too stunned to even cry. Pearl's footsteps trailed off into the kitchen. Now, only silence and poisoned air remained. *He doesn't want to see you.* Annie wanted to scream: *but he loves me, he said so in two voicemails, he loves me.* The impact of Pearl's words was so powerful that the light in Annie's heart went out.

"I called you a cab." Pearl stood looking down at Annie on the floor. "Go on. Get up. You can wait on the front porch."

48

Luke

Something's burning. It smelled like toast, like the time Luke tried to make some for his mom and dad as a surprise but started watching something on TV and forgot about the toaster until Daddy came running out of his room in his bathrobe. Luke, engrossed in the TV, didn't notice the smoke coming out of the kitchen. Daddy yelled at him, but when Luke told him it was a surprise, Daddy smiled and helped him make new toast, and together, they surprised Mommy.

Spiderman Legos surrounded Luke like a fortress. The bed was covered with them. He opened the instruction book and wished Uncle John were here to help him. He guessed he should wait until Friday when Uncle John came back, but he really wanted to make these now. Maybe Aunt Dale would help him later.

Something's burning. Grammy liked to eat English muffins for breakfast. It was too late for breakfast. Luke already had his cereal, but Grammy didn't eat anything. She just had orange juice. Maybe

Grammy was making English muffins now, for brunch. Mommy said brunch is breakfast and lunch put together.

Luke needed his green Power Ranger to help Spiderman fight the bad guys. He jumped off the bed and ran to the window where all his new Power Rangers rested against the glass. He grabbed the green one and ran back to the bed. *Wait a minute!* He tossed the Power Ranger in the middle of the Lego pile and ran back to the window. He squinted, trying to see. He saw someone sitting on the porch swing, but he couldn't see who it was. A lady? Tumbleweed, the cat, was in her lap. Luke pressed his face to the glass, then jumped up and down. *The lady, Annie!* He had to pee so bad, but he wanted to see the lady, Annie. He didn't know what to do. He ran into the bathroom and peed really quick and ran into the living room without washing his hands. He flung the front door open and stepped onto the porch, but the lady, Annie, was gone. The cat circled Luke's legs. He brushed him away and ran down the steps.

"Annie?" He ran all the way to the sidewalk and looked to the right and to the left. "Annie?" He ran up the driveway and into the garage. "Annie?" He ran around to the back of the house, all the way to the water. "Annie?" He picked up a rock and sat down on the chair. He threw the rock as hard as he could, but it didn't reach the water. He got up and trudged back to the house, then around the house, and back to the front porch, just in case. "Annie?" Of course, she wasn't there.

Luke ran into the kitchen and saw Grammy sitting with her head on the table. Her shoulders shook. He knew it. She burned her English muffins. He picked up a black disk, hard as a hockey puck, and sniffed. He wrinkled his nose and let it fall back onto the plate. Grammy looked up.

"Don't cry, Grammy." Luke patted her hand. "I can make you another English muffin. I know how to use the toaster."

"Go ahead, that would be nice. Do you want one too?"

Luke shook his head and pulled the package of English muffins out of the fridge. He took one out of the package, then got a fork and pried it open like he'd seen Grammy do. He moved a chair to the counter and climbed up. He put each slice in the toaster, pushing the lever all the way down. The metal turned red all around the muffin slices.

"They'll never cook if you stare at them like that," Grammy said.

"Yes, they will. They're cooking now. They're turning brown." The English muffins popped out, and Luke jumped, then laughed. Grammy got up and put the burnt ones in the trash, then gave Luke the plate. He plucked each slice out of the toaster, careful to not burn his fingers, and put them on the plate. Grammy carried it to the table and sat down.

Luke dragged the chair from the counter back to the table and sat beside Grammy. He picked at some crumbs, moving them around, turning them into the letter *L* for Luke. He tapped Grammy on the shoulder. She stopped buttering her English muffin and looked at him.

"I saw Annie," he said.

"That's impossible," Grammy said. She put more butter on her English muffin. "She left four days ago."

"I saw her, Grammy. I saw her on the porch. I was looking out the window in my room, and I saw her."

"Sweetie, that's impossible." She patted his hand. "You didn't see Annie."

"I did see her!" Luke got up and stomped his foot. "I saw her on the swing. She was petting Tumbleweed." His face felt hot. He put his hands to his cheeks and then covered his eyes. He wanted to scream but wanted to be good because Uncle John asked him to be good while he was gone. But he really, really, wanted to scream. He breathed deeply like Mommy taught him to do.

"I saw her Grammy."

"Luke, sweetie, you couldn't possibly have seen Annie."

"But I did, Grammy, I really did."

"She went back to New York, you know that." Grammy looked mad. "Now stop this, do you hear me? I want you to stop." Grammy stood up. "I'm going out to the Lanai. You're welcome to join me if you promise to stop this nonsense about Annie." Grammy took her plate and opened the back door. It slammed shut behind her. Luke went into the mudroom and out the garage door, retracing his steps back to the porch. He hoisted himself onto the swing.

"Tumbleweed." He called for the cat. "Here, Tumbleweed." He leaned back in the swing and tried to make it go. He stretched his legs all the way out, as far as they would go, sliding down the back of the swing, laying on it, trying to touch the ground. Halfway on the swing and halfway off, his toes touched the porch, and he gave a little push. He wiggled himself back up and tried to keep the momentum going by leaning forward, then back, then forward, then back. The cat appeared and jumped onto the swing. "Tumbleweed!" Luke stroked the cat's back.

Grammy was wrong. He saw the lady, Annie. Right here. On this swing. Petting Tumbleweed. He wanted his mom. He wanted his dad. He wished Uncle John were here. He brought his knees up to his chest and hugged them. *Maybe the lady, Annie, will come back. Maybe she went to the store and will be right back.* Luke would wait. He jumped off the swing and ran into the house to get his sock monkey. When he came back, Tumbleweed was gone, but that was okay. He had George. He climbed onto the swing and yawned. He laid down on the cushion and clutched George. He would wait for Annie to come back. Then Grammy would believe him.

"Lukey, wake up." A hand touched his shoulder, someone heavy on the other side of the swing.

"Annie?" Luke sat up and rubbed his eyes. He looked around. His sock monkey was on the ground. His arms and legs were sweaty. He touched his hair — it was sweaty too.

"No, Lukey. It's me, Aunt Dale." He threw his arms around his aunt and cried on her shirt. "Shhh. What's all this about?"

"Did she come back?" Luke pulled away and looked around the front yard. "Did Annie come back?"

"Lukey, she's in New York. She left on Christmas, don't you

remember." She squeezed his hand. "She didn't say anything about coming back."

"No, she was here. I saw her today." Luke slid off the swing. "I was in my room, and I saw her out the window." He bent down and picked up his sock monkey. "I came out here to see her, but she was gone."

"Are you sure it was Annie?" Aunt Dale held out her arms and lifted him back onto the swing. She pushed off with her foot, making the swing go almost as fast as Uncle John did. "Could it have been one of Grammy's neighbors?" Luke thought about this for a second. Grammy's neighbors were old, like Grammy. He shook his head. "It was Annie."

"Let's go talk to Grammy," Aunt Dale said. "Maybe she knows what's going on."

"No!" Luke jumped off the swing. "Grammy doesn't believe me."

Aunt Dale got off the swing and picked up her shopping bag. She took Luke's hand and led him into the house. Grammy was sitting on the couch reading a book.

"Oh, hi, Dale," Grammy said. "Were you able to find the lemon curd and leeks?" And then to Luke: "Did you have a good sleep?"

Aunt Dale sat down next to Grammy but didn't answer her question. Luke didn't answer her question either. He took the shopping bag and pulled out some weird things that he didn't recognize. He put them back in and ran to the kitchen with the bag, depositing it on the table. He ran back to the living room and flung himself on the couch next to Aunt Dale.

"Annie's coming back, I know she is."

"Luke, enough." Grammy was mad again. "You must have dreamed that you saw her."

"I didn't dream!"

"You didn't even like Annie that much, did you?" Grammy softened and tried to rub his back, but Luke moved out of the way.

"Uncle John is sad without her." Luke sniffed and wiped tears with the back of his hand. "I want Uncle John to be happy." He buried his face in one of the couch pillows. "I want my mom. I want my dad." Aunt Dale reached down and rubbed his back. Luke let her.

"Pearl, we should call John," Aunt Dale said.

Luke sat up. This was the best idea he'd heard all day. Uncle John wrote his phone number in the *Harry Potter* book last night. He jumped off the couch, ran to his room, grabbed the book, remembering what Uncle John said: *Call me if you need anything, okay, buddy? Push the numbers exactly like I wrote them. I'll see you on Friday.* Luke couldn't believe he didn't think of this before. He came out of his room quietly — Grammy and Aunt Dale were still on the couch talking — and held his breath as he walked down the hall and into the kitchen. He pushed a chair up to the counter, climbed up, and took the phone off its cradle. He opened the book and read the numbers out loud as he pushed each button. He did it exactly like Uncle John said.

49

John

John rented a car — cheaper than getting a cab, and he didn't want to waste time going back to his place to get his truck. He needed to see the house, Marina and Nester's house, needed to open the time capsule of a family that had been merrily planning a trip to Disney, oblivious to the fact that they would never return. Only Luke would return, but to a life so vastly different from the one he'd known. John hated leaving him in Florida like this, hated the quivering lip and the heroic attempt to be brave for *Uncle John*. Hated the chain of events that led him here, the unexpected twists and turns in a road that he would never have chosen.

He pulled up to the curb and got out of the car, leaving his duffle bag on the front seat. Halfway up the walkway, he went back for his bag, figuring there might be a few things of Luke's he could bring back, like some clothes and a special toy or two — toys that John would have to guess at the specialness coefficient. He swung the bag over his shoulder and limped up the walkway, still stiff from the plane. He stopped and stretched his bad leg, shaking the numbness out. Continuing up the sidewalk, he noticed that the Japanese maple — the one just next to the porch steps — had been cut down to the stump. He wondered what happened. Some years before he left, the tree had been treated for verticillium wilt, and like a trooper, it bounced back, bringing a flash of the brightest red leaves in fall. What a shame.

He tossed his bag onto the porch and took the steps carefully, the feeling in his leg not returning quickly enough. He bent down and lifted the doormat — one of several places he knew Marina would have left a spare key. Like a broken record, he'd nagged her about the reasons to not leave a key under the doormat — mainly that it would be the first place a ne'er-do-well might look. She never listened, always leaving one there when she went out on her walks. The night of the rape rushed through his mind. If it hadn't been Phil Riley with a key he had given him, it could have been a random bogeyman who found the key under the doormat. John sat down on the steps and sighed, knowing full well the likelihood of a random bogeyman finding the key under the doormat was slim. Very slim.

He put his head in his hands and tried to remember the other places he and Marina had, on occasion, hidden a spare key. He turned his head and saw the large ceramic planter in the corner on the far end of the porch. He stood up and hobbled toward it. Empty. Not even a thin layer of dirt. In all the years he'd lived in this house, that planter had never been empty. Never. He leaned against the house, thinking of ways he might break in. He and Marina never installed a security system. Maybe Nester had one installed. He supposed that might be a problem. He looked around for a *this home is protected by blah, blah, blah* sign, and didn't see one. No matter. He decided that breaking in and listening to a screaming alarm was worth the risk. Logically, he knew he could call Captain Murdoch and ask if someone from the department could let him in. But he wasn't thinking rationally. He was here now and his desire to go in and look around outweighed any thought of doing things by the numbers.

The weeping cherry tree! Of course! Two hand-widths from the left of the trunk. Forgetting his stiff and numb leg, he jogged across the porch and down the steps. He crouched in the mulch and dug until he felt the lid of the metal box that held the key. He pulled it out, suddenly afraid that this might be the old key — the key before he moved out, the key before Nester moved in, the key from his old life. He pulled his keychain out of his pocket and selected the one with the blue rubber cap — the key that he'd used every day for nearly twenty years — and held it against the key he dug out of the dirt. The two keys had no similarities in the hills and valleys of the cut. He took a deep breath and stuck Marina and Nester's spare key into the lock. It slid in as easily as Cinderella's foot into the glass slipper. John pressed down on the door handle, but the door didn't budge. He laughed, thinking about the damned door that always stuck — something he'd intended to fix but never found it to be a big enough priority. Nester apparently didn't think so either. He nudged the door with his shoulder, loosening it enough to push it open.

The faint scent of stargazer lilies, barely detectable, hit him hard. He scanned the entryway, and there they stood, in a tall purple vase atop the console by the stairs. Six of them, dead and dry, powdery yellow pollen all over the placemat beneath the vase. Marina had them in the house whenever she could get them. He tossed the spare key in the shallow bowl next to the vase — the catchall for their keys, spare change, random business cards. Today the bowl was empty except for a big rubber band, like the kind that held together asparagus bunches. Next to the bowl stood a wooden toucan with two pieces of outgoing mail in its spring-loaded beak. He pressed on the beak, and it opened, the two pieces of mail fluttering down to the floor like large confetti. He picked them up — a renewal for an art magazine and the water bill. Why Marina didn't just plop these in the mail before they left for their trip confounded him. So too did the toucan. Why couldn't she just lay the damned mail down on the console like they used to do when he lived there? This fucking toucan must have been Nester's doing. He whacked it off the console with the back of his hand and watched it bounce across the hardwood floor, a portion of its beak landing next to the coat rack.

John glanced back at the broken toucan as he ascended the stairs two at a time, holding tightly to the banister for support. He stopped just shy of the landing and sat down on the top step, taking deep breaths, not knowing whether his lungs failed him because he was old and tired or because he was on the verge of panic — brought on by simply being in this house. His lungs finally filled. He stood, careful to avert his eyes from his old bedroom, the one he and Marina shared, the one where she had been raped, the one she and Nester had tried and failed, to make a baby. Closing his eyes, he pulled the door shut and shuffled down the hall in search of Luke's room. Yep. The old guest room. Painted bright green on three walls, blue and white stripes on the fourth. A bunk bed, the bottom bunk unmade, the pillow at an odd angle, and the blanket in a ball partially hanging over the footboard. He picked up the pillow and fluffed it, then laid it down against the headboard. He untangled the blanket, gave it a good shake, and let it float down onto the bed, smoothing out the wrinkles with his hand. He plucked three stuffed animals off the floor — a penguin, an elephant, and a manatee — and arranged them against the pillow.

A framed photo on Luke's dresser made John's breath catch in his throat. He picked it up, his eyes filling with tears as he brushed his finger across the faces of Marina and Nester, then Luke, who sat laughing on top of Nester's shoulders, his skinny legs dangling down, blocking the *R* and *S* on Nester's Rutgers' hoodie. Red, orange, green, and gold leaves dotted the background — a recent scene, probably taken that fall.

He carried the photo to the bed and sat down, leaning his back against the stuffed animals. He lifted his legs onto the bed, his feet pressing against the footboard, and bent his knees until they touched his chest. He set the photo down and allowed himself to sob — for Nester, for Marina, for being so blinded by his own rage after the rape that he failed to consider, even for a minute, what having a kid — his own kid — would have meant. He sobbed for Annie and their broken relationship — broken for reasons he didn't fully understand and couldn't accept. He took a deep, shaky breath and allowed himself a thread of hope that Annie would take him back. He sobbed for Luke and wondered how he could be the sole person responsible for him. He sobbed for Shorty who knew nothing of this — John had been too overwhelmed to call and explain — and would have to deal with the fallout of John not being as available anymore. He sat up and rubbed his eyes. Shorty. He would drive over there as soon as he finished here and lay it all out. He slid back down and sobbed all over again, this time for the logistical nightmare of dealing with Marina and Nester's estate. And the years of therapy that Luke would likely need.

He buried his head in the pillow and screamed. At the top of his lungs, he screamed. He screamed and screamed and screamed. When he was finished, he felt like he'd just run a marathon. His eyelids grew heavy, and he suddenly felt like he hadn't slept in days. He yawned and opened his eyes wide, determined to not fall asleep, determined to not waste another minute. He needed to grab a few items for Luke and get the hell out of there. His eyelids, made of lead, had a different idea. They closed without his consent. Like the garage doors on Manhattan storefronts. Closing time.

JOHN SAT UP, the sound of a loud voice echoing through his head, confused and not fully aware of himself or his surroundings. *Where the hell am I?*

"On your feet," the voice shouted. "On your feet. Now!"

"Fuck!" John's head hit the bottom of the top bunk. He staggered away from the bed as his vision gradually came into focus. "What the hell?"

"Hands behind your head," the cop yelled.

John held his hands high above his head. Lucidity and logic hadn't kicked in yet — he didn't know his left from his right, or the fact that behind your head and above your head were two entirely different things. The cop rapped his hands.

"I said behind your head."

"What the fuck is this about?" John did as the young cop commanded and placed his hands behind his head, interlocking his fingers, growing more livid by the second. "Who the hell are you?"

"Officer Dobson." He pointed to his badge, then called on the radio for backup.

"This is fucking ridiculous." John started unwinding his fingers, then thought better of it. "I'm retired from the department. John Butterfield." He brought his left arm down to reach into his pocket for his wallet. He needed to clear this up. "What the fuck?" The pre-pubescent cop had his firearm cocked and ready. Reflexively, John returned his hands to their position behind his head. "What the fuck!"

"Butterfield?" Ernie Fuentes stormed into the room and screeched to a halt when he saw John. "What are you doing here? Dobson put your piece away. This guy's legit."

"Fuentes, thank God." John shook his hand. "What's going on? I'm here getting some stuff for Luke. He's in Florida with my mother."

"I'm so sorry about this." Fuentes looked at the young cop. "Dobson, go on and get out of here. I'll explain later." The young cop stood, paralyzed, eyes wide, seemingly unsure of what to do next. "Go!" Dobson snapped to attention and slowly backed out of the room, never taking his eyes off John.

"Thanks," John said, searching Fuentes' eyes. "It's been a hellish week. I didn't need this."

"I know. Crazy about Ness, huh? I can't believe it. Damn, what a shame."

"That ain't the half of it," John said. "Marina died two days ago."

"Oh, fuck. I hadn't heard. I'm so sorry. What are you going to do?"

"I'm not sure." John shook his head. "I'm really not sure." Then: "Why was that douchebag here? Who called the cops?"

"Your...I mean Nester's neighbor across the street. A guy in a wheelchair."

"Fuck. Mel." John closed his eyes and ran his hand across his forehead. "He didn't realize it was me." He sighed. "Fuck. He probably would have called even if he did know it was me. I'm basically persona non grata around here."

"Actually, he said he saw someone with a large bag digging around in the mulch. He said the person struggled with the door, then forced it open. He thought you were robbing the place." Fuentes looked around the room."Come on, let's get the things you came here for and get out of here. You still working at that pub in Jersey City?"

"Shorty's. Yeah, I am. I'm part owner these days." John didn't have the energy to explain about Luke being his son. "I'm headed there next. I need to take more time off and head back to Florida in a day or two. I'm looking after the kid until things get sorted out." He shrugged. "I guess I should have called Murdoch. One of you nuts could have let me in. Sorry for the commotion."

"Eh, not a big deal," Fuentes said. "Hey, call me when you're back for good. I'll buy you a beer." He gave John a quick hug, and together they filled the duffle bag with toys and games and a few changes of clothes. On the way out, John grabbed the photo, thinking it might make Luke happy.

JOHN CLUTCHED the steering wheel of his rental car. Still disturbed and agitated from having had a gun pointed at his head, he carefully navigated the streets of Maplewood as he made his way to the expressway. It took every ounce of concentration that he possessed to not drive off the road and cause an accident. He should have taken a cab. At least then, he'd have been able to close his eyes and fight the demons while someone else drove. Dammit. He couldn't shake the smell of Marina's wilted stargazer lilies from his nostrils. Why the fuck did the sense of smell have to be so damned powerful. He didn't want to remember. He needed to forget.

As if on autopilot, the car found its way to Shorty's. He parked in the lot behind the building and walked in through the back door, straight to his office. Lunchtime. The smell of greasy bar food stormed his nose like ninjas conducting a surprise attack. It knocked him a bit off-balance as it obliterated the stargazer lilies. He sat down at his desk and sniffed, breathing in this pleasant smell as if it were life-giving oxygen. This is what he wanted to remember. The pub. His life before the accident, his life before Annie broke his heart. He put his hand in his pocket and touched the ring. He didn't yet have a plan but knew he had to see Annie. He would give her the ring and beg her to remember how much he loved her. Yes, he intended to beg.

He bent down and reached under his desk to turn on the computer. It hummed to a winding start, having been asleep for the past week. He picked up a rogue pretzel near his foot, pushing his chair back far enough to reach the trash can. He leaned back and noticed something leaning against the side of his desk, the trash can holding it in place.

"Hey! What the hell are you doing back here? I could use your help up front." Shorty wiped his hands on his jeans and stood next to John's desk. "Welcome back. We missed you around here."

"I'm not exactly back," John said, standing. Shorty opened his arms for a hug, and John obliged, lingering longer than necessary, he was that exhausted.

"What do you mean you're *not exactly back*?" Shorty took a step backward. "You look like shit, by the way."

"Thanks." John laughed. "I haven't been sleeping." He sat down and put his head in his hands, the object leaning between his desk and the trash can — wrapped in festive holiday paper — long forgotten. The release valve on his tear ducts opened. Dammit. He thought he'd drained all of his grief through the millions of tears shed over the past week. How could he possibly have any tears left? Shorty squeezed his shoulders, bringing him back into the present. "Marina died two days ago."

"Oh. Fuck." Shorty's hand went to his mouth. "I am so sorry, man. I am so fucking sorry." He pulled his desk chair around and positioned it next to John. He sat down and put his elbows on his knees. "The last time we talked, you said she was making progress." He searched John's eyes. "What happened?"

"Her brain started swelling again. They took her into surgery, and she died on the table." John's breath caught. No! He wasn't going to cry again. He willed the release valve to close. Miracle of miracles, it obeyed. "That's not all. There's something else I need to tell you." He looked at Shorty, then at his computer screen, the *Shorty O'Rourke's Irish Pub* logo bright against the sullen conversation. "No questions." He pointed at Shorty. "I mean it. No questions." Shorty held his arms up in a gesture of surrender. John took a deep breath. "The kid is mine."

"They named you as a guardian?"

"No questions!"

"That wasn't a question."

"It sure sounded like one."

"Dammit, John." Shorty sighed. "You're such an asshole."

"I know," John said, smiling. "The kid is mine. Genetically mine. That's it. That's all I'm going to say." He suddenly remembered the strange object and reached around his desk for it. "What is this?"

"I don't know. Probably a painting of some sort. She dropped it off yesterday."

John's heart stopped. There would only be one *she* who would leave something shaped like that. But why would she leave it here? Why not just leave it at his house. Or better yet, deliver it in person.

"Did she say anything?" John held his breath, afraid of the answer.

"No, not really. She came in during burger night, you know how fucking busy it gets. I was pretty distracted. She just said she had something for you and asked if she could put it by your desk." Shorty raised an eyebrow. "What was she doing here, anyway? I thought she was with you."

"She was." John hung his head. "She was."

"Another long story?"

John nodded. He held the package against his knees. Starting at the far-right corner, he carefully pulled the tape that stood between him and whatever was inside. He looked up at Shorty.

"Can I have a moment?"

"Yes. Of course." Shorty patted him on the shoulder and started to walk out the door, then turned around. "Take as much time as you need. I mean, you know, later. If you need to go back to Florida, whatever. I'll be okay. A week, a month, half-a-year. It doesn't matter. We can talk about the kid then, okay?"

"Thanks, man." John watched Shorty leave, grateful for such a good friend and business partner.

"Hey." Shorty stepped back into the office. "As long as you're here." He smiled. "I could sure use a hand out there." He turned and walked out.

John closed his eyes and nodded, of course, he'll step out into the pub. But not just yet. He undid the tape on the other two corners and lifted the paper. Sure enough, an Annie painting, his boat, their boat, sailing against the backdrop of Manhattan under a winter sunset. Two people on board. One old and tall, the other with wild hair and his smelly sailing sweater hanging loosely on her body. He bent down and inhaled the varnish — a happy, happy smell.

THE PLACE SWARMED WITH PEOPLE, despite the odd hour — too late for lunch, too early for dinner. For the past two hours, John tried his best to blend in, taking orders, delivering drinks. The merriment betrayed his feeling of impending doom. Annie — his next stop — would seal his fate. He didn't know whether to treat the painting as a hopeful sign — a harbinger of reconciliation — or as a final goodbye. She obviously painted it before their world fell apart. Probably painted it to give to him for Christmas. He was balancing a tray of partially empty pint glasses when he felt his cell phone vibrate in his back pocket. He walked around to the back of the bar and set the tray next to the sink. He leaned against the counter and looked at his phone — the call had already gone to voice mail — and was surprised to see his mother's number on the caller ID. He pressed the button to listen to the message.

Uncle John. I saw her. I saw the lady, Annie. She was here, but Grammy doesn't believe me. Please call me back.

John tapped Shorty on the shoulder and pointed to his phone. He hurried into the office and closed the door. He sat down at his desk and listened to the message again.

Uncle John. I saw her. I saw the lady, Annie. She was here, but Grammy doesn't believe me. Please call me back.

Luke answered on the first ring.

"Hey, buddy, what's going on?"

"Annie was here."

"Hold on, now. When did you see her?"

"Today. I was in my room, and I saw her out the window. She was on the porch playing with the cat."

"What did you mean when you said Grammy doesn't believe you? Did you talk to Annie?"

"No. I went outside, but she was gone."

John tried hard to keep the frustration — driven by his need for data — out of his tone. Talking to a six-year-old indeed came with challenges.

"Okay, slow down. Tell me everything that happened."

"John?" His mother's voice usurped Luke's. He could hear Luke in the background, *I was talking to him, give me the phone.* And then, crying.

"Mother, what's all this about? He's not making any sense."

"I know he isn't. He thinks he saw Annie." In the background: *I did see her! I saw her! She was here!* More crying.

"Why would he think he saw her if he didn't actually see her?"

"I don't know. He was in his room napping and maybe dreamed it." *I wasn't napping! I was playing with my Spiderman Legos! I don't take naps! Naps are for babies!* Luke was screaming. John could hear his mother's voice — muffled, no doubt, from putting her hand over the phone — telling Luke to be quiet.

"Put him back on the phone," John said.

"No, he needs to calm down."

"Mother, please put him the phone."

Luke came back, hyperventilating, jabbering on, not making sense, crying, and hyperventilating some more. John waited, his heart pounding, ecstatic at the possibility that Annie had returned to Florida.

"Buddy, calm down," he finally said. "It's okay. I believe you." John wasn't sure what to believe. He wanted to believe Luke. Wanted to with all his heart, all his soul. "I believe you, buddy." He could hear Luke breathing hard. "Can you tell me exactly when you saw her? Was it five minutes ago? Or an hour ago? When?"

"It was after breakfast. Grammy was making an English muffin for brunch."

John calculated. Okay, brunch, typically ten-ish, maybe eleven. It was almost four now. He didn't know what to do. He supposed catching a flight back to Florida tonight made sense. But if Annie was in Florida, why wasn't she at the house? None of it made sense.

"I'll tell you what. I'm going to go to her house now and look for her there. If she's not home, I'll get on the next plane and come back to Florida tonight. If she's home, I'll stay here until Friday, like we talked about. No matter what, I will call you later and let you know what I'm doing. I promise."

"Okay, Uncle John."

"Do you promise to call me if you see her again?"

"I promise."

"Thanks, buddy. Put Grammy back on."

"Why are you giving him false hope," his mother said when she came back on the phone.

"Mother, I don't know what's going on down there, there better be a logical explanation. Let me talk to Dale."

"John." Dale sounded exasperated. "I really don't know what to tell you." She whispered into the phone. "I believe Luke."

"Thanks, Dale. I'm on my way to her house. I'll call you later."

50

Annie

Unlike this morning's flight to Florida, the flight back to New York City was crammed with people. Annie sat with her shoulders pressed against the cabin wall, wanting to be as far away from her seatmate as possible. The man tried to start a conversation — the usual, *where are you going and where are you from* pleasantries. Annie gave perfunctory answers then mumbled something about having to listen to a CD for work. She put her headphones on and tucked her CD-less Walkman between her thigh and the armrest. She looked out the window at the darkening sky, but the vast emptiness — even void of clouds — felt too much like the emptiness in her heart. She hadn't eaten since early this morning, and her stomach, used to being fed at regular intervals, barely noticed. In the cab ride to the airport she panicked and called John only to have the call roll straight to voicemail. She didn't leave a message, figuring Pearl was right, that he didn't want to see her, maybe even warning him that she might call.

Annie reclined her seat, closed her eyes, and pretended to be in deep thought. She sensed her seatmate craning his neck around her to look out the window. She pushed the button to straighten her chair, jamming her face against the porthole, laying claim to the empty sky as hers alone. The drink cart rolled up the aisle and stopped, tempting Annie to buy a glass of wine. She watched her seatmate get a mini-bottle of scotch and a bag of pretzels, images of her session with Mel temporarily distracting her from the misery of the moment. The flight attendant raised her eyebrows, and Annie shook her head, waving her off. Nothing she could put in her mouth would fill the void or take away her pain. Pain? She leaned forward and reached around her body, touching the spot on her back. Was she simply too distracted to notice her back pain? Or too distracted to notice its absence? She rubbed, pressing her fingers into her sweater, rubbing through the fabric. Nothing.

Lips loosened from his drink, Annie's seatmate began a lively discussion with the man across the aisle. She reached into her backpack and pulled out a CD. She fed it into her Walkman without looking to see what she'd selected. Vertical Horizon. Okay. Not what she felt like listening to, but better than the two men droning on about the NFL playoffs. Honestly, she didn't care to listen to anything.

The music failed to buoy her. She let it play as she kept her eyes glued to the window. The plane, on its final approach, now flew low enough for her to see the lights below, a bejeweled blanket covering the city. The colors of the dinner hour a mixture of vibrant and muted, both necessary in painting to create an image with depth. The colors of her soul felt muted, all vibrancy left on the floor in Pearl's mudroom.

The earth rose, and the buildings below became more distinct, the dots bigger, the yellow lights illuminating windows behind which the evening ritual of dinner went on without sympathy for Annie's heartache. She closed her eyes and recounted one particular evening at her childhood table, remnants of dinner soaking in the sink, she and her sister doing homework, her mother on the phone, talking to her aunt. *These are the subtleties of a ruined evening*, Annie remembered her saying, recounting the litany of things that had gone wrong that day. She didn't remember the specifics but remembered the phrase.

These are the subtleties of a ruined evening: being told he doesn't want to see you. A ruined evening. A ruined life.

51

John

The sensible people in John's life never tried to talk him out of getting involved with Annie. Nester, probably the most practical of all, blinded maybe by his love for Marina, simply said *go for it*. Not in one of those nonchalant ways that implied John would just do it anyway, so why bother offering an opinion or advice. No. Nester's words came out of a genuine place in his heart. When John's marriage failed, a few people assured him that marrying Marina had been a mistake from the get-go. As long as it had lasted — two decades — it had been a mistake, according to some. That they knew from the beginning that it would never work. He knew better. Had he not been so wrapped up in his own fucking self-righteousness, it might have worked. Maybe it was never a mistake.

John knew that anything worth doing is worth doing badly. A sentiment quoted often by his mother, painted on inspirational posters, said as encouragement before undertaking a feat like running a marathon or starting a new business. Shorty said it when

John balked at the offer to partner with him in running the pub. *I'm a cop*, he'd said. *I know nothing about the restaurant business*. Shorty shot back: *so, you'll screw up*. And here they were, six years later, running the pub like they'd been doing it their whole lives. John was, in some ways, happier behind that damned bar than he'd ever been on the police force. *So, you'll screw up*. And he did. Many times. Just as he'd screwed up with Marina. He should have stayed. Should have accepted her decision to not have an abortion. He eventually would have learned the truth. That he had a son. Maybe he would have screwed up. He most likely would have. Yep, anything worth doing is worth doing badly.

He pulled the car around to the back of Annie's building, determined to not screw up. Or, if he did screw up, he would own it, embrace it even, and remind her that anything worth doing is worth doing badly. He silenced his mother's voice, the voice that asked *what are you doing with that woman*? His falling in love with Annie, given her situation, made no sense. He freely admitted and acknowledged this. But what was he doing with her? Loving her. He needed her in order to breathe.

He turned off the car and sat, looking up at Annie's kitchen window. The darkening sky and the absence of a yellow glow from within flashed like a neon sign announcing *she's not here*. He called his mother's house, hoping to get Luke.

"I'm just checking in," John said, disappointed to hear his mother's voice. "Any sign of Annie?"

"Of course not," she said.

"Let me talk to Luke." John heard muffled voices and the shuffling of feet. It felt strange checking in with a six-year-old. But he'd promised.

"Hi, Uncle John."

"Hi, buddy. I just pulled up to Annie's house. It doesn't look like she's home. I'm going to knock on the door, and if she doesn't answer, I'll wait for a bit before making a decision." John paused. "Sound good?"

"Okay," Luke said, his voice quivering.

"Hang in there, buddy. Hey, is Aunt Dale around? Let me talk to her."

"Aunt Dale," Luke yelled. John cringed and held the phone away from his ear. "Uncle John wants to talk to you." Luke lowered his voice. "She's coming." And then: "Here she is."

"John, I'm going to hang up and call you from my cell, outside."

As John waited, he checked his phone for missed calls or messages from Annie. Of course, they existed only in his imagination. He'd tried calling her an hour ago, but it had rolled straight to voicemail. He didn't leave a message, worried that letting her know he was here might upset her. He needed to tread lightly, not ambush her. Yet here he sat, in her back alley, poised to do just that — ambush her. His phone buzzed.

"Dale, what's the hell is going on down there?"

"I'm not sure." Dale paused. "I called a few cab companies. Just a hunch. The second one I called confirmed that it dispatched a cab to this address at around eleven-thirty this morning."

"What are you saying?" John's confusion multiplied. Had Annie been to Florida or not? He didn't know what to think.

"The dispatcher gave me your mother's name as the person who called for the cab."

"But that makes no sense." Dale's words hung over his head like a rain-laden cloud. A lightning bolt shot through the darkness and into his heart. "Are you saying Annie came to the house, and my mother sent her away in a cab?" His heart pounded. "Why would she do that?"

"John, I have no idea." She sighed. "I mean, there's no more Marina to push you toward. I don't know why she would have sent Annie away."

"Did you tell her what you found out?"

"No. Hell no. Not yet, anyway."

"There has to be a logical explanation." John's blood boiled at the possibility that his mother would pull something like that. "Maybe Annie came, and my mother told her that I was in New York." He ran his hand through his hair. "But then why would she tell Luke that he'd imagined seeing Annie?"

"I don't know why, John, but your mother is lying to Luke." Dale paused. "I believe Annie came to see you." And then: "It's been hours now. I don't think she's here. I think she's there, in New York."

Light suddenly illuminated Annie's kitchen window. He took a deep breath and stared.

"John?"

"I'm sorry." He kept his eyes glued to the window. "I need to go." He looked at the top right-hand corner of his phone. "My battery is on fumes, and I didn't bring my charger. Tell Luke I'll see him on Friday."

THE ALLEY SEEMED ENDLESS. Darkness engulfed the city, the back row of brownstones brightened only by the two or three lit parking pads and the occasional fire escape wrapped with Christmas lights. John jogged as fast as his bad leg would allow. He brushed past a metal trash can and knocked it over, the sound echoing down the alley. A beer bottle rolled out when the trash can toppled, and John chased it down the street until it rounded the corner of a partial fence, stopping only when it rolled onto a patch of weeds sprouting from the blacktop. He picked it up and jogged back to the trash can, righted it, and tossed the bottle in. The crash of glass in an otherwise empty metal can startled a dog, inciting raucous barking up and down the alley. He picked up his pace — the last thing he needed was for someone to call the cops.

He should have climbed Annie's fire escape. He should have climbed it and banged on the kitchen window until she let him in. Not only would it have saved him precious minutes, but now, climbing the stairs at the front of her building and standing on the landing in front of her door presented a problem he hadn't anticipated: her neighbor Ted.

"John?" Ted stood in Annie's doorway with his hands on his hips. "You look like crap." He stepped out and closed the door behind him. "What are you doing here, anyway?"

"I was about to ask you the same question." John extended his hand. "Merry Christmas."

"Same." Ted shifted on his feet. "Look, Annie isn't here. I've been coming in to water her Christmas tree."

"So, you haven't seen her since she went to Florida with me?"

"She's been back for a few days. She told me she was leaving again." He shrugged. "So, here I am."

"Did she say where she was going?"

"Actually, no."

"What about when she'd be back."

"Again, no."

John reached into his pocket and pulled out his keychain, feeling for Annie's key and instinctively knowing it was gone. If a heart could fall out of a person's chest and bleed on the ground, well, his just did.

"I don't mean to pry," Ted cleared his throat and looked a the floor. "She told me the two of you are taking a break." He shifted from one foot to the other. "I'm guessing she wouldn't be thrilled that you're here." He looked at John. "Come on, I'll walk out with you." He shook his head. "I'm sorry, man. I feel for you, I really do."

John nodded, unable to speak, and turned around, practically sliding down the stairs, his legs weak and unable to hold his weight without concentrated effort, unable to move fast enough away from Ted, whose footsteps echoed behind him. On the sidewalk below, he turned left and walked quickly. People making their way home from their workday dotted the landscape — a woman in a red trench coat carrying a briefcase. Three men, two in hard hats, the third with his hard hat in his hand. A couple with two school-aged children trailing behind. And countless other nameless, faceless people who blurred by him, hopefully paying no attention to the hapless jerk with a limp, tears streaming down his face.

JOHN SAT on the top step in front of Annie's building. He didn't know how long he'd been walking — the now empty streets indicated that he'd covered a lot of ground. He opened his phone and pushed the button for her number. This time it didn't go directly to voicemail. He held his breath. After six rings, her recorded voice. So, Ted was right, she didn't want to talk to him. But why would she have gone to Florida? There must be some misunderstanding. Maybe someone came to his mother's door, who looked like Annie. A solicitor or perhaps even a person lost and needing a cab. It could have been anyone. Luke had only just met Annie — it would be easy for a six-year-old to confuse a random woman with *the lady, Annie.* John cried anew, remembering Luke's silly vernacular. *Fuck.* His phone went dead before he could leave a message. He set it down on the step beside him.

He stuck his hands — cold and numb — into his coat pockets. For the first time all day, he felt the bite of the late December evening. He watched the fog of his breath rise and fall in front of his face, tiny droplets huddled together against the cold. John didn't know what he was waiting for, exactly. If Annie honestly didn't want to see him, his presence on the front steps of her building would not be a welcome sight. He sat there anyway, with no expectation that she would even come home. Maybe she was at Alec's with Henry. Hell, for all he knew, she might have jumped on a flight to England to be with her sister. She could be anywhere. Maybe even hiding in Ted's apartment. None of it made sense. He didn't know whether to sit, stand, run, walk, drive, scream, or cry. He was in limbo. Purgatory. A bottomless pit. A black abyss.

John noticed the stars first, then the waning moon, bright as a lightbulb. He felt the emptiness of death — the death of the most beautiful relationship he'd ever had. He wanted to kick the damned moon out of the sky, knock it around until it broke into a million tiny pieces. Might as well knock each and every star out of the sky too. Then he'd grab the most powerful firehose on the planet and saturate the sun until it sizzled out, like the Wicked Witch of the West. *I'm melting. Oh, what a world, what a world.* The desperate witch from *The Wizard of Oz* echoing his soul. *Oh, what a world, what a world.*

He fished the ring out of his pocket and held it toward the moonlight. The diamond in the center of the compass caught the light, and

John twirled it around, like a lighthouse casting a beam. He brought the ring up to his mouth and for a fleeting second, considered swallowing it. He closed his hand around it, clutching it tightly, willing himself to not act on this strange impulse. It was no use. He dropped the ring back into his pocket and stood, the desire to get out of the cold stronger than the desire to spend the night on Annie's steps in the hope that she'd return and trip over him on her way up. The need to be back in his warm car overwhelmed him. He held tightly to the handrail and stomped his feet, ignoring the tingles and pain of limbs waking from slumber.

52

Annie

The day Annie's mother made the decision to enter hospice, she sat her two daughters down and talked frankly about what that meant. Annie remembered feeling insulted, spewing ugly remarks like, *I'm in college, Mom, I'm not an idiot, I know what it means.* Her sister, Kathy, the one more likely to fight fire with ugly words soothed and begged her to calm down, to just listen, to just let their mother talk. Annie often thought of that day after her own cancer diagnosis three years ago. So insensitive she'd been to her mother. Her own fears revealing themselves through a mask of arrogance.

Annie watched as the blur of the runway came into focus, the plane touching down and slowing rapidly from the howling reverse thrust from the jet engines. The pavement seemed to stand still until the wheels gradually returned to life and deposited the plane at the gate. Annie remembered one particular day during the more lucid moments in the last days of her mother's life. Propped up in the hospital bed, she breathlessly listed the things in her life that she wished she'd done differently. Everything revolved around Pops. *I would have been tougher on him, she'd said. I would have forced him into AA sooner. I wouldn't have put up with it.* Kathy reminded her that their dad had been an out of control drunk. This time it was Annie who soothed, Annie who begged Kathy to calm down, to just listen, to just let their mother talk.

"Excuse me." The woman in line behind her pressed into her back. Annie, too startled to respond, whipped her head around. "We're getting off the plane?" The woman's pointed statement, disguised as a question, jolted Annie into action.

"I'm in my own world, I'm sorry," Annie mumbled, flinging her backpack over her shoulder and marching toward the front of the plane, past the flight attendants and ignoring the cheery *Happy New Year* and *Welcome to the Big Apple* from the pilots. *There are still three days left this year*, she wanted to scream in their faces. Instead, she put her head down and stepped off the plane. The smell — a combination of jet fuel and other unidentified, airport-specific molecules — had always been pleasant, a smell that screamed travel, a scent that signified a break from the usual smells of the world. Annie had always loved this smell. Until now.

"Mom, there are a million tiny things I would do differently if I could do life over." She said to herself as she made her way off the plane. A million. At the end of her days, the one thing she knows she'll regret forever is screwing things up so royally with John.

She pushed past people on the crowded, moving walkway and tried, unsuccessfully, to drown out the cacophony of conversations and the background buzzing of rolling luggage on the rubber conveyor. She winced every time she heard the thud of someone's suitcase bounce off the walkway and onto the hard, shiny floor. All she wanted to do was get home, crawl into bed, pull the covers over her head and not come out for several days. At least not until Alec drops Henry off on Sunday, and she resumes her role as a fully functioning mother.

The terminal, buzzing with seemingly happy, excited people

unnerved her. The *I "heart" NY* signs all over the walls. The guy sitting against the wall at Gate Six flanked by his two large suitcases. Evidence of Christmas everywhere — from the wreaths placed strategically on the walls between the shops to the massive tree with its white lights and red baubles — for the sole purpose of enticing travelers into shops like Brookstone so they could buy useless crap. Crap that would one day end up in the back of a closet and eventually in a box labeled *to donate*. She was glad Christmas was over, relieved she didn't have to watch the disappointment on Luke's face when he opened all of the useless crap she'd picked out for him.

She walked past Starbucks on her way to the ground transportation area, suddenly aware that she hadn't eaten anything since breakfast. Pearl's words, *he doesn't want to see you* ringing in her ears throughout the day, made her stomach reject the very idea of food. But now she felt weak and light-headed. She needed something. She turned around and went back to Starbucks, angry and impatient, barely tolerating the people in line ahead of her. Finally, her turn. She ordered a Strawberry Frappuccino and stepped aside to wait.

"Strawberry for Annie," the barista called out. Annie grabbed her drink, frigid in her hand, and took a long, slow slip, bracing herself for brain freeze. She grabbed a wad of napkins and wrapped them around the drink, creating a barrier between the cold cup and her fingers.

She stepped back into the crowded terminal to the muffled tone of her phone ringing in her backpack. She hurried toward the nearest gate and sat down in an empty chair, frantically unzipping the pocket where she'd stuck her phone.

"Ted." She took a deep breath. She'd been so convinced that it was John, so hopeful — no matter how far-fetched the hope was, given Pearl's words that morning — that she didn't try to hide the disappointment in her voice. "What's up?"

"Where are you?"

"I'm here." She realized then that she hadn't told Ted where she was headed this morning, never even let him know when she would be back. "I'm at JFK, about to get a taxi home."

"I don't know how to say this."

"Did my Christmas tree catch fire?" Annie's eyes grew wide.

"No, no. Nothing like that." Ted suppressed a nervous laugh. "I went over to check your tree a little while ago, and who was standing in your doorway?" He paused. "John."

Annie, stunned to silence, unable to catch her breath, unable to open her mouth to speak, covered her eyes with her free hand, pinching them with her thumb and forefinger, unsure the precise nature of her tears.

"Annie?" She nodded but didn't speak, and is if Ted could sense this, he continued. "I told him not to go inside."

"I took away his key," she said, her voice a whisper. Remembering this set a wave of panic in motion. She sat up straight.

"I'm looking out my window." Ted paused. "He's sitting on the front steps of your building."

"What?"

"He's just sitting there, in the cold, in the dark." He sighed. "I don't know what happened between the two of you, but I feel sorry for the guy. I don't know whether to call the police, bring him a cup of hot cocoa, invite him to my place, or what." He cleared his throat. "My allegiance is to you, though. I'll do whatever you want me to do."

Annie grabbed her backpack and jogged, leaving the Strawberry Frappuccino on the seat where she set it down, laughing, yelling at Ted to let John into her apartment. She reached the taxi port out of breath but feeling more alive than she'd felt in days.

ANNIE CURSED the forty-five minutes it would take the taxi to wend its way from the airport to Brooklyn, longer with the evening rush hour traffic they would likely encounter. She clutched her cell phone as if holding it tightly would squeeze time and teleport her to her apartment. She opened the phone and pushed the speed dial button for John, feeling silly in her belief that this third attempt would be more likely to succeed than the previous two. Did she really think the call wouldn't roll straight to voicemail? She sighed, this time leaving a simple message: *please call me.* No need for salutations or identifications. Even without caller ID, they'd know each other by the sound of the breath taken before speaking.

"Isn't there another way you could go?" She leaned forward in her seat.

"Lady, the whole city is snarled. It's fucking rush hour. What did you expect."

"I'm in a terrible hurry."

"Yeah, you and everyone else." He shook his head. "Next time, try a helicopter."

"Fine." She rolled her eyes and let her body fall against the back of the seat. She pressed her forehead to the window and watched the street scene unfold before her. She closed her eyes, listening to the sounds of New York — car engines and horns, mostly — wondering if Ted would wait with John or just leave him alone in her apartment. She suddenly feared that John might get tired of waiting and leave. She opened her phone to call Ted, but he beat her to it.

"He's gone." Ted sounded winded and desperate. "By the time I got out there, he was already gone."

"Dammit, Ted!" Annie's tone horrified her. She put her hand to her mouth, then slowly let it fall back down to her side. "I'm sorry. I didn't mean to sound like that."

"Yes, you did." Ted sounded utterly defeated. "I get it, though."

"His phone keeps rolling to voicemail." She didn't want to ask this next question but couldn't stop herself, almost ready to pick a fight. "You didn't go out there right away, did you?" She felt horrible the minute she said it but didn't know how to take it back.

"I'm sorry, Annie." Ted sighed. "Donald and Elijah walked in. I got distracted, then I had to tell Donald what was going on. I'm sorry."

Annie shook her head, angry that Ted let John slip away. But isn't that what she, herself had done? Let John slip away? She didn't know how she would ever recover from her series of recent missteps.

"It's okay." Annie couldn't manage anything more than that. She closed her phone, too frustrated and upset to even cry. She looked out the window — about a mile to go. She could get out of the cab and walk the rest of the way home. Or run like Meg Ryan in *Sleepless in Seattle*, the Empire State Building's observation deck just minutes from closing. Only Annie didn't know what the hurry was anymore. John was gone and not answering his phone. For once, she actually wanted to cry and found that she couldn't. She must have finally run out of tears. She opened her phone.

"Shorty...it's Annie...he was? I'm in a cab. Yes, here in New York... I'll explain later...if he comes back in, please tell him to stay put."

53

John

The feeling had almost returned to John's feet by the time he reached the car. He pulled out of the alley, not exactly sure whether he would go to Shorty's or go directly home. He made his way up Pineapple Street in fits and starts, remembering all the times he and Annie laughed about the fruit-named streets in her neighborhood. Sitting in traffic on Hicks Street, he opened the glove compartment to see if the car rental company stocked it with a spare cell phone charger. Nope. He slammed it shut, determined to bitch about it when he returned the car. Dammit, why shouldn't rentals come with a spare phone charger?

The guy behind him laid on the horn. John rolled down the window and gave him the finger as he inched forward. Even with his bad leg, he could walk faster than drive in this fucking traffic. He was about to pop onto the ramp for the Brooklyn Bridge when he realized, horrified, that he'd left his phone sitting on Annie's front steps. He rotated his hips and patted his back pocket — the one he always carried it in — for verification. He made an illegal U-turn at the light and fought his way back to her building.

He didn't bother with the alley, choosing instead to double-park across the street, taking his chances that it would only take a few seconds to get his phone. He crossed the street quickly and climbed the steps. All the way to the top, then back down. On the sidewalk, he took several quick steps, then stopped abruptly and looked at the sky. *Fuck.* He let out a long slow breath — a white cloud in the cold night. He walked back to the steps and stood in front of them, scanning each one as if the phone would miraculously appear. He turned back toward his car, then changed his mind and walked toward the steps again. He grasped the handrail and lifted one foot onto the first step. *Why am I doing this? The phone is gone.* He let his foot fall to the sidewalk and ran his hand through his hair. On the verge of tears, he zipped his jacket all the way up to his neck. Fists to his head in utter defeat, he squatted and stayed like that for several seconds before standing up and trotting to the car.

"Are you looking for this?"

John turned around slowly, blood draining from his head, wondering if he had finally snapped. He closed his eyes tightly and opened them, fully expecting the ghost on the sidewalk to have disappeared in a mist. She stood, very much in the real world, wearing his old sailing sweater, the mist coming from their respective breaths, close enough to bond and mingle and rise together as one. She handed him the phone.

"I've been trying to call you," she said, smiling. "It's always a good idea to carry a charger when you travel."

He didn't know whether to laugh or cry or maybe do a little of both. He put his hand in his pocket, feeling bold, not wanting to waste another second. Holding the ring tightly in his palm, he went down on one knee.

"Damn, that hurts," he said, laughing, finally laughing. "Annie, there's something I've been wanting to give you..."

ACKNOWLEDGMENTS

When I set out to write my first novel, *Stay Back!*, I never intended it to be the first book in a three-book series. My characters had other ideas – they fledged and established lives of their own, demanding that their stories continue. Now that I've completed the series, it's going to be hard to let them go. They've become so real to me that I see and hear them in random people who cross my path. A wayward tuft of hair. A particular way of walking. A vocal nuance. Still, I need to let them live their lives outside the confines of the pages. Who knows, I may revisit them at some point. For now, though, it's on to my next project.

I give my heartfelt thanks to the following people: Debbie Herr Cornwell for suggesting the idea for Stay Here's plot twist. Christine LaMonica for helping me come up with the technical details that made the plot twist believable. Lisa Ray for her unmatched proof-reading skills. Maiden Maryland owners Tammy and Tracy Lynndee for taking a chance on me and carrying my books in their shop. And finally, my husband, Mike (a.k.a. Sweet Petunia) for his unconditional love, his support, his many read-throughs of my manuscripts, and for making me laugh.

ABOUT THE AUTHOR

Lynn Stewart lives in Cambridge, Maryland. This is her third novel.

For more books and updates visit:
lynnstewart.ink

ALSO BY LYNN STEWART

Stay Back!

Back And Forth

9 780999 890547